*He vowed to marry for money— until a beautiful slave girl offered him the greatest treasure of all . . .*

W9-BUN-134

## "WHAT DO YOU WANT OF ME?"

"Naught but two kisses," Rowan said. "The condition is merely that I grant you the first one and you return the second one in kind."

She rolled her eyes. "Aye, no doubt that first kiss will involve more than merely a kiss, but I will not succumb to your touch!"

"Kisses only," Rowan insisted. "And naught shall I touch but my lips to yours."

"Liar!"

Rowan smiled slowly. "Coward," he charged.

She stepped closer and raised her chin, her eyes bright with challenge. "Do your worst," she invited.

"Fear not," he whispered. "I shall do my best." He touched his lips to hers and set to the labor he did best of all.

~~~

*Dell Books by Claire Delacroix*

The Bride Quest series:

*The Princess*
*The Damsel*
*The Heiress*

# The Heiress

## Claire Delacroix

A Dell Book

Published by
Dell Publishing
a division of
Random House, Inc.
1540 Broadway
New York, New York 10036

This novel is a work of fiction. Names, characters, places, and incidents either are the product of the author's imagination or are used fictitiously. Any resemblance to actual persons, living or dead, events, or locales is entirely coincidental.

ISBN: 0-440-22589-2

Printed in the United States of America

Published simultaneously in Canada

September 1999

10   9   8   7   6   5   4   3   2   1
OPM

*For my Mom
and Dad—
with thanks and love*

# Chapter One

*London,*
*July 1172*

ROWAN DE MONTVIEUX WAS IN A FOUL MOOD.

Not only had he been ill beyond belief on the journey from LeHavre, but he was not at his intended destination. Indeed, the last Rowan had heard, the Thames was *not* in Ireland.

Which meant that he must endure another sea voyage, no doubt even less pleasant than this last, and that he must do so immediately in order to win the challenge he had accepted from his brothers.

Nay, he was not in a fine mood. He strode through the tangle of merchants on the docks, retrieving his horse and finding his squire Thomas with no small effort. They badgered him from every side, these hagglers with their shoddy goods, and he braced himself against thieves in the crowd. He deigned to purchase some meat pies from one merchant who looked more reputable than most.

But what he really needed was a measure of ale. Aye, then some song, and a solid measure of the sorry excuse for food in this country warm in his belly. Then blissful sleep. That would restore his interest in bucking his brothers' expectations. Rowan loved a challenge—at least when he was feeling hale—and the more desperate the stakes, the better.

*An Irish heiress!* For the love of God, what had possessed him to take such a dare? On a morn like this, with the taste of his own bile ripe in his throat, Rowan doubted he could charm even the most ancient and desperate crone alive.

Or that he wanted to.

"Oho! A fine knight just into port!" a slavemonger cried. The man was unshaven and unkempt, his dark hair hanging in his eyes and more than one tooth missing from his mouth. "I have just the wench for you, sir, and she is a bargain on this day of days." He leaned closer to whisper, his breath even more foul than Rowan's own. "I shall make you a special deal, sir, on account of your knightly status and recent arrival."

Rowan growled a dismissal and made to push past the man, his gaze drifting disinterestedly to the woman in question.

And then he stopped to stare.

'Twas not the bright red gold of her hair that captured his attention, nor even that her tresses were cropped short. 'Twas not the deep hue of her tan, nor even how that tan made her eyes appear ethereally blue. 'Twas not the ripeness of her breasts fairly spilling from her chemise, not even that she wore a boy's chausses, which hid none of her copious charms.

Nay, 'twas that she feigned insouciance nearly as well as he.

"She is not much of a lay, if that is what you seek," the seller confided in an undertone. He leaned closer to whisper. "Indeed, a corpse might serve a man better."

The woman did not even blink. Her stance remained unchanged, her arms folded across her chest, her bare feet braced against the ground. She was nearly as filthy as her owner, a rough length of rope knotted around her neck and tethering her to that man.

Rowan swallowed as he noted the mark of a chafe there. "Indeed," he said mildly. "I would have naught with which to compare." The man looked quizzically at him and Rowan lifted his brows. "Having never been intimate with a corpse." His squire chuckled at the jest, but the woman's steady stare did not waver.

The would-be seller, though, grimaced and turned away, muttering something uncomplimentary under his breath and giving the woman's rope a savage tug. She made no protest, obviously accustomed to his abuse, and strolled behind him with her head as high as a queen's. Rowan could not help but watch them go.

He imagined the man taking his pleasure with this woman, his sweaty bulk heaving atop her as she stared fixedly at the rafters. His stomach rolled mutinously and, though he stood on dry land, Rowan felt ill again.

"How much?" he called impulsively.

"Three silver deniers," the man cried, spinning to jab a finger at Rowan. *"Two* for you!"

"Outrageous," Thomas murmured.

'Twas a shocking price but Rowan found himself digging for the coins. "Margaux will be proud of me," he muttered. He fired a glance at Thomas. "Be sure to tell her of this. I may well be in need of her favor."

Thomas nodded. A mere heartbeat later, Rowan's purse was lighter and he held the end of the distasteful rope in his hand. The seller marched away, whistling.

But the woman surveyed him with the same cold manner. If Rowan had thought she might thank him for winning her release from that creature, he was clearly mistaken.

And that irked him. He had just bought a slave, for no good reason, a slave he did not want, expending coin he would have preferred to keep or at least spend on some amusement.

She could at least appreciate the gesture!

"For a smile and a word of thanks, I would release you," he offered pointedly, and her gaze flicked over him.

"Gratitude for paying him for his crimes?" she asked. "You will not have that from me, nor a smile."

"A smile would cost you naught."

" 'Twould cost me that very freedom you promise," she retorted dryly. Her eyes narrowed. "Or have you not noted the fine company we keep?"

'Twas true enough that the docks were swarming with unsavory characters, more than one of whom was making a thorough study of what filled her chausses.

" 'Tis your own fault for wearing such garb," Rowan felt compelled to observe.

The hint of a smile crossed her lips. "The embroidery on each and every one of my kirtles is being mended."

Thomas laughed, then looked to Rowan and stifled himself. Rowan fixed the woman with a dark glance, not liking that she made the jests instead of he.

His look did not seem to trouble her in the least, which was doubly vexing.

"At some point," he said sternly, "you donned that garb of your own choice."

"True enough."

"Why?"

Now she did smile, although the expression was more sad than might have been expected. " 'Twas a whimsy of long ago and far away."

"Why?" Rowan repeated, determined to have one answer from her.

Her smile disappeared. "I thought to disguise myself as a boy."

"You? A boy?" Rowan laughed. He could have done naught else. "A man would have to be blind to doubt your gender!"

The woman glared at him and Rowan felt a measure of pride for stirring some response from her. "I thank you for observing my foolishness. I might have doubted it otherwise, given my current exalted status."

Thomas snickered even as Rowan's smile was snatched away.

" 'Tis the mark of maidens in a convent to imagine that they can deceive the world, simply by donning boy's chausses and cropping their hair . . ." Rowan's voice faded as he stared at her in sudden comprehension. "You speak too well to have been raised in a gutter. Who are you?"

The woman's eyes flashed so quickly that Rowan almost missed the telltale sign that he had found a truth. "I am no one," she declared.

"You have studied in a convent," Rowan insisted.

"I labored in one," she corrected hastily, though Rowan guessed that was a lie. She shrugged, her composure in place once more. "Until I ran away."

"Shunning the compassion and care of the nuns for the charms of that one." Rowan jerked a thumb in the direction her former owner had taken.

"I did not expect . . ." she began hotly, then caught herself and said no more. She folded her arms across her chest again and glared at Rowan.

"You made a mistake," he acknowledged softly. "And I think you have already paid for it. Pledge to me that you will not flee and I will remove the rope."

"So much for your fine offer." She turned to Thomas. "Are your knight's words worth so little as that?"

Before Thomas could answer, Rowan clarified the matter. "I offered an exchange, but I have yet to have thanks and a smile."

Her full lips tightened. "Do not hold your breath."

"Then 'twill be a year and a day of labor from you," Rowan declared as if he made such arrangements all the time, "for I must have something from my coin."

In truth, he could not have cared less for the coin, but he would not give her the satisfaction of knowing she intrigued him.

She visibly gritted her teeth. "I shall not labor on my back."

"I would not expect you to."

"Nay?" Her skepticism was more than a little grating, and Rowan had the urge to provoke a response from her.

"Nay," he retorted. "I like my women lean and lithe."

Her eyes flashed dangerously and Rowan darted backward, not the least bit certain that she would not strike him. Instead she loosed a string of Gaelic so potent that it needed no translation. He knew she could not have learned that in a convent.

Ha!

Rowan grinned at her. "Your pledge, *ma demoiselle*?"

"If you touch me, I shall flee."

"Fair enough."

She considered him for a telling moment, her eyes no more than blue slits. "Then I swear it to you," she said finally, her reluctance to accept his very generous offer more than obvious.

Rowan unknotted the rope, catching his breath when he realized the chafing was more extensive than he had guessed. "This must hurt," he murmured, deliberately being gentle.

She averted her gaze. "One can accustom oneself to anything." She was cold and composed again, though Rowan yearned for another glimpse of that spark in her eyes.

"Have you a name?"

Her gaze flicked to his and away. "Ibernia."

"A lie," Rowan concluded with a smile of appreciation for her quick wits. It meant literally "from Ireland," something he would guess to be true judging by her earlier spate of Gaelic. "But 'twill do. And if you truly are of Ireland, then you can be of aid to me without rolling to your back."

"How?" Her suspicion could have been construed as an insult by one more sensitive than Rowan.

"I seek a bride, the most wealthy heiress in Ireland." He grimaced comically. "Sadly, I do not know her name."

"You seek a bride for her wealth alone?" she demanded with one fair brow arched high. "How very romantic."

Thomas—curse him!—chuckled again.

Rowan folded his arms across his chest, his good humor dispelled. "I seek her to answer a challenge from my brothers." Her curiosity was undisguised, so he elaborated. "I have been challenged to a bride quest, to find the most wealthy heiress in all of Ireland and make her my bride." He paused, looking the woman dead in the eye. " 'Tis a challenge I intend to win."

"My lord does love a dare," Thomas interjected.

"Oh, I should like to see you lose," Ibernia murmured with unexpected heat, "for you are too confident by far."

Rowan grinned that she once again revealed her thoughts. "Indeed, the near certitude of failure is what made me risk this quest."

Ibernia blinked. "Truly?"

"Truly." He spared her his best smile, to no discernible effect.

She straightened, a daring glint in her eyes that made Rowan's pulse quicken. "Then you will be delighted to know that the wealthiest heiress in all of Ireland is one Bronwyn of Ballyroyal."

"Why should that delight me?"

Ibernia smiled fully then. The result was so fetching that

Rowan nearly lost the thread of their conversation, and he considered the challenge of winning this woman's favor.

There would be high stakes of failure!

"Because she will not have you," Ibernia declared with resolve. "There is no doubt of the matter."

Rowan would not take that to heart so readily. He leaned closer and winked, well aware of his own good looks. "Because she likes her men less handsome? Less charming? Less amusing?"

Ibernia snorted with unwilling laughter, then lifted one hand to her lips to halt the sound. "Because she is already betrothed," she said with satisfaction.

"Perfect!" Rowan cried, laughing at his companion's startled expression. He gripped her waist and swung her into the air. " 'Tis hopeless! We shall proceed to Ballyroyal at once." He set Ibernia on her feet and touched one fingertip to her nose. "And you, my lovely *demoiselle,* shall guide us directly there."

She shook her head, clearly marvelling at his response. "You are mad."

"But oh-so-roguishly handsome," Rowan retorted, taking advantage of her surprise to quickly kiss the tip of her nose.

Ibernia darted away, scrubbing at her nose with her hand, her expression wary. There was a glint in her eyes, though, that had not been there before. Rowan knew enough of women to not be fooled.

"You have granted me license to flee," she reminded him.

Rowan's surety wavered for only a moment before he recalled her own comment about their surroundings.

He smiled and gestured to the unsavory characters surrounding them. "Indeed, you are free to do so." He bowed when she hesitated. "Although I should be honored to accompany you to Ballyroyal."

She folded her arms across her chest, pushing her fine

breasts to prominence. Contrary to his own claim, Rowan admired the view, less inclined to lithe and lean women as each moment passed. "How very gallant," she commented dryly, "to see my ends served to fit your own."

Rowan grinned, liking her quick wits very well. "And your choice?"

"I will accept your companionship," she said so regally that a blind man might have been convinced she had alternative options. Nay, this one was not bred in a gutter, Rowan knew it well. "If only to witness your failure."

"Do not be so certain of it as that," Thomas counselled in an undertone. "Matters have a way of turning unexpectedly in this knight's presence."

"Aye," Rowan agreed with a wicked wink. "By the end of this, even you will not be able to resist me."

That made Ibernia laugh outright for the very first time. There was a kind of satisfaction to be had in seeing her so surprised. Indeed, Rowan guessed that this year and a day might provide a very interesting pursuit, one beyond his brothers' quest.

He liked the sense of Chance mounting against him. Rowan would woo this Bronwyn of Ballyroyal to be his bride, *and* he would seduce Ibernia before they parted ways. And there, Rowan knew well enough, would lay the greater challenge of all his days.

He could hardly wait to begin.

*Ibernia.*

She almost smiled to herself at the apt choice. 'Twas a lie to be sure, but not a bad one, especially considering the sliver of time she had had to concoct a tale. Indeed, she had learned much of late, including the ability to use her wits with haste.

And she supposed there was no harm in this knight knowing the land of her birth. Indeed, it provided adequate explanation for her knowing the circumstance of Bronwyn of Ballyroyal.

Perfect. She matched her pace to his, noting that his retinue seemed to consist only of the fine destrier, a dark chestnut beast with a lopsided star upon its brow and one white sock. Its caparisons were of the same deep blue edged with white as this Rowan's tabard; his insignia, the spurs upon his boots, his sword, and his obvious wealth declared his knightly rank.

His squire was a young boy of ten or twelve summers, admiration in the bright gaze he oft bestowed upon his master, his hair so dark as to be almost black. The boy was neatly garbed in the knight's own colors, and he held a dappled grey palfrey beside the destrier. She was a much smaller steed and walked quietly, while the warhorse fairly pranced with cocky pride.

Not unlike his master. Ibernia swallowed her response, not wanting this man already so fond of himself to conclude that his company alone prompted her smile.

Though she was forced to concede—if only to herself—he was a good measure more handsome than her last master. And his touch had been gentle when he removed the rope. Its very absence made her feel free again.

Though she was not entirely liberated. 'Twas no small thing to realize that she must trust this man, this one who seemed to grant value to naught but a dare. Dread slipped through her and she feared she had trusted overmuch oversoon.

He had already challenged expectation with his fleeting kiss, though it had not been unpleasant.

Ibernia's mouth went dry. She knew naught about this knight, yet she was in his power. How oft had she heard the tale of a finely mannered man, even a handsome one, whose heart was as black as sin? Ibernia glanced quickly to the confident creature beside her and wondered at the wisdom of her wager.

God in heaven, had she impulsively made her lot worse *again*?

"Have you a name?" she demanded.

Her new companion winked, then executed a sweeping bow, right on the wharf, much to the amusement of all around him. Ibernia could just imagine what tales he prompted, making such a display before an obvious slave, and felt her cheeks heat.

This man would do naught without an audience, to be sure. That dread rose another notch as she wondered whether his gallantry would ease in private.

"Rowan de Montvieux, at your service," he declared with a solemnity undermined by the mischievous glint in his eyes.

Ibernia did not know quite what to expect of him. "And you are a knight?" she guessed. "A man of honor?"

He laughed then, a rich sound that turned yet more heads. "Now, there is an association, Thomas, that cannot always be held to be true."

"To be sure, my lord," the squire replied with enthusiasm. "We have met many men of *dishonor* with spurs upon their boots."

Such a claim did naught to feed Ibernia's confidence.

"And which are you?"

'Twas troubling how his amber gaze locked with hers, no less how her heart skipped a beat when it did. And that impish smile, well, she had best not to ponder its effect overmuch.

No doubt this Rowan considered its merit enough for both of them.

"You care mightily for my answer," he said silkily, and closed the distance between them with a quick step. His hand rose to her jaw and Ibernia did not dare give him a glimpse of her growing uncertainty. She held her ground, even as a tremble launched from her belly.

What would he do?

Rowan's gaze fell to the chafe on her neck. His eyes darkened. Ibernia's pulse leapt in terror, but his hand hovered above her skin, the heat so close to her own launching an unwelcome shiver over her.

To her astonishment, compassion gleamed in Rowan's eyes. "I suspect you have seen much of dishonor in this world," he murmured. His gaze locked with hers, and Ibernia did not know whether to flee or stare him down. She felt as if he could read her very thoughts; she had a fleeting conviction that he would kiss her again.

Perhaps not upon the nose this time.

Rowan's frown was so fleeting that she nearly missed it. Then he shrugged and stepped away, as if he were indifferent to her presence. He turned his back upon her, and Ibernia had the distinct sense that he hid from her as readily as she would hide from him.

Though that made no sense at all. What had a carefree man like this to hide from anyone?

"Indeed, it matters naught in this moment," Rowan said with a cavalier shrug. "For you have made your choice and will have to bear the price of it."

With that, he strode in the direction of the town, clearly expecting her to follow.

Ibernia did not.

His words had not reassured her, though his manner might have done. Indeed, she was sorely tempted simply to flee. With her knowledge of the wharf, she could disappear into the crowd and Rowan would never find her again.

Though undoubtedly another unsavory character would. And 'twould mean breaking her pledge.

But thus far, Rowan had kept his word. And she had a sense that he *was* a man of honor, despite his hesitation to make any such claim.

Ibernia would have liked to have waited until Rowan noticed she was not fast on her heels, if only to make a point. But an unshaven sailor leered at her. Another reached for her buttocks and she delayed no longer.

"Where are you going?" she called, disliking that this unlikely candidate was her best chance for a champion.

Rowan halted and turned, looking astonished that she was not immediately behind him. His features darkened when he saw the men circling around her. He marched back to her side and seized her elbow, his grip less forceful than she had expected.

"Fool woman!" He shook her slightly and forced her to match her pace to his. "I thought we had agreed!"

Yet Ibernia, instead of feeling threatened by his annoyance, felt oddly protected. She told herself that 'twas only natural to expect a knight to protect one, especially a knight who had paid too much coin to make her his slave.

She was a possession, no more than that.

"We agreed to go to Ireland," she clarified.

"Surely 'tis not too much for a man to partake of a meal and a measure of ale first."

Ibernia looked to him in alarm. "In a tavern?"

"Aye, likely as not."

"I will not enter a tavern!" Ibernia argued, for that was where her own troubles had begun.

"Whyever not?" Rowan turned to her, his expression slightly impatient. "Surely you can have no desire to linger here? When did you last have a hot meal? 'Tis not my intent to eat alone!"

Ibernia clung to her conviction, not daring to be tempted by the luxury of hot food. "We travel to Ireland." She deliberately took a more confrontational pose. "You vowed it to me."

To her surprise, dismay transformed Rowan's features. Then he smiled anew, and she wondered whether she had imagined his response.

Indeed, his tone turned cajoling. "But I have only just disembarked. Would you not have a meal in your own belly first?"

Did he mean to break his pledge? Ibernia folded her arms across her chest, not prepared to leave wharf for town without a battle.

Even if her empty belly was readily persuaded to join Rowan's side. "I think only of your quest," she declared archly.

Rowan looked skeptical. "Aye?"

"Aye. You would not want to reach Ballyroyal *after* Bronwyn had taken her marital vows." Ibernia shrugged, knowing from the brightness of his gaze that she had his attention. "Of course, 'tis *your* quest, and no doubt you know best how to pursue it."

The squire snickered until the knight cast him a dark glance.

"*After* her nuptials?" Rowan shoved a hand through his russet hair, the dishevelled result making him look appealingly boyish. His brows drew together in frustration. "When was she to wed?"

"Just past midsummer was the last I heard. And now 'tis—"

"Just past midsummer!" the squire crowed.

Rowan swore.

Once again Ibernia feigned indifference, knowing the knight's attention was fully snared. "Though indeed, 'tis long since I was in Ireland. The nuptials could have been delayed.''

''Or hastened,'' the squire commented, most conveniently, to Ibernia's thinking.

Rowan's expression turned grim in a way that she guessed was not characteristic. ''To what port must we sail?''

''Dublin, of course.''

His gaze slid over the numerous ships at anchor as if seeking an escape from keeping his word. ''Indeed, there may not be a vessel destined there.'' He nodded crisply. ''We shall seek news at the tavern while we eat.''

''On the contrary, that ship with the Venetian colors is destined precisely there.'' Ibernia pointed to the flag fluttering in the breeze with its familiar symbol of the winged lion of St. Mark.

Rowan's gaze turned questioning and Ibernia realized she had erred. She hastened on before he could even ask how she knew enough to recognize that banner. ''I heard the men talking as my former master and I passed.''

Which was partly true. She had heard them talking of their destination—but had recognized their insignia from her father's lessons.

Though she had understood their Venetian dialect from her father's lessons as well, that was less than pertinent. If Dame Fortune rode with her, Rowan would never catch her second slip.

Ibernia lifted her chin to face Rowan, wanting beyond all else to be on that ship, purely because it was destined to leave the soonest.

Rowan glanced to the ship and paled ever so slightly. ''Surely we can find passage on the morrow,'' he suggested.

Ibernia feared that time would change his thinking or that ale would muddy his intent.

"Perhaps we could." She smiled ever so slightly. "Or perhaps you do not truly wish to win your dare, after all."

She stepped forward, allowing a slight swagger in her walk, then glanced over her shoulder. "Or perhaps," she added softly, "you are *afraid* to measure your charm against the Venetians. One does hear that they are most handsome and gallant men, accomplished and discerning. A woman could readily lose her heart to such a man."

"Or something somewhat lower," the squire amended, his lack of innocence making Ibernia glance his way in surprise.

But Rowan cast his hands toward the sky, indifferent to the boy's comment. "I fear comparison with no man! How could you even suggest such foolery?"

"Then prove it," Ibernia whispered. Rowan glared at her and she felt suddenly very bold. "I *dare* you."

The air crackled between them and Ibernia's heart skipped a beat. The knight's eyes flashed. He strode forward so suddenly that his destrier started, and grasped Ibernia's elbow with purpose.

Ibernia slanted a sidelong glance his way and noted the determined set of his lips. She had a very definite sense that she was going to win her way in this. But that was not the sole root of the very odd thrill running through her as Rowan marched her down the wharf.

"Oh, I shall accept your dare and shame you for even making such a suggestion, of that you can be sure," the knight muttered through gritted teeth. "My charm so far exceeds that of mere merchants that even *you* shall swoon in my arms when you see the truth."

Ibernia chuckled despite herself. "Oh, I think not."

Rowan turned a sparkling glance upon her, his annoyance gone as swiftly as the wind. "Would you care to make a wager upon it, *ma demoiselle*?"

Oh, he was an alluring man, of that Ibernia had no doubt. Her breath caught in her throat. A strange warmth unfurled in her belly, and Ibernia wondered if she were becoming ill. Truly she had never felt so strange in all her days.

"What manner of wager?" Aye, even her voice was oddly breathless.

Rowan's eyes gleamed. His smile made her heart pound, the way his thumb slid across her arm prompting her to shiver. "That I can persuade you to share your charms with me."

"Willingly?" Ibernia's doubt made the squire chuckle again.

But Rowan arched a brow. "Of course." His gaze danced over her features, and 'twas as if he touched her. Ibernia's face burned and she leapt away from him.

"I will never willingly cede to a man's touch!" She granted him a scornful glance, though she wondered whom she sought to convince. "Especially a rogue like you."

Rowan watched her, his gaze too perceptive for Ibernia's taste. She wrapped her arms around herself, and glared at him. Both shivers and heat ran beneath her flesh. Clearly, she was falling prey to some foul illness.

Yet, if she fell ill, would Rowan take advantage of her then? She had witnessed how men thought of little beyond themselves and their pleasure. Oh, how she longed to be home and safe again!

When Rowan spoke, his voice was soft. "Then you have naught to lose by taking my challenge."

Ibernia studied him for a long moment. She was oblivious to the bustle of the wharf, aware only of the glow in Rowan's amber eyes and the hammer of her heart. "You will not force me?"

"Never." His slow smile heated her blood in a most uncommon way, or maybe 'twas the heat in his pledge. "I prefer to have women leap willingly into my bed."

Ibernia shook her head and stepped away. "I will not be the next. Not I."

"On the contrary, I suspect you will." Rowan offered his hand, in the manner of knights making a pledge, his manner so cursedly confident that Ibernia was tempted to prove his expectation wrong. "Let there be a new wager between us. I pledge to win your willing surrender—with no tool but my own charm."

Still Ibernia did not take his hand. "You will not force your affections upon me?"

Rowan snorted. "That course is for the vulgar alone." He arched a brow. "Perhaps a *merchant* might take such a course, but I would not stoop to such a deed."

"And what stakes do you set?"

He grinned. "Resist me until Ballyroyal and you shall have your freedom then and there."

Ibernia blinked. The man did indeed set a hefty measure upon his allure! "Instead of in a year and a day?"

"Aye." There was a twinkle in the knight's eye, one that reminded her of his desire to win at challenges.

But Ibernia knew she could withstand any such temptation. Sharing a bed with a man was no pleasure—and could be no different, even with one so handsomely wrought as Rowan.

She could fend off his advances for a few weeks, especially if the prize was her freedom—and to be home once again.

Home. She could be *home* before summer's end. And free.

'Twas an offer that could not be denied.

Ibernia took his hand without further hesitation. "Consider the wager to be made."

"That I do." Rowan's hand closed over hers with a warmth and surety that Ibernia found curiously reassuring. His eyes flashed and she had a warning only the span of a heartbeat before he quickly brushed his lips across her brow.

Ibernia danced backward, outraged that he would make such a gesture. "You!" The fleeting kiss seemed to burn against her flesh, and she scrubbed at it, well aware that the knight chuckled at her expense.

Oh, he was too confident by half! She would savor each refusal of his attempt to woo her!

"I but seal our bargain," Rowan teased with a confident wink, then turned toward the ship.

Without dragging her along, or binding her to his side, or otherwise compelling her to join him. But Ibernia followed, disliking that Rowan found her so predictable as that. She could have fled—aye, in a heartbeat!—but he was her best opportunity to achieve what she wanted. That alone was why she followed him.

And Rowan de Montvieux—curse him!—knew that all too well.

# Chapter Two

ROWAN STRODE TO THE SHIP SHE HAD INDICATED, NEEDLED by Ibernia's insistence that they leave immediately, no less her means to ensure she had him doing her will. 'Twas he who twisted women around his finger and turned them to *his* will! Rowan did not care for the change. Nay, there had never been a woman who compelled him to act against his will.

And he had wanted that hot meal. No less, a break from voyaging on ships and all the attendant discomfort. Aye, this was certainly not the circumstance he would have preferred, but Rowan had a weakness to which he seldom confessed.

The flash of fear in the lady's eyes had been his undoing. He was not one who liked to see women afraid. Perhaps his upbringing made him love to see women laughing and happy, to see welcome in their eyes. Rowan did not care. He would never force a woman beneath his hand, for to Rowan, that would take the joy of the moment from him as well.

The anguish in those clear blue eyes when he vowed to seduce her told Rowan volumes of what his new slave had endured at the hands of men. Clearly Ibernia—or whatever her name was—had not found happiness with men, and Rowan was not inclined to torment her.

He suspected she had been tormented enough.

Just as he suspected that she was more than she would

have him believe. There was something in the tilt of Ibernia's chin and the flash of her eyes that spoke of a life of privilege, a household in which a woman had the freedom to speak, a place in which her comments would be heeded.

There was a lilt in her voice that hinted at education, an assessing light in her eyes and keenness of wit that showed she had grown up surrounded by those who valued her view. Only a woman raised in pampered circumstance could imagine that fleeing that circumstance could win her anything better.

She was born wealthy, or Rowan would eat his saddle.

Though she hurried to cover her tale of the ship, Rowan was not fooled. She had recognized the insignia, an unlikely feat for someone who was "no one." The Venetians were not so common as that in this port outside the Mediterranean.

Rowan would guess that Ibernia was a merchant's daughter, schooled by her family in matters of import to merchants. 'Twas easy to conclude from that how she had become a slave. Perhaps she had travelled with her father or spouse on a journey gone awry, and become a spoil of war who had then been sold.

She lied about fleeing the nuns, of that there could be no doubt. Indeed, he was fiercely curious about that truth, and he knew he would have the fullness of the lady's tale before all was done.

If not much more of her favor.

But he would proceed with caution—even though there was clearly more to Ibernia than she would have preferred Rowan know, he also knew that she would not part with her tale readily. Nor that 'twould be readily disentangled from the falsehoods she had learned to tell to protect herself.

A sea voyage might indeed be the best way to win the lady's confidence and serve all of his objectives. Intimacy, few distractions, time they were compelled to be together. Perfect—if he did not spend all of the voyage with his head hanging over the rails.

Rowan refused to speculate on the possibility, though his innards churned at the very prospect of embarking on a ship so soon.

The vessel they sought was in the midst of activity. 'Twas not the most finely wrought ship in the port, and even more surprisingly, 'twas far from fastidiously maintained.

Rowan hesitated, unable to reconcile such a ship flying the Venetian insignia. The Venetians built their own vessels and were ferociously proud of them, so proud that he could not imagine they would acknowledge any lesser ship as their own.

Ibernia nudged him impatiently, and Rowan shook his head before he continued. Truly such details mattered naught—what mattered more was the manner of bargain he could make with this captain, if the ship was destined for Dublin.

Indeed, the only morsel of counsel his father had ever granted him was never to trust a Venetian, for their trust was bought and sold as readily as their goods.

'Twas an interesting accusation for a man like Gavin Fitzgerald—a mercenary devoid of trustworthiness himself—to make.

All the same, Rowan put one hand on his purse as he stepped forward, the other resting casually on the hilt of his sword. A man stood on the wharf, the foreign cut of his garb and his speech revealing that he was of the ship. He tallied and counted, obviously directing the loading of the vessel, and Rowan knew better than to trouble him.

Though the man's speech made Rowan smile slightly. Ibernia could have understood the men only if she had been tutored in the Venetian dialect.

*No one,* indeed.

He slanted her a telling glance. "How fortunate for you that when you passed earlier the men were not speaking their native dialect," he commented in an undertone. "Otherwise you might not have understood."

The lady, to her credit, flushed crimson. Her lips tightened though and she said naught.

Ha! Rowan would eat his *destrier* if she was not a merchant's daughter!

There was a man on the gangplank who supervised the repair of the rigging while he kept one eye on the loading. He stood with the confidence of a man well assured of his fine appearance. His full-sleeved white chemise was of fine linen, his chausses were of deep green wool. His boots were more finely crafted than most, his laced heavy leather jerkin was adorned with more than one battle scar. He was of an age with Rowan, trim and perhaps slightly shorter.

He was dressed so finely and directed with such authority that he could be none other than the captain of the good vessel *Angelica.*

Rowan hailed him with a wave and a shout. The man turned, revealing that he was ruggedly handsome, a fact that Rowan normally would not have noticed. In this moment, though, he was very aware of Ibernia beside him, no less her comments about the allure of Venetian men.

And how much did she knew of Venetian men? Or how well had she known them? Rowan found himself bristling at the unwelcome prospect of competition.

Was this captain the manner of man Ibernia found attractive? Rowan did not like the possibility of rivalry for her favors, not in the least, but he had taken her dare and would not back away from it now.

He stepped closer to the gangplank and raised his voice to call the captain again.

"I have no spices to sell," that man said haughtily, his speech accented, then made to turn away.

"I am not interested in spice." Rowan hastened on before the captain could dismiss him. "Indeed, I believe you sail for Dublin and would seek passage on your ship."

That made the captain pause and turn. He surveyed Rowan, as if assessing his net worth on the spot. His eyes narrowed shrewdly and Rowan guessed he had put the value close to the truth.

For the captain took a step closer. "You must pay in advance, in gold coin."

Rowan shrugged as if this were of no concern. Truly, 'twas not, for he always had a full purse, courtesy of his foster mother, Margaux. "Of course."

His calm agreement snared the captain's attention fully. That man waved to his sailors to continue their labor and descended to the wharf. The captain was tanned and well muscled, his stride revealing that he was a man of purpose who tolerated no foolery.

His flowing dark hair was tied back at his nape, his fathomless gaze danced assessingly over Ibernia. He shook out the lace at his cuffs until 'twas just so, then smoothed an errant strand of dark hair back from his brow.

Then he smiled slowly and solely for Ibernia.

Rowan stiffened but refused to look to see the lady's response to this example of Venetian masculinity. No doubt any hint of his curiosity would amuse her overmuch.

No doubt she glared at the captain.

But the captain's smile broadened, his own opinion of Ibernia's charms more than clear. 'Twas as if he found welcome in the lady's response. Before Rowan could look, the captain came to a halt before Rowan and met his gaze.

"For you and two others?" He rubbed his chin. "And a pair of steeds?" His gaze strayed to Ibernia once more, drifting almost absently over her garb. Rowan waited for an indignant outburst from the lady, but it did not come.

"I am not certain we can accommodate all of you," he mused, his smile becoming cold as he turned back to Rowan.

But he would take Ibernia, of that Rowan had no doubt! Rowan straightened with uncharacteristic indignation. "I suspect there is a price that will convince you to find the space."

The man grinned outright then and inclined his head slightly in acknowledgment. "Of course."

"Not on the decks."

"Nor in my hold," the captain retorted. "'Tis too precious a space to waste upon travellers."

"We would pay good coin."

"And my hold is already put to better use," he said crisply. "Travellers take considerably more room than other cargoes and fetch markedly less."

Rowan had no doubt the hold was stuffed from stem to stern with fine goods for trade. Before he could ask further, the captain chose to argue over the destrier. "They are trouble from start to finish," he claimed, walking around the steed.

Troubador tossed his mane and stamped his foot, as if that steed would persuade all that he was flighty. Rowan ground his teeth and glared at the stallion, who took no note of his response but fought the bit instead. The captain stood behind them all, his gaze straying rather obviously to Ibernia's legs.

"A fine *feisty* specimen," the captain murmured wryly, and Rowan disliked the glint in the man's eye.

Rowan suspected the captain was commenting upon Ibernia and glared at him. "The steed is sedate, you have my word upon it."

The captain shrugged. "Your word will be worth naught when the beast begins to kick."

Rowan gritted his teeth. "I shall, of course, compensate you for any damages sustained."

The captain looked up, his expression hardening. "You shall make a deposit."

Rowan held his gaze. "You shall render a clearly annotated receipt for any such deposit."

The men stared at each other, then the captain named a price. Rowan halved it, the captain laughed as if 'twas preposterous, and they argued good-naturedly. Both knew the deal would be made, both knew the price agreed upon would be in the vicinity of two-thirds the captain's original one.

But when they agreed and Rowan would have shaken the other man's hand, the captain instead captured Ibernia's fingertips. She started, her eyes widening, but he smiled and lifted her hand to his lips. His eyes glowed as if he had just spied a fullsome meal, then he bowed low over her hand.

"Beauty unrivalled," the captain purred. "Have we met, *ma bella*?"

Rowan was certain Ibernia would grant him a sample of her sharp tongue.

But she flushed scarlet and spoke quickly, almost breathlessly. "Never!"

The captain smiled, no one on the wharf in his eyes but the incomparable Ibernia. And 'twas clear enough that she was intrigued by the captain.

Rowan seethed.

*He* was the one who should be capturing the lady's eye. *He* was the one who had bought her freedom. *He* was the one who had offered her freedom, even from his own bargain.

And he knew he was possessed of greater charm than

some swarthy sailor. He would not pay for their passage and watch this man seduce her!

Ibernia, though, seemed to share no such conviction. She smiled for the captain, a fetchingly small, intimate, feminine smile that would have made Rowan's toes curl.

Had that smile been directed at him. But Ibernia eyed the captain as if he were so wondrously handsome that she could look no where else.

" 'Tis impossible that such a creature should be compelled to endure the hold, or even the chamber of one of my aides.'' The captain smiled smoothly. "I insist, *ma bella,* that you share my quarters on this journey."

That was enough! If Ibernia would not put the captain in his place, Rowan would!

" 'Twould be a most inappropriate circumstance for my lady," he retorted before even he guessed what he would say.

All eyes turned to him as one. The captain frowned momentarily, his gaze flying between Ibernia and Rowan, but Rowan was watching the lady. The color drained from her face, as if she could not imagine a more dire fate.

He was not that foul to look upon!

Ibernia opened her mouth, but Rowan glared at her and she frowned. Mercifully, she had the wisdom to say naught, and he was uncommonly relieved that she chose this moment to trust his choice.

He did not expect that impulse to last.

"Your lady *wife*?" the captain echoed with obvious skepticism. He scanned Ibernia's clothing tellingly and Rowan cleared his throat.

"We were robbed in this filthy port," he lied, summoning what he thought was a suitable measure of indignation. He took Ibernia's elbow in his hand and drew her close to him in a proprietary fashion. The captain's eyes narrowed and

Ibernia caught her breath, but Rowan pressed a chaste kiss to her brow.

" 'Tis tragic that my lady's fine garb and jewellery was the greater loss," he declared, unsettled by the hint of Ibernia's vulnerability. "As much as it troubled me, there was no choice but to grant her some of my own garb. As you can imagine, we would put this place behind us with all haste."

"Indeed." The captain did not appear to be deceived, his glance drifting over Rowan's clothing.

It would have been helpful if Ibernia had said something in this moment to aid Rowan's lie. She seemed, however, supremely disinclined to do so, apparently having been captured by this man's so-called charm.

The captain brushed his lips across Ibernia's knuckles once again—for she had not pulled her hand from his, even yet—his voice dropping confidentially. "It shows much of a man that he takes the finer things for himself," he mused, then smiled for the lady as Rowan's blood boiled. "On this voyage, perhaps I may be so bold as to show you the merit of a true gentleman."

"I should be delighted," Ibernia said with perfect composure.

Then she smiled anew at the wretch!

Rowan longed to speak his mind but did not want to jeopardize their passage. With an effort, he bit back his words, taking no consolation from Thomas, who clearly enjoyed himself overmuch.

"At the very least, let me see you garbed suitably," the captain purred, his excuse for charm enough to make Rowan long to push him into the mire of the harbor.

Ibernia's hand fluttered to her throat. "I could not so impose!" she declared, with the demure grace of a lady of the court.

"Ah, but 'twould be to my own delight to see such beauty suitably presented." The captain bowed low. "If I may be so bold—Baldassare di Vilonte, at your service."

"I will pay for my lady's indulgences," Rowan interjected coldly when this tender scene showed no signs of ending. "Of course."

"Indulgences." Baldassare clicked his tongue disapprovingly, then granted a consoling smile to Ibernia. "One would expect naught else from a man who does not truly understand women."

Rowan let his tone turn frosty. "Though you do me great honor by flattering my lady's many charms, there are those who could misinterpret your attentions."

"Indeed." The captain released Ibernia's hand with evident reluctance, his gaze flickering over Rowan as if he saw no threat to his amorous intent. "If I can be of any assistance, *ma bella,* please do not hesitate to summon me."

She smiled like a Madonna, her tranquil expression making Rowan's blood boil.

Where had these fine manners been when he bought her freedom from that slave trader with hard coin?

"I thank you for your gallantry, Captain," she said sweetly. "You are too kind."

"Baldassare," he insisted. "You must call me Baldassare."

Ibernia caught her breath. "Baldassare," she conceded softly. The captain blew a kiss to her, then returned to his post, a whistle on his lips.

And Rowan knew all too well why that whistle was there. He was doubly irked that Ibernia had been so charming to this rogue seaman and that he had not been able to think of a clever way to redirect the conversation.

It helped naught that Thomas was grinning hugely and that Ibernia still stared after the captain. Apparently she could not tear her gaze away from that man's retreating figure.

He was wrought too short, to Rowan's thinking, and dressed too richly for his labor.

"Do not let me interrupt your interlude with *Baldassare*," Rowan said testily. " 'Tis only the matter of paying for our passage and seeing us aboard that occupies me."

Ibernia glanced coolly up at him. " 'Twould have been less than wise to insult the man," she replied. "Venetians are greatly proud of their courtly skills, and there is no telling what he might have done had I spurned his simple gesture—"

Her words halted, as she belatedly realized her mistake. She gasped and raised one hand to her lips, her quick glance to Rowan telling him that she wondered whether he had noticed.

And notice he had. Rowan folded his arms across his chest and smiled. "For a slave, you seem to know much of Venetians."

The lady lifted her chin. "One hears tales, even from other slaves. We are not mute, after all."

"Indeed!" Rowan caught her chin with one fingertip when she might have turned away. She held his gaze warily, her uncertainty making him feel oddly protective of her. "Why did you welcome his touch?" he asked softly.

"I did not welcome it," she snapped. "I endured it."

"You enjoyed his salute."

She pulled her chin away from his touch, that intellect bright in her eyes again. "Do you know so little of men that you did not guess his manner had naught to do with me? He sought only to prick *your* pride." An unexpected smile danced over her lips. "Indeed, there is much between men in matters of prick and pride."

Thomas chortled at her unexpected earthiness, and

Rowan's mood worsened that she—once again—made the jest instead of he.

"And 'tis the way of a merchant to be concerned with ensuring a deal is made," he retorted, annoyance dismissing his intent to be cautious. "As well as to have knowledge of Venetians."

Ibernia's lips thinned only slightly before she met his gaze squarely. "What are you saying?"

Aye, there was a catch in her voice, one that a man who was not watching for a hint of the truth might have missed.

But Rowan was watching. He leaned closer to her, newly confident in his conclusions. "Only that you, *ma demoiselle,* are no slave of humble origins, regardless of what you claim."

She smiled as if this was ridiculous. "Do tell. What else might I be, in such exquisite garb? Have you forgotten my fine rope? Or my charming companion of earlier this day? Perhaps you have forgotten the coin that won you my companionship?"

Rowan glared at Thomas before he could snicker, though the boy grinned. "Make no mistake, you lie to me in this and I know it well. You are from a merchant family—there is no other way you could know of Venetians and of making deals."

"No other way indeed!" she scoffed. "Do not imagine that slaves do not witness the making of bargains. Any with eyes in their head can learn much of that with little effort. I have been in this port long enough to have learned something of matters!"

Rowan did not doubt that. Just as he did not doubt that her tale was not the truth.

"You lie," Rowan insisted.

Her eyes flashed dangerously, the sign of her temper doing marvels for Rowan's mood. He knew he was close to the truth when she could not hide her response.

"And you are as innocent as a newborn babe?" she demanded impatiently.

Ah, she was magnificent in anger! All sparks and flash, all color and heat. Truly, a part of him enjoyed matching wits with her, for he could not guess what she might say. Indeed, her manner made Rowan wonder how she would look in passion—a prospect so intriguing that consideration of it nigh distracted him from the conversation.

Ibernia, however, showed no such distraction. "What of *your* lie that we are wed?"

"I never said that we were wed." Rowan grinned. "Not *precisely*."

Ibernia's eyes shone with blue fire and she propped her hands on her hips. "Do not play games with me, sir! I am not so witless that I did not hear the words fall from your lips. You quite clearly said that I was your lady."

"And so you are." Rowan leaned closer, virtually daring her to deny the truth. He had a sudden urge to kiss this challenging woman, to kiss her fully, so deeply that she moaned for more.

"You *are* a lady," he insisted.

"I am no one." She folded her arms across her chest mutinously, clearly unaware of the enchanting view of her ripe breasts that the pose granted Rowan.

What had ever possessed him to admire lean and lithe women?

"A lady, to be sure," he insisted, "and by virtue of the coin I parted with, you are *mine*."

When he might have expected an angry retort, Ibernia's lips twisted and she lifted a hand to her heart. "Your gallantry overwhelms me," she declared, then fluttered her eyelashes. "Is this the moment that I should cede to your chivalrous charm?'' She turned to Thomas, her eyes wide. ''Indeed, how could any woman choose the fine manners of Baldassare over your master's boldly possessive claims?''

Thomas snickered in a way that was becoming most annoying. It helped naught that Rowan felt like a clumsy knave. Indeed, he sensed he had disappointed Ibernia and disliked the feeling most heartily.

Matters could not be said to be proceeding to his plan.

''And what was I to do?'' Rowan demanded, his voice rising that she should find him less than appealing. Especially in comparison to that Venetian! ''Let you share his quarters? He would make you no wager, of that I am certain!''

''Perhaps not.'' Ibernia shrugged and smiled, composed once more. ''Perhaps he would make a *finer* offer.''

''And you would willingly be his courtesan?''

She shrugged. ''Perhaps.''

'Twas infuriating that she should think so little of his offer of protection. And truly, how could one who loathed the touch of a man—as Ibernia claimed she did—even consider the possibility of becoming a courtesan?

''You do not fool me!'' Rowan retorted. ''You are not fond of liaisons with men, be they knights or merchants or sea captains. You would not roll willingly to your back for anyone!''

Ibernia's lips tightened, then she shook a finger beneath his nose. ''I will never roll willingly to my back for *you,* of that you can be certain!''

''So you have said, and so we have wagered upon the outcome.'' Rowan smiled slowly. He savored the sight of her bright gaze and the flush in her cheeks.

Aye, he angered her.

And anger did not come from naught. Nay, the lady was

aware of his charms yet determined, quite naturally, to win their wager by denying her attraction to him.

'Twas a fine prospect for this journey. 'Twould not be an easy seduction, but Rowan guessed the prize was well worth the price of winning it.

"Indeed," he mused, his confidence restored. "I cannot wait for the privacy of our small chamber on this ship."

Ibernia's eyes flashed. "There will be no small chamber and no such privacy between us!"

"Of course there will be." Rowan clucked his tongue. "One cannot expect a married couple to endure the open decks or share quarters with the sailors."

"We are not wed!"

"Ah, then you would prefer I tell the captain the truth and let you share *his* quarters."

She bit her lip and glared at him, her silence as much of an endorsement as Rowan was likely to win. "I could loathe you," she muttered, although the corner of her mouth quirked in opposition to her words.

Rowan grinned. "But I shall coax you to love me instead."

"You are most audacious . . ." She might have said more, but Rowan had already turned away.

"We shall have a cabin." He nodded with confidence. "This captain will see the way of it and will oust one of his men, no doubt encouraged by the beauty of your smile."

"You may be certain that I will not ask him for this favor."

Rowan shrugged in his turn. "Then a measure of coin will change his thinking, of that I am certain. You have my assurance that I shall try."

"You cannot do this thing!"

" 'Twill be done, Ibernia. You have my word upon it."

Suddenly she looked so agitated by the prospect that

Rowan bent close to reassure her. He whispered in her ear and felt her shiver at the warmth of his breath on her nape.

"*Ma demoiselle,* I steal naught that is not freely offered." Rowan let himself smile when she glanced up at him, surprised to find a shimmer of tears in her eyes. He felt the sudden urge to coax her smile or her anger.

Anything but tears.

He winked. "Though I am not adverse to persuading a lady to freely make such an invitation."

"Oh, your surety of your own allure is insufferable!"

Rowan cupped her elbow in his hand before she could step away, smiling determinedly for the captain who watched their exchange. "And until we reach Dublin, I am your spouse, however insufferable I might be."

"You cannot insist upon this!"

"Indeed I can, for I just have."

"I will not countenance your lie," she insisted. "I will tell the captain the truth of it at first opportunity."

"And he, no doubt, will be quick to assure you of his own charms. Do you truly wish to share his chamber, all the way to Dublin?"

The lady exhaled mightily. "Caught between the devil and the sea," she declared through gritted teeth, and Rowan did not want to know which role she believed him to fill.

He dropped his voice persuasively low, intent on reassuring her. "I made you a wager and I will keep it, Ibernia. Do not be so certain that others would do as much."

A consideration dawned in her eyes, as if she wanted to believe him but did not know whether she should. The hint of her vulnerability tore at Rowan and made him want to make her smile.

He pulled her closer and brushed his lips across her brow, liking that she did not fight him in this. "As for claiming you as my wife, well, do not forget, my Ibernia, that all is fair in love and war.''

'' 'Tis clear enough which this is,'' the lady murmured.

Thomas chuckled behind him and Rowan could not help but grin. ''Aye, when I turn my charm fully upon you, you will not be able to resist me,'' he teased. ''Love will make you swoon!''

The lady laughed, albeit quickly and unwillingly. The sight of her smile restored the last vestige of Rowan's good humor, though her comment was cutting.

''Indeed, has there ever been a man so smitten with himself?''

Even Thomas's snort of laughter could not dispel Rowan's optimism.

Aye, he would win their wager yet!

Infuriating man!

Ibernia's innards felt tangled. Her flesh tingled beneath Rowan's gentle grip, her temple burned where he had pressed his lips. She could neither catch her breath nor stop the shiver that tripped over her flesh whenever Rowan touched her.

Because he made her so angry, of course. Indeed, Rowan loved himself well enough for two. Oh, she would not cede to his touch, not on this ship or afterward.

She caught her breath once more as he did just as he had warned he would do. Truly, he made his victory in pursuit of that cabin look so easy it might have been predestined. Ibernia stood by, helpless to change the course of events and not liking it all, while Rowan negotiated for the navigator's chamber with smooth finesse. She hovered behind him as much as she was able, uncertain whether the captain knew something of her or not.

Baldassare's dark eyes told naught of the secrets he held. Ibernia did not know whether to be more troubled by the captain's courtly manner or by the possibility that he might know something of her true tale.

To be sure, she had erred in approaching this ship, but realized her folly too late. Ibernia had been terrified that this captain might have heard a rumor and guessed her true identity. It helped naught that he studied her so intently. Indeed, she had been so frightened that her guise would be stripped away when first they met that she had not been able to find a word to say.

That was not like her. Rowan and the response he spurred from deep within her had only confused her. She must be falling ill, there could be no other explanation.

Ibernia had never met Baldassare di Vilonte, that was no lie. But she favored her mother strongly in appearance, and Rowan—a pox upon him!—had quickly guessed aright as far as her father's occupation.

Had her father posted a reward for her return? Ibernia had no desire to become a pawn in any man's quest for coin— and there was something about Baldassare that prompted her distrust.

But as the captain turned away one more time, saying naught, Ibernia exhaled shakily. Perhaps she had feared wrongly, perhaps there was no risk here at all. Perhaps she would soon be home safely, secure in her father's home, able to make her own choice—and that more wisely than she had done before.

But there was still some measure of risk to be had on this journey. Aye, the reminder of that danced within her as Rowan laid claim to her arm once more, his warm touch making her want to lean against his strength.

Though Ibernia relied upon no one. Even when she was

ill. She straightened proudly and walked ahead of Rowan, turning quickly away when he winked at her.

Oh, Ibernia would grant him a reckoning of his charm!

The cabin they were given was so small that Ibernia doubted she truly could evade Rowan in such a cramped space. She nibbled her lip and studied the narrow bed mounted to the wall, the floor betwixt door and bed little wider than the pallet itself. Below and above the bed were bundles of goods lashed tightly—indeed, even the ceiling hung with more bundles!—and they were counselled not to so much as touch the goods.

"An inventory will be made before you disembark," the solemn officer informed them, his words stilted. "And any deficiencies deducted from your deposit."

"Of course," Rowan said softly as he dropped his single saddlebag to the floor. There was no real question in his tone, as if he knew the answer already. "Yet are we not to be witness to the initial inventory?"

The man smiled then disappeared into the shadows behind them, no answer evidently necessary.

Rowan muttered a curse directed at Venetians everywhere, then dispatched Thomas to check upon the steeds. "I shall be close behind you," he advised, then turned such an intent glance upon Ibernia that she shivered.

"There is a matter we must discuss," he declared.

Ibernia put the width of the room between them, feeling the cabin was already too crowded with only his saddlebag and herself over the threshold.

But to her dismay, Rowan stepped fully into the chamber and closed the thin wooden door behind himself. He visibly took note of the lock, then glanced over the goods once more. Ibernia knew they had been enclosed with the finer goods, thus the lock upon the door. Indeed, she could smell the spice.

Any loss here could cost Rowan dearly, and she assumed he wished to preserve whatever coin he had left.

"I will touch naught," she insisted, believing her compliance was what he wished to ensure.

" 'Tis not that I would discuss," he said surprisingly, his bright gaze fixing upon her. He took a step closer and smiled, Ibernia's heart leapt at his proximity. She stepped back and found the wall immediately behind her.

Rowan halted and frowned. "I will not hurt you."

"So you say!"

His expression hardened. "So I *pledge.* You have naught to fear from me, though as much may not be said of our travelling companions."

A footstep echoed overhead, the men called and the ship creaked. Rowan came close and dropped his voice. Indeed, Ibernia could barely hear his words over the clamor of her heart, his intense manner doing naught to ease her concern.

"I would suggest you remain within this room and unlock the portal only to me," he said.

"I will not be locked away like a chest of spice."

"You will not wander the decks in garb so revealing." Rowan propped his hands on his hips. "Ibernia, we voyage with men, none of whom have pledged gallantry of any kind, to you or likely any other women. 'Twould not be wise to offer temptation."

As much as she hated to admit it, his counsel made good sense. And her feminine pride was flattered that he considered her tempting, though she would have died rather than admit it.

Because she remembered all too well the price such temptation could bear.

Ibernia heaved a sigh and surveyed the confines of the cabin. "I shall go mad in this space."

Rowan smiled crookedly. "Then you shall have to persuade me to accompany you onto the decks," he said, and leaned incrementally closer. Ibernia caught her breath as he stared directly into her eyes. His were twinkling merrily, like amber struck by sunlight, making it impossible to fear his intent.

"A mere kiss would render me your slave," he declared, though his manner was so teasing that Ibernia knew he lied.

"You!" she declared, and made to strike his shoulder.

Rowan danced out of range and laughed outright, his merriment even coaxing Ibernia's smile. Then he sobered. "I ask only that you remain."

Ibernia was not inclined to agree so readily as that, simply because this man would read too much into such compliance. "And if I disagree?"

"Then I shall have to remain with you," he said easily. "For truly, you are beneath my care, at least until you win your freedom." Rowan pursed his lips and studied the cabin, his gaze lingering on the bed before he met Ibernia's gaze once more. There was a wicked glint of mischief in his eyes. "Though indeed, I wonder what we might *do* to pass the hours, the days, and the nights."

"You will never seduce me."

"Ah, Ibernia, I have yet to truly *try*!" Rowan winked. Ibernia swung her hand to swat him and prompted only his laughter as he ducked out the door.

To be sure, once she had shut the door and that insufferable man could no longer see her response, she smiled herself.

Now that she was alone, Ibernia allowed herself to marvel at her own certainty that Rowan could be trusted to keep his word. Indeed, he had shown her naught but good treatment in the short time they had been together, and she dared to expect only more of the same.

Optimism, her mother always said, was a healthy trait for a woman of merit. Nay, Rowan would not hurt her and he would not force her—he would only try to persuade her.

And none but Ibernia knew how futile those efforts were doomed to be. That made her smile broaden.

Only for it to fade shortly thereafter to naught. Even a merchant's daughter as knowledgeable about the ways of the world as Ibernia could err, for err she had. No sooner had the *Angelica* taken to the seas than the horrible truth became clear.

'Twas then that the ship's cargo moaned.

# Chapter Three

ROWAN WAS NOT IN A GOOD MOOD.

Already this day he had bought a slave he did not want; he had committed to keeping that slave he did not want; he had boarded a ship in much quicker succession than he might have preferred. Further, the ship was not one he would have chosen of his own volition, regardless of its destination.

For Rowan did not like this ship's captain, this Baldassare di Vilonte. There was something untrustworthy about the man, something that made Rowan less than pleased to have his own future in this particular man's care.

'Twas certainly not because Ibernia smiled for Baldassare when she refused to smile for *him*. That would have made no sense at all. Nay, Rowan de Montvieux cared naught for Ibernia, naught for any woman in particular beyond a desire to make them laugh.

Only Ibernia's refusal to laugh at his jests rankled, and that because it was contrary to the response of all women Rowan had ever known. Aye, and her apparent preference for a Venetian sea captain over his own copious charms.

'Twas unnatural.

And so, he led Troubador into the hold in markedly poor temper, what greeted them there doing naught to improve his mood. Rowan caught his breath, his ears pricking at the sound of very human whispers. The hold where the horses were to be tethered was veiled in shadows, and surrounded by three heavy wooden walls lashed with stores.

Above was a hatch to the deck, a rope ladder hanging down. Behind Rowan was the entry to the hold, the side of the ship that would soon be lifted back into place. 'Twould be nailed in place, then sealed with wax, Rowan knew it well. The horses would be effectively trapped there for the duration of the journey.

As were those he could hear *breathing* behind the solid walls.

He and Thomas exchanged a quick, horrified glance, Rowan painfully aware of the shipman supervising their efforts. He gave the pale squire a sharp look and continued as if naught was amiss. Even Troubador looked indignant, the smell of fear doing naught to counter the beast's inherent dislike of ships.

As Rowan shared that dislike, he was disinclined to be overly harsh with his mount. If he had been compelled to endure the voyage belowdecks, he would have been even more ill than was his custom.

Which said much, indeed.

But Rowan had made an arrangement. He had paid a healthy deposit for their passage, and had no doubt that it would remain in Baldassare's possession, even if Rowan and his party chose now to not journey on the *Angelica*.

Aye, Rowan's coin would go into the treasury of this rogue Baldassare, a man who made his fortune in spice and slaves. That revelation could do little to restore a man's humor.

'Twas Ibernia's fault that Rowan had impulsively arranged to journey on this particular vessel without learning anything about it, Ibernia's fault that he had been compelled to make a poor choice.

Truly, she tested his patience overmuch!

Troubador rolled his eyes and fought the bit, refusing to step further into the shadows. Rowan stroked the beast's flank and tried to calm him, but to no avail. It helped naught that the ship began to rock and Rowan's own belly began to churn.

"My lord," Thomas whispered as they tethered the steeds. "Must we journey this way? The ship has not yet left the port."

" 'Tis not my way to be faithless in a bargain made, Thomas," Rowan said grimly. "Even when 'tis made with a rogue."

"Aye," Thomas agreed faintly, his usual cheerfulness absent.

Rowan murmured to Troubador, who was having none of his reassurance. The steed stamped impatiently and tossed his head. The palfrey took his mood and became flighty, as she was wont to do. She danced sideways and refused to step up beside the destrier, let alone into the spot they had been assigned midship.

"We have not all the day and night to see this settled!" Their companion swore in Venetian, then raised a hand to strike the palfrey's flank.

Rowan moved quickly to intervene.

"No one touches my steeds!" he cried. "I have paid a king's ransom for passage—you will take naught more from the hide of any beneath my care!"

The man lowered his hand and smiled slowly. "A man of measure would endure no such foolery from any beast."

But Rowan would not be tempted to respond in kind. "A man of merit has no need to use force to win his way," he retorted.

The shipman snorted, unconvinced.

But Rowan would show him the truth of it. He retrieved

two lengths of linen from his saddlebag and blindfolded first the palfrey, then the destrier. The two steeds settled once they could not see the terrors surrounding them. Their noses twitched and their ears flicked, but the blindfold combined with Rowan's gentle murmuring calmed them. They shivered and leaned against Rowan and Thomas, who stroked and spoke to them.

Within a few moments, Rowan coaxed them into the assigned space. And not a heartbeat too soon. The ship heaved, there were cries from above and a last scampering on the decks. The gangplank behind was lifted, that hatch sealed as hammering echoed through the ship.

Trunks were hastily passed through the opening above and stacked behind the steeds, Troubador bristling at the noise of the men passing back and forth close beside him. Rowan scratched his ears and spoke softly, keeping a stern eye on how close the goods were packed to the horses.

Even such a measure of his coin, it seemed, had won them very limited space. Finally the men darted back above and more calls echoed.

"If you have pampered your beasts enough, we would depart," the shipman said wryly.

Rowan cast him a dark look. "I would remain for a few moments, to ensure the destrier settles." A shiver ran over Troubador's dark flesh even as Rowan stroked him. He could not abandon the beast when he was so afraid.

"We shall seal the hatch."

"You shall do no such thing," Rowan snapped. "My arrangement expressly allows access to the steeds throughout the journey."

"They must be fed!" Thomas interjected.

"Then their leavings must be shovelled, and that by you," the shipman snorted.

"I am well used to the duties associated with tending horses," Rowan retorted.

The men glared at each other for a long moment, then the silhouette of a man's head and shoulders was visible against the patch of cloudy sky. He demanded something in rapid Venetian; the shipman replied. Rowan had one last glimpse of the man leaning against his goods, his expression sardonic, then the hatch dropped closed and the hold was plunged into darkness.

"You must understand that with such a valuable cargo, I cannot leave you here alone," the shipman said, his voice soft in the shadows. "You have only to tell me when you are prepared to leave and arrangements will be made."

And Rowan understood that his own cry would not bring a ladder and the opening of the hatch. He felt the shadows press against him, he smelled suddenly the press of humans trapped around him.

The silk of Troubador's hide beneath his hand was suddenly smoother, the scent of horse stronger. The destrier shivered once again, the ripple that ran over his flesh passing over Rowan's own. Denied of sight, he was more aware of his other senses.

Thomas took a step closer. The boy was uncharacteristically silent, and now Rowan wondered at the wisdom of his choice.

Perhaps he should not have been so stubborn, or so anxious to win Ibernia's dare to win them passage on this ship. Perhaps he should have abandoned the coin to Baldassare—he could have afforded as much.

But 'twas too late for second thoughts.

Rowan's belly churned restlessly as the sounds of casting off echoed through the ship. The vessel lurched, the oars ground, the wood creaked, and the water splashed against the hull. The ship rocked, finding its own rhythm as it lurched out of London's docks and out to sea.

And when the first wave of the sea crashed against the prow, rocking the ship from stem to stern, Rowan could not withhold his response any longer.

He fell to his knees and vomited in the bucket left for the steeds, recalling its location all too well. It helped naught that the shipman laughed.

'Twas Ibernia's fault that he was at sea again in such quick succession, Rowan thought furiously, Ibernia's fault that he was trapped upon this specific ship. Aye, *she* had challenged him, she had chosen this vessel.

And she owed Rowan compensation for what she had wrought.

If Ibernia had any doubt as to what sound she heard, it was quickly dismissed. The moaning grew louder as they moved out to sea, clearly distinguishable from the creaking of the ship.

The hold of this vessel was filled with slaves. 'Twas a little too close to her own experience for comfort. Ibernia's breath caught in her throat and she closed her eyes, her ears filling with the sound. She could nigh feel that cursed rope around her neck again, and she itched to bring freedom to those below.

She knew she could not do it, just as she knew she should not be so foolish as to try. But that moaning tore at her heart.

She wondered how many of them there were.

She wondered where they had come from.

She wondered how many of them were ill or wounded, or heartbroken; how many separated from their families; and how many terrified.

When someone began to cry loudly, their wail winding through the ship, Ibernia could stand it no longer. Rowan's advice was forgotten, her hand was on the latch. She opened the door only to find the captain himself standing before it, his hand raised to knock.

He smiled at the sight of her. "Ah! I knew you would come to seek me out," he purred. His eyes gleamed as he stepped forward, his smile flashed in the darkness. "You are perhaps not so devoted a wife as your *husband* might suppose. And truly, there is naught awry with a lady seeing to her own pleasure." He arched a brow, obviously certain where Ibernia would find that pleasure.

She straightened and forced a thin smile, well aware that alienating her host would not be clever. "Indeed, I sought only a last sight of London."

Baldassare shrugged eloquently. "Ah, but 'tis inappropriate that you should walk the deck in such humble garb, despite your spouse's lack of generosity." His smile turned predatory and Ibernia took an unwilling step backward into the cabin. "I have a gift for you, *ma bella*."

Only then did Ibernia look past the captain, and when she did, her heart nigh stopped. Baldassare's smile did not falter, though the small woman behind him looked terrified. She was tiny, her dark hair matted, her dark eyes too wide for her face. She was trembling in her tattered garb and her feet were bare.

But 'twas the iron shackled around her neck, no less the length of chain held easily by Baldassare that made Ibernia's mouth go dry. She deliberately stood straight, hoping to hide her response, though her nails dug into the wood frame of the portal.

The captain nodded, apparently acknowledging that Ibernia could only be delighted by his generosity, then ducked past her into the tiny chamber. He locked the other end of the chain to a loop on the wall nonchalantly, tossed the key once in the air, then shoved it into his purse.

Ibernia had already wondered about that loop on the wall. Now she knew its purpose. The very thought made her feel ill with her own unwelcome memories. The woman watched the path of the key avidly, and Ibernia could understand her fear and suspicion.

Aye, they had much in common, they two.

"I had thought 'twould be fitting for you to have finer garb to wear," Baldassare said, his tone fitting for more social circumstance than this. "And thus I bring to you a length of wool more suitable to accent your beauty."

He snapped his fingers and a young boy bowed as he stepped into the room in turn. 'Twas becoming quite crowded in these small quarters! He presented a bolt of fine wool, woven in the tonal stripe typical of the weavers of Flanders, and dyed in wondrous hues of blue. Ibernia assessed its value despite herself and was impressed by the gift.

She knew this man would expect something in return for what he granted. At the same time, she doubted she could reject the gift without causing offense. Once again Ibernia was caught between two poor choices.

Baldassare gestured grandly to the wool. " 'Tis enough for a woman's kirtle, and my gift to you."

"I could not be so bold," Ibernia protested.

"I insist. 'Tis a fitting token of my admiration and one that I will not accept being refused."

"But I have no skill with a needle," she lied.

Baldassare gestured to the slavewoman without glancing in her direction. "This one is said to have talent. You may use her services."

"But . . ."

"But surely you would not wish to risk insulting my generosity?" He smiled warmly, a man looking to be indulged.

Ibernia knew she would not win at this, but still she would try. This was the manner of man who would force his choice upon one, if not given some challenge. She would at least make her unwillingness clear.

"You are indeed most generous," she acknowledged tightly. "But I fear the gift is too rich to be suitable." She touched the cloth, uncertain she should voice a question about the terrified woman crouched behind the captain. " 'Tis a fine weave."

"Aye, only the best will do."

Ibernia flicked a glance through her lashes. "My husband might be insulted, should I accept."

Baldassare's jaw tightened. "Then his argument would be with me," he said with sudden ferocity, then bowed with such graciousness that Ibernia thought she had imagined his fearsome expression. "If I might be so bold as to touch your fingertips?"

'Twas a concession, but a small one. Ibernia quickly debated her options and decided to grant this small favor. Baldassare, after all, could force them from his ship, and she wanted more than anything else to be home.

Surely she could keep his attentions at bay for the duration of this short journey?

Ibernia offered her hand, embarrassed at the state of her nails when Baldassare lingeringly kissed each fingertip in turn. He straightened and smiled genially. "Do not be so foolish as to grant her a knife," he said with a quick gesture to the woman behind him. She flinched tellingly at his gesture, a move Baldassare did not notice. "These people have no scruples whatsoever."

With that, he took his leave, the boy scurrying behind

him. Ibernia pivoted to eye her new charge, leaning back against the wall as she did so.

The woman was breathing heavily, her expression wary. She did indeed resemble a cornered creature in the wild. The ship rocked as the two women stared at each other, the bolt of cloth lying on the pallet to one side.

Ibernia wondered whether she had looked as frightened as this when Rowan found her on the dock.

"What is your name?" she asked gently.

The woman's eyes narrowed and she said naught at all, her gaze darting over the cabin as if she sought escape.

Ibernia could not begin to imagine what she had endured. Indeed, she did not want to.

Ibernia took a deep breath, striving to show herself harmless as she took a step closer and squatted to look the woman in the eye. She left her hands open on her knees. The woman watched her, easing back into the corner, her expression uncertain.

"Do you speak?" Ibernia kept her voice soft, all too familiar with the terror this woman was obviously experiencing. "Are you alone here? Where did you come from?"

When her questions merited no response, she tried Gaelic, though indeed the woman did not look like a Celt. She tried the dialect of the Venetians and noted only that the woman's expression grew more mutinous.

If she spoke or understood that tongue, she would not allow it to pass her lips. Ibernia eyed the heavy shackle and could not blame her for that.

But that shackle gave her an idea of how to proceed.

Though the sealed hold composed the better part of the galleon, the captain's chamber and those of his officers were built upon the back third of the deck, where a small kitchen was secreted. Here was where Ibernia should be awaiting Rowan behind a locked door.

Even Rowan was not fool enough to believe that.

He made his way back there, well aware of Baldassare's mocking gaze following his progress across the deck. Rowan had no doubt the tale of his illness had already reached the captain's ears. Thomas, well accustomed to his duties, emptied the pail over the side and followed Rowan without abandoning that pail.

Aye, 'twould be needed again, of that Rowan was certain. His ears burned at Baldassare's mocking smile, and he did not deign to acknowledge that man.

At least Rowan made it across the deck without having to flee for the rails. 'Twas a small victory, though likely one that had more to do with the hollow emptiness of his belly.

Rowan blinked at the darkness as he stepped into the tiny corridor, the smell of salt fish on the boil nigh enough to make his belly heave with all haste. With an effort, he swallowed his bile and made for the door near the end on the right.

Open. Of course.

Rowan gritted his teeth and stepped forward, intent on telling Ibernia of her foolishness, but the murmur of her voice brought him to a sudden halt. He frowned, surprised at her gentle tone, and gestured to Thomas to hang back. Rowan sidled closer, touching the door with one fingertip to ease it open wider.

Neither of the women within noticed. Aye, there were *two* women, one small and dark, shackled to the wall and as terrified as a cornered hare; the other, Ibernia, striving to reassure the first. A bolt of wool lay between them, and Rowan knew who had been so bold as to bring it.

First Ibernia, he resolved, *then* Baldassare.

As Rowan watched, Ibernia lifted her chemise away from

her neck, speaking softly to the other woman. Though Ibernia's back was to him, Rowan knew she showed the slavewoman the rope burns upon her own neck.

He was astonished that Ibernia of all women would admit to any manner of weakness, the very unexpectedness of this making him halt. He lingered in the protective cloak of the shadows, watching.

Her companion was evidently also astonished. The woman's eyes widened, her hand rose to the iron fastened around her neck. Ibernia nodded, her words falling low and fast, the cadence foreign and lyrical. Though the sound was pleasing, Rowan could not understand her speech, and neither apparently could the slave.

But on the matter of bondage, the women clearly understood each other.

Ibernia pulled up the hem of her sleeve, revealing a sorry welt on her left wrist, a sight that made Rowan's gorge rise.

Clearly Ibernia sought to reassure the terrified slave, sought to show the commonality between them to calm the woman's fears. 'Twas an act of compassion and one that left Rowan even more intrigued about his newly acquired captive.

The slave caught her breath and stared at Ibernia. Slowly her tiny fingers found what might have been called the hem of her tattered kirtle and she lifted it slightly, displaying an angry gash upon her leg. The wound had scabbed but would undoubtedly leave a scar.

Ibernia clicked her tongue and shook her head.

She squared her shoulders then, and Rowan knew she would reveal something even more painful than what she had thus far. How he wished he could see her features! Ibernia's hand landed on her belly and moved downward before it suddenly halted. She made some gesture with her fingers and averted her face from the slavewoman, as if her confession mortified her so that she could not look another in the eye.

Rowan's mouth went dry in sudden certainty of what had happened to her. No wonder she insisted she would never willingly turn to a man!

The slavewoman's face burned crimson. Her mouth worked silently as she touched the apex of her thighs through the worn kirtle. Her tears rose, a silent testimony to the pain she had endured.

Rowan felt ill, though 'twas not due to the movement of the ship this time. The woman spoke quickly, one sentence falling from her tongue in a rush. They were hot words, foreign yet filled with such anguish that any fool could have understood her pain. She curved her arms, as if cradling an invisible child, then flung out her hands with a cry.

She had been raped and she had lost a child; it did not matter whether that had been two separate incidents or one of cause and effect. Rowan shook his head in horror and dared not interrupt.

The woman inhaled sharply and bit her lip, clearly fearing she had said too much. Her wide eyes fixed on Ibernia, who murmured something low, reassuring by its very tone. A lone tear broke from the slavewoman's lashes and fell with a splash upon her interlocked hands.

Ibernia opened her arms. The slavewoman fell into her embrace and wept, while Ibernia cooed softly to her. She closed her eyes and held the smaller woman close, letting her pain spend itself in tears.

Rowan noted that Ibernia's cheeks were dry, and he marvelled at her strength. Maybe she had wept all of her tears already, though Rowan doubted it. Nay, 'twould be like Ibernia to never permit herself the weakness of tears. He leaned back against the wall and thought about this, content to grant the women whatever time they needed.

Moments later, the slavewoman pulled out of Ibernia's embrace. She rubbed her tears from her cheeks and took a few shaky breaths. Rowan held his breath, fascinated by this glimpse of Ibernia's compassion and not wanting to break the spell she had woven.

She touched her breast. "Ibernia," she said softly.

Then she reached across to the other woman. The woman inhaled sharply but she did not pull back, even when Ibernia's fingertips hovered a mere thumb's breath away from her own chest.

The woman's lips parted, but no sound came forth. 'Twas as if she had not uttered her own name in so long that she had forgotten it.

But Ibernia waited, infinitely patient, impossibly still. The woman licked her lips, she took a breath and swallowed, she tried again.

"Marika," she said hoarsely.

"Marika," Ibernia repeated, the name fluid on her tongue. She sat back on her heels and gestured to each of them in turn, speaking as one would speak to a child. "Marika and Ibernia."

A flush rose in Marika's cheeks and she lifted one hand hesitantly toward her companion. "Ibernia," she said softly.

Hesitantly she repeated the cradling gesture, those tears rising again. "Vassily," she whispered, her voice husky, and Rowan knew she named her lost child.

"Vassily," Ibernia repeated, and crossed herself. "God bless his tiny soul."

Marika crossed herself in turn, Ibernia's blessing of her child apparently understood and appreciated.

And when Marika tentatively smiled, Rowan knew that Ibernia had smiled first. Indeed, he wished he could have glimpsed that smile himself, but the lady still had her back to him.

All the same, he was touched by Ibernia's desire to forge a bond, however fleeting, between herself and this slave. He felt that he had glimpsed something that was not his to witness. But when he might have left the two to their new acquaintanceship, his stomach rolled ominously.

Marika glanced up, paling at the sight of him. She must have assumed him responsible for Ibernia's wounds, for she clutched Ibernia's hand, as if she would draw her close.

Ibernia herself started at the sight of Rowan but quickly lifted her chin with defiance. She eased to her feet, her leisure implying that she had meant to do so all along, and placed herself deliberately between Rowan and Marika.

Her implication that he could not be trusted was not welcome.

Rowan felt his lips thin. "You must have charmed our host, for him to share one of his slaves with you."

Ibernia's eyes narrowed. "There are more?" she asked, no question in her tone.

"Perhaps a hundred." Rowan folded his arms across his chest and leaned in the doorway. "They are sealed below, out of sight and thus impossible to count."

"Marika would know."

The woman started at the sound of her name, her anxious gaze flying between the two of them.

Rowan had a sudden feeling of dread. Surely Ibernia would not challenge the captain over his cargo?

He disliked that he could not be certain of that.

"It matters little, for there is naught we can do." Ibernia's eyes flashed at this claim, but Rowan held up one hand for silence. "You chose this vessel," he reminded her sternly, "and I have already parted with a goodly measure of coin to see us upon it. Do not imagine that I have the wherewithal to buy the freedom of an entire ship of slaves, especially from a Venetian well aware of their worth. And do not imagine that your friend Baldassare will sacrifice their value in any way.''

''You could set them free,'' Ibernia suggested, her words confirming Rowan's worst suspicions. ''You could begin a rout . . .''

''And have the Venetians put a price on my head? I think not!'' Rowan flung out a hand angrily. ''Do you know naught of the world? You must understand that the Venetians are everywhere, in every port, in every town. I would not survive a year!''

Ibernia squared her shoulders, her eyes taking a glint Rowan did not find encouraging. ''But indeed, you said yourself that you loved a challenge. Perhaps I should dare—''

''Do not even say it!'' Rowan roared, at the limit of his patience as he had never been in all his days. '' 'Twould be senseless foolery!''

Marika shrank against the wall as Rowan stepped into the room and glowered at Ibernia, marvelling that she could turn his mood so foul so very quickly. ''I will not take such a dare, even if you are so foolish as to utter it.''

Ibernia, supremely unconcerned, shrugged. ''Ah, then I see you are not the man you pledged to be, after all.''

She had done it again.

Rowan swore thoroughly, though it did naught to aid matters.

Had he ever met a more irksome woman? Rowan was quite certain he had not. He shoved a hand through his hair, paced to the portal, and swore again.

Rowan spun to face Ibernia and found her beginning to smile. ''You are an astonishingly vexing woman,'' he muttered, and she grinned outright.

''I thank you, sir,'' she said with a mocking little bow.

Her eyes sparkled with beguiling mischief and yet again,

Rowan was enchanted by her spirit. She defied even his own expectations, and he found himself sorely tempted to take her dare, to prove her wrong, to conquer the odds set against Marika and however many of her companions were locked in the hold.

'Twas folly of the worst kind. But Ibernia's eyes, eyes that glowed from within like fiery sapphires, tempted Rowan to do just that.

He braced one hand in the door frame and watched the lady, even as he tried to figure a way to best her in this. "And what if I did meet your challenge?" he demanded softly. "What would you grant me in exchange?"

Ibernia's smile faded. "The satisfaction of a match won."

Rowan shook his head, reassured that the balance had shifted once again. Now she was wary and *he* called the tune.

This was infinitely preferable to the opposite circumstance.

"Nay," he said calmly. " 'Twill not do, not for such high stakes."

"I have no fortune to grant you."

"Save your favor." Rowan grinned wickedly. "A more earthy satisfaction would be in order."

Ibernia folded her arms across her chest and her eyes narrowed. He knew she had already guessed the direction of his thoughts. "What do you want?"

"A kiss is all, one kiss from your sweet lips." Rowan blew the lady a kiss, to no visible effect.

"But, *husband,* you have the right to claim a kiss at any moment you so please." Ibernia's tone was as hard as a whore's heart, but Rowan was not fooled. She was afraid he would make precisely that claim, and as tempted as he was, he would prove that expectation of hers wrong.

He would prove her understanding of men and their desires wrong if 'twas the last thing he did.

Rowan let his smile broaden and leaned closer. Ibernia held her ground, as he had guessed she would, though he heard her quick intake of breath when he brought his lips close to her ear.

"Aye, *wife,* that I could," he whispered, and felt her shiver. "But the meal is so much sweeter when 'tis served willingly."

"I have told you that I will never surrender willingly!"

"Nay?" Rowan met her bright gaze. "I dare you to accept my challenge."

"What challenge?" Her voice was breathless, her eyes wide.

"For each slave I set free, you will shower me with kisses."

Ibernia's eyes narrowed to a sliver of blue, but not so quickly that Rowan did not note the way her gaze dropped to his lips. Indeed, a tinge of pink claimed her cheeks.

"One kiss," she argued breathlessly.

"Nay, 'twill not do." Rowan leaned closer, savoring how she caught her breath. Aye, she *was* aware of him. If he led her easily, she would follow him down the path of seduction.

The very prospect heated his blood, but Rowan strove to appear unaffected by her rejection. "Only hundreds of sweet kisses will compensate."

"Never!"

Rowan shrugged and sauntered toward the door once more. "Ah, well. Perhaps Marika is accustomed to her shackles."

"You!" Ibernia cried. Rowan glanced back to find her eyes flashing dangerously. "You would use one challenge to win the other."

"I?" Rowan feigned affront. "You would accuse me of

such dishonorable intent?'' He appealed to his amused squire. ''Truly, Thomas, have you ever heard the like?''

''Oh!'' Ibernia stormed after Rowan, shaking her finger beneath his nose. Her cheeks were flushed in a most intriguing way. ''You will not best me in this! You will not trick me into falling prey to your charms!''

Rowan smiled. ''Is that not odd? I was certain you believed I had no charms at all.''

Their gazes locked and held for a charged moment, then Ibernia looked away.

Rowan felt curiously compelled to reassure her. ''Kisses are not the same as surrender, Ibernia,'' he said quietly.

The lady's gaze lingered on Marika, all the anger fading from her expression as that compassion stole to the fore. The softening of her features made her look younger, and unexpectedly vulnerable. She lifted her chin suddenly, a warrior princess yet again, and Rowan's admiration surged.

''Marika first?'' she demanded.

Rowan was humbled that she would face her own fears to see to the good of another. Such a markedly selfless gesture gave him yet another glimpse of this lady's character. ''Of course.''

Ibernia squared her shoulders. ''I suppose a woman can endure anything once,'' she conceded, with enough reluctance to prick Rowan's pride. ''I accept your wager.'' Ibernia glanced up at him so quickly that Rowan had no time to hide his displeasure with her response.

''Because you think I will do it only once,'' he retorted.

A smile lifted the corner of Ibernia's full lips, the twinkle that lit her eyes nigh compensation enough for her insult. ''Aye. Clearly. Indeed, I suspect that you may lose interest in the chase before 'tis won.'' She arched a brow. ''I might not have to pay my wager, after all.''

Her pert manner was enough to challenge Rowan's control right then and there. The half-light favored the perfection of her creamy complexion and hid the scars of the rope. When she held his gaze like this, her own sporting a winsome twinkle, her lips full and half curved into a smile, Rowan could not imagine losing interest in this clever beauty.

'Twas time she knew the truth of it.

"Indeed?" Rowan eased closer, putting the narrowness of the space to work in his favor. Ibernia moved back a mere increment and he knew the instant her back encountered the wooden wall, for she blinked quickly. Rowan braced one hand on the wall over her shoulder, sheltering her beneath his body. He drew close enough that he could feel the heat of her flesh so close to his own, yet he did not touch her.

Save with a fingertip.

He held her gaze as his fingertip grazed her temple, slowly circled her ear, then traced a circle against the soft flesh beneath her ear. He felt her pulse leap beneath his touch as his finger eased across her throat, tracing the line of her jaw. He tipped her chin up further with that fingertip and held her gaze.

She did not seem to even breathe. He watched a flush rise over her throat and stain her cheeks.

"Indeed, *ma demoiselle,*" he whispered. "You underestimate your own allure." Rowan bent and pressed a gentle kiss beneath her ear, his fingertip still upon her chin. The flesh was so soft there, so sweetly scented and warm that he was sorely tempted to do more than leave that kiss there alone.

Well aware of her fears, though, and newly aware of the reason for them, Rowan left Ibernia ample room to escape. That she did not duck beneath his arm and flee might have been called a victory of sorts.

Or it might have been a sign that the lady was even more

stubborn than he. Rowan did not know and he did not care. She stayed. On some level, she began to trust him.

'Twould do, for the moment.

"Perhaps even as much as you overestimate my savagery," he breathed into her ear. Rowan felt Ibernia shiver, indulged himself with another tiny taste of her sweet flesh, then stepped away.

She did not so much as move—let alone speak!—until he had left the cabin. Rowan heard the latch dropped and allowed himself a tuneless whistle.

Aye, she would succumb to him before this journey was done, he was certain of it.

# Chapter Four

IBERNIA COULD NOT CATCH HER BREATH.

Indeed, her flesh burned where Rowan had deposited that pair of kisses. She tingled from head to toe, she wanted to shiver.

Illness, it could be naught else. Her mother had always said that a port was an unhealthy place, and she, to be sure, had frequented the most unsavory corners of this port. Though 'twas through no choice of her own, Ibernia feared she was about to bear the price of her own folly.

Again.

Ibernia was well aware of Marika's curious glance upon her. She took a trio of quick breaths and forced a smile. No doubt Marika had done naught so foolish as Ibernia had done to earn her sorry fate. Ibernia had heard many tales of how slaves came to be bought and sold—most were simply in the wrong place at the wrong time.

Or showed the poor judgement to be on the losing side of a war.

'Twould be no small thing to see Marika released. Ibernia willed her resolve to grow. Aye, if Rowan would see to Marika's freedom, if he managed this noble deed, then she would keep her word. She could do anything once and survive to tell the tale, as experiences of this sixmonth had already shown.

She had naught to lose in this wager, but a few kisses.

For indeed, she had less doubt with each moment that Rowan would keep his pledge. The man had a resolve about him, obviously one he preferred others not to note. But the fact remained that a dare taken against the odds could only be won with rare persistence.

Ibernia did not have a trouble believing that Rowan won most of his wagers. The man could be cursedly single-minded!

*Hundreds of sweet kisses.* Only this knight would have the audacity to ask so boldly for something so difficult to grant. Ibernia trembled within at the very prospect.

But she took a deep shaking breath and gestured to the cloth. Marika seemed to understand, her hands flying as she tried to indicate her needs to make the dress.

There proved to be a small bundle rolled within the cloth, a sack replete with needles and thread, a length of twine, a tiny sharp knife for cutting the cloth. Marika exclaimed with delight at the needles and—deliberately contrary to Baldassare's advice—Ibernia entrusted her with the knife.

Marika clutched it for a moment, clearly overwhelmed to be granted possession of what could be used as a weapon. They two shared a smile, then she began to chatter. Clearly she told Ibernia what had to be done, though she spoke in some incomprehensible tongue. Ibernia knew the order of the tasks, having made many kirtles herself, but she feigned ignorance.

'Twould be good for Marika to feel a confidence in her own abilities once more. Already she looked more vivacious and carefree. Ibernia's heart hardened against Baldassare a little more as the smaller woman talked with increasing animation.

To think that she had lost her child. Ibernia could not imagine the heartache Marika had borne.

Soon the two women were laboring together despite the language barrier, the door securely locked against the ship of men. Marika even began to hum under her breath as she measured Ibernia with the length of string.

But Ibernia could not ease the heat of those two tiny kisses, perhaps because she had so little to do. She wondered if there was a mark left upon her flesh from Rowan's sure touch.

*Shower him with kisses.* The echo of his words in her thoughts, the knowing glint in his eye, the hint of his smile as he uttered them, all conspired to distract Ibernia from the task at hand. Indeed, only a man so enamored of himself as Rowan de Montvieux could have conceived of such a deed!

Oh, if ever she had desired to see that knight lose a wager, that desire had just doubled anew.

All the same, she could not bear the thought of Marika not being free. Instinct told her that she would not have long to ponder the matter. No doubt Rowan, intent on securing his prize, already negotiated for Marika's release.

Then he would return to claim his due. Ibernia's heart skipped a beat with dread. He could return at any moment. How long could it take to part with coin, especially for Rowan, who seemed to scatter wealth readily in his wake? The man had no respect for hard-won coin, that much was for certain, and the merchant's daughter awaiting his return could not help but disapprove.

Yet even then Ibernia tried to imagine a way to avoid her duty in this. Was there some way she could keep her wager with Rowan, ensure Marika's freedom, yet avoid that fearsome toll of kisses?

Ibernia was a woman with her wits about her—men with teasing smiles to the contrary—and she struggled to think of a clever way out of her pending predicament.

◈

Yet Rowan, despite Ibernia's conviction to the contrary, was not ensuring Marika's release.

Naught could have been further from his mind, the pitching of the ship turning his thoughts in one direction alone. He hung over the rail, faithful Thomas by his side. Either the tide had changed more quickly than Baldassare anticipated or that man was incompetent. Rowan might have been able to enjoy that man's failure if he had not been so ill.

"For a man who has eaten little for three days, you have an uncommon lot in your belly," Thomas commented when the knight finally straightened.

He shot the boy a dark look. "I thank you for your solace."

Thomas grinned unrepentantly. He offered a damp rag and Rowan wiped the sweat from his brow. He accepted a sip of *eau-de-vie* and rinsed his mouth, spitting the liquor over the rail before repeating the deed. Despite the expense, he could not bear the thought of swallowing it.

His stomach soundly agreed with his choice, its rumbling more muted as they moved into the open seas. The wind lifted Rowan's hair, the fresh tang of the air doing as much to restore his spirits as the increasingly steady roll of the deck.

The grey water still churned too much for Rowan's comfort, so he deliberately looked to the horizon. The sea stretched in fathomless grey in all directions, the overcast skies and mist hanging over the water making the outlines of land distant and hazy.

The grey was unsettling, to say the least. Rowan gripped the rail and strove to remain composed. To the west, the channel betwixt the dim silhouettes of England and France seemed to boil. Rowan felt the blood drain from his face.

Aye, he would be ill all the way to Dublin.

'Twas not an encouraging prospect.

"I suppose 'twould be a waste of fine fare to invite you to share a meal this night," Baldassare commented idly, his voice unexpectedly close.

Rowan spared the captain the satisfaction of seeing him jump. He casually glanced to his side and met the amusement in the other man's eyes. There was a cold, mercenary glint to those dark eyes.

Fortunately, Rowan was well experienced with the motivation of mercenaries, having been sired by one.

He smiled, as if he had not a care in the world. "Aye, on this night 'twould be. Perhaps on the morrow would be better."

Baldassare smiled. "Perhaps. I would extend my offer of hospitality to your wife for this night, even in your absence."

Rowan smiled coldly, guessing that this man would not hesitate to press his suit if Ibernia was alone in his presence.

He had no intention of leaving her in such circumstance, especially now. "How very kind of you," he demurred, his words hard. "However, the lady will have naught to wear so soon. She would not wish to insult your board with her immodest garb."

Baldassare arched a brow. "Though she wore it on London's wharf? You overestimate your lady wife's modesty, I believe."

The two men glared at each other. "Perhaps 'tis not her modesty I overrate," Rowan said silkily.

Baldassare dropped a hand to his sword and straightened from the rail. "Do you insult my honor?"

"Of course not." Rowan leaned back against the rail, looking at ease though he was well prepared to respond if Baldassare drew his blade. He smiled tightly. " 'Tis merely my lady's preference to observe propriety. I cede to her will whenever possible.''

'' 'Twas not possible in London?''

''Not expedient.'' Rowan spread his hands. ''A man must balance his lady's demands. She could well have had new garb there, though she wished also to return home with all haste. One must choose the greater good, and on this, she and I were agreed.''

Baldassare's gaze brightened. ''You reside in Dublin? But you are unlike any other man I have met from that ill-fated land.''

Rowan shook his head, as if amused by the obligations invented by his woman. He would have to ensure he recalled this tangled web of lies—and that he told Ibernia of them before they did dine with the captain.

''My lady wife has family there,'' he said carefully, not entirely certain that was true, ''and has spent many happy days in that land. I fulfill her request to return there, though, indeed, I never imagined 'twould be a journey so fraught with adventure.''

He smiled directly into Baldassare's narrowed gaze.

''If your lady is familiar with the land, then 'tis doubly important that I speak with her. She may be able to aid me.''

''Indeed?''

At that question, Baldassare seemed to realize he had said too much. He looked away and spoke with sudden haste, the drop of his eyelids veiling the interest that shone in his eyes. ''Aye, of course. 'Tis difficult to find honest men in an unfamiliar port. Perhaps she could be of assistance.''

Baldassare smiled, a smile that never reached his eyes. ''I must insist upon inviting her to my table this night. Might I rely upon you to convey my invitation?''

Rowan straightened. ''My wife will not dine in your cabin without my accompaniment.''

"You would have the woman starve while you are ill?" Baldassare shook his head. "Surely even a knight is not so heartless as that. I offer naught but a fine meal."

"And you have been declined."

The captain shrugged. "If you will not convey my invitation, then I shall have to make it myself."

Rowan guessed that Ibernia would be standing nude in their cabin, as Marika measured and cut the cloth. Indeed, he had no doubt that Baldassare also assumed as much. He caught at the man's shoulder when that man turned away and schooled his voice.

"Truly, you cannot abandon our discussion so soon," he said smoothly. "I have yet to recompense you for the cloth you granted to my wife."

Baldassare smiled. " 'Tis my gift to the lady. Beauty to beauty, as 'twere."

"I must insist."

"I could not hear of it."

"Ah, well." Rowan jingled the coins in his purse and watched the captain's eyes light. "Perhaps another trinket would be more fitting."

"I have little to sell on this journey," Baldassare said quickly. "Much of my cargo is already vouched for."

"Indeed. What of the slavewoman who aids my wife?"

The captain blinked. "What of her?"

"My lady wife has taken a fancy to her, and I would match whatever commitment you have for her." Rowan smiled easily, the very image of a man intent on winning some trinket for his lady. " 'Tis good for women, do you not think, to have one they can confide in?"

"The slave would be very expensive. I doubt you have the coin."

"Name the price."

"I would not so insult you."

Rowan's smile broadened. "I insist."

Baldassare folded his arms across his chest and met Rowan's glance coldly. He named a sum that made Thomas choke. "As you insisted," he said archly. "Now that we have amused ourselves, shall we return to the issue of the evening meal?"

"Not just yet," Rowan declared. He counted out the coins and tossed them to the captain.

Baldassare caught them clumsily, bit the gold, then granted Rowan a surprised glance. Rowan did not miss the captain's glance to his purse and knew he would have to be certain the man did not take advantage of them.

Although it might well be too late. Curse Ibernia for forcing him to reveal his wealth in such circumstance! 'Twas a poor tactic at best—and he should have known better than to so openly win her dare.

Rowan gritted his teeth, less than pleased with his own decision in this. Aye, there was something about Ibernia that tempted him to forget his own few rules, if only to win a glimpse of her smile.

Or even hundreds of her kisses.

For a man who desired to live a life unfettered and devoid of responsibilities, as Rowan did, he was accumulating a hefty measure of both fetters and duties. A year and a day with Ibernia in tow would see him laden to the ground!

Meanwhile, Baldassare rummaged in his own purse, tossing Rowan an iron key with such abandon that it nearly leapt over the side of the ship.

Rowan guessed that was no accident, but he caught the key nonetheless.

The captain looked briefly disappointed as Rowan tucked it safely in his own purse. Then his eyes narrowed. "You are uncommonly wealthy, to so readily cast such coin aside."

There 'twas—the very conclusion he had feared.

"Not for much longer," Rowan retorted with a heartfelt chuckle. "My lady wife shall beggar me in short order if this continues." He shook his purse, ensuring that it made precious little noise. "Though I confess 'tis not easy to swallow any accusation that I do not sufficiently indulge the queen of my heart."

Baldassare's eyes lit with challenge. "Then you shall send her to my cabin, that she not miss her evening meal."

Rowan held his gaze. "We shall both be delighted to accept your invitation on the morrow."

"You will still be ill."

"Nay, I have no complaint upon the open sea," Rowan lied. 'Twas better for his belly there, but hardly ideal. He pursed his lips and scanned the sky, determined to needle this cocksure captain in exchange for the shocking amount of coin he had just cast aside. "Indeed, I would not have been in such discomfort had our departure been timed to the tides."

Baldassare's features darkened at this reminder. "One cannot completely trust the charts of foreigners," he snapped. "Particularly those of little experience upon the seas."

There was an edge to his words that awakened Rowan's curiosity. Venetians, he knew, plied their trade upon regular routes, often between ports where they maintained their own communities.

And Baldassare had already admitted to having no connections in Dublin. Now that Rowan thought about it, 'twas most odd that the Venetian had ventured this far. Venetian traders were much more likely to do business within the Mediterranean. Indeed, Rowan had never seen their ships in the northern ports of France.

"You had no Venetian charts for this port?" he asked with apparent idleness.

"None." Baldassare sneered. "And these foreigners know naught of timing a tide properly. 'Twas my own error for trusting their observations instead of making my own."

"And your ship is not Venetian either," Rowan mused.

Baldassare's eyes flashed. "An inconvenience, I assure you."

Why was Baldassare here? Was there something special about this cargo of slaves? And why did he desire Ibernia's assistance in Dublin? Rowan had assumed that Marika's price was high simply because Baldassare intended her to be too expensive for his purse, but perhaps there was more at root.

But he would have no chance to ask further. "If you will excuse me, my labor summons me once more." Baldassare bowed and walked away.

Rowan knew 'twas no coincidence that, within moments, they turned directly into the wind. High waves broke against the prow, rocking the ship so hard that it seemed it would shatter.

His belly turned again, even the prospect of Ibernia's shower of kisses doing little to ease his misery.

At least for the moment.

'Twas late in the day when Rowan finally returned, the meagre light within the cabin having faded yet more. Ibernia and Marika had made quick work of cutting and piecing the kirtle and were nigh completed. More hands, as Ibernia's mother oft said, made less of any task.

Though the work was a challenge as the ship pitched through the waves. Ibernia had more than one prick on her finger and feared staining the lovely wool with blood. In the shadows and without a lamp, such stains could not be readily discerned, if indeed they were there.

The waiting, the growing certainty that Rowan would return to claim his due, the knowledge that she had no clever ploy to avoid his touch, did naught to calm Ibernia, and she pricked her finger again.

And again, as she started at the jiggle of the door latch, though she had been listening for his return all the day long.

"Ibernia?" Rowan demanded gruffly. "Open the door, if you please."

"And if I do not please?" she taunted.

This time, though, her jest met with naught more than a growl of irritation. With a quick glance to Marika, who watched with alarm, Ibernia rose and unlatched the door.

"And what ails you this night?" she asked, striving not to sound like a discontented fishwife. "You have been long enough abroad to suit any tom."

Rowan frowned and staggered directly for the bed, not troubling himself with a reply. He collapsed on the thin pallet and closed his eyes, looking more like a cadaver than a cocky knight.

Ibernia had seen enough of men to know what trouble was at root. She had been right to insist upon leaving London rather than going to that tavern! Aye, a drinking man could not be trusted to keep his pledge.

She inhaled sharply and drew herself to her full height, exuding disapproval—though, indeed, she was more disappointed that Rowan had proven himself like all the others than disgusted with his choice of weakness.

"Drinking!" Ibernia declared, picking up her needlework with a sweeping gesture. "I should have known to expect as much. Aye, you wanted an ale so badly that you would have missed the sailing of this vessel."

"Aye, and what a crime that would have been," Rowan muttered, his tone uncommonly sour.

Before Ibernia could say more, he rolled to face the wall

of the ship, turning his back to her and ending the conversation. She exchanged a look with Marika.

Ibernia folded her arms across her chest and glared at Rowan. "Where am I to sleep, if you claim the only pallet for your own?"

"The bed is wide enough for two," he declared, without turning to face her.

How dare he assume she would join him so readily as that?

She tossed down her stitching, then leaned over him, her hands propped on her hips. "You do not fool me, Rowan de Montvieux," she declared. "Nay, I will not join you on this narrow pallet this night! I will not aid your quest to seduce me."

"Suit yourself" came the reply.

Ibernia glared at him for a moment, but his breathing deepened. Surely he did not go to sleep?

But sleep apparently was what he did.

Ibernia frowned. 'Twas not like Rowan to so readily abandon an argument. Aye, he was one who would have every eye in the place upon him, unless she missed his guess.

This must be a ploy to win her sympathy!

"You will not twist my heart," Ibernia informed him. "You will not win my compassion by looking so woebegone as this. I know well enough your objectives."

Rowan snored softly.

'Twas not precisely the manner of a man bent on seduction. Ibernia looked around the cabin, seeing that she still held Marika's attention.

"Well, at least you have shown the true measure of man that you are. A gentleman," Ibernia said haughtily, "would have granted the pallet to the lady."

She would have returned to her needlework, her chin high, but Thomas's unexpected words made her halt midstep.

" 'Tis a lofty ambition for a slave," he commented, his gaze bright, "to be treated as a lady."

Ibernia blinked and felt her cheeks heat. She had not realized the boy lingered in the cabin door. No less, her indignation with Rowan had been great enough that she momentarily forgot she was supposed to be no one of merit.

Instead of her father's privileged daughter.

She forced a smile. "A man of measure does not concern himself with such ranks of circumstance," she retorted, a poor reply that did little to mollify Thomas. Indeed, the squire snorted and rolled his eyes, though he said naught more to her.

He went instead to Rowan, carefully removing that man's boots and setting them aside. Oddly enough, the boy carried a bucket, which he set on the floor beside his lord's shoulder.

"We should see your hauberk removed," he murmured.

Rowan snorted softly. " 'Tis an unnecessary risk in this den of iniquity," he muttered, his words fading even as he uttered them. "I shall keep it."

Thomas sighed and frowned, clearly seeing that he could do naught more. He unfolded a blanket that was stuffed beneath his arm and carefully laid it over his lord with a care usually reserved for those incapable of seeing to their own needs.

"The bucket is here," the squire murmured. "I shall see the horses fed, then return."

Rowan grunted and Thomas turned away.

"He is drunk so often as that?" Ibernia asked archly. "You seem well used to accommodating him in his besotted state."

"My lord is not drunk," Thomas said sharply. "As anyone with wits can see, he is ill."

Ibernia's gaze flew to the knight once again, an array of

hints suddenly making great sense to her. He had looked pale upon his return, and his manner was not his usual one.

But she would not be persuaded so quickly as that. "How can he have fallen ill so quickly?"

" 'Tis the sea. His innards do not like its rhythm." Thomas shrugged. " 'Tis no doubt why he would have preferred to remain at least an hour on London's shore before departing anew. He has eaten little of late."

Accusation hung in the boy's words, and Ibernia realized that 'twas her dare that had prompted Rowan to depart so quickly. And against his own comfort.

She stared at the knight's sleeping figure as the squire departed and chewed thoughtfully on her lip. Perhaps Rowan was not quite the selfish man she had assumed him to be.

Or perhaps he merely sought to win her confidence. 'Twas quite a price to pay, however, and Ibernia could not credit that.

Perhaps she should not have been such a shrew. Perhaps she should have asked why he did not want to leave so quickly, why he wanted the bed this night, why he had remained on deck—instead of assuming the worst.

Perhaps Rowan de Montvieux *was* different from other men.

Ibernia got no further before there was another sharp rap upon the door. She started and Marika jumped back when Baldassare's voice echoed through the wood.

*"Ma bella?"*

Ibernia rose slowly. Rowan slumbered on, unlikely to aid her in this, so she smoothed her chausses and summoned her best smile. She opened the door a crack, unable to quell her urge to shelter Rowan from the captain's view. "Aye?"

Baldassare smiled broadly. "Ah, to look upon your beauty is like seeing the sun after a long spell of rain," he said, embellishing his claim yet further with a bow. "Dare I hope that your husband called matters amiss?"

"Which matters?"

"Ah, that you would not be interested in a fine meal this evening. To be sure, I tried not to offer offense in extending my invitation that both of you join me for an evening repast."

Food! Suddenly Ibernia realized that she was remarkably hungry. When had she eaten last? And when had she last eaten the fine fare of a captain's board?

All the same, she did not fully trust Baldassare, not with that lecherous gleam in his eye. "My husband is not disposed to dine this evening," she said, the lie nigh sticking in her throat.

The captain smiled. "Though 'tis most unfortunate that your spouse does not share my affection for the sea, still it seemed"—Baldassare apparently sought the right word—"*selfish* for him to decline on your behalf." His expression turned guileless. "Surely you are not so enamored that you cease to eat when he is ill?"

"Nay, of course not."

"Then surely we could share a meal together? I assure you, *ma bella,* that my intentions are purely honorable." He smiled wolfishly, his expression doing little to reassure Ibernia.

In fact, she would guess that his intentions were far from honorable. Ibernia decided to trust her instincts.

"I could not think of it," she said crisply and made to close the door.

But Baldassare slipped his boot into the space, his smile quick. "Then I must insist that you join me." Though his tone remained cajoling, Ibernia heard a thread of steel there. "'Tis not often that we have the delight of feminine company on our humble vessel."

She dug in her heels, though she smiled in turn. "I have naught to wear."

"Your presence alone will be ample grace for my board."

"Ah, but I could not so insult your hospitality."

Baldassare leaned closer, his eyes glinting. "Surely your husband called it awry to insist that you would prefer to pine for his recovery?"

Ibernia hesitated still.

Baldassare pushed open the door slightly, his expression turning scornful as he looked over Ibernia's shoulder. "Surely you can do naught for him while he sleeps like a child?" He looked Ibernia in the eye and his voice dropped low. "And surely, *ma bella,* you are hungry?"

Hungry? There was temptation difficult to deny.

"We have beef from London," Baldassare murmured, "and though 'tis rich and succulent, I fear it must be consumed this night before it spoils."

Ibernia's doubts wavered. How long since she had had meat?

Baldassare evidently saw that he had found a weak spot, for he pressed his case. "Fine young potatoes, ah, they are so sweet when they are small! And the last fresh bread we shall have before Dublin. A compôte of raisins and dates, a young wine—surely, *ma bella,* you will not leave me to indulge in such luxury alone?"

Ibernia's mouth went dry. Her belly was empty beyond all and there was truth in what the captain said. What could be the harm in joining him? Surely there would be others there?

She licked her lips without immediately realizing she did so. Baldassare's smile flashed and he stepped away. "Of course, if you feel you must watch your husband slumber instead, the cook can send you some biscuits from our stores."

"Biscuits?" They did not sound as delicious as the hot meat.

"Aye, they are decent enough fare." Baldassare shrugged. "A bit hardened after all our days at sea, but not so filled with worms that they cannot be consumed."

Ibernia could visualize those biscuits all too well and favored the alternative.

"And the salt fish." Baldassare gestured broadly, then shrugged. "There are those who enjoy it, I am told."

Just the smell of the cooking salt fish was enough to make Ibernia's belly protest. "Your cook could not send the beef here?" she asked hopefully, already guessing what the answer would be.

*"Ma bella!* What do you know of men?" Baldassare chuckled. " 'Twould be foolish to let my men so much as glimpse what fine fare is mine by rank." He shook a finger under her nose. " 'Tis the way of men to desire what is granted to another—a man of my position can only guard against such infidelities."

Oh, Ibernia could attest to the truth of that. She glanced back to Rowan, wondering whether he would even *know* if she took a meal with Baldassare.

Surely 'twould be a harmless indulgence?

That man waved his hand. "But if you will remain here, there is naught I can do to sway your choice. 'Tis a fearsome toll your spouse expects for loyalty, but 'tis not my place to comment."

As he turned away, the prospect of a hot meal going with him, Ibernia stepped forward impulsively. Aye, she could endure anything—especially in exchange for a good meal!—regardless of what Rowan thought of the matter.

"I would be honored to join you."

Baldassare's eyes flashed, he bowed low, then he offered

his arm. Indeed, he urged her a bit too close to his side for Ibernia's comfort.

And she realized too late that he also might not be immune to this desire of men to possess what was not their own.

Baldassare was delighted to find all as he had decreed. Three lanterns had been lit, their golden light casting an intimate glow over the finely appointed contents of his cabin. The wood gleamed, the hammered silver upon the table shone. His own sturdy chair had been drawn up to one side of the table—the other setting demanded that individual sit on the broad bed.

The linens were changed and turned down, a bevy of Eastern cushions at the ready to support whatever might need support. The wine gleamed red in the heavy glass pitcher.

And the chamber was devoid of anyone else.

He recognized the moment Ibernia realized the import of the setting. She caught her breath, spun to face him. Her eyes were wide, showing that remarkable blue to advantage, and Baldassare smiled as if he did not guess she would prefer to flee.

"Privacy, *ma bella*," he purred, "is important to any intimate discussion."

She watched avidly while he turned an ornate key in the lock, securing the door behind them. Her gaze followed the path of that key as he secreted it in his embroidered tabard. He was prepared to ply her with wine, with kisses, with food, with whatever was necessary to win his desire. The key ensured their privacy.

This woman would never find it, nor have any chance to flee, before Baldassare had what he wanted of her.

Fortunately, the evening was still young.

# Chapter Five

IBERNIA HAD MADE A MISTAKE.

Obviously. Oh, only too late did she realize she should never have succumbed to the temptation of a meal. She should have endured wormy biscuits instead of letting herself into this situation.

There was something about Baldassare's hungry gaze that persuaded Ibernia that he had only his own pleasure at heart. She had a fairly good idea that their objectives were not as one and cursed herself for not anticipating this most obvious ploy.

Ibernia was forced to concede that Rowan had been right in declining the captain's invitation to her. Oh, how she hated being at the whim of men!

Should she flee now? But how, when the key was so safely tucked away? Nay, 'twould be better to lull Baldassare into complacency, win his trust and *look* willing to savor his touch, then escape. Perhaps once he discarded his tabard, she could retrieve the key.

Ibernia could only hope that he would discard his garb. Aye, she had known those who did not, but then, Baldassare seemed most fastidious.

She would and could hope.

Baldassare watched her like a cat who had successfully cornered his prey. Ibernia retreated as he advanced, trying to look as if she intended to take that backward step all along. She thought furiously all the while but came up with naught that resembled a plan.

The smell of the meal distracted her, for she was hungry.

Ibernia covered her fear by casting an assessing glance over the table and lifting her nose appreciatively, still watching the captain from the corner of her eye.

"It smells wonderful," she said, hoping her voice was even. "How chivalrous of you to invite me to share in your meal."

She deliberately dropped to sit in the single chair. There was no way that she would perch on the side of his bed.

Baldassare prowled around the table, apparently untroubled by her choice. He adjusted the ruffle of his cuffs as she had seen him do before, he straightened the neck of his chemise. He brushed a speck of lint from his chausses, then turned a bright smile upon Ibernia. She had been so busy watching him preen—indeed, she had never seen a man do as much—that she was inadvertently pinned beneath his gaze.

"You must permit me to serve you," he murmured, "as my men are about their labor. And you must accept my humble apologies. 'Tis no fine table I can set here."

The table looked quite lavish to Ibernia. There was a white linen cloth on the board, an array of finely wrought dishes, a pair of goblets wrought of glass spun fine. She tried not to gape, but Baldassare noted her attention. He lifted one glass and turned it so that it caught the light.

"A fine specimen, is it not? 'Tis from the isle of Murano."

"I do not know this place," Ibernia lied when in fact she had heard a great deal about Murano glass over the years. 'Twas part of her father's fantastic tales of his home, though she had never seen a sample.

This glass was truly worthy of such high praise.

"Ah, but you should," he chided with a smile. " 'Tis in Venice and, indeed, home to the finest artisans in glass to be found."

"Surely some artisans elsewhere have similar skills?" Ibernia asked idly.

Baldassare shrugged. "Nay, not a one. The guild would not permit it."

Ibernia shook her head. "Surely you exaggerate. Artisans are seldom content to remain in one place, be there guild or nay. And many are inclined to share their skills with others. I have seen this often."

His smile was thin. " 'Tis why they do not leave Murano alive. 'Tis the way of the guild to ensure its own exclusivity in trade."

Though Ibernia's eyes widened in horror, Baldassare seemed untroubled by this practice.

In fact, he lifted the lid off a covered dish, showing her the tempting meat within. "May I?"

The smell nearly made Ibernia faint with hunger and partly distracted her from his tale of Murano. "Please do."

But his fine manners could not make Ibernia completely forget his easy acceptance of that guild's cruelty. She knew, beyond doubt, that she had to escape this night before Baldassare put his amorous plan into motion.

He might not even be as "gentle" as the two she had known before.

He served her a modest portion with fastidious care and Ibernia had a sudden idea how to repulse him. After all, Venetians were known for their love of fine manners—and Baldassare did not appear immune to that tendency.

Even as she had the thought, the lace-encrusted hem of his sleeve touched the dark gravy. His handsome features darkened, he dropped the ladle and immediately set upon removing the stain with a bit of water. Ibernia heard his exhalation of relief when it was clear there would be no lasting mark. He carefully added a bit of gravy to her portion, then stepped away to serve himself.

Ibernia chuckled, more than willing to let him believe her a savage if it meant her escape. "I am not a babe!" she protested, indicating the serving as if it were laughably small.

Baldassare blinked, then his smile returned. She sat with approval etched on her features as he served more. He hesitated, then, encouraged by her nod, added again to her trencher. Ibernia made no indication that he should halt, though she was not certain she could truly eat all this meat.

Baldassare frowned and served another measure. He paused, then added again, the gravy from the meat dribbling over the trencher and onto the linen.

He swore softly and made to wipe up the spill.

Ibernia saw opportunity and took it. She knew her fingers were clean, but Baldassare did not. She stuck her fingers in the running gravy before he could reach it and licked it off them.

"Marvelous," she declared, then looked pointedly into the dish. "Perhaps you should ensure that you have *some*." Her tone indicated that she had not yet had enough but was being gracious.

Baldassare hid his surprise quickly, serving himself an ample portion—though not nearly as much as was already heaped before Ibernia—then cast an inquiring glance her way. He tipped the pot, revealing a good bit more meat and a lot of gravy. Ibernia ran her fingers around her trencher to catch the running gravy, then busily licked them each in turn and ensured she made more of a mess on the linen than it would have endured otherwise.

Baldassare paled when he saw the fate of his linen, but he said naught.

"These trenchers are so thin!" Ibernia protested, knowing it was unspeakably vulgar to insult the offerings of his board. Her mother would have been appalled by such behavior, but Ibernia knew she had little other choice.

A resourceful woman used the opportunities at hand, after all.

She frowned and looked longingly at the remaining meat in the pot, considered her dripping trencher, then eyed the meat again as if she could not bear to decline it.

"You had best leave the pot here." She patted the board beside herself, leaving gravy fingerprints on the cloth.

Ibernia repeated her performance with every dish he served, until there was a ridiculous amount of food piled before her.

Rudely, she began to eat—noisily and with her fingers—before Baldassare even took his seat. She thanked him with her mouth full, savoring how he inhaled so sharply that his nostrils nigh pinched shut.

He reached for the wine pitcher and Ibernia cooed with delight, lifting her goblet toward him. The gravy on her fingers smeared over the Murano glass, a fact which the captain obviously noted. She frowned when he filled it only halfway, saluting him with the full glass so enthusiastically that the wine sloshed over the rim.

Another stain graced the white linen.

Ibernia took a healthy swig of the wine, before he could even pour his own, then dug into her meat with both hands. It was marvelous, and she wished she was in a situation that would allow her to enjoy it better.

She ate with gusto and deliberately left a bit of gravy on her chin. Baldassare stared at that adornment, clearly unable to say anything.

He did not eat.

Finally he cleared his throat. ''You indeed seem hungry this evening,'' he said, contenting himself with an elegant sip of wine. ''Does your spouse ever deign to feed you?''

Ibernia grinned, deliberately ignoring the fact that there was still meat in her mouth. ''It has been hours since our meal this morn,'' she declared, slurping her wine greedily. ''And, indeed, I had not packed nearly enough for the mid-day meal.''

Baldassare blinked. ''You have already eaten twice this day?''

''Thrice actually,'' Ibernia lied. ''Although a roast chicken at midmorning barely counts, does it?''

Baldassare stared at her, his own meal untouched. He sipped at his wine, his eyes narrowed as he watched her. She sensed that he could not bear to eat with the sight of her indulgence before him. His preference gave Ibernia an idea. She quickly quaffed her own measure of wine and held her glass out for more.

''No more for you?'' she demanded coquettishly. ''My mother said a woman should never respect a man who could not hold his wine.'' Ibernia dropped her voice. ''She said 'twas sign that he was not truly a *man,* if you know my meaning.''

Baldassare's lips tightened for a moment. Then he drained his glass in one gulp and filled it to the rim.

The wine would have more impact upon his empty belly than her own—and Ibernia could do much to ensure it stayed that way. She picked through her meat, discarding one piece or another. She scowled and rummaged through the contents of the pot, scooping up gravy in her fingers purely to appall her companion.

Finally she glanced up and eyed the untouched food still

before the captain. ''Do you intend to eat that fine piece of meat?''

Baldassare pushed his trencher across the table without hesitation. Ibernia shoved a choice morsel into her mouth, chewed with enthusiasm, then poked through the remainder. She grimaced. ''It needs more gravy,'' she declared, and before he could assist, tipped the pot at a generous angle.

The gravy surged forth and flowed across the linens, precisely as Ibernia had planned.

Baldassare swore.

''God in heaven!'' Ibernia declared, wide-eyed. ''What a shocking waste.''

Before Baldassare could recover from his obvious horror, she bent and noisily licked the gravy from the cloth. The captain paled, drained his glass, and poured another. He muttered something under his breath and withdrew slightly.

''A fine gravy,'' Ibernia murmured, smiling for him as she lifted her glass. She took a very tiny sip, wondering whether she could manage to summon a belch. She had eaten quickly, after all, so there was hope.

'Twould be the perfect end to her performance.

Baldassare gestured vaguely with one finger. ''You have sauce on your face,'' he said, the color rising on his own that he even had to call her attention to such a thing.

Ibernia ensured there was gravy on her fingers before she reached for her face. ''Here?'' she asked, landing one wet finger on her cheek. He shook his head and she touched other, feeling the first mark cool against her skin. ''Here?''

Baldassare looked away, his disgust clear. ''Nay, 'tis on your chin, though now there is more.''

''Ah well, then.'' Ibernia pressed her face into her sleeve and wiped her face with the length of it. To her delight and Baldassare's horror, she managed a respectable belch immediately thereafter. She sniffed and dabbed her nose on the opposing sleeve, then poked a finger in the meat again.

"I thought you said you had compôte," she said plaintively.

"Sweet Jesu," Baldassare muttered, and pushed to his feet. He drained his glass again, and Ibernia noticed how he steadied himself with one hand on the board before he stepped away.

"Does it have dried plums in it?" Ibernia demanded. "I adore dried plums when they are simmering in a compôte. Indeed, there is naught finer—I could eat them all the night long!"

Baldassare glanced back from the shelf where he evidently had left the compôte. "I had thought we might *talk* this evening."

Talk. Ibernia's heart skipped a beat, his intent glance telling her what precisely he meant by "talk." There would be naught verbal about it, unless she missed her guess.

"Suit yourself." She hid her trepidation, grinning broadly at him and leaning back in her chair. She deliberately sat like a peasant and used one fingernail to pick at her teeth, the task apparently taking all of her concentration. She examined her finger, as if she had retrieved something particularly worthy of note, then sucked it noisily from her nail.

Baldassare placed the entire serving vessel of compôte before her with a minute sigh of disgust, then took his place once more. He lounged back against the cushions, his gaze bright, and cradled his glass of wine in his hands. He watched her so avidly that Ibernia wondered whether she truly had fooled him at all.

"Are you of Ireland, then?" he asked with apparent idleness, only the glint of his eyes revealing his interest in the answer.

Too late Ibernia wished she knew whether Rowan had told

this man anything else. "Why?" She lifted a shoulder in a playful pose. "Do I look to be of the Irish?"

"I would not know," Baldassare countered smoothly. "Though 'tis said they are a lusty folk." His gaze drifted over the wreckage she had made of his table, then lifted to meet hers once again.

With her open enjoyment of food, Ibernia realized that she might have given him exactly the wrong impression.

Still, she would play the fool, as he seemed to expect little intellect from her. "Truly? My mother always said that I should not listen to the sayings of all and sundry."

"Your mother has much to say to you."

"Is that not typical of any noblewoman?" Ibernia ran a finger around the rim of the compôte pot, ensuring that she licked it thoroughly, then repeated the gesture.

Baldassare watched her gesture, then hastily took a restorative gulp of wine. "Then you *are* a noblewoman?"

Ibernia glanced up, determined to not be found out even though she had erred. "How else would I be wed to a knight?" she asked, then smiled with all the innocence she could summon.

Baldassare leaned forward. "A knight who insists you return to Ireland to visit family. Are you of Ireland, *ma bella*?"

Ibernia knew that she was on dangerous ground. There was not only her own suite of lies to Rowan to keep intact, but his lies to the captain to ensure their passage.

What else had Rowan told this man?

She plucked a plum out of the pot with her fingers, held it between finger and thumb, and sucked on it as she surveyed the captain. Aye, he was interested in her knowledge of Ireland, though why, Ibernia could not guess.

What had that to do with seducing her?

Unless he truly had recognized her and meant to capitalize upon his knowledge. Her heart stopped, then raced.

"I had no idea that you and my husband had the opportunity to talk on this day," she said, popping the plum into her mouth. "How wondrous that you became better acquainted." And she poked in the pot once more.

Baldassare visibly ground his teeth and his next words sounded strained. "*Ma bella,* do you or do you not have family in Ireland?"

Ibernia's thoughts flew like quicksilver and a knot of dread formed in her belly. She had been right! Baldassare knew something of her true circumstance! Why else would he care so much about such a detail?

Well, she would not be the one to confirm whatever he might have guessed. She had to escape his probing questions, and the sooner the better.

"Did you know—I have heard this said—that all the occupants of Christendom are related to the Irish?" Ibernia kept her voice light, as if she were indeed fool enough to believe as much. "Indeed, 'tis on account of the Celts, those men who once occupied nigh all of the lands from here to Outremer, and even 'tis rumored, farther east than that." Ibernia gestured expansively with her sticky hand. "Why, we could all be related! Is that not most amusing?"

Baldassare did not look amused. He drained his glass and set it heavily on the board, his gaze unswerving from Ibernia.

Sadly, he did not look besotted in the least.

Clearly, he had to drink more wine. Quickly.

"Oh, let me aid you," Ibernia insisted. She reached for the vessel of wine, intent on pouring him another.

But Baldassare's eyes widened at the mess of her fingers, no less where they would soon leave their mire. He reached simultaneously for his prized glass pitcher, their hands connected, and the pitcher wobbled.

Once she saw what was inevitable, Ibernia encouraged the pitcher to spill more quickly.

Red wine poured across the table like bloody river. There was linen that would never be serviceable again! It surged around Baldassare's discarded goblet, then ran off the edge of the table. He leapt to his feet as the wine evidently dripped onto his chausses, inadvertently bumping the table with his knee.

Ibernia, again, saw no reason not to aid in the chaos. She nudged the table a little further with her toe. Vessels, crocks, trenchers, goblets, gravy, and wine fell to the wooden floor with a resounding crash.

The Murano pitcher and pair of glasses shattered most satisfactorily.

Then silence filled the chamber. Baldassare stared at the mess of their intimate meal with horror, his mouth working soundlessly.

" 'Tis a shame, truly, that there is no dog upon this ship," Ibernia said pertly. "Our hounds would make quick work of this mess."

"You!" the captain roared. "You did this apurpose!" His face darkened with rage and he lunged toward her, his fine manners abandoned. Ibernia darted away, Baldassare landed one foot in the spilled gravy in the same moment that the ship rolled to one side.

He slipped, he swore, he landed hard. He scrabbled for a grip as he fell, the heavy table notwithstanding. Baldassare cried out as the table tipped, the corner of it catching him across the temple.

He slumped to the floor and did not move again.

The ship rolled the other way, the table slid back slightly, but Baldassare did not stir.

Ibernia stared at him for a long moment, her heart hammering. Did he mean to deceive her? But he did not move and she began to fear that her ploy had gone too far.

Ibernia crept closer. There was no blood upon his temple and he was still breathing. Baldassare was not dead—indeed, he might awaken soon.

And who knew what he would do when he remembered?

With not a moment to waste, Ibernia reached into his tabard. She quickly found the imprint of the key, though she had to feel through several layers of cloth before she could work it free. All the while she held her breath, convinced that Baldassare would awaken and make much of her actions.

But then the key was free. Ibernia did not hesitate. She fled for the door, unlocked the latch, seized a lantern, and fled into the corridor.

She was free!

For the moment, at least. She hoped that her father had not put too hefty a price on her retrieval—for a man like Baldassare di Vilonte would be more than intent to collect whatever he thought his due.

Then she hoped that Baldassare would have such an ache between his ears that he would forget all that had happened this eve.

'Twas unlikely at best, but Ibernia hoped all the same.

Ibernia jiggled the latch of the room she and Rowan had been assigned, unaccountably relieved when Thomas quickly opened the door. The boy was sleepy and he rubbed his eyes as he regarded her, squinting slightly at the light. Ibernia noted immediately that Rowan still slept. She could see Marika curled into a ball like a little cat, the other woman's eyes bright in the shadows.

"You smell like meat," the squire commented.

"Aye, 'twas a fine meal," Ibernia said breathlessly. "Sadly, the captain fell ill."

"How ill?"

"Not precisely ill," she conceded, locking the door behind them and leaning back against it in relief. "He slipped and hit his head. He will awaken in a sour mood, no doubt, but be none the worse for that." The boy's gaze was assessing, so Ibernia hastened on. "Did you eat?"

Thomas grimaced. "Biscuits."

There was a wealth of meaning in that single word, and Ibernia refused to consider what Baldassare had told her of those biscuits.

"If you are not overly proud, there is meat still in the captain's cabin," she confided. "You would have to be quick and stealthy, but 'tis there. Though the table tipped, much could probably be salvaged."

"Aye? It can only be finer fare than those biscuits," the boy said darkly. "And what of the woman?"

"Marika," Ibernia corrected, noting how lean the woman was. Aye, it probably had been long since she had eaten as well. "Perhaps you could bring her some."

"Why should she not simply accompany me? I would eat my meal elsewhere, now that you might at least watch my master. The smell of food might sicken him anew."

Ibernia cast the boy a dubious look. "There is the matter of her shackle."

Thomas grinned. "For which my master has the key. I would not be so bold as to take it from him, but since he told the captain that he bought the slavewoman for *you* . . ."

Ibernia gasped. "He bought Marika's freedom?"

"Aye."

"Then why did no one say so?" Ibernia did not wait for an answer. She crossed the small room and crouched beside the slumbering Rowan. He had rolled to his back, one arm hanging to the floor. His color seemed better, though maybe 'twas only the flattery of the lantern light.

And still he slept.

Surprisingly, she hesitated before reaching for his purse, feeling she pushed too far in this. Though she had had no such qualms about searching Baldassare for a key! What difference was there between Marika's freedom and her own? Ibernia shook her head and eased the purse from Rowan's chausses.

This time, though, she was achingly aware of the man so close to her hand, that hip beneath his fingers, his muscled thighs stretched to her right. She knew enough of men to know what she would see if she but lifted her gaze, and the very thought make her cheeks heat. She swallowed, knowing Rowan would savor any such hint of awareness in her.

Aye, this man was sure enough that all women desired him! Ibernia gritted her teeth and opened the purse with a quick gesture.

Too late, she feared he would awaken, but Rowan only grunted and slumbered on. Ibernia spilled the purse's contents into her palm. There were half a dozen gold coins, a few silver ones, a single key.

And a golden ring.

Ibernia's gaze lingered for a heartbeat on that ring, a ring clearly too small to fit Rowan's hand. She was almost curious, then told herself that his liaisons had naught to do with her. She took the key, poured coins and ring back into his purse, and replaced it as it had been.

Marika's eyes lit as Ibernia stretched to unlock the shackle. She was half afraid 'twould be the wrong key, that either Rowan deceived her or Baldassare had deceived him.

But the key turned smoothly in the lock. The shackle fell from the wall as Marika cried out in delight. The same key proved to open the shackle at her neck, the expression of joy on the small woman's features tearing at Ibernia's heart.

Then Marika fell on her hands and knees and kissed Ibernia's feet in gratitude. Ibernia felt the woman's tears fall on her skin and bent to hug her, her gaze straying to the sleeping knight.

Rowan had truly won her dare.

Even if he had done this purely to prove her wrong, purely to win her "shower of kisses," 'twas no less a fine deed for all of that.

Now she knew that he was not blessed with inexhaustible coin. Nay, if Rowan meant to court a wealthy bride and then return to France, then he had sorely cut into his finances to do this deed. And this while he was ill.

Despite herself, Ibernia's poor opinion of this knight was revised for the better.

Indeed, Ibernia's resistance to him softened in the lantern light. Aye, she knew what she had to do. She would keep her wager, just as she had pledged, just as Rowan had kept his.

But she would render her shower of kisses now, while Rowan slept, as tousled and harmless as he might ever manage to be.

He would not be able to argue whether her payment was sufficient. All the same, Ibernia was less than confident in her skill and did not savor the thought of witnesses.

No doubt Thomas would be highly amused, for he must have witnessed many an elaborate seduction and would find her efforts laughable.

Ibernia urged Marika toward the door. "Go with Thomas," she instructed, gesturing with her hands until the woman nodded. "Go and find what food you can, then go with Thomas."

"Would you not have her return to you?" Thomas asked.

"Nay." Ibernia smiled. "I have a debt to render to your master, and 'tis a deed best done in privacy."

The boy grinned, then chuckled. He bowed to Marika, indicating that she should precede him, then paused on the threshold.

"Be gentle with my lord and master," he counselled, a wicked glint in his eyes. "He has lately been ill and might not be able to withstand a lengthy shower of kisses."

Ibernia's smile was tight. "I shall keep that in mind." She latched the door behind the two and faced the knight, still sleeping peacefully.

How many was a shower of kisses, precisely? Rowan had said hundreds.

Ibernia's belly quivered. She rubbed her stomach, then looked down at herself. She was smeared with gravy, stained with wine, and wearing a measure of the compôte's sticky sauce. She was still dirty from her travels, her clothing was torn and disreputable. The sight almost made her chuckle, though surely 'twould be unappealing to the knight should he awaken.

Perhaps she risked less here than might be imagined.

Ibernia glanced to him again, watching his chest rise and fall. Even in sleep, there was something about this man that defied expectation—and she was not as certain of her undesirability to him as she might have hoped.

Nor was she so certain that she did not find him desirable. Nay, the sight of Rowan, all long and lithe strength, his jaw stippled with a day's growth of russet beard, his hair tousled, made Ibernia tingle deep inside. Her lips already burned, just as her neck had burned where he pressed those kisses, and she knew that she must truly be falling ill.

Ibernia heaved a sigh. 'Twas better she delivered her due while she was mostly hale, no less while the man was asleep. There was no telling how he might turn her own touch against her otherwise.

A woman could endure a task only once 'twas begun, she told herself grimly, and stepped forward.

Rowan dreamed of chickens.

Aye, he was in the kitchen garden of Montvieux, all of six summers again. The sun was shining, Marie was scolding him for stealing a pinch of bread, complaining to the cook that Rowan would never escape the taint of his roots. Her prized chickens scattered as Rowan fled across the garden, then returned to their incessant pecking of the ground.

Marie cast grain across the ground, venting bitterly about the trouble young boys made underfoot, then let the chickens in the green of the garden proper. They clucked and fluttered and scurried, then they pecked at the pests on the crops growing there. They scratched and clucked, their necks working as they greedily gobbled up grubs and insects.

Rowan watched in horror, wondering what 'twas like to be an unfortunate grub, destined for a chicken's belly. He watched them peck and peck, imagining the surprise of the insects that were merrily enjoying themselves when disaster struck unexpectedly from above. He even protested, but Marie swept his words aside, her attention bent on encouraging her flock to become fatter.

They pecked and gobbled and pecked some more, pecking the ground, pecking the grubs, pecking the insects.

And then they began to peck at him. Rowan could feel them. They began gently at first, then with increasing fervor. They pecked at his brow, his nose, his cheeks, his jaw. He twisted and turned, but the chickens could not be deterred.

Rowan felt the sweat trickle down his back. They would

peck him to death! He tried to run, he realized 'twas naught but a dream, he fought to escape its clutch.

Yet all the while, the chickens mercilessly pecked.

His eyes finally flew open. His heart was pounding. Rowan clutched the sides of the narrow bed nowhere near Marie's garden, momentarily uncertain where he was.

Then Ibernia bent to bestow another kiss upon him. Her eyes were tightly shut, her lips were puckered so tightly that they paled. Her entire expression was one of distaste.

When she bent and pecked a tight kiss upon his brow, Rowan could not help but laugh aloud. This was the chicken who would peck him to death!

Ibernia's eyes flew open and she jumped back, her wary expression quick to cover her surprise. " 'Tis so amusing as that to find me rendering my debt?"

"What debt?"

"A shower of kisses."

Marika! Rowan glanced to the place where the woman had been shackled and saw her gone. "Thomas?" he asked, and Ibernia nodded.

There was no delight in her expression, though, and Rowan was momentarily irked that he had slept through her discovery.

Rowan swung his feet around so he was sitting on the bed. To his delight, his belly seemed to have settled. "That was a kiss?"

Ibernia propped her hands upon her hips. "Ninety-eight kisses, to be exact." She lifted her chin and stepped closer. "If you should be so kind, I will pay the remainder of my due and have this labor behind me."

Rowan sobered, wishing he had not missed the other ninety-eight kisses. Though, if they had been of the same ilk as that last one, he had not missed much. Indeed, it appeared he was to have little credit for his good deed.

Which only meant the remaining kisses had to be worth remembering.

Rowan shoved a hand through his hair and offered the lady his best grin. "And I am to simply sit here, while you drop one hundred and two more such kisses upon my brow?" he asked.

Ibernia's eyes narrowed. "Two and two alone it shall be."

"Hundreds," Rowan retorted, emphasizing the plural and enjoying how her eyes flashed before she hid her response. He pushed to his feet, noting her quick step backward. "Although even I have little appetite for a hundred and two more kisses like that."

She lifted her chin, those eyes bright with defiance. " 'Tis all you will have of me. That or naught at all."

Rowan eased closer. "I shall settle your debt for two kisses alone, on one condition."

"We agreed on no conditions."

"That we did not." Rowan halted a mere step away from her, noting how her breasts rose and fell more quickly now that he was so close. "But I offer to lessen your obligation in exchange for a small consideration."

The lady arched one fair brow. "Small to you, no doubt, but considerable to me."

"Oh, I shall do my best to ensure 'tis not so onerous as that." He leaned closer, savoring the way she straightened, and blew softly on the side of her neck.

She shivered, then stepped aside. "You try to force yourself upon me."

"With a breath? I think not. 'Twas only your strange adornment that captured my curiosity." Rowan traced the line of her throat with a single fingertip, lifting a spot of gravy while he did so. He held her gaze and slipped his finger into his mouth, licking the sauce from it thoroughly and enjoying how she blushed.

"Delicious," he purred, and she abruptly looked away.

"What do you want of me?"

"Two kisses, 'tis all."

"In exchange for what?"

"Naught but those two kisses," Rowan insisted. Ibernia looked back at him, curiosity lighting her eyes. "The condition is merely that I grant you the first one and you return the second in kind."

Ibernia rolled her eyes. "Aye, no doubt that first kiss will involve more than merely a kiss. You would ensure you win your other wager, one way or the other, but I will not succumb to your touch!"

"Kisses only," Rowan insisted. "And naught shall I touch but my lips to yours."

"Liar!"

Rowan smiled slowly. "Coward," he charged in a whisper. The lady's eyes flashed fire, the sight quickening his blood. "But if you are so very afraid that you might enjoy that kiss, that you might want more than one other, then take the easier path. We shall count the hundred and two due together."

She stared at him and Rowan decided to push her just a little more. "Do you not think that a shower should cover a man from head to toe? Not merely his face?"

"You!" Ibernia exhaled hotly. She stepped closer and raised her chin, her eyes bright with challenge, her lips set. "Do your worst," she invited in a low voice. "Truly, you love yourself enough for two."

Rowan refused to take offense, knowing she would not be so annoyed if she were not tempted by the prospect of his touch. He stepped closer, letting his gaze rove over her features, bracing his hands against the wall over her shoulders. He leaned closer, until they were nearly nose to nose, and watched her anger fade into fear.

His heart clenched and he knew that he must persuade her of the merit of men, of himself, of the pleasure of touch, and all of this with a single kiss. Even Rowan, after all the kisses he had shared, felt a increment of doubt in his abilities.

So much rode on a single embrace!

"Fear not, my Ibernia," he whispered, his own smile gone. "I shall do my best, not my worst."

Her eyes widened slightly, she stiffened. Rowan grazed her full lips with his once, twice, thrice, and felt her soften slightly.

He touched his lips to hers ever so gently, felt her quiver of fear as surely as if it had been his own. He moved his lips slightly, coaxing and cajoling. Ibernia made a little sound in the back of her throat, she shuddered, then she parted her lips.

Rowan was not a man to decline such an invitation as that. He slanted his mouth across hers, swallowed her gasp, and set to the labor he did best of all.

# Chapter Six

THOMAS PEEKED AROUND THE EDGE OF THE PORTAL AND surveyed the disarray of the captain's quarters. Even with the spilled food and shattered pottery, 'twas clear the captain lived well.

Though that was hardly Thomas's concern. He could smell stewed meat, and that was enough to make his belly complain. Marika's stomach grumbled from behind him, and he glanced back to find her hand clamped over her midsection. They shared a smile and Thomas indicated she should remain outside the chamber. At her nod, he crept into the room.

The captain lay on one side of the chamber. Thomas wondered for a heartbeat what had transpired here, then reminded himself that the doings of others were not his trouble.

Though he ensured the captain was alive. The man had a bruise rising on his temple but otherwise appeared to be sleeping.

Thomas's belly urged him to make haste. He checked the scattered meal and found a large pot with a good bit of gravy unspilled within it. There was naught amiss with the thick bread trenchers, to his thinking, and he stuffed them into the pot. A survey of the table revealed naught else worth eating, though this would be fine enough fare and plenty for the two of them.

Thomas turned to leave and halted in surprise. Marika had come into the chamber behind him silently. She was staring at the fallen captain, such hatred in her eyes that Thomas's blood chilled. She spat on his tabard, her expression so furious that Thomas could not bear to look upon her.

In all his twelve years, he had never witnessed such animosity. Thomas turned blindly to the table and feigned ignorance of her presence, even though he was startled by the change in her manner.

It seemed at odds with the sweetness Marika had displayed thus far. Indeed, he wondered what kind of person she was truly; what had happened between herself and this captain; what the entire tale was.

Yet he was not certain he wanted to know what could inspire such passion.

She made a sound of approval and Thomas glanced up with trepidation. The Marika he had glimpsed previously was returned, shyly offering an apple he had missed. She smiled and Thomas nodded with haste, uneasy with how quickly she changed expression.

Truly, she was so charming from that point onward that Thomas began to doubt what he had seen. All the same, he felt uncertain of her smiles, uneasy in her presence as he had never been with a woman before.

The pair found a corner in the kitchen that was warm and snug, and consumed the contents of the pot. Marika giggled and blushed like a young maid, though he knew she was at least ten years his senior.

She was unexpectedly pretty when she smiled at him. There was a dimple beneath one corner of her full lips and a dint high in the other cheek that made her look like a woman who laughed often. The sadness that occasionally stole through her dark eyes tempered that impression and left Thomas with a thousand questions.

Which he could ask, but she could not understand.

Perhaps it was only the meat, but long after Marika had fallen asleep, Thomas lay awake. Aye, he was not quite certain he wanted to sleep alone in this woman's presence. In fact, he kept one hand upon the hilt of his knife, though he told himself 'twas just caution having its say.

For if Marika did more than spit upon the captain, they all could pay the price.

Ibernia had never felt anything like Rowan's kiss. His touch awakened a yearning deep within her that she had never guessed she possessed. 'Twas no fever that claimed her, for this illness showed itself only beneath this knight's touch. Too late Ibernia realized it was desire that made her knees weaken.

Rowan's kiss was possessive yet gentle, tender and persuasive, entirely different from the way any other man had touched her.

It made Ibernia long for more. It made her want to savor this fleeting embrace, made her want to understand the full reason why others found lovemaking held such allure. She had no doubt that Rowan could show her all she desired.

But she had to resist him if she was to gain her freedom in Dublin.

To her own surprise, Ibernia realized that she trusted Rowan to keep his word, to take naught more from her than this kiss, to force naught upon her. Ibernia knew that he would suffer her to step away at any moment—yet at the same time, he was not unaffected by her embrace.

Aye, she could feel the heat of his arousal just a handspan

from her own belly. Just as he pledged, he touched her with his lips alone.

He waited. He pleased. He urged her to join him.

And he savored. She peeked and found that Rowan's eyes were closed, his expression blissful. That made her feel somewhat more desirable than she knew herself to be, and sent a feminine surge of pride rolling through her.

Rowan's kiss was shared, not inflicted, and he was apparently as concerned with her response as with his own. She had some power in this match, she had some ability to coax his response, she had the right to halt their embrace.

And that alone persuaded her to continue.

Surely it could hurt naught to enjoy a single kiss? Surely she would be a fool not to savor such a moment?

Her decision made in a heartbeat, Ibernia opened her mouth to Rowan. He eased his tongue between her teeth, the way it flicked against hers making her heart pound. Ibernia closed her eyes and surrendered to that kiss; she let her tongue tangle with his.

Rowan caught his breath. He came yet closer, his lips more demanding than they had been before. 'Twas as if they fed from each other's passion and coaxed the embers of a blaze to burn high. No less, they did it together, and that, for Ibernia, was the telling ingredient.

When Rowan finally lifted his head, she was honest enough to admit—at least to herself—that she was disappointed.

Then Rowan opened his eyes, revealing how they had darkened with desire. He smiled that slow smile that made Ibernia tingle, his gaze falling to her lips like a caress. She noticed that both of them were breathing quickly, that the cabin seemed astonishingly warm.

"Ninety-nine," Rowan whispered. He arched a russet

brow, clearly challenging her to not try to escape her wager.
" 'Tis your turn, I believe."

There was a challenge in his voice, a hint that she would
not keep her word, or that she would not return his kiss with
the same gentle ardor he had shown.

But Ibernia would show Rowan that he was not the only
one possessed of allure! She smiled, then eased an increment closer, ensuring that her breasts were a mere finger's
breadth from his chest.

She heard Rowan catch his breath and shook a finger
gently at him. "Your hands will not move," she reminded him.

Rowan swallowed and nodded once, his gaze dancing
over her.

Ibernia had a fleeting sense that he did not know what to
expect from her, and she savored the change of roles. She
stretched to her toes and framed his face in her hands. She
echoed his attack, sliding her lips across his several times
before she slanted her mouth across his own with gentle
demand.

Rowan moaned softly, the minute sound heating Ibernia's
blood yet further. She felt the tension within him, heard him
catch his breath, felt the moment he surrendered to her embrace.

'Twas she who set the stakes this time, she who was in
control. This was a new experience for Ibernia and one she
intended to enjoy. She kissed Rowan with increasing intensity, nibbling on his lip, tangling her tongue with his, savoring the smell and the taste and the feel of him.

He kissed her back, matching her passion though he did
not move his hands. The heat rose faster between them this
time. Ibernia fairly tasted the heat of Rowan's desire, his
erection brushed against her belly, his every muscle drawn

taut. Yet he stood and let her take her pleasure, let her kiss him however she wanted.

That he would let her do this, that he would not seize what he so obviously desired, drove Ibernia on. She felt filled with a power that she had never sampled before. She was desirable, she was desired, yet she alone would say what came of it.

But when she finally broke their kiss, Ibernia knew her cheeks were flushed. Her breathing came quickly, even as Rowan's did.

Their gazes locked and held. The air seemed to sizzle between them, naught but the creaking of the ship carrying to their ears.

Ibernia leaned back against the wall, feeling the heat of him, smelling his skin, seeing the way his hands had knotted into fists where they still were braced against the wall.

"One hundred," Rowan whispered, his voice more uneven than Ibernia had expected. He exhaled shakily, then made to run a hand through his hair. He could not seem to tear his gaze away from her, though, and he did not step away.

That made Ibernia smile. She had shaken his composure, this knight who had more confidence than any she had ever known. She felt suddenly bold and impulsive—'twas the same impulsiveness at the root of her current troubles, but Ibernia did not care.

The sense of being in charge of her own destiny, however fleeting that influence might prove to be, was impossible to deny.

She eased closer, her gaze locked on his. She saw Rowan's eyes widen, noted how his jaw tightened. She reached up and slid a fingertip down the side of his face, much as he had touched her earlier. She traced the strong line of his jaw, let her finger meander across his firm lips.

She lifted her gaze to Rowan's as she decided to succumb to temptation.

She stretched to her toes, fanned her fingers across his cheek, and let her breasts touch his chest. Rowan shivered. Ibernia smiled.

"Ninety-nine and a half," she whispered with a wanton's boldness, then touched her lips to his once more.

Rowan slanted his mouth across hers with purpose, and Ibernia surged against him. The hardness of his chest made her feel soft and feminine; the way his hands remained on the wall emboldened her. She ran her hands down his neck, across the breadth of his shoulders, then back to tangle in the luxuriant thickness of his hair. She arched against him as he kissed her deeply, knowing only that she wanted yet more and more.

Rowan groaned and he caught her against him. The strength of his hands bracketed her waist and lifted her against him. He backed her against the wall, one hand rising to cup her jaw as he kissed her thoroughly. Ibernia could only hold on and enjoy this unexpected pleasure. She matched him touch for touch, too lost in sensation to care at this path's destination.

Until Rowan reached into her chemise and cupped her breast in his hand.

Ibernia caught her breath at the intimacy of his warm palm against her bare flesh, shuddered as his thumb slid across her nipple. She gasped and tore her lips from his, but Rowan, his expression intent, only bent to capture that tightened nipple in his lips. He suckled her gently and Ibernia closed her eyes. She clung to his shoulders, feeling faint with pleasure, until she suddenly realized what he did.

He was merely winning another wager. Rowan meant to seduce her with his touch, just as he had pledged, but the prize that hung in the balance was Ibernia's freedom.

"Nay!" she cried, and pushed him away.

To her relief, Rowan immediately released her, though his eyes smoldered with desire. He surveyed her, his gaze lingering on the breast that now grew chilly without the luxury of his touch. He looked tousled and displeased, and Ibernia knew an inkling of dread that she was not truly in command of this situation.

"You pledged not to touch me," she declared, hating how tremulous her word sounded. "You swore to keep your hands upon the wall."

Rowan snorted, he shoved a hand through his hair. "Ye gods, Ibernia, a man can only bear so much," he muttered, then paced the narrow expanse of the cabin. It took only two of his steps, but when he turned, Ibernia was glad of even that minute distance between them.

"I knew that you meant only to win our first wager with the second," she charged.

Rowan arched a brow. "I beg you make your accusations more clearly. My thinking is addled at this moment."

Ibernia wondered whether that was true. He looked so composed so quickly that she doubted as much. She pulled her stained chemise closed and folded her arms across her chest, wishing she could hide the fullness of her breasts from his gaze.

"We wagered that if I did not succumb to your charm before arriving at Ballyroyal, then you would release me there, rather than in a year and a day. And when you demanded a shower of kisses in exchange for Marika's release, I knew you would make the most of that to win the first wager."

Rowan looked unconvinced. " 'Twas you, Ibernia, who made that last kiss what it was." His gaze bored into hers, as if he would read her very thoughts, as if he guessed that she had truly desired him.

Against all good sense. Ibernia abruptly turned away.

Silence reigned in the small cabin, though there was a tension in the air. Ibernia hated that she was too well bred to leave the matter there.

"I thank you for winning Marika's release," she said grudgingly.

"The prize was well worth the price."

Ibernia glanced up to find Rowan's gaze warm upon her. She felt herself flush and hoped the poor light would hide her response. "You must say that to all the women you persuade to abandon good sense."

He chuckled then, clearly not insulted by her cross tone. He sauntered across the cabin, but Ibernia defiantly held her ground. Her pulse quickened but she fought to hide any sign of her awareness of him.

Rowan halted before her, eyes twinkling merrily and tapped one fingertip playfully on the tip of her nose. "Ah, *ma demoiselle,* 'tis difficult to say who was most persuasive just moments past." He surveyed her, his eyes gleaming gold. " 'Tis not everyday that I abandon my pledge to a woman, no less that I forget it completely beneath her beguiling kiss."

Ibernia's cheeks heated and she heartily disliked how his confession pleased her. "Rogue! You only seek to win another kiss." She straightened and refused to be charmed. "You have not enough coin to be buying the freedom of slaves in exchange for mere kisses. How do you intend to court a wealthy bride with so little left to your name?"

Rowan's brow darkened. "How do you know how much coin I have?"

Ibernia shrugged. "I had to fetch Marika's key, of course."

Rowan glanced away, obviously displeased by this revelation. His fingers strayed to the purse, and Ibernia sensed that he was anxious to check its contents.

The very insinuation that she might be a thief was infuriating. "See for yourself," she declared haughtily. "I took naught that was not mine to take. Indeed, if Thomas had not confessed that the key was there, I would never have opened your purse."

To her disgust, Rowan did dump the contents of his pouch into his palm. How dare he not trust her? But 'twas not the coin that Rowan counted. Nay, his expression eased only when he saw that the golden ring was yet there. He ran a finger across it, almost reverently, then put everything back in place.

Ibernia watched him with narrowed eyes. "That ring is not worth so much to make a difference in your suit," she observed.

Rowan impaled her with a glance. "Indeed, for *no one,* you know much of the value of jewellery. Nay, I would wager that you are a merchant's daughter, that you fled a convent and had fortune turn against you."

Ibernia backed away from his bright gaze. "I keep my ears open and my wits about me, 'tis all." She tried to change the subject, to deflect his curiosity. "What is the import of that ring? Its value must be sentimental is all I imply, though I would never have guessed you to be sentimental."

Rowan's lips drew to a taut line. " 'Tis not of import. I should prefer to know more of your tale."

"And I should prefer to know more of that ring," Ibernia retorted, well aware that they both were trying to turn the conversation in the direction they favored. " 'Tis a lady's ring, for 'tis too small for you, and too finely wrought to favor a man's hand."

"So, you are a goldsmith."

"Nay, I am a woman with eyes in my head." Ibernia made an intuitive guess. " 'Tis the ring of the only woman who ever held your heart, I would wager, a token of her affections and a memento to cherish. What happened to her, that you are alone and so quick to·spread your seed?"

Rowan's features hardened. "You know naught of what you speak!"

The very glimpse of his anger told Ibernia that she was close to the truth. "Or is it the ring of the only woman you ever loved?" she challenged. "Perhaps the only one who ever spurned you?

Rowan's eyes flashed. To Ibernia's astonishment, he did not grace her guess with a reply. He spun and marched to the door, the speed of his departure telling her that she had hit upon the truth.

He said naught but walked straight out, his footsteps echoing solidly down the corridor, then fading away. Ibernia sagged against the wall, knowing in her heart that he would not return this night. She also knew she should not be troubled to know that Rowan's heart was so securely held in thrall.

But troubled she most certainly was.

It must be the unfamiliarity of meat in her belly, Ibernia resolved. Aye, such a treat could hard upon a body. That alone must be why she could not sleep, even in the peaceful solitude of the cabin.

It could be no more than that.

Rowan did not like losing control of his passions. 'Twas unlike him, and the certainty that he had done so—no less with the infuriating Ibernia—was enough to keep him awake most of the night.

Aye, he wanted her, and he was not inclined to wait.

But he would not break his pledge. Even if the lady showed remarkable resistance to his kiss.

Perhaps that alone was key to her appeal.

Rowan paced and he prowled, he drummed his fingers, he whistled tunelessly. When the sky began to pinken, he took to the decks, pacing off his frustration. He found Thomas and Marika asleep in the kitchen and ate part of a trencher of bread soaked in gravy.

His belly, to his relief, did not spurn the offering.

Rowan did not return to their cabin, for he did not know what he would do if he did. 'Twas not the most reassuring thought he had ever had.

Even hours absent from her presence and long after his blood should have cooled, Rowan stood on the deck desiring Ibernia.

And she had made her own lack of desire for him more than clear.

'Twas no good sign that she seemed intent upon unveiling the few secrets Rowan had. He closed his hand possessively over his purse and took a deep breath of the salt-tinged wind.

Even when he closed his eyes, he could see her. The way she faced him with defiance, the snap in her eyes, the proud tilt to her chin. The curve of her breast visible though the gape in her stained chemise. The sweet weight of that breast in his hand. The sigh that escaped her lips when she yielded to his touch.

Rowan's mouth went dry as he recalled the look of wonder in Ibernia's eyes when she stretched to kiss him that last time. That kiss had not been due; she had offered it of her own volition.

Without fear. Aye, there had been desire shining in the sapphire depths of her eyes.

The sight of it had nigh been his undoing. The woman

addled his wits, there was no doubt about it. Why else would he have revealed the import of that ring? Rowan heaved a sigh at his own weakness, clenched his fists at his sides, and walked.

Ibernia was naught but a woman. Another woman in a long string of women for Rowan, her willingness naught unusual in his experience. Only the thrill of victory intrigued him, the prospect of changing her fear to delight. Aye, she was naught but a woman who, soon enough, he would never see again.

After all, he was a man who desired naught in his life. No obligations, no responsibilities, no due owing to any master. 'Twas why he sought an heiress, a woman who would continue upon her own course with no need for him.

Rowan preferred women who expected naught and had naught to lose. Widows. Whores. Perhaps an heiress. She might want a son, but that was a duty he could fulfill. Aye, Rowan had seen evidence enough that marriages had naught to do with shared lives or even shared objectives. He was confident that he could strike a bargain with any woman he chose to court.

'Twas fortunate for him that Ibernia would not be among the candidates. There was a woman who defied every expectation!

Rowan deliberately summoned the visage of the charming widow he had sampled in Paris; the two sisters at his brother Burke's wedding festivities just weeks past at Montvieux; the enthusiastic romp he had savored en route to those festivities with . . .

Rowan frowned, displeased when Ibernia's rare smile intruded upon his recollections.

Nay, that one had not been blonde. Her hair had been long, he had been certain of it. Curly, aye, that was it, and her face was . . .

Impossible to recall.

Rowan took a bracing breath of morning air as the sun nudged over the horizon and paced with new vigor. He had to loosen Ibernia's grip upon him—the fact that she denied him seized his imagination, no more than that.

'Twas decided in that moment. Rowan would win his wager with Ibernia, and before this ship docked in Dublin. After all, he should not be pondering the seduction of his lovely slave. There were greater issues at hand. He was on a bride quest, after all.

Aye, Rowan *should* be thinking about the courtship of one Bronwyn of Ballyroyal. That was the matter that should consume his attention. There was the victory he needed to prove not one but both of his brothers—and his foster-mother—dead wrong.

The stakes were not small. Failing to win the hand of the wealthiest heiress in all of Ireland could ensure that his purse was never readily loaded with coins again. Rowan felt a shiver of dread. Would Margaux truly cut him off from her fortune?

She was riled, there was no doubt of that. And when Margaux was angered, she struck with the surety of a viper.

He stared at the ruffled surface of the sea, now tinged with a fine coral hue, and knew he had to win his brothers' dare.

Even though Ibernia was right that his coin thinned overmuch. Rowan would have a hard time lavishing gifts upon this heiress, no less because undoubtedly she was already in possession of everything she had always wanted. And he knew well enough how pampered women loved expensive gifts.

Why had he not considered this before? He should have brought treasures from Paris, wonders that would catch such a woman's eye, silks and perfumes that she would not know!

But he, characteristically, had been too impatient to begin, too impetuous and assured of success, to trouble himself with such petty details.

Rowan's lips thinned as he acknowledged his flicker of doubt. He wished Ibernia had not been so very right about his disappearing coin.

He wished Ibernia had not kissed so very sweetly. The errant recollection of her nipple tightening under his hand tormented him in that moment.

Nor indeed that she should have been so hesitant to share her charms. The woman was a distraction and one most unwelcome! Rowan growled in frustration and made to pace the length of the deck once more.

But when he pivoted, 'twas a disgruntled Baldassare di Vilonte he found in his path. The man was angry and rumpled beyond expectation, with a reddened bump on his temple. He looked fit to fight, and Rowan took a wary step back.

"A good morning to you," Rowan said with false cheer. He added a smile designed to melt any opposition.

" 'Tis no good morning and you know it well," the captain snarled. " 'Twas a black day that ever I took the lot of you aboard my vessel, and it cannot be soon enough that I am rid of you."

Rowan deliberately hid his alarm. This man could not put them ashore sooner than Dublin! Not only could he not bear to endure another arrival and departure, another ship and another negotiation, but he doubted he had the coin to see the matter resolved.

'Twas a new sensation, to fret over coin, and one most unwelcome. Rowan did not intend to let it become a permanent situation in his life. But he knew all too well that there were many ports along the way and 'twould be far too easy to direct this vessel to one.

Baldassare did not look indulgent this morn.

Rowan wondered where he had acquired that bump on his

brow and felt a slight inkling of dread. It could not be insignificant that this fastidious man allowed himself to be seen in such a state.

What had happened last night?

"I have paid more than adequate passage to Dublin," he said with bravado. "And 'tis only in Dublin we shall disembark."

"Only because I have not the time to enter another port." Baldassare snarled. "But you will not be about the ship, and you will not leave your cabin, and you will not buy the freedom of slaves, and you will not allow your wife to cross my path again."

"Again?"

"Again. That is no gentlewoman you wed, and, indeed, I pity you the humiliation of enduring her sorry excuse for manners."

Rowan frowned, sensing that he had missed part of this tale. "What would you know of my lady's manners?"

"What would I not know of them!" Baldassare snorted. "'Twas *disgusting* to watch her lay waste to a decent meal and a fine table! Indeed, I cannot imagine the magnitude of crime that would compel a man to witness her eating again. You shall keep her confined to that cabin, for 'tis rightly said that a woman has no place upon a ship."

Rowan folded his arms across his chest, having a very good idea what had happened. Aye, Ibernia's chemise had been stained last eve when he awakened, but not before.

"What meal would this have been?" he asked, letting frost filter into his tone. "I specifically recall declining your kind invitation for a meal last eve."

Baldassare snorted. "A woman should not starve because her spouse is ill. Indeed, the very fact that you expected as much inclines me to believe that you two barbarians are deserving of each other!"

Rowan dropped his hand to the hilt of his blade. "You will not insult my lady wife!"

"And I shall not bear the cost of the damage she has wrought," the captain retorted. "Clearly I erred in fearing the steed's wreckage alone."

"Damage? What damage?"

Rowan saw then that Baldassare carried a pot. The man produced it from behind his back and shook its contents at Rowan. Whatever the shards within it had been, they glittered in the morning sunlight like gemstones.

Shattered gemstones.

Rowan lifted his gaze to the other man, summoning every increment of his disdain. "And this would be?"

"A fine pitcher and two wine goblets wrought of Murano glass," Baldassare supplied hotly. "They were particularly fine specimens, of my collection, and I demand compensation for their loss."

Rowan arched a brow. "I should recompense you for these shards, on the basis of your own assessment alone? I did not even see these goblets before. How am I to know their worth?"

"By my word!"

"Which will set the measure of your own compensation?" Rowan shook his head. "I think not."

Baldassare took a step forward, his expression grim. "You will pay, or you will swim."

Rowan deliberately gauged the distance to the shoreline misted in the distance, as if he had a choice. In truth, he had none, and Baldassare knew it, but Rowan would not be extorted so readily as that. "You have my deposit already."

"And 'tis clear I may need its reassurance, given the damage already sustained. Indeed, we are but a single day out of London's port. St. Mark himself could not guess what you might manage in the three days passage remaining!"

Rowan hoped 'twas less than it had been thus far. "Surely 'tis only reasonable to consider my wife's tale of events?"

The captain's eyes narrowed. "Do you call me a liar?"

"Nay, but 'tis clear you held this glass in affection and, like any token held in esteem, you may have overrated its charms." Rowan softened his charge with a smile, though he held the captain's gaze steadily. "I would have my wife's assessment to compare with your own." He shrugged. " 'Tis simply good business."

"This is no business wager!" Baldassare cried. "This is an *insult*, an insult that requires compensation. The longer you wait, the higher the price will be."

He clamped his lips tightly and seemed to rein in his emotions, then leaned closer. His eyes were so cold that Rowan stifled a shiver. "Do not imagine, sir, that you could not disappear from this vessel, never to be seen again."

"How much?" Rowan put as much impatience into his tone as he dared, as if he bored of the discussion.

Baldassare named a price and Rowan, even though he had braced himself, very nearly flinched.

"And I thought you were a merchant, not a thief," he muttered.

Baldassare held out his hand.

Rowan exhaled mightily, then dug in his purse, cursing Ibernia under his breath. The woman would see him beggared.

And had she not said she would love to see him lose his suit for this Bronwyn's hand? Rowan's fingers stilled in sudden realization.

Had she done this apurpose?

He could not discredit the possibility, given her obvious desire to win her wager. 'Twas a tactic fitting of his usual deeds with his brothers! Ye gods, he would teach her not to push him overmuch!

The other man snatched up the coins as soon as Rowan presented them. Baldassare would have marched away, but Rowan hailed him. "The glass, if you please."

" 'Tis of no use to you!"

"I would argue that. And indeed, I have just paid a hefty price for it."

"I would keep it."

"Then you truly are a thief, not a merchant, as you so claim."

The men glared at each other for a long moment, then the captain spat once on the deck. He tossed the crockery vessel to Rowan, then marched away, his mood not visibly improved. He ran one hand over his tabard, evidently intending to smooth its rumpled state, then looked at his hand in horror.

Rowan, however, was not interested in whatever souvenir Baldassare had found. He shook the contents of the pot until they jingled and felt his lips thin.

He had other matters to resolve.

Before Ibernia spent every last coin he possessed.

# Chapter Seven

SINCE SHE COULD NOT SLEEP, IBERNIA SPENT THE NIGHT mustering her resistance. Aye, if she did not steel herself against Rowan, she would yield to his touch and lose the possibility of early freedom. 'Twould be too painful to be home and be unable to remain—and who knew where this unpredictable man might find himself in a year and a day? Ibernia did not even want to imagine.

Nay, she had to *win*.

So she could not afford to think about Rowan. Not the gentleness of his touch, not the languor of his kiss, not the way his eyes gleamed when she brushed her lips across his.

Certainly not the pleasure of his lips exploring hers.

Nay, anything but that!

Ibernia rolled over in the narrow cot. She could not think about how tall or how broad Rowan was, how alluring his smile, how cursedly cocky he was about his handsome features. She would be better to not even acknowledge that he was handsome, certainly not to admit that he was the most handsome rogue she had ever met. The twinkle in his eye tempted her to smile too readily, so she had best ignore her recollection of that.

She certainly could not afford to think about the weight of his hand upon her bare breast.

Ibernia shivered involuntarily and rolled to her other side.

If her flesh had burned from his kisses, that was naught compared to the tingle in her nipple that would not cease. Aye, it throbbed, even now, as if it yearned for his touch again. His hand had been so warm, his fingers so strong, yet his touch was tempered with tenderness.

'Twas all a ruse, and Ibernia knew it well. The man manipulated her with his charm to bend her to his will. But she would not fall prey to Rowan de Montvieux. Nay, not she. She was clever enough to foil his plan. She knew the truth of relations between women and men, she had experienced enough of how men were.

Even if Rowan defied expectation at every turn. Ibernia gritted her teeth, stared at the ceiling, and mustered her resistance with every increment of determination she possessed.

But 'twas all for naught in the end. For the very moment that Rowan sauntered over the threshold of the cabin, that resistance abandoned her.

Completely.

Ibernia sat up, fighting her urge to study Rowan openly. Instead she lifted her chin and met his gaze, hoping hers snapped with defiance. "What do you want of me?"

Rowan smiled and shook his head, that wicked twinkle in his eyes not aiding Ibernia in the least. "Now, there," he murmured, "is a weighted question indeed."

Their gazes locked and held across the narrow space. Ibernia could not seem to take a breath; she could not halt her gaze from dropping to his lips. Her own burned in recollection of his kisses, she felt her nipple rise to a point, as if it would welcome his touch once more.

Curse its betrayal—'twould beckon him closer.

Rowan had the audacity to smile. He smiled slowly, as if to remind her of how his lips felt against her own.

'Twas a practiced feat, no doubt.

Ibernia rose abruptly and folded her arms across her chest in an attempt to stifle the annoying tingle. "Why did you return this morn? If 'tis for more kisses, you are destined to be disappointed."

"Am I?" Rowan strolled into the cabin, his presence making the space feel even smaller than it was. His eyes narrowed as he halted just a pace away from her, and it seemed his smile chilled slightly. "You may be fortunate to escape with merely a kiss after what you have just cost me."

Ibernia knew better than to fear this man. He would never hurt her and she knew it well. "I cost you naught but an affront to your pride!"

He laughed then. Ibernia glared at him and jumped when he brushed the tip of his finger across the end of her nose. It was a surprisingly playful gesture, one that caught her unawares, one that still made her thrum with yearning for more of his touch.

And he knew it well. She set her lips and held his gaze as if unaffected, wondering whether he truly was fooled. Rowan seemed untroubled by her response, though he looked down so quickly that she could not see what lingered in his eyes. He lifted a crockery vessel and shook it between them.

The jingle made Ibernia look within it.

"I am told that you were responsible for the destruction of this particularly fine Murano glass."

Ibernia flushed. She stared at the shards of glass, feeling Rowan's gaze upon her. She swallowed as she noted the distinctive swirl of a goblet stem, the twist of a pitcher handle.

She glanced up to find Rowan considering her and did not doubt he had glimpsed her guilt.

One russet brow arched high. "Interestingly enough, it seems our captain did not lie."

"Nay, but neither did he tell you all of the truth," Ibernia replied. "What else could I do? He locked me in his cabin, he intended to have his due from me. I fended for myself as well as I was able."

Rowan's eyes gleamed as he leaned forward, his voice dropped low. "But what were you doing in his cabin, *ma demoiselle*?"

She swallowed. "I was invited."

"I had already declined that invitation."

"I know, but . . ."

Rowan's eyes flashed. "You *knew*, but still you went willingly to a private meal with this man? What of your promise to remain in this cabin, with the door barred?"

"You cannot tell me what to do!"

"Nay?"

"Oh, indeed, you have *bought* me, so now you believe you can decree whether I eat a hot meal or not. How could I have forgotten?"

"Sarcasm does not favor you." Rowan shoved one hand through his hair and frowned at her. "Ibernia, you were welcome to eat, but not with him."

"Will you approve of all my activities? Truly I have never had a master so very diligent!"

"Ibernia!" Rowan bit back something and clearly fought for control. He backed her into the corner and she felt a flicker of uncertainty at the unholy blaze in his eyes. "Is it so reprehensible that I have concern for your welfare?"

'Twas not reprehensible and he knew it, just as Ibernia knew she had erred. She had broken her promise but she dared not admit it, for fear of softening to his appeal. "You would save me only for yourself," she charged, though there was no heat in her words.

Rowan made a sound of frustration. "I thought you were a woman with some wits about her! Could you not see that this man is concerned only with his own advantage? Merchants can be bought and sold like so much chattel—and our captain is no different!''

The insult against her own family's class would not pass uncontested—if it was, Ibernia would look overlong into Rowan's amber gaze and forget all her reasons to resist him.

She certainly would not admit to this man that he was right.

''You are quick to condemn the merchants!'' she countered. ''How many tales does one hear of *knights* changing loyalty to the side most likely to win? Of landowners caring only for their own advantage? Why, you have only to look at happenings in Ireland of late to see that nobles are not above seeing their own needs served first!''

''You pose a spirited defense of merchants.'' Rowan's voice was soft, his gaze assessing. ''As if you have a personal interest in their dignity.''

Ibernia drew back and considered him, realizing too late that she had said too much. Her heart began to pound.

Rowan shook the glass between them. ''I have had to pay recompense for this foolishness of yours, a payment which cuts yet again into my increasingly limited finances.''

''What do you want from me?''

''A better bargain.'' He smiled, though the expression was not reassuring.

Ibernia thought of hungry wolves and backed into the wall without realizing that she did so. ''I will not surrender to your touch.''

Rowan shrugged. ''You will, but 'tis not of import to this discussion.''

His confidence did little to ease Ibernia's fears. Indeed, the words she managed to force past her lips sounded too strained to be her own. ''What do you desire then?''

Rowan set the pot between them on the floor and propped his hands upon his hips as he studied her. "Honesty."

The word was so unexpected that Ibernia blinked and stared at him. This man wanted *honesty* from her?

Rowan's sudden grin caught her by surprise. "And your aid in winning the hand of Bronwyn of Ballyroyal."

"What could I do to persuade this stranger to take your hand?" Ibernia scoffed. "And what further honesty do you want of me? I have told you all you need to know."

"Liar." Rowan enunciated the word carefully, though there was no censure in his tone. "I do not condemn you for keeping your secrets to yourself. But you know more of the ways of Ireland than you admit, and I would wager my own blade that this Bronwyn is no stranger to you. Are you friends? Confidantes? You could do much to aid my suit."

Ibernia lifted her chin. "But I would so like to see you lose," she declared with a measure of her usual spirit.

Rowan chuckled. He braced his hands on either side of her shoulders, and Ibernia knew he heard her quick intake of breath.

To her surprise, his expression was deadly serious. "But I am not inclined to lose this wager, even if it costs me all else. You will aid me." He nudged the crock with his toe. "For indeed, you have already seen my resources quickly depleted. You owe me this."

"I owe you naught!"

Rowan shrugged and turned away. "As I truly owe you naught."

Ibernia felt a sudden dread. "What is that to mean? You bought me!"

"And I can sell you." Rowan seemed to be feigning indifference, and she wished she could read him well enough to be certain. "Is that not what merchants do? Buy and sell to suit their own advantage? Truly, Ibernia, you are woefully expensive as a slave, particularly one who grants little value to her master."

Ibernia caught her breath. "You would not do it! We have a wager and a bargain for my winning my freedom."

"And you have already accused my rank of being faithless." Rowan's tone was most reasonable. "What little 'twould cost me to prove you right in this. Truly, my purse could use the coin."

"But there is none to whom you could sell me," she challenged, her eyes widening in realization as Rowan smiled.

"*Ma bella,*" he murmured, his gaze filled with mischief.

Ibernia's mouth went dry. "You would not. You could not." She sought a reason why he should not do this thing and found none. Indeed, she had relied heavily upon his sense of honor, and could think of no other compelling reason for him to keep her.

Because the problem was that she could not guess what Rowan would do.

And he knew it, curse him!

He arched a brow, his eyes gleaming, as if he would dare her to tempt him. What a vexingly unpredictable man he was!

Oh, she should have sacrificed herself to his touch last evening! Perhaps then he would believe she had value.

Though none of her other masters had.

She met his gaze and summoned her most challenging stare. "I do not believe you would do this thing," she declared. "I believe you have more honor than that."

Rowan chuckled, not the most reassuring sound he might have made. "Why do you not dare me?" His words were silky soft and Ibernia guessed that any challenge would do little to change his mind. He was determined to win the wager already made with his brothers, and that alone would guide his choices.

Regardless of how that affected her.

But still she had to try to sway his choice. Ibernia could not quickly compose the dare to ensure her goal was achieved, the fact that Rowan eased closer doing naught to aid her concentration. He halted before her, her mouth went dry, and she stared at the floor as she tried to muster the words she needed.

Sadly, the lean strength of his legs interrupted the view and distracted her from the argument.

"You intrigue me, *ma demoiselle,*" he whispered, and she closed her eyes against the waft of his breath far too close to her ear. "Other women would offer kisses or more to win their way, but you argue like a man." His lips feathered across her cheek and Ibernia felt herself tremble. "Do you think your feminine charms so little worthy of merit as that?"

The heat of his mouth closed over her earlobe and Ibernia's resistance slipped dangerously. All too soon, she sagged against the wall, felt herself turn to touch her lips to his.

Rowan's lips closed over hers and Ibernia's will dissolved beneath his sure touch. For the moment, she did not care that he manipulated her apurpose. For the moment, she wanted naught but Rowan's kiss.

Though, indeed, that kiss granted her the answer she sought.

Ibernia told herself that she had to surrender to stay his hand. Proving her value to Rowan was far preferable to becoming a possession of Baldassare di Vilonte. Even a year and a day beneath Rowan's hand—a man who had shown himself to be reasonably fair—was far preferable to lifetime in slavery to one who had proven himself precisely the opposite.

'Twas no more than a sensible decision that had Ibernia opening her mouth to that kiss. She immediately felt dread well up within her, for that deed between men and women had never been a sweet moment for her, but Ibernia knew what she had to do.

A woman of resolve could endure anything once.

Rowan had never expected Ibernia to welcome his touch. He certainly had never expected her to surrender with a sweet yearning that made him both anxious to please her and desperate to have her.

'Twas too tempting to have his desire find an echo within her. Rowan slanted his mouth across hers possessively, fully expecting her to twist away, but Ibernia opened her mouth to him.

She lifted her hands to his shoulders. Her eyes fluttered closed and, almost as an act of will, she leaned against his chest.

Rowan's heart thundered. He felt her trepidation, sensed her uncertainty, was awed that she put her trust in him. There was a plea in her kiss, an entreaty for tenderness, that a man less experienced in the arts of love might have missed.

But Rowan heard it and it tore at his heart. His certainty that he was glimpsing a vulnerability that Ibernia would have preferred to hide made him feel protective of her. She was by no means a weak woman, yet he could wound her deeply, at least in this moment.

Rowan had no intention of doing so. Clearly she had been hurt by her couplings with men in the past. If naught else, he would leave her with an understanding of both her own al-

lure and the pleasure that could be found between a man and
a woman.

Indeed, Rowan could not have thought of a candidate
more perfect for the task than himself. He caught Ibernia
against him, deepened his kiss, and revelled in her unwilling
moan of pleasure. Oh, he would be thorough, he would
make the most of this opportunity. 'Twould take a goodly
measure of the morning, or perhaps the day, to see matters
set to rights.

He almost smiled in anticipation of the way she would
thank him.

Rowan lifted his head reluctantly when Thomas knocked
on the door. He watched Ibernia's eyes open, noted her
quick glance upward and the faint flush that stained her
cheeks. Rowan smiled down at her, taking his leisure in
ensuring that she understood he, too, was pleased.

"My lord?" Thomas cleared his throat.

'Twas only when Ibernia tore her gaze from Rowan's and
swallowed that he turned to his squire with a grin. He surrendered the lady's embrace with reluctance, anxious only
to ensure their privacy once again.

With certain amendments to the current situation.

"Good morn, Thomas."

"You are better this morn, sir?"

"Aye, I am as hale and hearty as ever I was." Rowan
winked. "Though whether 'tis the open sea or the pleasure
of the company, I cannot begin to guess."

Rowan watched Thomas look between the two of them
and grin. "I trust you slept well?"

"Aye, my lord." Thomas bowed. "The steeds are tended
already this morn and seem well enough, though Troubador
is feisty."

" 'Tis only natural he be restless in such confinement,
though there is little that can be done for it. And Marika?"

The slavewoman peeked out from behind Thomas, offering a shy smile. "She seems well enough, my lord, but . . ." Thomas's brow knotted in a frown.

While Rowan could imagine that the boy did not appreciate the woman's company, he was disinclined to do much about it in this moment.

"But naught, Thomas," he said firmly. "You do me a great favor in ensuring she is well. I have a task for you this morn, and then you may amuse yourself."

"Aye?" The boy's countenance brightened.

"Aye. Ibernia and I have need of a decent bath." Rowan heard Ibernia inhale and almost smiled. 'Twould be a fine way to spend the morn, and telling that she was too shocked to protest.

"Several pails of hot water will suffice, if you can persuade the cook to part with the water. I suppose we could bathe in salt water if naught else can be had. But it must be hot, and I will part with no more coin to see it done."

Thomas nodded and bowed, and Rowan beckoned to Marika as the boy darted away to complete his task.

Rowan gestured to the pieces of wool and made a stitching motion with his hand. "You must finish this today," he told her, uncertain how much she understood. He gestured to Ibernia. "So the lady has something to wear." He touched Ibernia's chemise and grimaced.

Marika nodded in quick agreement and undoubtedly would have sat on the floor to take up her work, but Rowan shook his head. "Nay, you must take the work with you." She looked up at him, her expression blank, and Rowan gestured to the door.

Marika promptly abandoned her needlework and made to leave.

"Nay!" Rowan scooped up the wool and pressed it into her hands. Marika considered him with some confusion, then shrugged and sat down again, preparing to thread a needle.

Rowan looked up and found Ibernia smiling. The very sight quickened his blood and made him anxious to have Marika on her way. He quickly repeated his gestures, confusing the slavewoman all over again.

Rowan refused to concede that his mother had been right when she counselled him to be more diligent with his studies, that awareness of languages would serve him well. Though French was his first language, he fared well enough in the common tongue of England.

Marika, sadly, seemed familiar with neither of his options. Rowan gritted his teeth, preparing to repeat the whole ordeal once again for lack of other choice, but Ibernia intervened. She flashed Rowan a sparkling glance so unexpected that it struck him silent for a moment.

Then he realized that she was laughing at him, at his incompetence, and was doubly irked. Trust all to go awry when he meant to seduce this woman! 'Twas one thing to tempt a woman's laughter by choice, another to unwittingly prompt her laughter by one's inabilities.

Not that Rowan had many of those. Ibernia seemed to bring out the worst of them. He folded his arms across his chest and watched as she bent over the slavewoman.

He would not admire the ripe perfection of Ibernia's buttocks. Rowan thought again of her intent to pass as a boy and nearly snorted aloud.

It seemed he was not alone in foolish whims, and that realization did much to restore his mood.

Ibernia spoke softly and though she said much the same thing as Rowan, she gestured differently. She pointed to Marika and the needlework, then made a sewing gesture. Marika nodded with enthusiasm, then chattered away in some incomprehensible tongue, her hands moving like quicksilver. Ibernia nodded approval, then took the woman's hand, lifting her to her feet and ensuring that all of the sewing was in her arms.

Marika looked confused and Rowan folded his arms with satisfaction. Here was where the matter became troubled! He knew Ibernia would fare no better than he.

But she pointed to the door, giving Marika a little push, ensuring she held on to the wool when she might have put it down. Marika frowned. She pointed to the floor, then repeated the movement of sewing. Ibernia pointed to the hall, following with the same gesture. Marika's gaze slid between Ibernia and Rowan and she pursed her lips.

She indicated herself once more, made the sewing gesture, and pointed emphatically to the floor. Ibernia shook her head, pointed to Marika and the hall. Then she indicated herself and Rowan, pointed to the narrow pallet, and pushed her right index finger into the loose fist she made of her left hand. She pumped it a couple of times, to ensure the meaning was not lost.

Marika gasped. Both women blushed. It seemed Marika could not look at Rowan any longer, and though he dearly wanted to laugh, he did not dare to do so. The slavewoman hastily gathered up all of her materials, then fled out the door without a backward glance.

Before Rowan could say anything, Thomas returned with two steaming buckets of water, his expression mutinous. "I have to haul slops in exchange," he said darkly.

Rowan's grin finally broke free, though Thomas undoubtedly thought it poorly timed.

" 'Tis not amusing in the least!" the boy complained.

"Nay 'tis not," Rowan agreed, and bit back his errant smile again. "Take but one bucket and disappear. The cook has no business demanding your aid. And after all, you must ensure Marika's safety. If he troubles you about the matter, tell him to speak with me.''

''Aye, my lord.'' Thomas grinned then ran back out into the shadowed corridor. ''Marika!''

Rowan flicked the door shut with his fingertips. The latch fell into place with a click. ''Now, where were we?'' he mused, leaning back against it and surrendering fully to his impulse to grin. ''Ah, I know. You were teaching Marika obscene gestures.''

Ibernia did not smile. ''It worked, did it not?''

''Indeed.'' Rowan bowed low. ''I am much impressed with your cleverness.'' He stepped closer and caught her hand in his. Ibernia stared at him, her eyes wide and the flicker of a pulse at her throat. ''As I was impressed by your fleeting smile.''

The lady looked away.

''Smile for me,'' Rowan cajoled.

''I cannot.'' Ibernia shook her head, her expression grim. ''Not now, not when this prospect is before us.''

''Ah, but that is precisely when you should smile.'' Rowan bent and bestowed a feather-light kiss on one corner of her mouth. Ibernia watched him, almost poised to flee.

'Twas galling to realize how she dreaded this, no less what must be at root of her fears. Rowan's admiration for Ibernia's resolve redoubled.

He kissed her on the other corner of her mouth. '' 'Tis not so very difficult to smile,'' he whispered, his lips a finger's breadth from hers. ''I have seen you do it.''

She was pale with the fear of what they would do, and Rowan knew they would do naught unless she could summon some enthusiasm for the deed. He brushed his lips across hers gently and she shivered.

''I would never hurt you,'' he murmured, holding her gaze as if he would persuade her with his own steady glance.

Her uncertainty might have been unflattering to a man less convinced of his own abilities than Rowan.

He brushed another fleeting kiss across her lips, lingering tellingly for the merest heartbeat. "Have I ever hurt you?"

"Nay."

"Then why imagine I would now?"

Ibernia swallowed. " 'Tis unavoidable."

Rowan chuckled and treated himself to another taste of her lips, letting his mouth tease her lips until she parted them in response. "Only to clumsy fools." He lifted his gaze to hers once more. "Do you believe me a clumsy fool?"

"Nay." Her word was breathless, but that fear still lit her magnificent eyes.

"An inexpert lover?"

Ibernia released a soundless laugh, though still there was no smile. "Nay."

"A man whose kiss is offensive?" Rowan treated her to his most engaging grin. "Poorly executed?"

"Nay," she whispered, then caught her breath when Rowan stole another tiny kiss. "And nay."

He grazed his lips along her jawline, noting how her lips parted and her eyes closed. Her body at least seemed amenable to his plans. Rowan could work with that.

And indeed, he would. Slowly, languorously, thoroughly.

Ibernia's breath caught as he kissed beneath her ear. He let his hand trail down her neck on the other side, his fingertips enchanted by the softness of her skin. He cupped her jaw in his hand, kissed her ear, her temple, her cheek. He hovered just above her lips, waiting for her to open her eyes and acknowledge him before he claimed her lips again.

Her eyes flew open, all wide clear blue. Her gaze raked over him, and she seemed to recall herself. She straightened, her first instinct clearly to fight or flee, but Rowan had seen this in her before.

He would see her shaken of these impulses before he halted. He bent, pleased that she did not pull away. He closed his mouth over hers, his kiss slow and deliberate. There was no rush this day, and he continued his leisurely kiss, coaxing her lips to part, touching his tongue to hers, urging her to embrace him in return.

He knew the very moment she responded. Her gasp was like a flint being struck. She shivered and rose against him, her hands tentatively twining around his neck.

But 'twas how Rowan favored this lady. Determined to grant and to have her own share. She must have been sorely used to abandon that stance in any facet of her life, and its return fed his desire as naught else could have done. He cradled her face in his hands and kissed her deeply, ensuring that he pushed no further than she was willing to go.

When he finally lifted his head, her cheeks were flushed. There was a sparkle in her eyes that he glimpsed just before she averted her gaze.

"No smile?" he teased.

Ibernia flicked a quick half smile his way, though her gaze fixed on the steaming buckets with apparent fascination.

"You should grant the gift of your smile more often," he said softly. " 'Tis bewitching."

The lady stepped away, her smile fading to naught. "You do not fool me," she charged, though her tone was more breathless than scathing. " 'Twas the obscene gesture—or better yet, its import—that bewitched you."

Rowan laughed, he could not help it. "Nay, I was bewitched afore," he admitted, his words turning more husky than he had anticipated. "When you smiled on the docks."

Ibernia pivoted and stared at him, apparently uncertain whether to believe him. Their gazes locked and held for a timeless and telling moment. Indeed, neither of them took a breath; the cabin seemed suddenly overwarm from the steaming water.

Rowan knew 'twas true, there had been something about Ibernia that touched him as no other woman had done, even on that first day. He hoped he saw a similar acknowledgment in her eyes but could not be certain whether his hope colored his vision.

But either way, he was concerned that he not disappoint the lady. He told himself that was only because he took pride in his labor, even a labor of love, but Rowan knew that was a lie. 'Twas the way Ibernia's eyes widened, the flick of fear that she quickly suppressed, the hundreds of tiny signs that told him she had not savored her adventures abed. She was uncertain, but she was forcing herself to trust him.

*Him.* Rowan had never felt the weight of responsibility quite so acutely. To his astonishment, the burden was not so ungainly as he had always expected it to be. Perhaps that was only because their objectives were as one in this.

And Rowan knew, without doubt, that his fascination with Ibernia would end with the having of her. If he was not sated the first time, then the third or the sixth or the tenth would see it done. 'Twould be easy to walk away once they reached Ballyroyal, both he and Ibernia having won their desire.

Rowan looked into the fathomless sapphire of her eyes and was not quite as certain of that as he would have liked to be.

He made a jest to cover the moment, as was his wont. "What man of merit would not be intrigued to know what lingered beneath this gravy-embellished garb?"

He lifted his fingers to the knotted tie of Ibernia's chemise. He bent and pressed a kiss beneath her ear, feeling her tremble and feeling less alone in his trepidation.

"We must hasten before the water cools," he whispered.

"Aye," she agreed breathlessly, and pushed away his hands. Her own dropped to the ties of her chausses and shook as she undid the knot. As Rowan watched in surprise, she wiggled out of those chausses and kicked them aside, rolling to her back on the narrow pallet and parting her thighs.

He did not even have the chance to enjoy the lean perfection of her legs, the hued tan of her flesh, the glimpse of the treasure between her thighs.

"I am as prepared as ever I will be," she said briskly. She closed her eyes, clearly expecting him to leap atop her and do the deed, then turned her face to the wall.

Rowan's enthusiasm waned in the face of her manner. He turned away crossly and hauled his tabard over his head. "Indeed, *ma demoiselle,* I have had whores who showed more desire than this."

"Is enthusiasm not what they are paid to feign?"

"That is not the point," Rowan retorted, then took a deep breath. When he continued, his voice was more steady. "You misunderstood my meaning. I intended that we bathe first."

"Ah, my lack of clean garb disgusts you. I understand." Ibernia's words were toneless. She straightened and reached for a cloth, but Rowan caught at her hand.

"You have misunderstood me," he said in a low voice when her gaze rose to his in alarm. "I ask that you cease in your efforts to hurry events."

"What do you mean?"

"There is no need for haste," Rowan assured her. "I ask only that you cease to fret, that you savor the moment."

But the expression on Ibernia's face told him that she could not even conceive of doing that. Well, Rowan de Montvieux was not a man who surrendered a challenge readily, and, clearly, seducing Ibernia was going to be a greater challenge than even he had anticipated.

'Twas fortunate indeed that she had chosen the right man for this task.

# Chapter Eight

IBERNIA WAS TERRIFIED. NOT ONLY WAS ROWAN GOING to take his pleasure with her, but he intended to take days at the task. She did not know how she would survive—indeed, what intimacy she had endured had lasted but moments and left her in pain for a long time afterward.

If he were as thorough as he threatened, she might never walk in comfort again. All the same, Ibernia knew that whatever Rowan demanded of her, 'twould be small in comparison with whatever Baldassare believed his due.

She would not question her faith in that, though she hoped hers was not some misguided optimism.

Or impulsiveness. She closed her eyes and cursed impulsiveness soundly.

Rowan had already discarded his hauberk, the clatter of its fall to the floor making Ibernia jump. She watched through her lashes as he shed his chemise with a casual gesture, his gaze averted from her own. Ibernia's eyes widened at the sight of his nudity, the tanned expanse of his chest, the russet river of hair on his chest. He seemed to fill the cabin, even more than he had before. Ibernia could smell the heat of his flesh; she found herself watching the flex of his muscles as he lay his belt and scabbard aside.

And she was profoundly grateful that he seemed oblivious

to her presence. That alone granted her the opportunity to study him, a deed she would never have imagined to interest her, certainly not as much as it did.

He had folded his tabard and his chemise, much to her astonishment, and took care in laying his belt aside. The scabbard with its fine sword and his dagger were handled with even greater care, and she realized that though Rowan would have all believe he cared for naught, that was far from the truth.

She wondered what he valued most of all and knew she could die wondering. This man would confess naught to anyone, especially a slave with whom he took his pleasure.

She wondered whether he would tell Bronwyn of Ballyroyal such secret truths, then his efficient movements distracted her from that direction of thought.

He would soon be nude.

He would soon be atop her.

She would soon be hurting and unable to aid herself. Ibernia gripped the pallet in dread.

Rowan shed his boots and set them aside, then reached for the tie of his chausses. Ibernia swallowed, knowing full well what came next. Neither of her former masters had troubled to undress themselves fully, but Rowan would not differ in the deed itself. She stared at the wooden wall, bracing herself for the worst.

'Twas then she heard a splash. Ibernia darted a glance Rowan's way to find him quickly washing himself. His back was to her, so she took the opportunity to study him, noting the strength of his legs, the tightness of his buttocks. He was tanned from head to toe, a sign that he was not afraid to let the sun touch all of him, but then, that boldness did not surprise Ibernia.

Rowan was not a knight interested in convention.

When he started to turn, she squeezed her eyes tightly

shut and waited for the worst. She thought she was prepared for anything, but soon learned differently.

For she was not anticipating the warm caress of a cloth on her foot. Ibernia jumped and she sat up in alarm, instinctively pulling her feet beneath herself.

Rowan crouched at the end of the pallet, a wet cloth in his hands and an impish twinkle in his eyes. But she could see his aroused state and knew that he was not so boyishly playful as he might pretend.

"Your feet are filthy," he charged.

That was a fact. Ibernia heaved a sigh of concession and cautiously stretched her leg back out again. A harmless enough indulgence, she supposed. The cloth was rough, and Rowan stroked it across the bottom of her foot like a caress.

Ibernia leaned back, closed her eyes, and endured.

He scrubbed the bottom of her foot, then pushed the cloth between her toes, leisurely cleaning each in succession. Ibernia tried not to clench her foot; she sought to appear at ease with all of this. She was quite certain she failed—her grip on the sides of the pallet hinted at the truth—especially when his thumb eased across the nail of her second toe and she caught her breath. It was a move she felt she should have anticipated.

Ibernia took a deep breath. It was not so bad, truly, to have a man wash her feet. She gritted her teeth, deciding to savor this moment and not think of the one to come. This alone was rather pleasant, the thoroughness with which Rowan worked doing much to ease her agitation.

Aye, he was tranquil and oddly quiet. Ibernia listened to the rhythmic creaking of the ship. The men's voices were so distant and muted that she and Rowan might have been alone. She could smell the spices from the bundles knotted overhead, the steam from the water apparently having loosened their exotic scents.

When Rowan completed one foot and moved his attention to her other one, repeating gesture for gesture, Ibernia resolved this *was* enjoyable. To be clean again was no small thing. Aye, she had felt encrusted with filth for the better part of a sixmonth, and this change would be a welcome one.

There might be some benefit to ceding to the touch of a fastidious man. The telltale splashing of water and absence of Rowan's touch revealed that the cloth was being rinsed and wrung out.

Ibernia prided herself on the fact that she did not so much as stir when the warm cloth and Rowan's hand closed around her ankle. He scrubbed the skin with gentle diligence, his thumb sliding into the nook beside her ankle bone with sensuous ease. Ibernia told herself it was just his manner to move so deliberately, that there was naught amorous about his touch.

She was proven wrong when he kissed the sole of her foot.

Ibernia gasped. She sat up and Rowan chuckled at her response. He watched her, a glint in his eyes that dared her to pull away once more. Ibernia's heart was thumping but she would not prove him right in this. Though she stiffened, she did not retreat.

She did not miss his satisfied smile. He nibbled the side of her big toe, he kissed it, he slid his tongue between it and that next toe. He caught her foot in his hand, his thumb sliding across her instep with persuasive ease. His lips followed suit, caressing her instep, nibbling on her ankle bone, the heat of his breath driving her to distraction as he kissed every increment of skin.

Rowan watched her all the while, his gaze searching. There was concern in his eyes, Ibernia was certain of it, and she had a sudden conviction that a single protest from her lips would halt his progress.

'Twas a heady thing, to feel that she had a say in this. Even more remarkably, she did not want him to stop.

Ibernia felt that foot tingle. She lay back with a thump and stared at the goods knotted over the bed, unwilling to let Rowan see her response.

She felt as she did when he kissed her. Her flesh tingled, she wanted to shiver, she was achingly aware of his breath, his kiss, his touch, his heat.

And his heat awakened an answering passion within her. Ibernia swallowed, locked her hands around the edge of the pallet, and reminded herself of her talent for endurance.

Rowan, though, was disinclined to rush. As she might have guessed if she had been able to hook two thoughts together, he proceeded to wash her legs. He was as slow and thorough as before, each stroke of the cloth languid.

He followed the progress of the cloth with his hot kisses, the weight of his body easing up the pallet alongside her. His touch and his kisses stoked that burgeoning heat within her belly to a flame, pushing her fear further away with each slow stroke.

Ibernia learned things about her body that she had never guessed before. Who would have imagined that a man's hand, locked around her ankle, would be so pleasant? Who would have guessed that a slow kiss on the inside of her thigh, just above the knee, would make her yearn for more of his touch?

Rowan knew. Rowan understood her own body better than she. 'Twas only because he was a practiced seducer of women, Ibernia knew this well. All the same, she was disinclined to stop him. Indeed, when he halted at the crest of her thighs, she was almost disappointed.

But not quite. Her fear still flickered in the back of her

thoughts, her certainty that all could not proceed without pain was unshaken.

Rowan's lips quirked, as if he guessed as much, then he got smoothly to his feet and crouched to rinse out the cloth again. His back was to her and Ibernia found herself studying him through her lashes, lest he turn quickly.

"You shall have to remove your chemise," he said, his calm tone in marked contrast to Ibernia's racing heart. "Then roll to your belly so I can wash your back."

Ibernia did not wait for him to reconsider his offer. She was not so brazen that she could bare herself before a man and look him in the eye, yet truly she longed to be clean from head to toe. Ibernia shed her chemise and cast it on the floor, quickly rolling over in case Rowan tried to catch her unawares.

But he did no such thing. The cloth was dunked and wrung out one more time before he came to her side. Ibernia closed her eyes and bit her lip when he sat on the pallet beside her. Her heart began to pound. She knew full well what part of him was so close, knew that they both were nude and there was naught to stop him from taking what he would have of her.

The pain would surely come in a moment, and her determination to prove her usefulness to him nearly deserted her.

But Rowan cradled her buttock in his hand and squeezed, the slow slide of his thumb across her flesh making Ibernia's eyes fly open. He used both hands to wash the small of her back, his fingers nearly closing around her waist. Ibernia felt her lips part and acknowledged that this attention was not so difficult to endure.

Indeed, that heat in her belly had been joined by a shiver, and the combination was not all bad.

Rowan washed her back, the heat of his skin dangerously close as his lips trailed the cloth. Ibernia's flesh sang beneath his caress, then his strong hand slid up the back of her neck. Water trickled around her, escaping down between her breasts. Ibernia shivered, though she was uncertain whether that was due to the water or the possessive way Rowan slid the weight of his fingers into her hair.

He caught her shoulders in his hands, bracing his weight on his elbows as he leaned over her. Ibernia exhaled shakily when Rowan pressed a hot kiss into the curve between neck and shoulder.

His tongue traced a path up her neck and he kissed her earlobe again, making her shiver as he had before. He lingered there, teasing her with his tongue and awakening the same yearning she had felt when he kissed her before. The strength of him was almost against her back, the hair on his chest tickling her shoulder blades.

Ibernia was shocked to realize that she wanted to press back against him, even knowing all she did.

But Rowan eased away, rolling her to her back with an easy gesture. Ibernia let him do it, telling herself this was the moment of reckoning. She could not bear to look at him, to see the twinkle purged from his gaze when lust claimed him. Or even worse, she would not see his expression at the truth that she was far from lean and lithe.

Aye, Ibernia was tall; she was not fat, but she was buxom. Her mother always said her figure was all womanly curves, and even these months of scant provisions had not changed that.

No doubt Rowan would be appalled. He said naught, but she felt his gaze linger upon her and her face burned. Then he rose to rinse out the cloth once more. When he returned and she met his gaze, he smiled and Ibernia's heart thumped in a most awkward manner.

He captured her hand with the warmth of his, his gaze unswerving, as if they stood at court in all their finery. His smile broadened as he eased the dirt from her hand. And when he was done and Ibernia was more flustered by his attention than she knew she should be, Rowan inclined his head and kissed her palm. He closed her fingers over the burning imprint of his kiss, nibbled his way up the tender flesh of her arm, and kissed the inside of her elbow.

Ibernia could not breathe. Rowan, his eyes closed in an expression of perfect bliss, pushed his cloth higher. His kisses followed suit until he grazed his teeth across her shoulder.

His eyes flew open as Ibernia stared at him. He grinned wickedly and winked so quickly that her heart leapt. He pressed a kiss in the hollow of her collar bone, then turned his attention to her other hand.

Ibernia stared at her own curled fingers, still holding that kiss safe while he washed the other hand. She felt oddly cherished by this man, pampered and spoiled by his touch, savored and appreciated in a way she had not been before.

Ibernia closed her eyes and leaned back against the pallet, certain her bones were melting beneath his persuasive touch. Rowan washed her wrists, her arms, her elbows, her shoulders, and her throat. His lips grazed a trail right behind while Ibernia held fast to the kiss that still heated her palm. He washed her neck, then rinsed the cloth and washed her face. He kissed her brow, her temple, her closed eyes, the tip of her nose.

To her astonishment, Rowan did not kiss her lips.

To her greater astonishment, she felt cheated.

His kisses moved down her throat, even as the cloth moved lower. Her breasts, she was certain, had never been so clean as when Rowan finished with them. Indeed, he seemed fascinated by them, so intrigued that he abandoned the cloth on her belly, cupped one breast in his hand, and bent his head.

Ibernia cried out when his mouth closed over her nipple. She gasped and twisted beneath him, wanting escape and, in the same breath, wanting only more. Rowan suckled and teased; he flicked his tongue across the turgid peak, he stroked her curves with those strong fingers.

When Ibernia thought she could bear no more, he turned his attention to the other breast. She felt the heat of his erection pressed against her thigh and was startled to find that it did not frighten her as it had before.

Nay, she was anticipating the heat of him filling her.

Before Ibernia could puzzle over that, Rowan's questing lips moved lower. He rolled his tongue in her navel, then he kissed her hips. He cupped her breasts in his hands, his thumbs sliding across the tight nipples over and over again, driving Ibernia to distraction.

Slowly his fingers and the cloth moved lower and slid between her thighs, his touch sure and gentle. Ibernia found herself rising to meet his touch with a brazenness unexpected. She saw only the knight's fleeting smile before he cast away the cloth with a flourish.

Then his kiss followed his fingers where none had ever kissed Ibernia before. She might have protested if she had not been so quickly captivated. His tongue flicked against her, and Ibernia realized how much she wanted his touch there. She parted her thighs, that hint the only encouragement Rowan needed to cup her buttocks in his hands and feast upon her.

Rowan knew Ibernia was his the moment she let her thighs fall apart for him. He might have felt triumphant but there was yet too much to do. He tasted and teased, ensuring that this time, Ibernia felt the pleasure lovemaking could bring.

She fought a battle and Rowan knew it well, for experience could be a hard master.

Fortunately, he had three days to undo whatever lessons she had learned. Rowan settled in, savoring the taste of her, the little gasps she made when he surprised her. He coaxed her further and further, one step at a time, smiling to himself when her fingers dug into his shoulders in silent demand.

He had been a fool to ever prefer lean and lithe woman and could not imagine now what he had ever seen in their boyish figures. Ibernia was all ripe curves and sun-kissed skin, she was womanly in every sense of the word. She was soft and strong, she was feminine yet resilient.

Rowan desired her as he had never desired another, and it was not only the lady's ripe curves that enchanted him. He was intrigued by the fiery flash of her blue eyes, by her determination to conquer the odds, to see matters resolved as she would choose.

He delighted in the knowledge that he was surprising her now. She moaned, the helpless sound feeding his own passion. She writhed but did not try to escape his touch. Rowan could fairly feel the heat rising beneath her flesh. She was wet and hot and achingly sweet. 'Twould take more than one sampling of Ibernia's charms to sate him, he knew.

And he did not care.

Rowan felt her quickening, he urged her on. He kissed and tempted her anew. He seized her foot in one hand and ran his thumb across her instep, having already seen how it made her shiver. Ibernia shivered this time with gusto, she cried out and arched off the pallet. Her nipples tightened, her hips bucked, she cried out as she peaked, then she collapsed, trembling.

Rowan stretched out beside her, holding her in his arms as the last of the quakes slipped through her lush body. She was flushed and so astonished that she twined her arms around his neck before she realized what she did.

She opened her eyes and looked at him in wonder. Rowan granted her his most charming grin, and she almost smiled as she rolled her eyes in disgust.

"Cocky rogue," she muttered.

"Surely I have earned a smile for that," he teased.

Ibernia pinkened, but she did smile for him, looking so delightfully tousled that Rowan could not resist her. He kissed her impulsively and deeply, and liked that she hesitated only a moment before she returned his kiss in kind. His hand slid down the smooth length of her, his fingers easing between her thighs. She gasped when he touched her again and Rowan swallowed the sound, caressing her undeterred.

And she rose to his touch once again. Instinctively Rowan knew how she had been compelled to service men who did not see to her own pleasure, and he resolved to make this experience as different as possible.

Nay, he would not feed her fear. He would not pin her down. He would not make her feel trapped and cornered.

There were far more interesting ways to make love.

He forgot his clear thinking when Ibernia shyly eased her tongue between his teeth. Rowan caressed her and swallowed her moans, he coaxed the flame anew, every hint of her arousal feeding his own. When Ibernia could not keep her hips still, when her kisses became so fervid that Rowan did not believe he could last much longer, he caught her in his arms and quickly rolled to his back.

The lady sprawled atop him, her eyes wide with surprise, her magnificent breasts inviting his kisses.

"You are mad," she protested. "What is it you would do now?"

Rowan grinned up at her. "What else?" He caught her hips in his hands and urged her to straddle him.

She took one downward glance and paled. "I cannot do this."

"Of course you can." Rowan held her gaze. "And this way, 'tis your choice when to start and when to stop."

Her lips parted as she stared at him and Rowan thought she might have blinked away a tear. He reached for the bounty offered by her breasts but did not manage to kiss her anew.

For Ibernia's hand closed around his erection with a surety that made Rowan jump. He had only a glimpse of the determination in her face before she pushed him into her.

He fell back against the pallet, fighting for a measure of control, reminding himself to be slow. But Ibernia was hot, wet and tight, the grip of her upon him nigh enough to make him swoon. And heavens knew that he desired this woman beyond all else.

But matters were not aright. Rowan gritted his teeth and opened his eyes. Ibernia might have moved to please him, but her expression was strained and Rowan was not fooled.

This would not be a foul task to be endured! He halted her with a touch, the vulnerability in her eyes making his heart clench.

"There is no need for haste. Does it hurt you?"

Tears glittered in her eyes. "Less than before."

Rowan smiled to reassure her. " 'Tis not good enough."

"Let us see the deed done."

"Nay, there is only one way we shall see this done, and that is when we both find pleasure together."

She stared at him as if she could not comprehend his words. Rowan reached between her thighs and touched her again, his own erection swelling within her when she trembled with desire.

She whispered his name, the unsteadiness of her voice feeding that unfamiliar protectiveness again. Rowan gritted his teeth and compelled himself to wait until the lady was ready.

Oh, he had never been so chivalrous as this, and the shame of it was that his mother would never know. This deed could never be counted in his favor. This deed was only between himself and Ibernia.

And that—oddly enough considering his mother's current threat to disinherit him for his unworthiness—suited Rowan well. He had no opportunity to consider the puzzle further.

For Ibernia sat up and leaned back, her head falling back and her fine breasts jutting forward. 'Twas a sight to feast upon, one that scattered any thought beyond desire. Rowan could have stared at her for all his days.

He touched her with gentle persuasiveness, fighting his body's demand for release. He watched the flush spread from her breasts, watched her bite her lip. She moaned softly and then her hips rocked against his of their own accord. She gripped his hand demandingly, her lips parting soundlessly, her neck arching.

Ibernia stiffened with a tiny cry, then fell forward. Her breasts brushed against his chest, her gaze blazed into his. "More," she whispered. "I want more of you." And she rolled herself against Rowan, driving him to a frenzy.

Rowan was only too happy to comply. He gripped her hips and let her set the pace, easing farther into her with each stroke. Her heat seemed to swallow him, to cradle him, to coax him closer. They moved together, each stroke driving them higher and higher.

And just when he thought he could endure no more, Ibernia framed his face in her hands and kissed him. Her tongue tangled with his, her hunger unmistakable. Rowan fleetingly thought she would devour him whole, then there was naught but her tongue, her lips, the heat of her surrounding him.

Aye, he was overwhelmed by the most beguiling woman he had ever known. His hands were full of her, he wanted as he had never wanted before. Her womb tightened around him convulsively as she shivered from head to toe, and in that same moment, Rowan slackened his reins of control.

There was naught but Ibernia. Rowan broke their kiss and arched back, gripping her buttocks and roaring as his own release filled his veins with stardust.

Aye, Ibernia was his alone.

Ibernia collapsed atop Rowan, her thoughts spinning incoherently. She could do naught but feel, and what she felt was fine enough to satisfy.

The first thought she managed was the acknowledgment that she had never felt so marvelous.

She had never imagined that there could be such pleasure, that a man and a woman could grant each other such a gift. She steadied her breathing and realized that there was something of merit in lovemaking, after all.

Especially with this man. Ibernia opened her eyes and studied the profile of the man beneath her. She was still lying atop Rowan, he remained on his back, his hands warm on the back of her waist. He was breathing as heavily as she, his eyes were closed, and she could see the erratic leap of his pulse at his throat.

His heart hammered nigh as quickly as her own. Ibernia swallowed a smile that she had been able to please this man, this man who was clearly no stranger to pleasure. He opened his eyes and smiled at her in that moment, his gaze so warmly appreciative that Ibernia blushed.

Rowan heaved a contented sigh and ran one hand up her

back with evident admiration. His hand slid to her breast, that nipple still responding pertly to the caress of his thumb.

He cupped her jaw, smiling to himself as he studied her. "And there is that bewitching smile again," he teased softly. "I knew 'twould be worth the wait." With that, he drew her down to kiss her again.

They parted reluctantly some moments later, only because of the discomfort of their position, and Ibernia could barely catch her breath. Who knew she would rise to his touch again so quickly? Indeed, this was a day of marvels. She sat up and folded her knees together shyly, aware of her nudity but not wanting this moment to end.

Rowan watched her as if she were the greatest marvel in all of Christendom, a heady sensation indeed.

"I cannot imagine that I knew naught of such pleasure," she confessed, feeling her cheeks heat.

Rowan shrugged and grinned, pushing to his feet easily. Ibernia watched the ripple of his muscles unabashedly, knowing full well that he preened slightly before her.

" 'Tis only because you have not coupled with me before," he said cheerfully, grimacing when he found the water had chilled. His attention moved to the door, and he appeared to be deciding whether to call Thomas for another bucket.

Ibernia could not believe his audacity. "You have a confidence in your own charm!"

Rowan cast a sparkling glance her way. "Practice makes for perfection," he confided with a merry wink, then reached for his chemise as if he had not a care.

Ibernia regarded him in shock. She had been naught but another willing woman to him—and he had shaken her to the core! 'Twas unfair to realize in this moment that she had been right in guessing that naught mattered to this knight beyond himself.

"And how close have you come to perfection?" she asked coldly.

Rowan grinned wickedly. He crossed the cabin and caught her face in his hands, bending to kiss her deeply, his move so smooth that she had no chance to evade him. Much to her own disgust, Ibernia felt her annoyance with him fade.

Curse the man, he knew the moment she yielded to him. He lifted his lips from hers, a knowing gleam in his amber gaze. "My technique is fully perfected," he purred, then bent to fetch his abandoned chemise, a whistle on his lips.

"Well, I have had better," Ibernia retorted, purely to prick his pride.

Rowan granted her a confident smile. "I should think not." He hauled his chemise over his head, that victorious whistle making Ibernia grit her teeth.

"I sought only to ensure that your pride was not wounded," she retorted haughtily. "But truly, the coupling was mediocre."

Rowan stilled. Ibernia braced herself, but he pivoted slowly, his expression intent. "Mediocre?" His voice was dangerously soft, his eyes narrowed. That cursed whistle was silence. "None have ever called me a *mediocre* partner."

Ibernia smiled, pleased to see that she had unsettled him. She reached for her own chemise, hoping she looked as if such encounters occurred every day of her life. "There is always a first, I suppose."

Rowan's eyes flashed. He crossed the cabin and caught her arm in his grip. "That was *not* mediocre!"

Ha! Now she had his attention. "Nay?" Ibernia shrugged and reached for her chausses. "If 'tis of import to you to believe as much, then I suppose I must agree."

"You were pleased, I ensured as much!"

"Aye." Ibernia kept her tone light. "As were you. But

truly, is that not the least of what one expects?'' She turned away before he could see how boldly she lied, though she heard him mutter a curse.

''You expected far worse than what we shared,'' he asserted, such conviction in his voice that Ibernia knew he had not been fooled. ''You feared my touch.''

''Only because I was not certain you would be aware of anything beyond your own pleasure.'' Ibernia cast a glance over her shoulder, only to find Rowan's amber gaze blazing. ''Some men are thus, you must surely know.''

He folded his arms across his chest, a chest she had been nestled against only moments past, a chest that was warm and reassuringly solid. Aye, she had felt sheltered in his arms.

But she had only been the next conquest.

She would not make this easy for him.

''And was I?'' he asked, frost in his tone.

Ibernia summoned a chilly smile. ''Your competence cannot be questioned.''

''Competence!'' Rowan roared, more infuriated than she had ever seen him. ''I am far more than *competent* in the arts of love! Never have I been so insulted!''

''Then perhaps you should put more effort into your labor,'' Ibernia said lightly, bending her attention on the tie to her chausses. Her fingers were trembling still and she tried to fasten quickly before he saw the telltale hint of her response.

That was the only reason she was surprised when his hands landed on her shoulders. 'Twas no less surprising to find his breath on her nape, nor even his lips against her ear.

Ibernia shivered, much as she would have preferred otherwise.

''Mediocre,'' he whispered, then rolled his tongue into her ear so slowly that Ibernia's eyes closed. She felt herself lean back against him, powerless to stop herself as desire flooded through her. Aye, he was wickedly talented in this, and when he touched her, she found it nigh impossible to resist him.

Especially after what they had just shared. His hand slid around her waist and under her chemise, those fingers rising to tease her nipple again.

Ibernia just barely managed to bite back the moan that threatened to fall from her lips. Her sole consolation was the press of Rowan's erection against her buttocks, and she rubbed herself against him, like a wanton, before she knew what she was about.

"That was far from mediocre," Rowan murmured. "And the next time, you will have to admit as much before I grant you release."

Ibernia's eyes flew open at that threat and she turned quickly to face him. "What do you mean? You have to release me in a year and a day, 'tis our bargain!"

Rowan's slow smile only made her traitorous heart pound. "I meant your release abed," he whispered, lifting one hand to trail his fingertips across her cheek. "Although you raise an interesting possibility."

His lips landed on her cheek like a butterfly, but Ibernia swatted off his touch and danced backward, needing to keep her thoughts clear. She took a step farther away, though this seemed to amuse him mightily. "What madness do you talk now?"

Rowan arched a russet brow, untroubled by the fact that he wore no chausses as yet. Had she ever seen a man more at ease in his own skin? If naught else, such confidence was grating!

"You complain about my lovemaking. And truly the only way to improve any deed is with diligent practice."

"One coupling was all I intended to grant!"

He chuckled. "But surely not a *mediocre* one? It would only be chivalrous of me to ensure you were"—he licked his lips and surveyed her slowly—"sated."

Sated?!

"Oh, I am sated with you! You need have no fear of that!"

But Ibernia's words fell too quickly to be believable. Rowan's grin widened and he touched a fingertip to her lips. Ibernia caught her breath and knew he heard it. His eyes gleamed as he traced the outline of her lips, their gazes clung, his fingertip meandered over her collarbone.

Ibernia knew where that fingertip was destined, but she would not give him the satisfaction of stepping away. The moment that that finger and thumb found her nipple, she knew that her body at least would do naught to support her ruse.

The nipple came to an aching point with embarrassing speed. Rowan turned his gaze upon it, the admiration in his expression making Ibernia catch her breath. He slid his palm across her breast, then back again, as if he could not help but be fascinated.

The man was practiced in making a woman feel appreciated, there was no doubt of that.

Even if his attention was too fleeting for Ibernia's taste.

She heaved a sigh deliberately and forced boredom into her tone. "Are you finished toying with me? I would check upon my new garb."

He glanced up quickly, then his cocky smile returned with all its radiance.

"Liar," he whispered, leaning closer to her. "You are a liar, *ma demoiselle,* and I shall win the truth from you yet."

She held her ground stubbornly, squeezing her eyes shut when he bent and kissed her erect nipple, even through her chemise. The sensation was exquisite, and made her want him again. She had an urge to drive her fingers into his hair, to drag him back to that narrow bed and spend the entire day there.

But not if it meant so little to him.

A woman of merit had to have some pride.

To her dismay, Ibernia misjudged his timing and opened her eyes to find Rowan nigh nose to nose with her, his fingers having replaced his questing lips. He smiled slowly, his gaze dancing over her features as if he saw something there she would prefer to hide.

"Mediocre, indeed," he purred, his tone almost affectionate. "I shall prove that you lie, Ibernia, regardless of what that task demands of me."

And he kissed her so quickly that she had no time to escape his touch.

"You!" she cried when he stepped away. "You have an audacity, and 'tis most unwelcome!"

But Rowan, laughing, was already tying his chausses and ducking out the door. When she heard him whistling a moment later, Ibernia glared after him.

Well, she had already surrendered to his touch, and though it had been a marvel, Ibernia did not welcome the sense that she had been naught but the next wench in a long line of Rowan's pleasures. Nay, she would have a surrender from him, she would coax his astonishment as he had hers.

Or she would die trying.

Aye, perhaps she could so astound him that he would grant her freedom at Ballyroyal, after all. Or indeed, he might be inclined to indulge her, if he grew fond of her. The very possibility made Ibernia smile.

For if Rowan intended to court Bronwyn of Ballyroyal, the goodwill of Ibernia could not be underestimated. Aye, in the end, 'twould be she who outwitted this cocky knight.

That was consolation indeed.

# Chapter Nine

I F REVENGE WAS A DISH BEST SERVED COLD, THEN Baldassare's serving would be most satisfactory. He was within grasp of settling a debt that had gone due for over twenty years, and he was anxious to redress the balance.

For the sake of his father's memory.

Fortune had deigned to smile upon Baldassare of late, after long turning her attention away. He had a ship, he had a cargo that would see his debts paid, he even had a rumor of the man who had set his course on misfortune. Baldassare was hot on the trail of vengeance and knew Fortune would not fail him now. He stood, impatiently scouring the horizon for the first glimpse of Ireland.

Where debts would finally be settled. Oh, he had been wise to defy the advice of others and seek his prey beyond the shelter of the Mediterranean. He had taken a chance, and Chance would see him rewarded.

Baldassare was still there when the woman who had caused him such trouble the night before came on to the deck. She was a barbarian, of course, as he had learned all too well, yet she was not without some appeal. Her silhouette was decidedly feminine against the grey hue of the sea and sky, the faint sunlight glinted in the gold of her ridiculously short hair.

The blue wool favored her, better even than he had anticipated, though Baldassare was not surprised. He had an eye
for trinkets that pleased women, and to be sure, anything
that made them look their best was always a welcome gift.

He scowled with the recollection of how his gift seemed
to have done little to soften Ibernia toward him. Nay, she
had not been helpful. The more Baldassare reflected upon
the matter, the less he was persuaded that she was as much
of a fool as she would have had him believe.

Anger had a way of blinding Baldassare to anything beyond it, and he had been sorely angered by the shattering of
the token of his homeland. He had gone through much to
preserve that pitcher and glasses, so seeing their loss had
enraged him beyond reason.

The jingle of coin did salve the wound, though.

Baldassare might have hauled into a port and dumped
them all ashore, if he was not increasingly certain that
Ibernia knew something that could aid his quest. He
watched her for a long moment, noted that the knight did not
join her, and deigned this as good a time as any to approach
her again.

There were things he had to know, after all, and Ibernia
was the one most likely to know them.

"Good afternoon, *ma bella*," he murmured when he
reached her side. She jumped slightly, then turned, her smile
as cautious as the glint in her eyes. Baldassare was startled
anew by the change in her appearance.

Not only was she garbed in a kirtle fitting of a lady, but
she was clean. Her features were more fairly wrought than
he had imagined, her complexion clear, her eyes bright and
luxuriantly lashed. She stood like a lady of the court, her
chin high, her gaze steadily meeting his. Indeed, the trepidation he had sensed had already been dismissed.

If it had ever been there. How had he ever imagined that this one was not high-born?

Indeed, there was something elusive in her appearance— the line of her jaw perhaps or shape of her eyes—that vaguely reminded him of a man he had sought off and on for two decades.

Was she related to Niccolo? Was that why he spied a fleeting ghost of his old enemy in this woman's features? Baldassare's heart skipped a beat, and he wondered whether he truly could be so fortunate as that.

Or did he see what he desired to see?

"Good afternoon," she said crisply, her gaze wary.

Baldassare claimed her hand and raised it to his lips. "Your beauty leaves me speechless, *ma bella.*"

A ghost of a smile touched her lips. "It seems not, sir."

Baldassare chuckled despite himself, much more at ease with her dressed this way. " 'Tis a shame you have no fine jewels to ornament your beauty."

She lifted a shoulder carelessly, her gaze slipping back toward the sea. "They are but trinkets, and their possession oft fleeting."

Baldassare leaned on the rail beside her, fully aware that she would have preferred to dismiss him. "As you learned on London's docks."

Her gaze flicked to him so quickly that he knew he had found a lie. So, there had been no theft in London! He had suspected as much.

Was Ibernia truly the knight's wife? There was a chafe on her neck left visible by the cut of the kirtle—such a mark as might have been wrought by a rope tied too tight—that hinted otherwise.

Who was this woman truly? More important, did she know what he sought to learn?

She recovered herself as he pondered his course and inclined her head in acknowledgment. "As you say," she agreed carefully. "I had tried to push that tragic theft from my thoughts."

"Then I am a knave to have reminded you." He granted her a smooth smile, and after a moment's consideration of him, she responded in kind.

" 'Tis naught."

Baldassare looked out to sea and waited for the question he knew would come. Let her draw the information from him—it was less likely to rouse suspicion than if he had willingly confessed all.

"Do you sell spice in Dublin?"

"Nay. 'Twill fetch a better price in the ports of northern France." Baldassare watched her from the corner of his eye, nearly smiling when she swallowed visibly. Her curiosity about his intentions was a fine portent.

"The slaves, then?"

"Nay. They are destined for the south, for Mediterranean nobles who will appreciate their fair skin." Baldassare shrugged. "I am thinking that Granada might be a suitable stop, as there is much wealth to be had there."

"I would know naught of such matters," she said hastily, and Baldassare smiled.

He patted her hand. "Ah, 'tis not so troubling as all of that to be a slave in such circumstance. Many of them have a finer life than they might have had in their own lands. The women, particularly, are much indulged in return for little but their favors. You have denied the pretty one of your choice much leisure, to be certain."

Ibernia turned away, her words tight. "Do you not know her name?"

Baldassare laughed at the thought. "Of what possible use is her name? I know her worth and that is enough."

The lady's fingers tightened on the rail, the gesture amusing Baldassare. Women were such fools in thinking the luxuries of the world were not assessed by their value in trade alone. Though he had known men who found such nonsense charming, fortunately he had been spared such misguided thinking.

He knew what was of import.

"Why *do* you sail to Dublin, then?" Ibernia's voice was tight.

"There is a task I must fulfill," Baldassare said, carefully watching her reaction.

"A task?"

Baldassare smiled and braced his elbows upon the rail. "You see, *ma bella,* I made a pledge many years ago." He watched his companion avidly and suddenly realized something he should have noted sooner.

'Twas odd that this couple had known his destination, when he had told none, though Baldassare knew his men talked on the wharf.

But his men only spoke Venetian among themselves. Was it knight or noblewoman who understood that tongue? There was one way to discover the truth.

Baldassare dropped his voice and leaned closer, slipping easily into the Venetian dialect. He spoke low and fast, watching her eyes to see whether she comprehended him. "I seek an old friend, a Venetian, with whom I have a debt to settle."

She caught her breath tellingly, then shook her head.

Before she could protest her ignorance, he continued. "He is a man who has seen fifty summers, he is tall and dark of hair, he has a merry laugh and heavy purse. Rumor is that he wed a woman with fair hair, not unlike yours, *ma bella,* and fled to the refuge of her family estate. Of late I have learned that she was of Ireland, perhaps from the vicinity of Dublin. Would you know a man by the name of Niccolo? He was called the Falcon, because he traded so brilliantly and swept from port to port."

The lady paled. "I do not understand," she argued, though her voice lacked its previous resolve.

Baldassare nearly hooted with victory. He was so close!

"Would you know him, or know of him? 'Tis imperative, you see, that I find him." Baldassare smiled, as if he were not talking about a man's potential death. "I am a man who keeps his vows and this debt is long overdue."

Ibernia's fingers rose to her lips, then she abruptly straightened and shook her head.

"I cannot understand what you say," she confessed, though there was a tremor beneath her words.

"Can you not, *ma bella*?" he demanded amiably in the tongue she favored. He bowed low, intending only to hide his smile. "My apologies. 'Tis the mark of a man abroad to slip into his mother tongue, without expectation."

They eyed each other for a long moment, the wind whipping at her curls, hatred chilling her eyes. Oh, she had understood—he had said naught in this rough tongue of the English to prompt such sudden dislike.

"You have yet to tell me your mission in Dublin," she chided, her smile forced.

Baldassare smiled easily. "I seek a friend, that is what I said. No more than that. It is always welcome to find a friend in a foreign port."

The lady inhaled sharply before she turned away.

"Perhaps I know this friend," Ibernia said, the way her voice hardened over the last word most revealing.

"His name is Niccolo."

Her sidelong glance was cool and composed once more. " 'Tis not a common name among the Irish."

"Precisely why I thought you might recall him. He has

the dark hair of the Venetians, which must be uncommon as well."

"There are many dark-haired Irish."

"But not with skin of golden hue." He smiled when Ibernia looked his way. "Do you know him?"

She shook her head quickly, too quickly. "I know of no man named Niccolo in Dublin. Perhaps you seek him in the wrong place."

Baldassare was undeterred. This lady's response hinted that he was close, very close, to his prey. "Perhaps he changed his name."

"Why would your friend do such a thing?"

He shrugged. "Perhaps he wished to fit in among the local folk with less commentary. Perhaps his new neighbors could not say his name as he preferred. Perhaps his wife did not care for it." He paused. "Perhaps his child could not pronounce it."

Ibernia's sidelong glance was hasty. "You know that he is married and has a child?"

Baldassare smiled. "Nay, I merely speculate upon the child."

Ibernia shook her head again. "A man of your coloring would not go unnoted in Dublin. I should know of him—he must not be there."

She turned a steely gaze upon him, as if she would will him away from the port by her own determination alone. The look alone nigh stole Baldassare's breath away. Her expression was strangely reminiscent of the way a certain man had looked when he had struck the killing blow.

She was *kin* with Niccolo!

"You would be better served to seek your friend elsewhere," she said crisply.

"Do you know all the men of Dublin so well as that, *ma bella*?" Baldassare teased, to cover his own surprise.

She had the grace to blush. " 'Tis not a large burg."

"And you are not there now. How long have you been gone from that port?"

The lady clamped her lips together and looked out to sea. "Not so long as that."

"But long enough that a ship could arrive and a man could take up his abode in the town without your awareness of him."

Ibernia's lips thinned. She nodded barely and with obvious reluctance. Every line of her figure was tight with disapproval and anxiety—aye, Niccolo had been there when Ibernia left.

Played skillfully, she would lead Baldassare directly where he wanted to go.

"You have yet to tell me of your abode," he prompted.

She flashed a glance his way, then veiled her alarm. " 'Tis not pertinent," she argued.

"Perhaps you could grant me accommodations," he suggested, noting her terror even though it was quickly veiled. Baldassare captured her hand and lifted it to his lips, watching her as he brushed his lips across her knuckles. "Perhaps I seek only the gift of seeing your smile again."

The lady pulled her hand from his grip and looked away. " 'Twould be inappropriate. My husband would not approve."

Aye, she did not like the thought of him being near.

Baldassare shrugged easily, though he sensed he was finally close to victory. "Ah, well, I shall find other accommodation."

"Surely you do not intend to linger in Dublin?"

"I see no harm in spending a few days seeking this friend of mine. After all, we have come so far—'twould be a shame to miss encountering him again." He smiled. "Perhaps a week in Dublin should see my goal achieved."

Ibernia looked at him with such shock that Baldassare nearly rubbed his hands with glee. Anger began to simmer in her gaze.

Better and better. She sought to protect Niccolo by urging Baldassare away, but he was not so easily swayed as that. He bowed again and excused himself, having no doubt that he left the lady with much to consider.

Aye, she would flee to warn Niccolo of Baldassare's arrival, of that the captain had no doubt, perhaps as soon as they touched the shore in Dublin. He would follow her, of course, to settle a debt that had festered overlong.

Niccolo would finally pay for his treachery.

Ibernia feared she would be ill. She hung on to the rail and stared into the distance, desperately wishing she knew how long it might take to arrive in Dublin.

'Twas daunting even to consider an attempt to outwit Baldassare di Vilonte. The man toyed with her, as a cat did with a mouse, and she was not entirely certain he had not read her thoughts. He had a streak of cruelty that could not be ignored.

But yet, Ibernia could not do *naught* when a life so precious to her hung in the balance. How quickly could she make her way home? Could she evade Rowan? 'Twould mean breaking her word, but she did not have a year and a day to wait! She would have to steal a steed, perhaps she would take Thomas's palfrey. If naught else, she could return the beast later. Somehow.

What was critical was that she return home with even more haste than she had expected. For home was where the man who had once been Niccolo the Falcon believed himself to be safe.

Her father was wrong.

He was not safe, not in the least, and against every assurance he had ever granted her mother, his past returned to claim its due.

Ibernia had to warn her father.

She stared out to sea, her gaze tracing the distant silhouette of land even as she strove to recognize some curve of the coast. 'Twas impossible, though, and she could not gauge their distance from Dublin. She wanted to pace the decks in frustration, she wanted to shout, but she dared not give any hint to the watchful Baldassare that his words reminded her of an old tale.

Ibernia considered briefly the idea of confessing all to Rowan, for that would surely win his quick wits to her dilemma at least. It might be of aid to have a knight like Rowan by her side, instead of facing adversity alone.

What addled her wits? Rowan would not take her cause to his heart! He would certainly not risk his life to see Baldassare thwarted in this. Nay, Rowan was a man who valued lovemaking and pleasure, not a warrior intent on setting matters to rights.

Rowan would ensure his own ends, no more than that. If there was any chance that Bronwyn of Ballyroyal could not be his bride, or if he discovered that Bronwyn was not the wealthiest heiress in all of Ireland, or if the truth itself came to light, Rowan would be gone in the blink of an eye. He had impressed upon Ibernia that he would not lose this wager with his brothers, not at any cost. If she relied too much upon him, his inevitable departure could prove most inopportune.

It would be better to not rely upon him at all. Ibernia folded her arms across her chest and hugged the truth to herself. She stared out to sea, chilled to the bone, and wondered how quickly she would be able to flee home.

'Twas then she realized that fleeing home was precisely

what Baldassare expected her to do. After all, he *knew* she had understood him. If she raced to warn her father, he would simply follow her.

Ibernia gripped the rail, her knees suddenly weak. She could prove to be the link that provided her father's destruction. Nay! It could not be thus! But she had to return home, for she had no other means of earning her keep.

Except upon her back. Her lips tightened. She knew that starving in the streets of Dublin was no guarantee that Baldassare would not find her father anyway.

And kill him.

Ibernia's throat tightened. She had to do *something*.

She must not lead Baldassare home. That was what he expected, that was what he waited for. If Ibernia could not warn her father, there must be another solution that would save his life. Her mother had always said that a woman with wits about her could find the key to the riddle.

What if Baldassare could not follow her?

What if Baldassare met with an *accident*?

The possibility of violence falling from her own hand nigh stopped her heart. Ibernia closed her eyes and forced herself to think of her kind-hearted father, a man who had wanted naught but to step away from the shadow of his past. She thought of her gentle mother, the woman who glowed in that man's presence. She thought of the home those two had made, the happiness they had found in each other, the love they shared.

And she deliberately thought of Baldassare di Vilonte stealing it all away. She could not let him do that. She *would* not let this mercenary captain steal so much away from the two people she loved most in the world.

Not at any cost. Yet as long as he was alive, 'twas clear that was what Baldassare intended to do. Ibernia knew that her father would not return to Venice willingly; he had sworn as much long ago.

Which left only one choice.

Ibernia wondered what had happened to the wickedly sharp blade that had been granted her for the cutting of the wool. She had not seen it when Marika finished the kirtle.

Indeed, she had not seen it since the day before.

"Do not tell me that you are falling ill now," Rowan teased as he leaned on the rail beside Ibernia. Though her new kirtle favored her wondrously, she was deathly pale and her hands were knotted upon the rail so tightly that the knuckles shone white.

"I am fine," she declared, and made to brush past him.

Rowan caught her arm in his hand, keeping her from walking away, and frowned at the chill of her skin. "You shall fall ill if you remain so cold for long," he chided, and shed his cloak. He cast it about her shoulders, noting that she seemed uncommonly distracted.

And not by him. This was not precisely how a man hoped to meet a woman after they had loved with such passion. Aye, she ought to be recalling all they had done and be anxious to return to their cabin!

But Ibernia frowned and stared across the sea, apparently oblivious to Rowan's presence.

He touched a fingertip beneath her chin, compelling her to glance his way. "Are you ill?"

"Nay."

"Chilled?"

"No longer." A faint smile touched her lips. "Thank you."

Her gaze slid away from him once more. She nibbled her lip, evidently disinterested in his presence once more.

'Twas irksome how readily she could dismiss him, and even more irksome that he had been able to think of naught but her while they were apart. That she was spared the answering affliction did little to please the knight.

Rowan eased closer and redoubled his charm. "Does the kirtle please you? To my eye, it favors your coloring wondrously." He bent and brushed his lips across her temple. He ran a fingertip down the side of her neck, frowning as he paused beside the chafe mark. "If you had a suitable chemise, 'twould hide this blemish. Does it still trouble you?"

"Nay." Ibernia's response had all the interest one saved for brushing away a fly. She frowned and drummed her fingers upon the rail, shooting a sudden and very blue glance his way. "Did you take the knife?"

Rowan blinked. "What knife?"

"The one Marika used to cut the cloth."

"I did not even know there was a knife." She pursed her lips and Rowan bent to offer a smile. "You are welcome to the use of my dagger, if you have need to cut more cloth."

"Nay, 'twill not do." Ibernia's words were crisp. "It must be the other."

"Why do you have need of it? Your kirtle is done and my blade is sharp enough for any task you have."

But Ibernia shook her head impatiently and frowned. What in the name of God was she thinking?

She impaled Rowan suddenly with a glance, her eyes so bright that he thought her feverish. "How long until we reach Dublin?"

Rowan leaned against the rail to consider her, more than puzzled by the change in her manner. "Why?"

"I would simply know how long we are to be at sea."

He spared her a winning smile. "What reason is there to care?" He lifted a finger to trace the line of her jaw, disappointed when she did not shiver as was her wont. "We have each other and privacy—perhaps you are only concerned that we spend enough time abed.'' He leaned closer, his own thoughts consumed with that very question, and kissed her temple with a gentle persuasiveness that never failed to win results.

To the knight's surprise, Ibernia stepped abruptly away. She gritted her teeth and glared at him. ''Is it so impossible to imagine that I might want to know something that did not concern bedding you?''

Rowan grinned cockily, reassured by her annoyance. ''Aye, 'tis.'' She rolled her eyes and might have stepped farther away, but he caught her in his arms and trapped her between himself and the rail. 'Twas good to feel her curves against him once more, though she seemed immune to the pleasure Rowan felt.

''Your affection is inappropriately timed.''

''On the contrary, 'tis perfectly timed. Do you think all of these seamen did not fail to note your solitary presence here? Or your lovely curves, so fetchingly displayed in your new garb?''

Rowan gathered her closer, taking satisfaction in ensuring that all aboard the *Angelica* knew this woman to be his own. Her back was against his chest and he folded his arms around her waist, leaning his chin on her shoulder as he followed her gaze across the sea. The curve of Ibernia's buttocks against him awakened a part of him, and he guessed she knew her effect upon him.

Rowan nuzzled her neck. ''Am I alone in seeing that there is no chemise beneath this kirtle and wondering how the wool feels against your bare flesh?''

''Rowan!''

He pulled back to look deliberately into her eyes. ''Does it chafe your nipples? If so, 'twould only be chivalrous of me to soothe them with kisses.''

She flushed scarlet, not nearly so unaware of him as she might have had him believe. "Your attention is unwelcome."

"Indeed? I have no doubt that any one of this crew would be pleased to offer his companionship instead, if you would prefer to be devoid of my company. Perhaps even Baldassare would take leave of his duties to entertain you."

Ibernia stiffened and stared resolutely out to sea.

"He did come to speak with you," Rowan guessed, a cold kernel lodging in his gut and tempering his desire. There was that protectiveness again, though, indeed, he had proof aplenty that Ibernia had no need of his protection.

The lady fared well enough on her own, it seemed.

Though that truth was surprisingly annoying.

"Did he trouble you? Did he touch you?"

"He but wanted thanks for his gift."

Rowan heard the hard edge to his own words. "And how did he have that thanks?"

Ibernia shrugged. "As pretty words, no more than that."

"That was the end of the matter?"

The lady averted her face. "More or less."

That was not the end of the matter and Rowan knew it well. He knew equally well that she was not inclined to tell him of it.

"He said something to trouble you," Rowan guessed, whispering the words into her ear.

Her reply was slightly breathless. "Nay, naught."

"But you are troubled."

"Nay, not I."

Clearly she was not going to confide in him. Though the realization stung, Rowan knew one way to earn another increment of the lady's trust—not to mention, to win her attention fully. He slipped a hand beneath the cloak she now wore and closed his fingers around the swell of her breast.

Rowan smiled when Ibernia caught her breath, satisfactory proof that he could be irresistible.

"There is something preying upon your thoughts," he murmured, his thumb coaxing her nipple to a peak with satisfying speed. "Perhaps you reflect upon our coupling of this morn and fear you must wait until this evening for another sample."

She laughed then, a quick startled sound, and flicked a glance over her shoulder at him. "You have no lack of confidence."

Rowan grinned, boldly touching her beneath the refuge of the cloak. Ibernia's smile faded and a flush stained her cheeks as her tawny lashes fluttered against her cheek. "Perhaps I was mistaken then. Perhaps you have no interest in returning to our cabin. Perhaps you would prefer to while away the days here on this cold deck rather than warm and cosseted below."

He made to lift his hand away.

Ibernia caught at his fingers, staying his move, her fingers entwining with his. "You are a wicked tease," she charged, her eyes sparkling so merrily that Rowan caught his breath.

He might have argued that *she* teased, but her other hand slipped between them and closed unexpectedly over his arousal. Even through the layers of cloak and chausses, her grip was sure and Rowan jumped slightly.

She turned in his embrace, her grip unyielding, and met his gaze knowingly. When her hand moved, her gesture making him catch his breath, he locked one arm around her waist and did not relinquish the weight of her breast from the other hand.

He dragged his thumb across the tightened nipple and watched her catch her breath.

"You have a choice," he fairly growled into her ear. "You may walk demurely and immediately back to the cabin, or I shall toss you over my shoulder and take you there.''

Ibernia lifted her chin, the bold glint that fired his blood lighting her eyes. ''And if I decline either option?''

Rowan grinned. ''Then I shall have you here, and the crew will be vastly entertained.'' He winked. '' 'Twill be a long and thorough loving, for I should be determined to ensure that you were pleasured beyond your wildest dreams.''

She flushed scarlet and flicked a glance over his shoulder to the crew. ''You would not!''

He caught her against him with a wicked grin and let his voice drop low. ''That sounds like a dare, *ma demoiselle*. Do you challenge me to prove you wrong?''

''Nay!'' Ibernia jumped and might have darted away, but Rowan was not prepared to let her go. Indeed, he did not intend to release her from his embrace, not before he sampled her charms once again.

He caught her around the waist and saw the delight touch her face. She knew what he was going to do and laughingly began to protest, her expression captivating Rowan as naught else could have done. He tossed her over his shoulder, his grin broadening when she twisted to fight his grip. She muttered a string of insults in Gaelic, though there was a thread of laughter beneath her words.

The crew whistled and shouted approval, her hip bumped against his cheek. Rowan gripped her knees and waved merrily to the crew, whistling as he headed for their cabin.

''Beast!'' Ibernia declared. ''Incorrigible creature!''

Rowan laughed aloud, knowing she was not so incensed as she would have him believe. '' 'Twill be made worth your while and you know it well.''

''Aye, and you will be poorly served in exchange for your services,'' she retorted so crisply that he laughed again.

''You were the one who declared it was mediocre,''

Rowan retorted. "I would merely practice to ensure your pleasure."

Ibernia growled though she did not fight to be released. Rowan found his anticipation rising with every step he took toward their cabin.

"Oh, I shall make you moan, Rowan de Montvieux," she declared grimly. "I shall leave you so in awe of my touch that you will cede to my every whim."

"Indeed, my lady, I challenge you to win that very result." Rowan kicked the door closed behind them and dropped the latch into place before he put Ibernia down.

He deliberately reached beneath her kirtle, the bare silk of her skin beneath his hands firing his blood. He cupped her buttocks in his hands and let her slide down his front, halting her course when they were eye to eye. Her feet still dangled above the floor, her kirtle bunched around his wrists.

"You bold creature," she charged, a twinkle lighting the sapphire of her eyes. That smile was what addled his wits, Rowan was certain. Not to mention her rare but merry laugh. Aye, he would make the lady's eyes sparkle before this day was done!

Rowan feigned shock. "I, bold? 'Tis you who wear naught beneath your kirtle!"

Ibernia bit back her smile. "I had no choice. The chemise was so soiled that I could not don it beneath the new kirtle."

"And too well used to stand another wash."

She grimaced. "In all likelihood."

"Then you shall have a chemise of mine," he offered quickly, refusing to consider that he had never granted a woman a personal token before. Ibernia's lips parted, perhaps to protest, but Rowan dipped his head and took advantage of the opportunity.

He kissed her deeply, gripping her buttocks in his hands

and loving the press of her breasts against him. She wrapped her arms around his neck and opened her mouth to him immediately, her ready capitulation only feeding Rowan's raging desire. She lifted her knees, the move making her buttocks into riper curves in his hands, and locked her ankles around his waist.

Only then did Rowan recall her threat—and realize he could hardly wait to savor whatever she chose to do to him.

By the time they were done, Ibernia would not be longing to reach Dublin; she would be begging to remain in his company yet longer. But this indulgence would ensure that Rowan was fully free of the intoxicating novelty of her touch by the time they reached Ireland's shore.

'Twould be so much easier to set her free that way.

He was certain of it.

# Chapter Ten

FAR AWAY, TO THE SOUTHEAST OF PARIS, MARGAUX DE Montvieux was troubled. 'Twas some commentary on the mood of Rowan's foster mother that she found herself within Château Montvieux's chapel and that her steps turned in the direction of the altar. Though she sought solace of a kind, 'twas not absolution of a religious nature that would do.

Margaux had been trained young to apologize to her father directly, without evasion or delay. His death changed naught but the location where that apology was rendered.

The weight of her legacy hung heavy on this day and 'twas, Margaux knew, because she had done naught right. She strode to the altar in the chapel, pausing long enough on the threshold of a darkened doorway to take a flickering torch in her hand.

The golden light spilled down the curling staircase before her, making her path look more welcoming than she knew it was. With cane and torch, Margaux had no hand to steady herself upon the wall, and she was doubly wary of the crooked flagstones underfoot.

She would have to have them reset again, lest she take a fall as she had once before. Her cursed hip had never healed aright, but that was no excuse for catering to its complaints. The joint ached as she descended, as if 'twould protest her return to this place, but Margaux had other matters on her mind. She could have called for aid on this day, but that would have interfered with her privacy.

She gritted her teeth and descended, one careful step at a time. The staircase wound tightly, the opening to the chapel lost to the shadows behind by the time she had taken half a dozen steps. Margaux shivered, though not due to memories of that fall. Though she would have admitted it to none, she dreaded coming to the crypt, just as she had dreaded going to her father as a child.

All the same, she could not conceive of staying away.

Her father demanded her presence, as commandingly as if he still drew breath. Her father missed no fault, he never had. No misdemeanor went unpunished, no slight went without remark.

Margaux came to a halt at the foot of the stairs, leaned heavily on her cane, and stared at her father's tomb. Beyond the stone sarcophagus lurked the shadow of another—that of her grandfather—and behind that was yet another. She needed no further reminder that the lineage of Montvieux culminated in her—and ended with her.

Margaux lifted the torch higher, willing the light to banish the shadows lurking in the corners of this place. 'Twas damp again, the must making her nose twitch.

Aye, the river had risen high last spring. That caprice of the season felt like another failure, another inadequacy, another instance of a sole daughter failing to measure up to the expectations of her lineage.

Margaux realized suddenly that she had loathed her father, almost as much as she had revered him. Was that the gift of age, that all should become ambiguous?

She lifted her chin and stepped farther into the crypt, realizing even as she did so that it was foolish to try to impress her father with bravado. He was naught but dust and bones after all these years, and even in life, he had not been one apt to be deceived.

She slid a hand across the sarcophagus and found it fitting that he should slumber forever thus, encased in stone as set and as cold as he had always been.

Then she chided herself for her impertinence. Just the measurement of the sarcophagus reminded her of how tall he had been, how broad and strong, how magnificent his booming laughter, how terrifying his anger. She rubbed a fingertip along the edge of the stone and felt tears prick at her eyes.

Margaux blinked quickly and composed herself. She *never* cried. She slipped the torch into the sconce to one side and eased down on to her knees, wincing at the pain that shot through her hip. She braced both hands on the head of her cane, inclined her head, and submitted to the overwhelming tide of her failure.

She had failed Montvieux. She had failed her father. She had failed the legacy of the ages, and she had done so even more thoroughly than her father had ever feared. There was no son to seize the reins of power, no blood heir to rule this estate, so long the pride of her family.

Margaux had sacrificed everything for Montvieux, and, in the end, she had only Montvieux to show for it.

It had proven to be precious little consolation. Alone with only her father's tomb as her witness—and that of his father and his father before him—Margaux permitted herself to cry. She did so silently, her shoulders shaking as the tears rolled down her face.

She had fulfilled every dire prediction her father had ever made. Despite herself. And how she hated that, in the end, he had called the matter right.

Margaux truly had not been as good as a son.

She was so lost in her misery that she did not hear the

scrape of a boot on the stairs behind her. 'Twas only when a man cleared his throat that her head shot up. When she saw who 'twas, she struggled to her feet, hoping against hope that the torchlight hid her tears.

"Gavin," she managed to say with a measure of her usual reserve.

For indeed, none other than Gavin Fitzgerald, the spouse she had taken hastily and nigh as hastily regretted, stood framed in the doorway behind. The man she had wed to defy her father, the man she refused to divorce lest she grant her sire another complaint against her, had returned.

God only knew what he wanted from her.

"Tears, Margaux?" Gavin shook his head and took a step closer. He was a rough man, and age had done naught to aid his looks. His complexion was tanned as dark as a peasant's and nearly as thoroughly lined. His brown hair was shot with silver these days and was thinner on the top than when she had last seen him.

But all the same, there was a certain vigor about him. Indeed, he looked cursedly hale. And that shrewdness still lingered in his eyes. Margaux braced herself for a verbal sparring.

" 'Tis unlike you to weep for anything," he continued, rapping his knuckles on her father's tomb with annoying familiarity. "Especially this old bastard."

Margaux stiffened. "You will not speak of my father this way."

"Aye, 'tis too late for that." Gavin pursed his lips. "I wish I had told him what I thought of him whilst there was a chance."

"He thought naught of you!"

"Aye. He made that clear."

Their gazes met for a long moment and Margaux abruptly

recalled another reason she had wed Gavin Fitzgerald. There was something ruthless about him, to be sure, a self-motivated streak that was not unfamiliar to anyone raised at Montvieux.

But in Gavin, that selfishness found its greatest outlet in passion. There was no compromise with him abed—he wanted all the pleasure he could sample and he demanded that she match him touch for touch. Margaux's heart skipped a beat and she quickly averted her face from unwelcome reminders of the past.

"What do you want?" she asked sharply. "Why have you returned here after all these years?"

She felt rather than saw Gavin fold his arms across his chest. "Is it so unsuitable to visit one's spouse?"

"You are no longer my spouse!" Margaux spat. "It has been over twenty years since I cast you out, and you still are not welcome in this place!"

"Because I ask questions you would rather not answer?"

"Because you are a wretched liar! Because you despoil all you touch, like a vagrant dog!" She pointed imperially to the portal. "Get out."

But Gavin smiled slowly. His eyes glinted and there was a knowingness in his smile that quickened her blood. "Ah, Margaux, I always recalled the fire in your eyes. 'Tis good to see that has not changed."

Margaux backed away hastily, afraid he would touch her, then regretted showing such weakness when he obviously noted the gesture. "You are not worthy of me, you never were."

"But you wed me all the same." He knocked on her father's tomb again, as if he would awaken that man. "Tell me, Margaux, how much did your choice have to do with me—and how much with him?"

He was too perceptive by half. 'Twas one of the things she had always loathed about Gavin.

That and his need to utter whatever words came to his lips. Oh, he was rough and crude, a barbarian unworthy even to kiss her slippers.

Margaux recalled him kissing her slippers once when she had made such a charge, and all that had ensued. She felt her cheeks heat. "You dare overmuch!"

He chuckled, not in the least bit insulted. " 'Tis why we are two of a kind."

Margaux gasped in outrage, appalled that he should compare them favorably. "We have *naught* in common," she snapped. "I wed you because I wanted one thing of you and one thing alone. Even that, you were knave enough to steal from me."

"That," Gavin echoed, enunciating the word clearly. "No doubt our son Burke would be pleased to know that he was but a trinket you desired above all else." He took a step forward. "Does he know that you loved him only for his prick, for his future as the next Lord de Montvieux?"

Margaux folded her arms across her chest. "Get out."

But Gavin raised a finger, feigning recollection. "Oh, he *does* know, does he not? Is that not why he declined to accept suzerainty of Montvieux? The only son you ever wanted and he refused the legacy you had so carefully saved for him." He folded his arms across his chest in turn and clicked his tongue, surveying her with far too much satisfaction in his gaze.

"He spurned you first!"

Gavin inclined his head. "Aye, that he did. In the end, we have even more in common."

"You poisoned his thinking!" Margaux cried. "You turned my boy against me! You stole my son from me."

"You have more than one son, Margaux."

"Not with the blood of Montvieux in his veins. Luc is *your* son by your first wife and Rowan is *your* bastard."

"You raised Rowan."

"The crime of the parents is not the burden of the son. 'Twas not his fault he was born of a whore and cur."

Gavin chuckled to himself. "Ah, your tongue is still as sharp as a viper's kiss. I always did love that about you."

"Liar! You loved naught in me!"

He sobered and watched her carefully. "You do me disservice."

"As you did me!" Margaux settled her weight on her cane and let her anger loose. "You twisted Burke to your view, you tried to make a mercenary of him that he might follow in your lead and be damned to hell fast behind you!"

"Nay, Margaux." Gavin shook his head. "I might have tried," he admitted softly, his gaze searching hers. "But in the end, there was too much of you in his blood."

The unexpected words hung between them. "Why are you here?" Margaux demanded, turning hastily away. She saw his shrug from the periphery of her vision.

"I did not know where else to go," Gavin admitted, his uncharacteristic thoughtfulness making Margaux glance again his way. He frowned at his finger, tapping it against the cold stone. " 'Tis unsettling to have the purpose of one's days and nights snatched away." He looked up suddenly, his gaze snaring hers, and Margaux turned away that he might not see how affected she was by his mood. "It makes a man wonder whether he was wrong."

But Margaux had no reassurance for her mercenary spouse. "They have tempted even Rowan to leave me, with some fool wager," she declared instead, her words heated. "Now there is not even laughter to be found in this hall— nor will there ever be, if he does not return."

Gavin was clearly unsurprised by this tale. "Rowan will return." He smiled. "He loves the scraps that fall from your hand too much."

"Rowan may not have a choice," Margaux snapped. "You know what a fool that boy is when he believes he can win a challenge. Naught stands in his way!"

"You fret for him." The amusement lurking in his words did naught to appease her.

Margaux shot a lethal glance his way. "I fret for no man."

Gavin chuckled and leaned a hip against the stone. "I knew you cared for Rowan. Were Rowan your own fruit, I daresay you would love him best of all."

Margaux was appalled by the very suggestion. "Lineage is not the point! Rowan will die and I shall never see him again!"

"The boy has more wits than that." Gavin shrugged. "You might even approve of his bride. You do have a fondness for heiresses."

'Twas galling that he could simply appear and know as much as she did of matters. Margaux averted her face. "I suppose you have heard all the news, then."

Gavin shrugged. "I paused in the village and bought a round of ale."

But there was one thing he did not know, could not know from there. "Did they tell you that Burke's Alys is with child?"

His surprise was obvious and satisfactory. "Nay. When?"

"In the spring."

"They spoke of it already? 'Tis only past midsummer."

"They did not speak of it," Margaux said bitterly. "They did not need to. I know Burke, I know him as a woman knows her son, and I saw it in his manner to his wife." She cast Gavin a dark glance. "Do you know what this means?"

He lifted one brow. "That you will be a grandmother?"

She exhaled in frustration. "Use your wits, Gavin! It means that Burke will *never* return to Montvieux."

And the cur laughed. "Margaux! Surely you already knew as much?" Gavin held Margaux's gaze when she glanced up. "The boy took from both of us and grew to become his own man, to make a life of his own choices."

Margaux snorted. "So now you are a philosopher." She sneered. "You who can read naught and cannot make a sum or even sign your own name." She paced across the low vault. "I am not only a failure in my father's eyes, but blind to the truth in the eyes of my unlettered oaf of a spouse."

Gavin snorted in turn, the sound so feeding Margaux's annoyance that she crossed the room to stand before him.

"A failure! Do you understand the import of that? I have proven my father perfectly aright in this. I have not proven to be as good as a *son*!" She flung out her hand. "A son. 'Twas the only thing he wanted and the only thing I could not be. This legacy will crumble to dust when I die and 'tis all my fault!"

Gavin clicked his tongue. "So, an education does not necessarily ensure one cannot become a fool."

His implication angered Margaux as naught else could have done. Fury fired through her like quicksilver, for he had never understood anything of merit.

Her palm cracked loudly against his cheek, the sound echoing loud in the stone room. Gavin turned his head from the force of the blow, he blinked, he opened his mouth and closed it again.

Margaux's hand shook as it fell back to her side. She had never struck another, she had certainly never struck *this* man, and she feared belatedly what he would do.

But she would not back down.

To her surprise, when Gavin met her gaze, a slow smile eased across his lips. He had a roguish charm, a rough allure that Margaux had never been able to deny. Indeed, he was like an animal in his passions, wild and untamed, oblivious to everything but what he wanted in that moment.

She saw in his eyes that he wanted *her*.

A part of Margaux admired his bold desire. Even now, after all these years, that glint in his eye awakened a flicker of white heat that reminded her what it had been like to be young.

With Gavin.

"I invite you, my lady wife, to vent your anger upon me. You know full well that I can answer to your passion as none other."

"Knave!"

Gavin stepped closer and Margaux realized suddenly that he was clean. Aye, her nose told no lie. He had washed to meet with her, a fact not without portent.

Had he returned to Montvieux to court her anew?

She stared into his eyes, incredulous, as his smile broadened. "I should even hold you, if you should cry beneath the burden of the old bastard's expectations." He touched his finger to his lips. "And I should tell none of what I witnessed."

She could not summon a protest to her lips. Just the clean smell of his skin was enough to remind her of their bodies tangled together, of the way they had nearly devoured each other in their desire, of the feel of his tongue upon her flesh. He would do anything for pleasure, he would anything to please her.

He had agreed, many years ago, to wash before he came to her bed. When he lifted his fingertip from his own lips and touched it to hers, her knees weakened at the rough edge against her lips.

Aye, she *remembered.*

"Why are you here?" she demanded, her voice more breathless than was her wont.

Gavin's smile widened. "I wanted to see you," he said with quiet heat. "I needed to know whether you took Burke's choice better than I." He swallowed. "But mostly, I needed to know whether there was still fire in Margaux de Montvieux's eyes."

"You came to steal Montvieux," she charged.

But he laughed beneath his breath. "Nay, Margaux. Though 'tis true I once thought to seize the prize of Montvieux by wedding you, I know now that Montvieux will never be mine. It matters naught."

"You came to die in comfort, to live out your days here at Montvieux."

Gavin shook his head. "Nay. I will not stay."

Margaux could not comprehend the softening in him. Was it truly as he declared? "You lust for Montvieux alone," she charged, only half certain that was the truth. "I knew your intent when we were wed and I know it now."

"And you wanted naught but a son from me." Gavin arched a brow. "Ours was not a match wrought of love or even of dynastic alliance, Margaux, and we are each as guilty as the other in that. At least we were equals, as few others can say."

Margaux looked away, because there was no argument she could make to the truth.

"But in the end, despite all that has passed between us and all the women I have lain with, 'tis the memory of you that haunts me."

Margaux tried to be skeptical. "And all the riches you left behind, no doubt."

"Aye," Gavin agreed with startling ease. "And you were

the richest of them all, though I realized the truth too late.''
With that, he took a quick step to close the distance between
them, framed her face in his hands, and kissed her.

'Twas not an embrace born of finesse, nor was his manner
filled with grace. 'Twas not his way. But there was a hunger
there, a hunger Margaux well recalled, a hunger she had
never been able to deny or to resist.

Because that same hunger burned within herself. In that,
he was right—they both accepted no compromise abed.
They both were greedy for pleasure. And when they
touched, some alchemy made them insatiable for each other,
driven to grant and seize as much pleasure as could be
wrung from the moment. Margaux leaned against Gavin,
closed her eyes, and abandoned herself to sensation, admitting only to herself that she had missed this.

She had missed *him*.

If he did not intend to stay, she had best make the moment
count. When Gavin finally lifted his head, her lips felt
bruised from his devouring kiss. His eyes had darkened, as
always they did in desire, and Margaux felt younger than she
had in weeks. Perhaps years.

"Take me to your bed, Margaux," he said quietly. "For
all we had, and all we never had."

Margaux laughed, the weight of failure and years shed by
that single kiss. "Nay," she said, savoring her spouse's surprise. "I would not wait so long as that."

"Here?" he demanded, incredulous.

"You have a fine wool cloak and I see 'tis lined with fur."
Margaux permitted herself to smile. "And 'tis time that I
did something to shock him once again." She rapped her
cane on the sarcophagus to make her point.

Gavin began to laugh. Margaux stepped into his embrace
and ensured he had naught to laugh about for a long time.

'Twas just before the dawn the next morn when Gavin Fitz-gerald rose from his wife's bed. They had indeed ended up there, when joints and old bones complained overmuch of the hard flagstones, despite the luxury of that fur-lined cloak.

He shook his head as he stared down at Margaux, her strength of will formidable even in sleep. Her hair had turned from ebony to silver, her once-smooth flesh was lined, her lips had thinned. But she was still the beauty he once had glimpsed and then had wanted so badly that he ached.

He had never met a woman like her.

He knew he never would again.

Yet she believed she was a failure. That was enough to break even his hardened old heart. He could not tell her that he saw the old bastard in the steel of her spine, in the glint in her eye, in her determination to see her will done at all costs.

In her desire to shackle her child to the servitude of her dream.

Nay, that truth would be too cruel, even for Margaux. Gavin dressed quickly, intending only to slip away from a place where he had never been welcome, his curiosity sated. But Margaux's insistence upon her own failure echoed in his thoughts.

She had confided in him, as he had never known her to confide in another. He felt as if she would compel him to set matters to rights, as if she alone believed he could accomplish anything of merit. As if she still would demand of him the only thing she had ever said that she desired.

An heir for Montvieux.

How like Margaux to keep a reckoning, to remind him of his debt unpaid.

It would have been simple for the man he once had been to turn away. But Gavin was not the man he had been. He had fought all his life to create a fitting legacy for Burke, for the son he had always dreamed of having, only to have Burke decline the gift.

That refusal had shaken Gavin and forced him to reconsider all he had held dear. Now it seemed that he had matters backwards 'round, as if he had always chased what in the end had no merit at all.

And abandoned what might have been his greatest treasures.

Gavin lingered when he should have gone, watching the dawn's fingers creep through the window and paint a rosy hue over his wife's flesh. It made her look like a girl again, though, indeed, Margaux had never been like other young girls.

There was some truth in her accusation that he had stolen Burke from her.

There was more truth in his reply that she had more than one son.

He had come to Montvieux, finding himself rootless, seeking some purpose, instinctively guessing that his estranged wife might hold the key. And she had indeed offered him a quest to guide his footsteps.

Aye, Gavin would ensure that Margaux did not confront the old bastard in the beyond as a failure, he would give purpose to his own days and make his last goal a noble one.

He would fetch Rowan back to Montvieux.

For Margaux.

His course decided, Gavin turned and left his lady's chambers for the last time. He would never see her again, he knew it in his very bones. Though the knowledge saddened him, for once he had no complaints of how they parted.

'Twas probably the sole time he could have said as much about himself and Margaux—and that prompted Gavin to smile as he seldom had within the walls of Château Montvieux.

Even the clatter of his steed's hoofbeats had faded by the time the sun crested the horizon and shone upon Margaux's lonely prize.

But Gavin Fitzgerald never looked back.

# Chapter Eleven

BERNIA SNUGGLED DROWSILY AGAINST ROWAN'S warmth and refused to think of more practical matters. The first pale light of the morning crept into the cabin and made the walls glow a pearly grey. She had been easily distracted from her mission, she supposed, but there was still time to ensure her father's safety.

After all, while they were at sea, Baldassare could do naught.

The cabin was chilly, but Rowan's heat was wrapped around her back, his cloak tossed over them both. The pallet was too narrow for two, but after all they had done upon it, Ibernia decided that sleeping should be no challenge at all. They had pleasured each other plenty, and Ibernia admitted to herself that Rowan's sure touch had eased her consternation.

Rowan's hand swept over her in a long lazy caress and she smiled without opening her eyes. He kissed her neck, taking his time as he explored the curve of her shoulder.

Truly, Ibernia had never imagined that coupling could be so fine. Trust Rowan to know the truth of it, and teach her of it. Though she would never admit to him that she was impressed. The man needed no reassurance of his own allure.

That he had a considerable measure of allure could not be denied. In fact, a woman could be fooled by Rowan's lighthearted manner, fooled into believing that this knight held naught within his heart.

But Ibernia had seen his concern for Thomas, his determination to ensure that Baldassare did not take advantage of her, and she had a deep suspicion that Rowan was more honorable than he might have wanted anyone to believe.

She smiled to herself, imagining the look upon this knight's face if she charged him of honorable intentions.

"It was enough to make one smile, was it not?" the man in question mused.

Ibernia sighed contentment.

A rap on the door and a whisper revealed Thomas's presence, and Rowan rose, returning to the bed with biscuits. Ibernia surveyed hers critically, not having the heart to tell Rowan what she knew when he devoured his so quickly.

In the end, he ate hers as well.

Then he eased closer, muttered something under his breath. Ibernia felt him reach back and glanced over her shoulder to see him fighting to pull the end of his cloak out from beneath their weight.

"Little did I knew I slept with a thief," he declared, the twinkle in his eyes mitigating his mock scowl.

"A thief?" Ibernia feigned innocence, though she guessed what he was about. The sleek strength of his buttocks were bare to the cabin's chill air. She gave the cloak a playful tug, baring his thigh to the cold and cast an admiring glance over him.

"Aye, a thief of the worst order!" he charged. "One guilty of the lowest crime known to man—thievery of *covers* when 'tis cold." Rowan gave the cloak a tug but Ibernia resolutely hugged it closer around herself.

"But the view is so fine!"

"Teasing wench!" he charged and she giggled.

" 'Tis wondrously warm," Ibernia purred, and deliberately snuggled deeper into the cloth, flicking one corner of the cloak away from his feet and capturing it beneath her own.

Rowan cried foul, his eyes sparkled, then he dove against her just as she had known he would. He tickled her, and Ibernia laughed, managing somehow to keep the cloak wrapped around herself.

Rowan's eyes lit when he found an opening and Ibernia cried foul in her turn when his cold fingers landed on her bare flesh.

"You are too cold!"

" 'Tis your own fault." He chuckled under his breath, his eyes dancing wickedly. "And I shall make you pay."

Ibernia squealed and tried to retreat. Her move made the gap wider when Rowan made a sudden grab for her. He hooted in victory when he found a ticklish spot beneath her ribs and Ibernia squirmed to no avail.

Then she started to laugh and could not halt, gasping for breath as Rowan tickled her mercilessly. He granted her no quarter, and she laughed until she thought she would burst with it.

Then he tickled her some more, his laughter mingling with own. Their legs tangled together, the forgotten cloak fell down around Ibernia's waist. Rowan was atop her, his legs holding hers down as she kicked and wriggled.

Finally she arched her back and stretched out her hands. "I surrender!" she cried breathlessly. "Just cease tickling."

"Ah, but for what price?"

Ibernia squeaked as his fingers found another ticklish spot. "Anything!"

Then he stopped. His hands froze upon her and Ibernia looked up, gasping, to meet the glow in his eyes. Her blood heated at his proximity and suddenly she felt the chill air no longer. Rowan grinned slowly, bracing his hands on either side of her shoulders and bending closer.

"Anything," he echoed, the way his eyes widened making Ibernia's heart skip a beat. "Now, there is an offer that cannot be refused." He dipped his head and kissed her fully, swallowing Ibernia's sigh of delight.

'Twas only then, when he virtually pinned her to the pallet with the weight of his body, that Ibernia realized she was not afraid. Not in the least. Not of Rowan, not of his obvious ability to overpower her, not of his weight atop her or his strength within her. She should have feared being trapped beneath him, especially after all she had endured beneath other men, but Rowan was different.

He was tender, he was gentle. Ibernia blinked, catching her breath as he nibbled a course toward her ear.

Rowan truly did desire her participation in this moment, and just as he had vowed, it did make the feast they shared much more enticing. He had granted her a wondrous gift, in slaying her fear and simultaneously teaching her of this pleasure. Ibernia studied the russet waves of his hair, raising her hand to tangle within its thickness and liking the look of her fingers in his hair.

She trusted Rowan, as astonishing and unexpected as that was. She wondered whether 'twould truly be so terrible if he did succeed at his bride quest.

The very prospect made her mouth go dry.

"I should have bought a longer cloak in London," he muttered against her throat. "This one has ever been too short."

"But 'tis wondrously fine," Ibernia said absently, her fingers kneading the cloth into pleats as she pondered the root of her unexpected confidence in this man, of all men.

Rowan valued the merit of his pledge, he did what he swore to do, he protected her and savored her. He taught her of wonders, he made her laugh. Truly, she had never matched wits with a more worthy opponent.

"You should never have found the same quality in London," she continued with a small smile. "The weaving for sale in that port is shoddy indeed."

"Indeed?" Rowan kissed her earlobe in that way that turned her bones to butter.

Ibernia gasped and arched her neck, fighting to hold the thread of the conversation—if only to challenge his own belief in the power of his touch. She could feel his smile and knew he deliberately teased her.

"Aye, their cloth is vastly inferior to that of Flanders," she said breathlessly. "This twill could have come from nowhere else, given its fine weave and rich green hue."

"Trust the daughter of a cloth merchant to know more of such matters than a mere knight," Rowan mused, then closed his hand over her breast.

"You are no *mere* knight," Ibernia protested before she realized what she had done. She gasped, just as Rowan propped himself above her on his elbows.

"Aha!" he declared, his eyes alight. "You *are* the daughter of a cloth merchant. I knew it well!"

Ibernia sputtered but could see no logical means of denying the truth. Instead, she took umbrage in his deceit. "You tricked me!"

"No more than you tricked me." Rowan settled his weight over her again, grinning as he entwined her fingers with his own. "Your father is a Venetian cloth merchant, is he not?"

Ibernia's heart hammered. "I do not know what you mean."

"Grant me some credit, Ibernia!" Rowan rolled his eyes. "You comprehend the dialect and 'tis the most reasonable explanation. And how else would you know so much of cloth? How else would you be so educated? Truly, I am not so witless as that.''

Nay, he was not. Ibernia stared at him, unable to think of a compelling lie with his length pressed against her. She could feel the hair on his chest against her breasts and her nipples tightened.

'' 'Tis clear enough that you are the victim of some adventure gone awry,'' Rowan continued, not a shred of doubt in his tone. ''Any fool knows that the loser in a battle against pirates wins only slavery, especially a beauty such as you.''

Ibernia opened her mouth and closed it again, silenced by the confusing rush of pleasure his compliment sent through her.

Rowan's eyes filled with concern and his voice dropped low. ''Was your father injured? Was that why he could not defend you?''

Ibernia swallowed and looked away from the compassion that she knew would loose her tongue. ''He was not there,'' she admitted, without having any intention of doing so.

Truly, her wits were addled!

Did it matter that Rowan knew her origins? If she trusted him, should they not have honesty between them? Or was her cursed impulsiveness advising her false again?

She could not think the puzzle through, not with his warm fingertips sliding down the length of her throat. Ibernia could fairly feel his gaze upon her; she swore she could hear him delving into her thoughts.

To trust Rowan with her touch was one matter, but could she trust him with her father's life?

''What I cannot understand''—Rowan continued, his tone conversational and his breath warm against her throat—''is why you would choose to flee to *Ireland*. Surely Venice would be a more reasonable choice? But then, I hear the training of a convent in your voice—perhaps 'tis in Ireland that you were consigned to the sisters and their education. Is this how you know Bronwyn of Ballyroyal?''

Ibernia glanced to him in alarm. The man was too quick-witted!

Rowan smiled engagingly. '' 'Tis clear you know her, for her name rose quickly to your lips. What harm is there in admitting your friendship? Truly, it aided me that you had such a ready answer.''

Ibernia swallowed. "I know her.''

"Are you friends from afore? 'Twould make sense. Or perhaps you believe your friend would shelter you, now that all has gone awry.'' He smiled slightly, his eyes dark as if he were solving a trying riddle. ''Is that why you would flee to Ireland? Do you hope to find safety there?''

Ibernia looked to the wall once more, gritted her teeth, and decided her course. She had had enough of lies and was not certain she could find another within her, at any rate.

She did not trust by half measures, after all.

"I was raised there,'' she confessed. '' 'Tis home to me, so only natural that I would return there.''

Rowan's eyes narrowed. "Then how did you find yourself in this fix? You must have been far from Ireland's shores.''

Ibernia took a deep breath. "I ran away.'' She almost smiled. ''From an arranged marriage I found unsuitable.''

"And you thought to fare better on your own?'' Instead of compassion for her circumstance, Rowan's eyes flashed in anger. "Truly I thought you had more sense than this!'' Rowan shoved a hand through his hair. "Ibernia, you could have been killed!'' he declared, giving her shoulders a min-ute shake. "You could have fared worse than even you have! Look at Marika! You could have shared a similar fate and for what? Because the spouse chosen for you was too fat?''

"Too old," she corrected mildly, marvelling at his anger with her.

No less her own response to his protectiveness.

But Rowan swore. "Whimsy!" he declared. "What seized your thoughts that you should endanger your very hide for such foolery?" He shook his head, his glare still fixed upon her. "Truly, I thought you were more clever than that!"

Ibernia shrugged, unable to explain that she could ever have been so foolish as she had been. " 'Tis abundantly clear in hindsight that mine was a sheltered life. As you say, I was fortunate to have fared no worse." She shrugged as if her experience mattered less than it did. "I knew naught of what I would find and acted like a fool."

Rowan's expression softened, the look in his eyes making Ibernia's heart clench. He bent to brush his lips across her brow, and what little resistance she had melted to naught.

"To be innocent is not the same as to be a fool," he whispered, his words like balm on a wound.

Ibernia closed her eyes, hating that the weakness of a warm tear slid from beneath her lashes. She felt drawn to this man in a way she had not expected, and she was oddly tempted to confess every vestige of the truth to him.

"I do not have to endure the burden of innocence any longer," she admitted, meaning to make a jest, but her voice broke over the words.

Rowan drew back slightly, cupping her face in his hands and compelling her to look at him. "Innocence is over-rated," he declared, then smiled slowly. "You are remark-able, a strong and resilient woman unlike any I have ever known before. That is more alluring than innocence or even foolery ever could be."

Ibernia managed a smile, though her vision clouded with

tears. Again she tried to jest. "And you have known a great many women, so would know the truth of it."

Rowan grinned and flicked a fingertip across the tip of her nose. "Aye, I have, many of them remarkable indeed." He sobered then, bending to touch his nose to hers. His golden gaze searched hers, as if he would reassure her of her own worth.

"Do not underrate yourself, Ibernia," he murmured, his words low and intent. "You are incomparable."

Ibernia caught her breath. When he regarded her with that admiration in his gaze, that teasing curve upon his firm lips, a glint of seriousness in his manner, she could have easily surrendered her heart. She could have been the only woman in all of Christendom, the only one worthy of his attention, the only one to whose charms he would ever fall prey.

Her heart skipped a beat as she wondered whether he had called any others *incomparable*. She had to know, and she had to know immediately.

Rowan bent to kiss her, but Ibernia halted him with one hand on his chest. He met her gaze, his own filled with a question.

"Tell me of the woman whose ring you carry," she urged, hating her breathlessness. "Was she incomparable?"

Rowan stiffened, he caught his breath. He looked as if he would evade her question, then he glanced down to her eyes. "Does it matter?"

"Of course!" She responded lightly, pretending his answer did not matter overmuch to her, but Rowan studied her for a long silent moment. Ibernia did not know what he saw, but that slow smile curved his lips once more, as if his uncertainty was allayed.

"Then I shall make you a wager, *ma demoiselle*."

She held his gaze, well prepared to meet any challenge he offered and not caring if he knew. "What is that?"

He winked. "Tell me a tale and I shall tell you one in exchange."

"Your tale will be of the ring."

Rowan inclined his head in agreement. "And yours will be of your journey to slavery."

Ibernia exhaled and might have looked away, but Rowan caught her chin in gentle fingers. The ship rocked slightly, the wood groaning as the wind rose, but there was naught in her world beyond the steady gleam of this knight's eyes.

"All of it," he insisted grimly, apparently sensing her impulse to decline. "And I shall tell my tale first to show you that you will not lose in this bargain."

Ibernia nodded, wanting to know more of this ring he treasured yet at the same time uncertain she wanted to know details of the woman who so captured his heart.

Aye, her wits were addled this morn!

Rowan rolled to his back abruptly, carrying Ibernia with him, and she ended up nestled against his side. He settled back and stared at the ceiling. Ibernia propped herself upon his chest, intent upon watching his expression change, for clearly this tale would not be an easy one for him.

Though his tone was light when he began.

"Once upon a time, long ago and far away, there was a man who lived in a fine castle. He had a wife and a son and wealth incomparable, but he was the manner of man who wanted all he saw. He made his trade as a mercenary, fighting for a share of the spoil, and had been successful enough over the years that he owned estates throughout Christendom. His wife was noble, his son was handsome, but this man wanted only more.

"Perhaps it was because he was universally loathed that no amount of treasure would suffice. At any rate, his temperament was perfect for his chosen profession—his loyalty could be bought, his temper was ferocious, his manners were appalling, and he spared no concession for morality or ethics.''

He spared her a significant glance. ''He was said to never laugh, which tells you as much of the man as anything else.''

Ibernia shook her head in mock severity, relieved that this story seemed less emotional than she had feared. ''A true barbarian.''

''Indeed.'' Rowan frowned, his fingers beating a staccato against Ibernia's hip. ''One day, a travelling troupe of entertainers came to the gates of his castle. A tragic miscalculation on their part, for none within those gates would spare hard coin to be entertained, but they had no way of knowing as much.

''There is no doubt in my mind that this mercenary intended to cheat them, to have his pleasure of them and send them on their way without a denier, but they were not so guileless that they did not take such possibilities into account. Truly, there is always an element of risk in what they do.''

Clearly he felt an affinity with these entertainers. ''What manner of entertainers were they?''

Rowan smiled as if he had found a fond memory. ''Ah, an old troupe with all the usual array of skills. There were musicians and singers, acrobats and conjurers, a storyteller and a jester. They entertained at weddings and festivals, they were quick and merry and very funny. Their garb was in a thousand colors, oft wrought of luxurious scraps sewn together.

''They were mad, of course, eccentrics all, but embued with a joy of life that could not be contained. They owned naught and they owed naught, they lived beneath the sky and saw the wonders of the world as they labored. They danced and sang, even when there was none to pay for watching. They were happy, in their own ways.''

Rowan sobered. ''Among them was a woman, a dancer so lithe and beauteous, so winsome that every lord's heart was captured with a glance. Her hair was the color of a flame and it hung to her knees, moving with a grace all its own. She loved to dance as much as she loved life itself. She was gifted, there was no doubt of that, for she danced with the seductive grace of the East.

''Yet remarkably, she was a chaste woman, a clever woman, a woman determined to wed well despite the odds.'' A smile touched his lips again. ''They said she was a dreamer, a romantic and a fool, but she knew she was destined to be loved. She clung to the possibility that a man would sweep her away from the life she led and make her his wife.''

Far overhead, the crew shouted and Ibernia heard the heavy flap of the sails being unfurled to this new wind. She heard the cry of birds and guessed that they were close to some shore. The ship rocked again, then steadied its course.

She could not, would not think of what this particular woman meant to the knight beside her.

Rowan grimaced. ''Of course, men do not think the same way as women. A man confronted with a beautiful woman dancing with sensual abandon knows he has found a whore. The dancer was always beset by offers, and the troupe, being protective as such groups often are, had learned to defend her chastity from her many admirers.''

Was the seduction of this woman a challenge Rowan had lost? 'Twould ensure he recalled the woman, of that Ibernia had no doubt, though she found the possibility of him dreaming of another most troubling.

Which made no sense at all.

"The mercenary was captivated by her." Rowan's eyes narrowed and he glanced away, his voice strained when he continued. "I do not know how it happened, indeed, I am not certain I desire to know how it happened, but he of all men consummated his desire."

Ibernia caught her breath. "He raped her."

"I do not know. It would not have been surprising if he had, for he was one concerned only with his own desires." Rowan's darkened gaze locked with hers. "But when the troupe left that castle, they fled while the mercenary slept. The mercenary's wife was said to have orchestrated their departure, ensuring that they had no time to take even what few belongings they had. Nine months later, the dancer bore a son."

Rowan gritted his teeth, clearly fighting for control of his emotions. Had this woman been his lover later? Had Rowan healed her fear as he had healed Ibernia's?

He flicked a glance to her and their gazes held. "Four years later, the dancer died of an ague, her dream of marriage unfulfilled. Others in the troupe said that she had died of a broken heart, for her pregnancy had ensured that no man treated her with any courtesy again. I do not know, for I barely recall her."

Ibernia frowned in incomprehension but had no chance to ask before Rowan hastened on, his words embittered.

"What I do recall is that the troupe decided that the boy could not remain among them without his mother. Perhaps they did not know how to care for a child. Perhaps they could not bear a reminder of the dancer in their midst. Perhaps the boy was right in believing their earlier affection for him had been a lie.

"It matters little. In the end, they deposited him outside the gates of that castle where he had been spawned, for they knew the mercenary was the child's father. They left him

alone outside the gates, a child of four summers. He faced
the most merciless man in all of Christendom, armed only
with a golden ring that the mercenary had entrusted to the
dancer and the flaming red hair upon his head that so resembled his mother's own.''

''You,'' Ibernia breathed in sudden understanding, her
gaze flicking to the auburn hue of the knight's hair. Aye, red
hair oft darkened thus over the years, she had seen it many
times.

Rowan shrugged as if untroubled, but the shadows clung
to his eyes. ''Me.'' He pulled his purse free of his discarded
chausses and Ibernia had the definite sense that he was
avoiding her gaze. He shook out the contents and picked up
the tiny ring, turning it so that the gold caught the light.

When he continued, his voice was low. ''Then I learned
the lie that is called love, and 'tis a lesson I have never
forgotten. The myth of love is used by others for their own
convenience, and those who profess to it merely leave themselves open to exploitation.''

The silence hung between them. Ibernia did not know
what to say, for though she did not agree, she doubted he
would listen to her counsel. The pain in Rowan's eyes startled her, the depth with which he felt this wound made her
want to console him in turn.

How could she have imagined, even for a moment, that
Rowan cared for naught? This rejection was as a fresh
wound to him and evidently its bite was deep.

Rowan cleared his throat. ''As you might imagine, the
mercenary was disinclined to acknowledge the child—
'twould only have been to his detriment, to be sure. But his
wife was another matter. As fierce as a peregrine left hun-
gered is Margaux de Montvieux. She demanded an accounting of her spouse, she demanded the truth about the ring,
and even he did not have the fortitude to deny her.''

Rowan shook his head. "And then she cast him out."

Ibernia leaned on his chest, entangling her fingers with his own. "What of you?"

"She raised me as her own, after dispatching her husband for his faithlessness." He swallowed, turning the ring restlessly in his fingers. "I shall never forget it. She chose me over him."

Ibernia squeezed his hand and saw an opportunity to present her defense of love. "Because she loved you?"

Rowan snorted. "Nay! Margaux merely recognized that she could not reform Gavin, that that cause was lost. She thought to shape a child to her own ends."

Ibernia was not fooled by his dismissiveness. Rowan was grateful to this woman and there was affection lurking in his tone when he spoke of her. Margaux might have been uncompromising and unyielding, but he appreciated what she had done for him.

Regardless of how he might pretend otherwise. Aye, Ibernia was learning to read this man, who was not nearly so indifferent to emotional ties as he would have all believe.

"And I would guess that you took pleasure in defying her expectation?" she asked with a smile.

Rowan grinned outright. "It was too tempting by half! Indeed, there was no risk in disappointing her, for she had already a perfect son and heir. Burke was a golden boy, he could do naught amiss, and Margaux clearly had ambitions for him." He shrugged as if indifferent. "She did not need me. Perhaps it was a greater gift to live among those who are open about their selfishness than to be caught in an illusion that the world is otherwise."

He frowned and looked away, but Ibernia nestled closer. She plucked the ring from his restless grasp and pushed it on to the smallest finger of his left hand.

" 'Tis the only token you have of your mother," she

chided. "You should wear it as a reminder of her love for you." She let him think about the matter, settling against his shoulder again. "Just as Margaux loved you in her turn, regardless of what she said of the matter."

Rowan looked alarmed. "I should think not!"

"Why else would she keep you and clothe you, feed you and educate you? Rowan, use your wits! Someone paid for you to earn your spurs, for that fine destrier, someone ensured that you should have coin in your purse. Obligation does not open a purse with such vigor. She loves you, else she would desire something in exchange for her largesse."

Rowan grimaced. "Well, you are wrong in that, for Margaux's gifts are *not* without their price. She has called an accounting."

"What do you mean?"

He flicked a heavy glance her way. "I am to be disinherited by the Yule if I do not follow her bidding."

"Aye?" Ibernia propped herself up on her elbow to watch him. "What would she have of you?"

"A bride." Rowan winced. "I must return to Montvieux with a bride, one that my half brothers have decreed should be the wealthiest heiress in all of Ireland."

"Half brothers?"

"Aye, I have two: Burke, the son of my foster mother Margaux and my own father; and Luc, the son of my father and his first wife. 'Tis Burke, though, I know best, Burke with whom I have matched dares all my life."

"And they together have dared you to find this bride?"

"Aye. They think I cannot do it." He grinned impishly. "And I, I was fool enough to accept their dare, if only because it seems so hopeless. It makes the matter rather more interesting than it might be otherwise."

Ibernia could not believe that he sought a bride for no more than that woman's dowry, even though he had said as much before. How like Rowan, she now perceived, to hide his emotions behind insouciance.

On this day, she wanted the truth between them.

"So you would bind yourself to a woman for the rest of your days, solely on the weight of her father's purse?" she scoffed, hearing her hope that conclusion would be denied.

But Rowan laughed. " 'Tis a good sensible foundation for my match." He winked and she could not glimpse any seriousness in his manner. "Ah, you should see how I can dispense with coin when in a feckless mood!"

Ibernia straightened, dismayed by his manner. "I have already seen you cast coin to the winds with unholy abandon," she retorted, hearing her father in her words. "What will be left of your marriage when the coin is gone?"

Rowan grinned. "But that is why she must be *incomparably* wealthy—to ensure that the coin is never gone."

The use of that particular word, the one he had so recently used to compliment her, annoyed Ibernia to no end. He could not know who she was, he could not know the weight of her father's purse. He could not have tricked her.

Could he?

"Why would this heiress have you, if you have no other desire than to spend her inheritance?" she demanded, feeling suddenly cold. "An heiress oft has a measure of intellect."

Rowan smiled slowly, his hand sliding over Ibernia's flesh, clicking his tongue as he chided her. "I do possess some charm, Ibernia. The lady will not lack for pleasure in exchange." He bent to kiss her, but she evaded him.

Ibernia sat up hastily, not liking the glint of humor in his eyes. Surely this could not be all a game to him? "This then is the wager you would make for marriage? Pleasure for coin? 'Tis a bargain for whores, or courtesans!"

Rowan laughed merrily. "I suppose 'tis, but the wrong

way around." He pursed his lips. "Do you think my bride will keep me as pampered as a prized courtesan? 'Twould not be a bad way to live out one's days. And truly, I am not a man enamoured of obligations and responsibilities. 'Tis better to live unfettered, in my estimation, as those entertainers did."

Rowan leaned back against the wall, folding his arms behind his head and looking supremely male. "Aye, that is the way a man should live. Do you think my heiress bride will be persuaded to indulge me in exchange for savoring my charms?"

Ibernia stared at him, incredulous that she could have misunderstood him so much as this. "But what of love?"

Rowan shook his head, as if she was dimwitted child. "Love is not to be relied upon, Ibernia."

"Of course it is!"

"Nay, it is not." There was naught in his eyes but total conviction, a conviction that chilled Ibernia to her marrow. "Love is fleeting, at best, and an empty claim, at worst. A claim of love is too oft used a tool to win an end to have any merit at all. Everyone sees to their own advantage alone—why should I not do the same?"

There was disappointment in his voice that Ibernia did not miss. "You must have known love at some point in your life."

"Who is to say? 'Tis not a claim that can be validated—and truly, in my experience, all who swear to it want something in exchange."

Ibernia's heart chilled. Surely he did not count himself among their number? "But your mother . . ."

Rowan's lips thinned. "Felt some obligation to ensure I did not die in her wake, no more than that. Perhaps she wished to have vengeance for my father's deeds. It does not matter in the end." He leaned closer, his eyes gleaming.

"Come back beside me. Let us make the pallet groan again."

But Ibernia was immune to any such temptation, as she might not have been just moments past. She pushed from the pallet and hastily got to her feet, anxious to put distance between them. She donned the chemise he had granted her and glanced back at him, savoring the surprise in his eyes.

Her father had always said that what was bred in the bone would come out in the flesh. Here indeed was Ibernia's proof of that. She had been charmed by this knave, as no doubt had countless others before her. Trust the son of a mercenary to see a pledge of love as a means to an end!

What was troubling was that she held the prize that this son of a mercenary wanted for his own. Was that why he bedded her? Was that why he sought to please her?

Oh, she had been such a fool!

" 'Tis too early to rise." Rowan patted the edge of the pallet. "Come back and be warm."

"Nay. I would rather be cold than lie entangled with the likes of your father's son."

Rowan sat up hastily. "What is that to mean?"

"You would wed a woman for her legacy alone, as if she were naught more than a warm body beneath you when you so choose! What of what *she* desires of a match?"

Rowan folded his arms across his chest. "I should see her pleased. I should see her indulged!"

"With her own coin." Ibernia heard her voice rise. "How romantic!"

His eyes flashed. "Romance is of no merit in this!"

"Clearly not!" Ibernia leaned closer, her fury bubbling to the fore. "Is it not the precise kind of match this Margaux made with your father?"

"I am not like him!" Rowan roared and bounded to his feet. "He is a ruthless scoundrel!"

"You are *precisely* like him, 'tis more than clear! You see only how matters can be wrought to your own advantage and care for naught else!"

"You know naught of what you speak!"

"I know that no woman should have to endure a match made for convenience alone, a match devoid of love, a match arranged to forge dynasties." Ibernia's words flowed low and hot. "I believe this in every fibre of my being, 'tis what brings me here to this circumstance, 'tis what compelled me to flee my father's home."

Rowan folded his arms across his chest to survey her. "You fled an arranged match with an older man."

"A *loveless* match, one that would serve my father and his interests but not mine!" Ibernia stepped closer and lifted her chin in defiance. "My choice was borne of ignorance of what I might face, but even knowing all I do now, I would do it again."

Rowan gasped, but Ibernia was not done.

"I would do it in a heartbeat to avoid a lifetime in a loveless match." She glared at him. "I would do it to avoid a man seeking only a fortune, a man who saw a pledge of love as a necessary concession to his own victory, a mercenary just like you."

Rowan's eyes narrowed. " 'Tis fortunate then that I do not seek your hand."

" 'Twould be, if that were true." Ibernia laughed, though the sound was cold and obviously disconcerted the knight before her. "My name is Bronwyn of Ballyroyal," she declared regally. "And I assure you again that you will never win my hand."

She might have lingered to savor the shock on his features but Ibernia was too furiously angry with herself. To think she had thought there was tenderness in this man, that they might have something in common, that she could have been bending to his touch.

Out of the fat and into the fire. Truly she had a gift for such a course! Bronwyn was even more a fool than she had been six months before!

She hauled her kirtle over her head and stalked out of the cabin, not caring for the disarray of her garb and the glances of the busy crew. The sails were snapping overhead, the wind sending waves against the prow, the elements echoing her mood.

A smear of green marked land ahead, birds circled above, their wings silhouetted against the dark rolling clouds that hastened to obscure the sky. She knew a moment's jubilation that Ireland was so close, for land so green could be nowhere else.

'Twas only when she gripped the rail and lifted her face to the bite of the wind that she realized the magnitude of the error she had made.

She had told Rowan her name. Now he would never release her willingly. Once again, impulse had steered her false.

She spun slowly as horror dawned, only to find a grim-faced Rowan striding across the deck, his burning gaze fixed upon her.

God in heaven, what had she done?

# Chapter Twelve

T WAS NOT OFTEN THAT ROWAN WAS SURPRISED, EVEN less often that he was surprised by a woman. They were cursedly predictable in his experience—especially to one so perceptive as he.

With one notable exception.

That exception stood on the deck, her pose defiant and her eyes flashing, as if she would dare him to question her claim. She knew little about him if she thought he would simply walk away from this!

For she had not only surprised him, she had deceived him. Ibernia had used him for her own ends, and Rowan did not like the revelation.

Not Ibernia. Bronwyn. Her name was *Bronwyn.*

He was appalled at what remarkably good sense it all made. She wanted to go home. He wanted to find an Irish heiress. She named herself, challenged him to press his suit, which incidentally ensured that she would be home quickly. When he might have lingered, she goaded him to depart sooner. She insisted that she knew Bronwyn would not have him, challenging him to prove her wrong.

Rowan had never guessed how she could know so well what Bronwyn thought. What a fool he was to fall for such artful trickery! She had addled his wits.

The deck rolled beneath his feet as Rowan strode toward

her. He saw suddenly the ominous clouds gathering quickly overhead, noted the churning shadows of the sea.

Rowan nearly growled. The last thing he needed was a tempestuous sea. He had best deal with Bronwyn first, before illness claimed him again.

The prospect did naught to improve his sour temper. How dare she best him at his own game? Rowan came to a halt before the lady in question, met her rebellious gaze, and felt a wave of admiration so strong it nearly took him to his knees.

She *was* incomparable. At least he had not called that amiss.

Though that was small consolation in this moment.

Rowan glared as well as he was able, but Bronwyn was undaunted. He took a step closer and glowered—she held her ground.

"You did not think it pertinent to tell me the truth sooner?" he demanded coldly.

"If I had my wits about me, I would not have told you at all!"

Naught she could have said could have restored Rowan's mood more readily than that admission.

She was addled by him as well. Now, there was encouragement!

"Indeed?" Rowan leaned against the rail, watching her as he grinned with undisguised satisfaction. "And what happened to your wits, Bronwyn of Ballyroyal?"

"Naught of import." She folded her arms across her chest and stared at the distant coast. A faint blush tinged her cheeks, the sight heating Rowan's blood.

Rowan was most reassured to know that he was not alone in losing the battle against sensation here. He leaned closer and whispered so that his breath feathered across her throat.

"What could have distracted you from your clear thinking?"

"I said, naught of import." She took a step away and cast an arch glance his way. "Though you may have distracted me once, rest assured that you will not do so again."

"A challenge!" Rowan made to close the distance between them, but she moved away before he could capture her in his arms. He considered her for a long moment, then stepped quickly after her.

But not quickly enough. Indeed, her eyes began to dance with mischief that she vexed him again, the sight dismissing any sense of victory he might have felt.

How irksome that she could guess his intent so readily as that! He greatly preferred to be considered unpredictable and did not care that this lady seemed able to read him so well.

Rowan folded his arms across his chest and glared at her, a choice that *Bronwyn* seemed to find amusing.

"Truly. When did you intend to tell me the truth?" he demanded.

She arched a fair brow. "With luck, never."

"Never!" The word exploded from Rowan's lips. "And how did you intend to manage this deed? How did you anticipate that you would lie to me when we crossed Ballyroyal's threshold? Do you imagine I would not notice that you and my intended were one and the same?"

Bronwyn rolled her eyes. "Oh, you are not so blind to all around you as that."

"I thank you for that meager credit."

"But you would never have come to Ballyroyal."

"What is that to mean?"

"Only that I would have fled your side in Dublin and you would have found some other kirtle to chase in my stead." She shrugged and turned out to sea. "You are, after all, a man unenamoured of obligation.'' She cast another glance his way. ''Why would anyone imagine that you would keep any pledge?''

Rowan scowled, uncertain what to say. To live a life unfettered by obligation was indeed his ambition, though it sounded far less noble a pursuit when Bronwyn stated it so.

''I mean to win my quest,'' he insisted.

''Aye, purely so that your foster mother does not disinherit you. How noble an intent! What manner of fool are you to not perceive that winning this quest will only win you all you say you do not desire?''

''What nonsense is this?'' Rowan took a step back.

''Oh, do not feign ignorance with me!'' Bronwyn's eyes flashed like sapphires in the sun. ''If you win this heiress bride, then Margaux will not cast you out, is this not so?''

''Aye,'' Rowan agreed warily.

''And so, you will be indebted to the bride and her father, no doubt answerable to various duties and responsibilities. And this Margaux will burden you with an estate, or an inheritance, or some matter that persistently requires your attention.''

''Nay, not Margaux . . .'' Rowan began to argue, but then he recalled that Burke had declined his mother's legacy. And Luc had his own mother's holding to call his own, not to mention that of his heiress bride.

Margaux had no heir. Rowan's heart stopped at the truth of it.

Ye gods, this could not be right! Margaux would not entrust him with anything of value.

Would she?

But even if she did not, there was the matter of the heiress's holdings. He supposed it was not unreasonable to conclude that duties might be expected of him there.

Though he had never thought that far.

Bronwyn lifted her chin in triumph. "You will have responsibilities if you win this wager, Rowan de Montvieux, of that there is no doubt. Fortunes do not fall into hands unwilling to labor for their maintenance."

Rowan stared at her, marvelling that he could have missed something so painfully evident. It seemed rather foolish to admit in this moment that he had seized upon the challenge of his brothers and thought no further than that. He had been dared and he had accepted the terms, purely because the odds of success were so long.

But Bronwyn's explanation made it clear that he was striving to win the one thing he was certain he did not desire.

She stepped closer and tapped a fingertip in the middle of his chest. "Do not offer me the lie that you did not see the truth of it," she said softly. "You are keener of wit than that."

He apparently was not, but Rowan was not inclined to make his lack of intellect clear—though he would not question why he cared what she thought of him.

"I do not want any responsibilities and Margaux knows the truth of it," he declared, his calm tone in marked contrast to his pounding heart. "She would never entrust anything of import to me, at least not if she wished to see it maintained."

He grinned, hoping he achieved some measure of his usual disregard. Bronwyn did not smile, and Rowan had the distinct sense that she was disappointed in him.

Not that that was of any import at all.

"Well, you should know that Bronwyn of Ballyroyal is *not* the wealthiest heiress in all of Ireland." Her tone was cool and composed, as if she were discarding naught of greater import than an old stocking. "I lied to you to ensure you took my dare."

Rowan found this appalling, no less that she so readily admitted to her crime. That must be why her claim stung.

'Twas not often that Rowan was tricked, and never so successfully. Perhaps this was admiration he felt for her. Clearly he felt something, for his heart hammered and he could not summon a clever word to his lips as he regarded her.

"You can seek your fortune elsewhere, now that we understand each other."

That she could dismiss him as readily as that, as readily as he was wont to dismiss former lovers, was not welcome in the least.

Rowan propped his hands on his hips, feeling the need to argue the point. "But I pledged to win you."

"But you must succeed by the Yule." Bronwyn looked him straight in the eye. "I assure you, Rowan de Montvieux, you will not win me before this Yule or any other. You had best seek to win your wager elsewhere."

"Do you imply that my word is worthless?"

Bronwyn laughed. "Aye! What else would I assume of a man who desires no responsibilities! To keep a pledge or fulfill an oath is an onerous weight indeed. Nay, you are not the manner of man to cling to mere words." She smiled brightly, her acceptance of this annoying as naught else could have been.

Rowan glared at her, but the lady was untroubled by his response.

" 'Tis fair enough that you cannot find what you desire in me," Bronwyn declared, her manner so blithe that Rowan's eyes narrowed as he watched her. "And truly, 'tis enough for me to be so close to home. We should part in Dublin and each pursue our own path."

Rowan could not find the precise argument as to why this course would be unsuitable. He certainly had no particular affection for this vexing creature, even if Bronwyn was unlike any woman he had ever known.

Aye, he should seize this chance and abandon the entire quest! He should let Margaux disinherit him, he should find a troupe of travellers and live unfettered as he so desired. Bronwyn was right—he desired naught he could win by success in this.

But Rowan could not summon the words to declare he would do precisely that. He supposed that was because he owed Thomas a decent training as a knight. Aye, an *obligation* at root! Once Thomas won his spurs, then Rowan would walk away from this knightly life.

But 'twould be five years before that was done.

Rowan leaned his elbows against the rail, ensuring he was close to Bronwyn's side but not touching her. He could smell her skin, and the lazy thread of desire that unfurled in his belly brought words other than a ready agreement to his tongue.

"Nay, that cannot be done," he said amiably.

"What is this?" Something flashed in Bronwyn's eyes then was quickly subdued, though Rowan knew he had struck a chord.

He smiled at her, feeling as if matters were shifting in his favor once more. "It cannot be done," he insisted mildly, liking the way her eyes flashed in anger. "Though 'tis true that I hold naught in esteem and my word is worth less than naught, the same cannot be said of you."

She took a sharp breath, her gaze fairly cutting him in half. "Me?"

"Aye, your sworn pledge is naught with which to trifle and, as I recall, you did pledge to serve me for a year and a day." Rowan let his smile widen. "In exchange for your freedom."

Crimson flooded her cheeks and steam high rose from her ears. "You would not compel me to that!"

"Indeed I would," he agreed easily. Rowan told himself that his intent was solely to annoy her as she annoyed him, and there could be no doubt that she was infuriated.

He leaned closer, determined to twist the knife in the wound. "In fact," he reminded her cheerfully, "you might recall that I granted you a chance to win your freedom sooner, yet you failed the test."

She looked fit to kill him with her bare hands.

The very sight of her fury cheered Rowan immeasurably. He grinned at her, reached out, and flicked a fingertip across the end of her nose.

"Imagine, we have only just begun to explore the pleasure we can grant each other," he teased, waiting for the flash of her eyes before he whistled between his teeth. "An entire year of satisfying each other's every desire. It should grant you even your fill of me. Perhaps I should become a male courtesan, after that." Rowan grinned, bracing himself for a spate of angry words condemning his vanity to hell and back.

He was not prepared for the slap of Bronwyn's hand across his face.

Nor for the force of her blow.

He jumped back, affronted that she had struck him. "Ye gods, what was that?" He touched his burning cheek with his fingertips, but the lady was not ready to back away.

"That was for being even less worthy of merit than could be believed!" she snapped, her eyes flashing and her cheeks flushed. "That was for your shameless seduction, that was for feigning that you had any heart at all. And that was for denying me the one thing I want most in all the world, solely because you can!"

Rowan spread his hands. "I am all yours."

She cast him a look so lethal that he took a step back. "Bastard!" she muttered through her teeth.

Rowan inclined his head in agreement. "Indeed."

"Shameless knave!"

"Undoubtedly." He grinned. Indeed, he was tempted to kiss her soundly, even if there was a risk of her slapping him again.

She leaned closer and whispered through her teeth. "Mercenary!"

That charge hit home as naught else could have done. Rowan straightened angrily. "Nay, *ma demoiselle,* it is you who used me for your own ends, seeing only to your own advantage."

She lifted her chin, her eyes widening as she mocked him. "Woho, the pot calls the kettle black."

"Then you do concede your trickery?"

"I concede naught to you."

"You have before and you will again."

She laughed then, as never a woman had laughed when faced with the prospect of Rowan's lovemaking. Her eyes flashed as she leaned toward him, the creamy length of her throat leading his gaze to the top of her untied chemise. *His* chemise. She looked so desirable, so determined to challenge his every expectation, that Rowan could think of naught but dragging her back to their cabin once more.

"You will never touch me again, of that you may be assured, Rowan de Montvieux."

'Twas not precisely what the knight longed to hear. "You desire me, you know you do," he insisted, but her arched brow said otherwise.

Her eyes, though, were bright, and he knew that anger such as this did not come from naught. Nay, she cared for him, she desired him, and Rowan knew the truth of it.

Why else was she so concerned that he hold love in esteem? Rowan chuckled at the truth of it. Aye, he would have Bronwyn begging for his touch before they were done! He stepped closer, savoring how her eyes narrowed assessingly at his move.

Oh, she would be his again within moments.

The captain's voice rose as he changed the course and Bronwyn raised her gaze to look over Rowan's shoulder. A faint smile teased her lips and her expression turned welcoming, that look bringing his advance to a halt. When she waved and smiled, Rowan spun to find the captain granting her a salute.

Something dark twisted in his gut, though Bronwyn's next words stole his breath away.

"I desire a man of substance, not some knave whose word cannot be trusted," she declared under her breath. "Is Baldassare not a handsome man? Aye, a man with fine manners and a fat purse, a man who knows how best to treat a lady." She sighed. "Perhaps 'tis the call of blood to blood, but I cannot resist the allure of a Venetian man. And now that you have shown me the pleasures to be found abed, well, I cannot resist *him.*"

She brushed past an astonished Rowan, her gaze fixed on the other man. "I would guess his lovemaking would not be *mediocre,*" she murmured.

Nay! This was not right! Bronwyn's desire could not be so fleeting as that! Her desire could not be so fleeing as his own oft was!

Could it?

"You cannot do this!" he bellowed

"Watch me," she muttered through her teeth, casting him a glance so stubborn it nigh stole his breath away.

Rowan lunged after her. "You cannot go to him! You cannot leave *me* to pursue *him.*"

Bronwyn resolutely kept her gaze fixed on the captain, a

smile upon the ripe curve of her lips. " 'Tis precisely what I intend to do." She untied her chemise a little more, casting Rowan an arch glance.

But Baldassare was not a man of honor and Rowan knew it well. Neither was Rowan, at least by his own claims, but that seemed of less import in this moment. The ship rolled beneath his feet, but he gritted his teeth and fought back a wave of nausea, knowing only that he had to keep Bronwyn from doing something foolish.

Again.

Rowan stepped into her path and seized her shoulders in his grip, forcing her to meet his gaze. The determination he found in her eyes stunned him. "You cannot go to him! You know he is not a man of merit."

"I thought you were a man of merit, though now I know better." She shrugged. "It seems my perceptions go awry. And what does it matter in the end? I have naught to lose by coupling with as many men as I might desire." Bronwyn smiled up at him. "Is pleasure not the only thing that can be relied upon?"

"You cannot believe that!"

"Can I not?" Her eyes were as bright as a cat's, her expression one that dared him to prove her wrong.

But her argument was too close to his own thinking for Rowan to summon an argument against it. "He will take advantage of you."

Bronwyn tilted her head to regard him, her own filled with that mingled intelligence and spirit he found so beguiling. "As you would not?" she scoffed. "Tell me what other reason is there for you to compel me to remain by your side for another year? You mean to trick me at some point into wedding you so you can win your cursed dare. Why else would you want me to remain?"

Her tone pricked at Rowan's pride, her gaze locked with

his own. He sensed that she would urge him to claim something other than what he knew to be the truth, some false reliance upon her presence, some need to have her by his side.

But that was nonsense.

"I would merely hold you to your sworn word," he insisted, and the lady's gaze flickered before she looked away.

Her lips tightened to a grim line. "Then I will break it. I am told—by a knight, no less—that it is not a matter of import."

"Ibernia!" Rowan shoved a hand through his hair in frustration. "Bronwyn," he growled. "What makes you imagine that Baldassare will make a pledge of love to you?"

"Ah, but there is your error," she said, sadness clouding her eyes. "There is something other than a pledge of love that I would have from Baldassare di Vilonte."

Rowan blinked at her, completely confused by her words. Why did she go to him, then? Was love not the sole thing she desired? He shook his head in confusion, but the lady abruptly gripped the hilt of his dagger.

"You did say I might borrow this," she reminded him, and moved the dagger into her own belt before he could protest.

Rowan frowned but the captain called again and the ship changed course once more. Immediately their passage became rougher, the waves breaking against the hull with shuddering blows.

The bottom dropped out of Rowan's gut just as Bronwyn brushed past him. He would have called after her, but he made the mistake of looking to the sea.

The waves swirled and tossed, their rhythm nearly enough to make him lose his footing. He seized the rail and surrendered the contents of his belly, shuddering as he leaned his brow against the wet wood.

By the time he turned to lend chase, Bronwyn and Baldassare were too absorbed in each other's company for his taste.

It had seemed like a good idea at the time.

Bronwyn realized belatedly that that could have been the theme for much of her life and certainly all of her choices in the past sixmonth. All the same, she kept walking toward Baldassare, holding his gleaming gaze, unwilling to back down from her course.

She knew what she had to do. Indeed, when she was feeling murderous, it had seemed good sense to put the impulse to throttle Rowan to better use.

She fingered the hilt of Rowan's dagger, overly aware of its unfamiliar weight in her belt. Indeed, she would not have minded if he came after her in this moment and halted her impulsive course, though she would never have told him as much.

But there was no sound of Rowan giving chase. She glanced back quickly and noted that he was bent over the rails. Compassion unexpectedly shot through her, but Bronwyn steeled herself against it.

Nay, she knew the manner of man Rowan was—he had made the truth more than clear—and she was clearly best without him.

Which meant she must solve her own problems, including this one.

Bronwyn summoned what she hoped was an alluring smile for Baldassare and stepped closer, half certain the man could read her every thought. "Good morning."

"Good morning, *ma bella.*" He bowed deeply, the wind tossing his dark hair and crisply white shirt sleeves. He was indeed a handsome man, though there was a chill in his eyes that unsettled Bronwyn.

When he smiled, there was no answering warmth in those dark eyes. His gaze dropped to the slight display of her cleavage and his smile broadened, the change making him look even more predatory. "Dare I hope that you have pondered my question?"

"Your question?"

"Aye, about Niccolo." Baldassare studied Bronwyn as her heart hammered in her throat, then shook his head as if saddened. "Perhaps 'tis too much to hope that we might be reunited after all these years. I so hoped to see him again, for 'tis not often a man has a chance to relive old times. Perhaps another in Dublin can aid me in this quest."

Anger rose hot in Bronwyn's throat and she knew he would see the evidence of it in her eyes. Mercifully, a crewman called, his foreign speech readily comprehensible to her.

"Captain! The wind takes us too close to the shore!"

"Nay, there is naught to fear," Baldassare called. "My chart insists there are no shoals in these waters. As long as we remain clear of the coast itself, all shall be well." He waved to the crewman. "Hold our course!"

"Is something amiss?" Ibernia asked as if she had not understood.

Baldassare smiled and cupped her jaw with one of his hands. She forced herself to endure the gesture, knowing that 'twould infuriate Rowan if he saw it. "Nay, *ma bella,*" he murmured. "There is naught that you need to fear. I am a man who can be relied upon to finish what he has begun."

Bronwyn forced a smile, trying to hide her fearful response to his obvious reference. Aye, he would see her father killed and she knew it well. He was the one her father had tried to escape.

She had no choice.

First, she had to ensure they were alone, that there were no witnesses to her crime. Bronwyn could think of only one way to manage that deed.

She would worry about managing the crime later.

"Baldassare," she murmured. "There is something about your reassurance that makes a woman"—she sighed—"feel safe."

"Aye, *ma bella*? And what cause have you to feel unsafe?"

Bronwyn flicked a glance over her shoulder, noting that Rowan was straightening and looking no less grim than before. He turned his steps in their direction, his eyes dark, and she spun back to face the captain.

"My husband!" she whispered, trying to feign panic. "He is a man of great passions, and I fear I have vexed him overmuch. There is no place I might hide from his fury!"

Baldassare's eyes narrowed. "I saw you strike him."

"Aye, and he will have vengeance for that blow!" She knotted her hands together, relieved when the captain glared at Rowan and drew her behind him. "Oh, I had hoped he would be ill again, but he already recovers."

"You have no need to fear, *ma bella*. I will protect you."

Bronwyn flicked a glance in Rowan's direction, her heart taking a little skip at both his determined expression and his proximity. "If we could retire to your cabin, Baldassare, I should feel much safer."

The captain frowned, he eyed the sky. "I am not certain that 'tis a good time for such a course . . ." he began, but Bronwyn clutched his arm. She brushed her breast against his arm, but his smile turned rueful. *"Ma bella*, there is no time for such pleasures on this day . . ."

But Bronwyn was not about to surrender this chance. "I must tell you about Niccolo."

Baldassare's eyes blazed and she had his attention fully. "You know him?"

"Aye! I remember!"

It took no more than that to have Baldassare seize her arm and turn her toward the corridor to his cabin. He strode so quickly that Bronwyn had a hard time matching his pace, and she knew the moment was nigh upon her. The crew called again, but Baldassare waved off their fears. Rowan shouted, but the captain only increased his pace.

She gripped the hilt of the knife, steeling herself for what must be done. The deck began to pitch in a wild manner, the first drops of rain fell heavily on Bronwyn's cheeks. She spared a glance at the angry sky as a crewman cried a warning.

"Shoals! We will run aground!" roared a crewman, others shouting in the wake of his cry.

Baldassare spun in the shadow of the corridor. "Incompetent fools!" he cried. "I should never have relied upon these charts again!" He swore with a thoroughness unexpected and shoved Bronwyn aside. He might have returned to the deck, but Bronwyn seized the only chance she was likely to have.

She plunged the dagger into Baldassare's midriff, into the space between his leather hauberk and his chausses. 'Twas harder than she expected to do so, and the knife did not go deep.

But a great deal of blood flowed almost immediately. Baldassare cried out in pain, blanching. His eyes widened when he saw the blade. He swore and grabbed for her. Bronwyn stepped backward, and Baldassare lunged after her. A panicked Bronwyn turned to flee and ran directly into Rowan's chest.

Rowan quickly shoved her behind him and reached for his

sword. Bronwyn realized in the same moment as he that it was still in the cabin beyond.

Baldassare did not miss the omission either. He roared and lunged at the knight. The dagger fell from Baldassare's wound and danced across the floor as the men circled each other.

Baldassare dove for the knife. Rowan stepped on his hand. A bone crunched, the captain paled, and the dagger slid out of the way. The pair slipped and went down, each struggling for supremacy, rolling back and forth in the narrow space.

The knife scuttled out of their reach as the ship was tossed about the sea. Baldassare pounced on the dagger when the ship rocked again. When Rowan moved to deflect him, the captain came up with another knife.

Bronwyn gasped, for this blade must have been hidden on his person. Baldassare's blade caught Rowan across the thigh, a thin line of blood showing on the knight's dark chausses. Rowan kicked Baldassare's hand with a growl, the knife bounced down the hall out of range, and they circled anew.

The ship groaned, Bronwyn falling against the wall as the deck tipped. The dagger skidded toward her, Bronwyn scooped it up and watched the fight, trying to gauge where she could best lend her aid.

"I will kill that deceitful bitch!" Baldassare roared. He leapt for Rowan, and the pair struggled mightily before Rowan slammed the other man's head into the wooden walls. The captain sagged, Rowan leaned over him, but Baldassare's hands locked around the knight's neck with lightning speed.

"Nay!" Bronwyn cried, and leapt into the fray. She raised the dagger high and brought it down heavily into the captain's shoulder. The blade sunk deep this time and Baldassare caught his breath.

He cried out and fell backward, his eyes rolling closed so slowly that time seemed to have stopped.

He did not move. Bronwyn stood with shaking hands, the trembling spreading through her entirety as she watched the captain grow even more pale.

His blood flowed onto the deck with alarming speed.

Rowan gripped the wall and watched the other man bleed for a long moment, the rasp of his breath filling the corridor. The skies burst open and rain pounded on the deck beyond, flowing into the corridor and mingling with the captain's blood.

Rowan's golden gaze rose incredulously to hers and Bronwyn found herself backing away. "What seized your wits?" he demanded. "If you did not want the man to touch you, then you should not have taken matters so far as this."

Bronwyn bridled at his tone. "This was not because he meant to touch me!"

Rowan flung out a hand. "Oh, you simply thought it a good plan to murder the captain? Aye, none were likely to notice *that*! We shall have all of the republic hunting our sorry hides for this crime!" To her astonishment, he shouted at her. "Are you mad? Ye gods, Bronwyn of Ballyroyal, I thought you were a woman of some sense!"

Bronwyn folded her arms across her chest and glared at him. "He was going to murder my father. I had no choice."

Rowan stared at her, stunned to silence. He shoved a hand through his hair and swore with a thoroughness unexpected.

When he stepped toward her, his eyes were flashing so furiously that she flinched from his touch. "I suppose 'twould have been too much for you to simply tell me the truth."

"Aye, 'twould have." She flung out a hand. "What would you have cared for the *obligations* of my blood?"

Rowan opened his mouth, no doubt to make an angry

retort, but the sudden groan of ship stole his words away. The vessel lurched and shook from stem to stern, its unexpected halt throwing them both against one wall.

There was a sound of shattering wood, then the crewmen shouted to each other. The ship trembled mightily, waves thundered against the hull. Far below, the trapped slaves began to scream, and rushing water could be heard echoing in the hold.

And a destrier whinnied in terror just before he began to kick with resounding rhythm.

They had run aground.

"Are you injured?" Rowan demanded.

"Nay." Bronwyn felt overwhelmed by all that had just transpired.

"Can you swim?"

"I do not know."

The knight cast her a grin that was less cocky than usual but still managed to reassure her. "Well, *ma demoiselle,* I suspect we shall shortly find out. Fortunately for both of us, I can." Then he stepped onto the chaos of the deck and shouted. "Thomas!"

# Chapter Thirteen

OR A DAY THAT HAD BEGUN WELL ENOUGH, THIS ONE
seemed intent on abandoning any promise at all.
Indeed, Rowan heartily doubted he would survive it.

He could hear an infuriated Troubador wreaking havoc
belowdecks and did not dare to imagine what that beast
might accomplish before he got to the steed's side. At least
Baldassare would be unable to take issue with the damage.

Rowan refused to think about what had just happened,
much less what he might do to set matters to rights.

First matters first.

To Rowan's relief, they were not far from shore. A glance
revealed that the ship had run aground on a rocky shoal. If
the waves had not been whipped so high by the commencing
storm, the ship might have perched there long enough to
allow all to disembark.

As it was, the vessel creaked ominously and there was no
telling when 'twould plunge into the sea.

Or shatter to a thousand pieces. The sea churned angrily,
and Rowan already guessed that Dame Fortune had abandoned him the moment he accepted his brothers' dare.

With the exception of finding Bronwyn. He could not
think about that either, nor the wave of protectiveness that

had so caught him unawares. There was proof that responsibilities were trouble!

And Bronwyn was trouble unrivalled.

Thomas came quickly, his manner sober. Marika was right behind him, her eyes wide in fear. She cringed with every shout from below, and Rowan realized that she might have friends or family still in the hold. Bronwyn cast him an appealing glance and he knew well enough what her expectation was.

He reminded himself that if he saved her from this disaster, he could have the pleasure of killing her himself. Murdering the captain! And distracting that man when they were so close to shore. Had he ever witnessed such foolery?

Even if for a noble cause. His heart twisted that she would take such a risk out of love for her father, then he forced such consideration from his thoughts.

Indeed, there was no time for it now.

"Take Marika and Thomas with you and make for the shore as best you are able," he bade Bronwyn. "I will try to free steeds and slaves."

She balked, as he should have expected. "I will not!"

"Is naught ever simple with you?" Rowan flung out his hands as the ship creaked and tipped a little farther into the sea. "I but request you save your hide!"

"And I but insist that we shall all be saved together."

"Or, more like, all die together."

"I will not leave you here to die alone."

"You have no choice! I entrust you to see these two safe, and as a woman who welcomes responsibility, you should be delighted to ensure their welfare."

Even with that, she hesitated, though Rowan could not imagine why. Surely she could not desire to die? "There is an opportunity to get yourself onto the shoal and thus make the shore, even if you cannot swim."

Before the lady could protest further, Rowan caught her chin in his hand. "Go, Bronwyn, or I truly shall believe you are witless!" Her eyes flashed and he kissed her quickly, striding away before she chose to discuss the matter further.

For there was no time to argue. Rowan cut a quick path to the hatchway, threw it back, and nearly stumbled at the stench of terrified horse.

And terrified human. A pungent blending of sweat and fear and excrement assaulted Rowan, the pulse of rain doing naught to aid matters. Troubador evidently saw the light above—or Rowan's silhouette—for he snorted and kicked with new vigor. His rear hooves slammed against the hull of the ship and wood splintered noisily. The palfrey whinnied, her feet stamping a staccato as she took the destrier's foul mood.

Before Rowan could descend, Troubador snapped at his tether with vigor and the bolt to which his reins were secured was ripped right from the wall. The bolt clung to the reins, moving with vigor each time the destrier tossed his head. The bolt flew around the small space, threatening to dislodge an eye.

Better and better. Rowan gritted his teeth, not surprised the frightened beast did naught to aid in his own survival. The destrier was strong and more clever than most.

Except when he was afraid. Then there was no reasoning with him, nor even any way of swaying his conviction in whatever madness he took to mind. On this day, clearly the beast had decided to fight his way free.

Rowan hoped that neither of them was injured in the attempt. He threw an arm over his face and made his way to the side of the ship that had been closed behind the horses to make the exterior of the ship. The tipping of the vessel had left this side slightly skyward and Rowan's fingers worked madly as he sought the seal.

Troubador frothed. The bolt caught Rowan once in the back of the shoulder. He winced at the brutal sting but knew there was naught that could calm the steed.

Naught but freedom. Seawater pooled in the far corner. Troubador began to snort and stamp that his feet were in the chill water. That was no good reminder to this beast that did not favor the sea.

The palfrey screamed and shook, her frenzied cries nearly shattering Rowan's ears. The slaves cried for mercy in an incoherent babble for which Rowan needed no knowledge of foreign tongues to understand.

If he had had any wits, he would have fled and seen to his own safety. But Rowan scrabbled at the edge of the door. Too late he realized that it was nailed from the outside and he could not open the hatch by himself.

Troubador raged and kicked again, Rowan just barely escaping the impact of those flying feet. He pressed himself back into the corner, watching as the beast kicked again and again and again, evidently recalling even in his fear how he had come to be trapped in this place.

And the wood was beginning to fall prey to the stallion's assault. Rowan cringed back into the corner, hoping against hope that the beast could achieve what he could not.

'Twas then that he saw the key. It hung from a hook, dangling just above his head, in a corner that would be out of sight when all was at rights. Rowan seized it, guessing its purpose immediately, and fell upon the lock that secured the slaves in the hold.

He had no sooner turned the key than the base of the gangplank shattered beneath the destrier's assault. The rain slanted in coldly, the sea rushed in to swirl around his feet.

A trio of bedraggled men raced out of the confining hold, their eyes wide with fear. They headed directly for the light and put their shoulders to the broken wood, so fearful that they were oblivious to the panicked horse. The infuriated destrier shoved his way through them, intent on reaching freedom as soon as the hatch fell open, the palfrey immediately behind him.

Rowan found Bronwyn unexpectedly by his side. He had no time to chastise her before she plunged into the bowels of the ship, her questions flying quickly in a succession of languages.

He would not admit that her ability was of any aid.

"Bronwyn! The ship is easing free of the shoal! You must flee." Rowan lent chase, only to have the lady in question press a child into his arms.

"We cannot abandon them," she chided, undeterred by his displeasure. "Quickly, Rowan. Many have not the strength to walk."

She spoke aright. Rowan blinked as she faded into the shadows and the babe in his arms began to cry. He was achingly aware of the unsteady rhythm of the ship and did not trust it to hold its place for long.

Which meant only that they must hasten.

A man spoke to him from behind. Rowan turned and passed the child. He won a grateful smile that settled around his heart with a glow.

"Hurry!" Rowan cried, the rushing water now past his knees.

They settled into a rhythm quickly, each able-bodied slave coming free of the hold as quickly as possible. To Rowan's relief, none here was shackled, the security of the hold apparently deemed sufficient.

But there were so many of them and they were so weakened by what they had endured. His heart clenched as he lost sight of Bronwyn yet again.

As if in echo of Rowan's thoughts, the ship gave a shuddering moan. "We must be gone," Rowan cried.

"I heard a moan," she insisted, her voice distant.

Rowan rolled his eyes and dove into the darkness in pursuit. 'Twas dark as pitch within and the smell was enough to turn his belly again. The water had joined with countless other substances here to make a mire that now rose to his waist. Something bumped against his leg and he feared it was too late already for many here.

The ship began to creak loudly.

And he did not know where the lady was.

"Bronwyn!"

"Here!" Rowan reached back and found her hand in the same instant that the ship shuddered and creaked ominously. There came a shout from overhead and Bronwyn cried out.

The ship was slipping off the shoal!

Rowan recognized a last chance when he saw it. They would never survive if the ship sank with them in its belly. He caught Bronwyn in his arms and lunged for the light. The seawater suddenly rushed against them in an angry grey torrent, keeping them from the portal. Bronwyn clung to his neck and Rowan snatched at the wooden frame, fighting with all his might to see them free.

'Twould not be his fault if Bronwyn died trying to save the lives of strangers.

For a man disenchanted with responsibility, Rowan de Montvieux showed a remarkable drive to ensure all who were his responsibility—and a great many who were not—lived to tell of this day. Bronwyn was astonished by his determination, no less by his strength.

And she was grateful for it. After his confession, she had not been certain that he would aid the slaves in escaping, but he had already released them when she arrived in the hold.

She could not blame him for not guessing their sorry

state. 'Twould be beyond his experience to know the circumstance of slaves.

But Bronwyn knew all too well. Rowan's shocked expression and his grim resolve once he witnessed the truth told her that she had called the matter aright.

When the wave rolled through the portal, Bronwyn was glad that she knew the truth about his character, even if that was the last thing she would ever learn.

But Rowan was not so inclined to cede defeat. Bronwyn could never have moved so quickly as he did, even with her caught in his arms. Even as Rowan raced forward, she feared that she would keep him from surviving.

They reached the opening as the ship rolled into the sea and the cold water closed over them with a vengeance. Bronwyn knew they were lost forever beneath the silver waves, trapped within the maw of the sinking hold.

But Rowan grabbed the wooden frame and held fast as the ship rolled. He fairly shoved Bronwyn through the opening, and her heart leapt at the aqua gleam of salvation high overhead. Rowan kicked and urged her toward the surface.

'Twas far, much farther than she could have imagined, and she was not a swimmer by any definition. When she might have faltered, Rowan caught her beneath his arm and pulled them higher with bold strokes. Bronwyn's chest ached and she thought she would faint for lack of air, but she kicked valiantly, trying to aid his efforts to save them.

They broke the surface as one, gasping with painful vigor. Rowan's arm still locked around her waist, holding her afloat.

They both gulped greedily of fresh air and Bronwyn trembled in the wake of their escape. She had never been so glad to feel rain on her face as she was in that moment. She felt Rowan's muscles move so close against her own and realized he was keeping them both afloat.

"I can manage this," she insisted, not wanting to be more of a burden than she already was. Bronwyn moved her arms in mimicry of his movements, and Rowan released her with a nod.

Bronwyn had a moment to gasp in alarm before she sank like a stone. Rowan dove after her, his arm locking around her waist with resolve as he hauled her again to the surface.

"You cannot swim," he declared through gritted teeth.

"I could not know until I tried," she answered, trying to lighten the mood. Rowan flicked a glance her way and she smiled. "Thank you."

Rowan averted his gaze quickly, though it might only have been because of more pressing matters at hand. He moved through the water with surety and an elegance she envied, then hauled her to an outcropping of rock.

"Hold on here," he instructed, and Bronwyn gripped the stone. It was a rocky tip of the shoal that had claimed the ship. Through the mist of the rain, she saw others clinging to rock as they could, a few heads in the distance, and—praise be!—many standing upon a shore that was not too distant. Bronwyn nearly wept in her relief.

Bronwyn looked over her shoulder, her heart clenching at the ship's masts protruding from the sea. They were at a hard angle, the rest of the ship already hidden by the waves. She shivered at their close escape, not wanting to think about those who had not been so fortunate. She caught her breath when she realized Rowan had slipped away from her.

"Fool horse," he muttered, his brow dark. "Rest here a moment. The tide will not change so fast as that."

He swam with powerful strokes, cutting through the water, his chemise clinging to his muscles. Bronwyn looked beyond him to spy a pair of steeds, resolutely swimming in the wrong direction.

"Troubador!" Rowan shouted.

The destrier started, then swam on with increasing speed, the palfrey fast behind. Bronwyn knew enough of horses to see that the steed was terrified.

Which meant he would heed naught.

Rowan muttered something foul that even Bronwyn could hear, and she bit her finger as he ventured out farther in his steed's wake. "You fool creature!" he roared. "Are you so witless than you cannot even smell the shore?"

He swam after the horses with determination, though Bronwyn was dismayed by how far he went. Rowan plowed through the water and managed to seize the rein that trailed behind the horse. He gave it a tug.

"That way, you mad beast!" He tried to direct the steed back toward the shore.

The palfrey broke ranks with the larger stallion, her nose rising as she turned shoreward. Bronwyn breathed a sigh of relief that the horse had forgotten her fear long enough to smell the lush grass of Ireland.

But the destrier fought the bit and shied in the opposite direction. Knight and steed both slipped lower in the water as Bronwyn watched and chewed her lip in fear. The stallion began to swim in a broad arc, clearly a horse determined to swim until he could no more.

The horse would continue until he was so exhausted that he faltered and drowned, Bronwyn could see the truth. Indeed, if the destrier kept that course, that sinking would be inevitable.

The stallion whinnied indignation when he realized that the palfrey had left his side. That steed folded her ears back and swam steadily for the shore.

"That way!" Rowan bellowed in frustration, his voice fading slightly.

The destrier seemed oblivious to him, and, indeed, moved away from his voice as if frightened by the sound. Rowan swam after the beast when the rein pulled from his grip, but his strokes grew less powerful. Bronwyn straightened, knowing with sudden certainty that the knight swam too far.

He must be tiring. Rowan could not be lost trying to save a steed! Not after all he had done this day.

"Rowan!" she cried, her fingers clenching together. He turned, clearly alarmed by her cry, and a wave crashed right over his head.

She screamed his name as he disappeared from eyesight. The destrier redoubled his speed in the opposite direction. Bronwyn clung to the rock, though she could not leave this spot until she knew.

'Twas an eternity before Rowan broke the surface again, more pale than before. He shook out his hair, checked that she still was safe upon the rock, then looked after the steed. She could see his arms moving beneath the surface as he stared after the stubborn if misguided horse. When the knight turned back in her direction, his expression was grim.

He swam back to her, every stroke that brought him closer reassuring Bronwyn. She would not consider why she was worried for him. 'Twould just be the injustice of his not surviving a noble deed, no more than that. Though injustice could not have explained the relief that flooded through Bronwyn when Rowan's hand landed heavily on the rock beside her.

His expression was strained, and it was some commentary on his state that he accepted her aid in climbing on to the rock.

"Fool beast," he muttered, turning to stare after the creature again. He breathed so heavily that Bronwyn thought he must be exhausted beyond all.

"I thought you might not have the strength to swim back," she confessed without any intention of doing so.

Rowan looked at her quickly, his expression uncharacteristically serious. Then he winked merrily. "Ah, but you owe me a tale."

"What?" she demanded, incredulous at his manner.

"This morn we agreed to an exchange. I have yet to hear the tale that you promised to me."

"I am surprised you recall as much, after all of this," Bronwyn said crisply, and turned away. How could he make a jest at such a time as this?

"Oh, I may be a faithless wretch," Rowan countered cheerfully, "but I am not a man to miss out on a story I am due."

Bronwyn looked up in surprise. He grinned so broadly that she nearly smiled in turn. His hair clung to his brow, all dark and disorderly, and his skin was still pale.

There was a mischievous gleam in his eyes, though, and she was very glad to be by his side. Rowan was vibrantly alive, and she saw that he savored every challenge his life had cast his way. Naught seemed to halt his course and she found herself admiring him.

Something must have shown in her expression, for Rowan eyed her intently. The twinkle in his eyes faded to something that made Bronwyn's mouth go dry.

"I owe you thanks," she admitted softly. "I should never have survived without your aid."

Rowan shrugged as if he had done naught. "It seemed only fitting," he said lightly, "since so many others lived because of your aid." He flicked a playful finger across her chin and winked. "Incomparable."

Bronwyn did not know what to say to that. She felt her cheeks heat beneath Rowan's steady regard, then he studied the distance to the shore.

"We should hasten ourselves before we both are swept away."

Then Bronwyn recalled the blow he had taken. "Is the cut deep on your leg?"

Rowan shrugged. "It seems well enough. If naught else, the salt-water will have completely cleared the wound." He made a grimace that was too fierce by half, and Bronwyn laughed, though she knew that was why he had done it. "I shall live to seek my pleasure on another day, *ma demoiselle*. Now, come along, before you grow chilled."

There was naught to argue with in that.

The outcropping was a long shoal wrought of sand. The fact that it disappeared quickly beneath the waves was what had caused the ship's misfortune. From the location of the wreck and beyond, the shoal was hidden beneath the turbulent sea, but to the left, its arc could be clearly seen. It proved to be increasingly shallow, the other survivors having walked its length back to the shore.

They made their way toward the shore in silence, Bronwyn puzzling whether Rowan's concern was protective or merely polite. His salute left a warm glow in her belly that was not unwelcome, though she knew that Rowan sought naught from her beyond the victory her hand could give him.

She knew more than enough of Rowan de Montvieux's expectations and dreams, did she not? He had told her the truth. He might well be more nobly inclined than he cared to admit, he might hold emotion in greater esteem than he acknowledged, but his view of wedlock was abundantly clear. Aye, she was not the bride for him.

Even if the conclusion did hang on her heart like a leaden weight.

The rain, now gentled, fell on the unfamiliar beach, low cliffs adorned with verdant grass rising beyond. The air was sweet and warm, more strongly so with every step. Bronwyn was close to home and glad to be so.

But her jubilation was not matched by her companion's mood. Nay, Bronwyn did not miss the way Rowan periodically glanced back, frowning at the bobbing head of his destrier swimming determinedly for England's far shores.

"Do you think he has turned?" he asked finally, his eyes narrowed. "Perhaps he will follow the palfrey this time."

Bronwyn did not even trouble to look. Willful destriers— like knights—did not change their ways so readily as that. She took Rowan's hand silently and led him toward the shore, his sigh telling her that he knew the beast was lost. The palfrey had vanished into the distance and one could only hope she reached shore.

Bronwyn thought it a poor time to remind Rowan that 'twas his desire to live a life unfettered.

There were about forty survivors upon the shore, most of whom were exhausted by their most recent ordeal and weakened by their incarceration. Bronwyn could not fathom a guess as to how many had not made it to safety, though the grim expressions on many faces were eloquent. Bronwyn and Rowan were the last to reach the shore, and she noted disappointment on more than one face that no more followed.

For a man who did not welcome responsibility, Rowan had a natural tendency to lead. Every soul on that beach turned to him, and Bronwyn watched, marvelling, as he coaxed smiles from even the most despondent among them. Only one or two seamen had survived, and they had been quick to separate themselves from the others and disappear.

Clearly many of the slaves believed they owed their lives to Rowan, but the knight shrugged off their expressions of gratitude, giving credit instead to Bronwyn. He made a circuit of the survivors, coaxing smiles while he ensured that none were sorely wounded. 'Twas equally clear that he did not intend to abandon these people to whatever fate might find them.

Rowan only glanced once to the horizon as he strode back to Bronwyn, and she could not keep her unruly heart from skipping when his gaze locked with hers. He smiled that slow smile and her blood heated, though she dropped her gaze when he came to a halt beside her. His words fell low between them and it took Bronwyn a moment to realize that he sought her council.

"No one here is injured," he commented with a thoughtful frown. "Though they are tired and hungry. Do you think there is a village nearby?"

"I do not know where we are." Bronwyn scanned the length of the beach, the distance obscured by the misty rain. She raised her gaze to the hills that she could just glimpse rising high to the west and wondered if they were the Wicklow Mountains.

And if so, how far along that range's length they found themselves. "Though I assume we are to the south of Dublin yet. I smell no peat fire and see no easy course to where there might be a road above."

"In this weather, 'twould be tricky to climb."

"It could be a long walk to any sort of dwelling," Bronwyn supplied. "This coast bore the brunt of Strongbow's attack—though many died, many others simply left."

"Your family?"

She smiled thinly. "Live beyond Dublin and have too many powerful connections throughout Christendom to have been targeted for attack." She arched a brow. "We merchants are useful subjects."

Rowan considered her for a long moment, then glanced over the survivors. Most had huddled in the lee of the cliff and were for the better part out of the rain. Thomas had slumped against the shallow cliff, his eyes barely open, and Marika dozed beyond him.

" 'Tis not cold. I suppose 'twould hurt little to remain here for one night."

Bronwyn could only agree with him. This party had not the strength to go far, and at least here, they were out of the better part of the downpour.

"I think 'tis the best course. Even if the rain does not cease, all will be stronger on the morrow."

"Even you?" Rowan teased.

Bronwyn slanted a glance his way. "And what is that to mean?"

"I am not accustomed to you being so biddable," he declared with a wicked wink. "It must be a sign of exhaustion."

Bronwyn propped her hands on her hips. "As I recall, you were the one so intent on arguing! You were the one who called me witless."

He rolled his eyes. "And I was to congratulate you on the splendid good sense of killing the captain? You are fortunate, Bronwyn of Ballyroyal, nigh as lucky as I have been in all my days and nights, for the sinking of the *Angelica* has hidden your deed for all time."

The bile rose in Bronwyn's throat along with recollection of what she had done. "You know the truth of it," she acknowledged, needing some reassurance from him of his intent.

His sidelong glance was quick. "And you think I will use this against you?"

"Would you? If there was something to be gained for yourself?"

But Rowan scowled. "What manner of man do you think I am?"

"A man who prefers pleasure to responsibility," she echoed carefully, hoping against hope that he would prove her wrong. "Was that not what you told me of yourself?"

Rowan bent to study the wound on his thigh, but not so quickly that Bronwyn did not see his expression darken. "Well, I am not so shameless a cur as that," he said gruffly. "I will tell none of your deed, upon that you can rely." He impaled her with a quick glance. "But you will tell me the reason for it before our paths part. Surely that is not too much to ask."

"Nay, 'tis not," Bronwyn agreed simply, stunned by his offer to cover her crime. It was unexpectedly generous—and yet more unexpected that she did not doubt in the least that he would keep his word.

But then, her wits had been addled since this man showed her the pleasure his touch could bring. She watched his hands as he parted the cloth of his chausses, so focused on the gentle strength of his fingers and the recollection of them upon her that the blood surprised her.

Bronwyn felt a chill pass over her as she stared at the ribbon of red seeping from the long shallow wound. She could not tear her gaze away from the insistent trickle of blood.

She had murdered Baldassare.

Willfully. Deliberately. She had killed a man. Though she had done as much to save her father's life, still she was certain that this sin could never be absolved.

She would rot in hell for this.

"You should bind that," she said, her voice sounding unnatural even to her own ears. But she had to do something, she had to be rid of the sight of the blood. Her fingers trembled as she tore a length of cloth from the hem of her kirtle and faltered as she tried to tie it around Rowan's thigh.

"You do not need to do this," he protested, lifting her

hands away. He frowned down at her, the chill in her fingers apparently seizing his attention. " 'Tis not so bad a wound as that. Are you well?"

"I am well enough," she argued, feeling faint. Her gaze fell to the blood once more, the sight reminding her of how Baldassare had bled. He had fought her, fought Rowan, well aware of the stakes. He had not slipped into death unawares, not as quietly as she had hoped.

And that was all her fault. She could at least have killed him quickly and painlessly. Bronwyn swallowed in recollection of how his blood had mingled with the rain and been slick on the deck.

Were it not for the sea, she would have the captain's blood on her feet as well as her hands.

Bronwyn closed her eyes as the world cavorted around her and she felt her bile rise. Rowan caught her before she fell, and lay her in the minute shelter offered by the overhanging low cliff.

"What ails you?" he asked, with obvious concern. "Are you hurt?"

Bronwyn leaned her head back and kept her eyes closed, knowing that what troubled her would not cause a knight to turn a hair. After all, a knight made his living at war.

"Well?" Rowan prompted.

Bronwyn licked her lips. "I killed a man."

She felt Rowan studying her, then he eased down beside her. He did not touch her, though she could feel his warmth. "And this sickens you?"

"Aye."

"It seems a most natural response," he conceded unexpectedly. " 'Twould be more troubling if you enjoyed the deed."

Bronwyn opened her eyes and looked at his profile. "Have you ever killed a man?"

Rowan seemed to find this amusing. He smiled and shook his head, bending his attention on binding his thigh. "I? Never. You forget that I avoid all unpleasantries with diligence. Murder is, after all, somewhat unpleasant."

Bronwyn sat up to study him. "But you must have gone to war. You are a knight, after all."

"I have not." He grinned, as if proud of his achievement. "I always found an excuse, when Margaux would have put me to work, and truly I believe she tired of the game."

"Because you did not wish to labor at all?"

He met her gaze steadily. "Because I did not wish to kill, regardless of who endorsed the matter." He shrugged and looked to the sea again. "It seems there is no shortage of men anxious to kill others to win their own advantage."

"Including your father?"

Rowan snorted. "He kills enough for an army. I told you I was not of his ilk." Before Bronwyn could ask anything, he turned a bright gaze upon her. "And what of your father? You said you did this deed for him. What is his tale?"

" 'Tis part of the tale you are owed."

"Aye, and I would collect while I can." Rowan smiled, though Bronwyn was not encouraged by the reminder that their paths would soon part.

Aye, he would seek another heiress, one more wealthy, one more biddable, one perhaps more incomparable. Bronwyn did not cherish the thought.

She drew her knees up beneath her chin, her gaze dancing over the others who had managed to reach the beach. The rain fell in a gentle, incessant patter, and the sea rolled in fathomless grey. Debris from the broken ship could be spotted periodically, then it disappeared again.

She was in no rush to hasten away from this place, nor indeed from Rowan's side. She told herself that was only because she was tired but admitted in her heart that was a lie.

Bronwyn pleated the wool of her kirtle between her fingers, feeling how the salt was drying in the weave. 'Twould be stiff later, of that she had no doubt.

"You said that Baldassare wanted to kill your father," Rowan prompted. "Why? Did they know each other?"

"Perhaps, once," Bronwyn admitted. She shivered and did not protest when Rowan slid his arm across her shoulders. Its weight was welcome, his presence beside her comforting. She took a deep breath and decided 'twas past time she told him what she did know.

"My father's name was Niccolo, at least before he came to these shores. He was a Venetian trader, a captain known for his skill in making new discoveries and ensuring his voyages made profits for his investors. He always saved the finest wares for his home port and was a man of wealth and repute there. He was called the Falcon, for his sharp eye and his ability to drive a hard bargain."

"How did your father come from Venice to here?"

Bronwyn smiled. "He met my mother. She says he tried to cheat her, by paying less for her wool roving than its worth. He insists that he wanted only to draw out the negotiation to ensure that they spent more time together."

She focused on her fingers busily pleating her kirtle and missed Rowan's rueful smile.

"And they fell in love. My mother would not abandon her family, so my father offered her passage on his ship. He wooed her all the way to Dublin, though she insists they went by way of the Atlantic. He says that was only because she was too stubborn to admit the truth."

She glanced up to find Rowan smiling slightly. "They sound well matched."

"Indeed, they are still smitten with each other, and these

differences of opinion oft end with much laughter from their chamber.''

"So, Niccolo courted her, and he won her.'' Rowan pursed his lips. "But why would a Venetian find himself so far north? 'Tis not common now and could only have been less common twenty years past.''

Bronwyn focused on the wool between her fingers. "My father was fleeing an enemy.'' She felt Rowan's gaze upon her and did not need his question to be prompted to continue. "Once upon a time, before my father left Venice, he had a trusted partner. They two had roved many a sea together, found many a new opportunity, and made a tidy living at their trade.

" 'Twas my father who charted their course, listening as he did to rumor and intuition. He oft declared that he wished he had not heard the tale of a distant port where gold could be traded for salt. He and his partner agreed they would make this their next destination, and salt they loaded aplenty. They found the port and 'twas exactly as rumored. They were the first Venetians ever to visit, perhaps the first from Christendom, and the gold was of such quantity that the eyes of all the crew widened.

"The voyage went awry from that point, my father said the gold made his partner turn mad. He could not have enough of it. He swears his partner would have loaded enough to sink the ship like a stone. They argued heatedly, for the first time in all their days together, and in the end, their men drew sides. There was much bloodshed and many good men died before the ship had even left the harbor, including the partner who had so changed. In the interest of security, his discontented followers were put ashore, against their will, and abandoned in this foreign port.

"My father returned home to acclaim, but what he had witnessed weighed heavily upon his heart. He doubted that he could ever trust another fully, for he had shared so much with his partner, only for their companionship to come to ruin in the end. He had no desire to return to this port of gold. In fact, he wished never to set sail again, but his patrons insisted otherwise.

"My father's investors would not outfit his ship without his pledge to return to the golden city, and my father refused to return or reveal its location. I think he believed the place itself was cursed and a source of wickedness, for naught else, to his thinking, could have turned such good friends against each other."

"What was the partner's name?"

" 'Twas forbidden to utter his name in our home, so great was my father's heartache." Bronwyn shrugged. "At any rate, my father lingered in port too long. Word came that the rebels were making their way back to Venice, with vengeance hot in their words. My father decided he would not wait to hear their false accusations. If he could not leave with a ship, he would leave on foot. A trusted servant accompanied him.

"My father left his homeland. He left all he knew. He travelled north with naught more than he could carry, wanting only to put distance between himself and the lust for gold that made men mad." She granted Rowan a smile. "Eventually, he reached the North Sea and his yearning for the sea reclaimed him. He and this servant who had become his friend worked on ships, and though my father told no tale of his past, his skills saw him quickly promoted."

"And then he met your mother?"

"Aye. And when he won her, he changed his name, for he could not bear that she should undertake the burden of his past. Always in the back of his thoughts was the fear that his partner was not truly dead—he mentioned once that the man had a son who had been on that fateful voyage.

"My father promoted this servant and friend to captain in his own stead and made a new life for himself in Ireland. Eventually his friend returned to his side and tempted him into a new partnership. My father missed his trade and his travel, though now he only invests in his new partner's journeys."

Rowan looked surprised. "But he loved the sea, you said yourself."

"Aye, but he feared for my mother—and later for me—if he was recognized."

Rowan frowned, as if he could not imagine making such a choice.

" 'Tis the power of love to sacrifice what you hold of import to see another safe, or happy," Bronwyn insisted, seeing in Rowan's eyes that he knew naught of such power.

Nor even of such love.

Her heart cringed a little for that small boy and all he had lost when his mother died so suddenly. Her gaze fell to the ring glinting on his hand as she realized that one twist of faith had shaken that child's conviction that he was lovable.

And this was the crux of the matter. That boy had learned a telling lesson, that he should never treasure anything, that he should expect naught for himself, that he was of no merit to those around him.

The man he had become clung to that lesson as if 'twere the only certainty upon which he could rely. Rowan feigned indifference to all so that he might readily care for naught— or that he might *pretend* to care for naught.

But the truth might be that he cared too much. Bronwyn's heart leapt to her throat at the prospect.

"And love is why you had to stop Baldassare?"

Bronwyn met Rowan's gaze steadily, seeing the question that lurked in those amber depths. He truly did not understand. Once she saw the truth of it, she could not hold his gaze. Bronwyn looked away, feeling suddenly more fortunate in having known her parents' love than she ever had before.

She would not torment Rowan with fond recollections of a childhood so very different from his own.

"My parents are happy," she said quietly. "My father is a good-hearted man, and I believe the tale as I have been told it. Baldassare could be none other than that partner's son. When he declared that he sought my father and called him by his Venetian name, I knew the truth of it, I saw the wild hatred in his eyes. I could not have stood by and done naught."

"You would protect your father from such a threat, regardless of the risk to yourself, without another thought?" Rowan gripped her shoulder, his touch prompting her to turn. "How could you put your own welfare aside? You could have been killed!"

He leaned closer, the flash of fear in his eyes taking Bronwyn by surprise. "Baldassare was not a weak man, not by any means. What if he had turned upon you? Or what if the ship had not sunk? His crew would have taken compense for his loss from your very hide."

Bronwyn blinked and swallowed. "I had not considered the risk, and even if I had, 'twould not have stayed my course."

He watched her so long that she wondered whether he had been struck dumb. Then he tilted his head, regarding her with narrowed eyes so that she could not discern his thoughts.

"Just as you did not consider the risk when you fled your parents' home?"

Bronwyn felt suddenly like a willful child, determined to see her way alone. He must think her foolish indeed! "I suppose I have been impulsive in my time."

Rowan chuckled and she looked up in surprise. "Impulsive is the least of it! I have never met a woman so persuaded that she can set matters to rights as you are."

Bronwyn felt her cheeks heat, though she lifted her chin proudly. "I was taught that a woman could achieve all that a man might, if she but had the will to try."

"And you have the will?" he asked, the glow in his eyes making Bronwyn's heart pound.

"Aye. Aye, I do."

Rowan smiled. "Incomparable," he whispered, then brushed his lips across hers, leaving a burning tingle in the wake of his touch.

Bronwyn looked back to the sea, stunned by the wave of desire that swept through her, and pulled free of the welcome weight of his arm. She knew she should not encourage this man's touch, knew she should not rely upon him, knew she should not let herself be seduced.

But she also knew that she loved him.

The realization stole her breath away and left her blinking blindly at the rhythmic lull of the sea. She loved Rowan, a man who knew little of love, who did not trust love, who did not hold love—as she did—in greatest esteem.

'Twas foolish, more foolish perhaps than anything she yet had done, but Bronwyn could not deny the simple truth of it.

Nor did she know what to do about it.

The silence stretched between them and Bronwyn grew certain that Rowan had drifted off to sleep. Indeed, the man had earned a rest, and she was tempted to slumber herself.

So, when Rowan finally spoke, his low words startled her. "I would have a promise from you, Bronwyn of Ballyroyal."

She looked back to find his gaze dangerously bright and not sleepy in the least. "What is that?"

"That you will confide in me, from this moment until our paths part, instead of resolving matters yourself."

Bronwyn's mouth went dry. "Why?"

He smiled then with his usual confident air, when a sweet confession might have changed all. "Because I would not want to reckon with your father, if you arrived home in worse condition than you are now."

"You are not returning home with me!"

But Rowan shook a playful finger at her. "A year and a day, my lady. We have a wager, and I shall hold you to it."

She did not have it in her to ask why.

Indeed, Bronwyn feared that if she did, he would tell her a truth that she did not want to hear. She might be no more than the spoils of a wager to Rowan, he might well walk away a year hence as if there had been naught between them, she might have to watch him win another heiress for his own.

But she would not compel him to tell her as much. She folded her arms across her knees and watched the waves rise and fall, achingly aware of the man behind her.

Perhaps Rowan was wrong about himself. Perhaps he knew more of love than he would admit. Perhaps he secretly yearned for love yet did not know how to pursue it. Bronwyn closed her eyes and found the image of a young Rowan in her mind.

'Twas all she needed to chart her course. Aye, if Rowan showed any hint that he was coming to hold love in esteem, if there was any indication that he was prepared to abandon what path he had taken through his life thus far, she would aid him. Bronwyn would step forward and show Rowan the way, for clearly he had no way of finding his path himself.

She knew enough of love to know that one could not force another to love in return, but she could show Rowan the prize he had been missing.

'Twas no more than he had done for her, when he dismissed her fear of lovemaking.

Bronwyn waited, hopeful and silent, but Rowan said naught more. The light changed as the sun moved, the shadows drew long, and when she finally dared to glance back, he was asleep.

# Chapter Fourteen

OWAN WATCHED THE SUN RISE THE NEXT MORNING, HIS mood grim. He should have been pleased and he knew it well. He had achieved his lifelong objective, and that with scarcely any effort on his part. He had naught to his name, no steed, no hauberk, no blade, no coin, not even a saddlebag or a cloak to call his own. He had naught but the garb upon his back.

And he had no decent prospect of changing that state.

'Twas precisely what Rowan had always desired, or so he had long told himself, but the achievement was less than satisfactory.

Aye, he could not help but think of his lost cloak when he saw Bronwyn shiver in her sleep. He could not help but think of those two lost gold coins and how much bread they would have bought for all these hungry captives, now freed upon a foreign shore.

He would not fret over how he might fulfill his obligation to Thomas, nor even how he might see Bronwyn safely home without coin or blade. He certainly would not think of that great destrier swimming valiantly in the wrong direction, nor indeed that he would miss the fool creature.

The cut upon Rowan's thigh burned like hellfire, teaching him the agony of salt pressed into a wound, but he ignored that as well. He struggled to be unaware of Bronwyn, sleeping beside him, though it was difficult not to steal the occasional glance at her, her lovely features so soft in sleep.

But she was not so soft as that. He knew now what she expected of marriage, of men, of the life before her. He knew she demanded more than he could ever give and that she would never compromise. Rowan knew he was not the man for her.

He was not prepared for how irksome that realization was. Indeed, he was unaccountably restless as the sun pinkened the sky and turned the sea to glittering glass. He was irritable and anxious to be on his way.

Wherever he was going.

'Twas impatience, no more than that, impatience with the obligation he felt himself to have to all these slumbering souls. Rowan pushed to his feet, careful not to wake any around him, and set out to pace. The beach was long and narrow, the gentle lapping of waves luring his footsteps closer.

The sky had cleared over the night, and the rain had stopped. The air was fresh and clean, tinged with the salt of the sea, yet also with the verdant scent of rich grass. Rowan walked along the lip of the sea, marvelling that it could look so harmless after all that had happened the day before. He checked the summit of the cliffs and still saw no hint of hut or fire.

It might be days of walking before they found a hearth, let alone that of one inclined to grant alms. Rowan remembered all too well the skepticism of the locals when he set out on Brianna of Tullymullagh's bride quest nigh a year past. They were dubious of foreigners, and fairly so, given the invasions this land had recently weathered.

But Rowan was already cursedly hungry, though he supposed he was not alone in that. He also was not alone in looking more like a beggar than a knight, a fact that would do little to aid his cause.

Rowan ambled close to the lapping waves, letting the water slap over his boots and telling himself to appreciate the lack of burdens he bore, even if that was more challenging to do than he might have expected.

The tide was retreating, leaving a line of debris upon the beach that he was not interested in studying. Rowan thought of Bronwyn as he walked, the spirit in her eyes and the valor that made her risk her own life to see others safe. Ye gods, the woman could not even swim and she ventured into the hold of a ship to help strangers.

Rowan kicked at the sand and decided that he would see her home, if only to ensure that she had no further misadventures.

'Twas only good sense, no' more than that. Perhaps Bronwyn's father would introduce him to another heiress, though Rowan had to admit that he had little taste for his brothers' quest any longer. That was surely why the prospect did little to improve his spirits.

Better yet, perhaps he would find again that travelling troupe of entertainers, the ones he had sent to Tullymullagh to coax a princess's laughter, and join their ranks. Was that not the fate he had oft longed for? To join a troupe, to travel wherever his footsteps turned, in the way he had known as a child.

Of course. Rowan could juggle reasonably well, and he had been known to coax a laugh or two in his time. Perhaps Bronwyn's father would see to Thomas's return home and remove the last obligation that rested upon Rowan's shoulders. Aye, the prospect of disappointing Thomas alone stood in the way of his enthusiasm for this course.

Rowan's stomach grumbled and he recalled only now how often he had been hungry as a boy.

And cold.

Frightened and uncertain.

Not that any of that was of import, for a man with his wits about him could ensure he had a hot meal once in a while. A child was prey to the whims of those around him. Indeed, 'twould be good not to set foot upon a ship anytime soon. Rowan should be relieved to be here, alive and in possession of an opportunity to make his life what he would.

Then why did his footsteps feel leaden? Lack of sleep, he reasoned, lack of a hot meal, exhaustion in the wake of an ordeal. No more than that. He would soon feel hale again.

Rowan deliberately lifted his chin and strode down the beach, rounding a little jut of land. He took a deep invigorating breath of the morning air, told himself he was happy and let the sun fall on his face.

It did not work, so he tried harder.

So engrossed was Rowan in his efforts that he tripped over the debris on the beach before he saw it. He frowned and turned to give whatever had tripped him up a hearty kick, sending it back to the sea and venting his annoyance with his own dour mood, but one glance stopped his foot.

Rowan halted and stared at his own saddle.

His own caparisons still clung to it, though the silk was shredded and part of the length was gone. The sea gently wafted around the saddle, the silk billowing as the water advanced, then falling flat against the sand as each wave retreated.

Rowan bent to run a hand over the curve of its seat. The leather had come from Milan, the saddle itself had been fashioned near Montvieux. It had been a gift from his foster mother when he won his spurs, a gift to match the destrier that she also granted him.

It had been a gift he knew he did not deserve, just as he had not deserved those spurs. Nay, he had jested his way through the bulk of his training and played practical jokes on all the household. He had tried everything once, bested every dare, astounded his patron's household with his audacity time and again.

Rowan had been severely reprimanded by his patron more than once, that man apparently being the only soul in Christendom immune to Rowan's charm. Aye, the old cook had chided him before the others, as had the marshall, though both indulged Rowan when he was alone.

'Twas typical of all of Rowan's life—a jest and a smile always set the worst crimes to rights.

His patron had argued with his foster mother, refusing to knight Rowan, though Rowan had shown the old cur wrong in the final accounting. Rowan had excelled at the test devised to prove his incompetence, not because he deeply desired to be a knight, not because he cared for his patron's respect, but because he dearly wanted to prove that man wrong.

He had not been prepared for Margaux's pride—nor, indeed, his own rush of pride in her display of affection. His foster mother showed her feelings not with gesture or word but with the opening of her purse, and the treasury of Montvieux had yawned wide on the day Rowan had been granted his spurs.

Rowan bowed his head in recollection and crouched down beside the saddle. He ran his hand across the leather, now worn smooth in places, wet from the sea and encrusted with salt. In his mind's eye, he saw a younger version of Troubador, a wild glint in his eye and a rakish white star on his brow.

And one white sock. Rowan smiled and shook his head. How had Margaux known that only the most feisty stallion in her stables would do? How had she guessed that the steed's unruly nature would meld so well with Rowan's own? How had she guessed that racing on this beast's back, his knees gripping tight and the wind in his hair, would become Rowan's greatest pleasure?

Here he thought he was unpredictable, but it seemed his foster mother knew him overly well.

Rowan lifted his head and looked out across the shimmering sea, knowing he should not. The water danced beneath the sunlight, unmarred as far as the eye could see.

This part of his life was over and Rowan knew it well. He would never be so indulged again. He told himself not to mourn what was lost, reminded himself that he had never truly wanted it anyway.

Even if the loss did sting.

Rowan turned away from the sea and his memories, only to find Bronwyn lingering behind him.

Her hem was torn high and revealed her bare feet in the cool of the sea. Her kirtle was wrinkled, its hue somewhat less than the fine blue it had only recently been. Her skin was dirty again, her eyes yet as vibrantly blue as when first they met.

His heart clenched once, hard, at the sight of her.

Bronwyn gestured aimlessly with one hand. "I did not want to disturb your thoughts." Her gaze fell to the saddle and Rowan nudged it with his toe.

" 'Twas mine," he said, his voice unexpectedly hoarse. He offered her a smile that he knew was not as cavalier as he might have liked. "But I do not have need of it any longer."

Rowan looked away, ashamed to find tears rising, but Bronwyn came to his side. She laid a hand upon his arm and he had to glance into her eyes, though the compassion he found in those blue depths surprised him.

And then he could not look away. Why could this woman alone prompt him to abandon his own intent?

"I am sorry," Bronwyn whispered.

There was no pity in her manner, nor even any scorn for his weakness. Instead of moving away, as might have been his first choice, Rowan was tempted to linger by her side.

" 'Twas his own choice," he said heavily. "There was naught anyone could do when he took a thought into his head. He was cursedly stubborn."

Bronwyn chuckled under her breath. " 'Twas not a trait he shared with his master?"

Rowan almost smiled, her words so close an echo to his earlier thoughts. "Aye, I always suspected 'twas no coincidence that he was chosen as a gift for me."

"Two of a kind."

He shrugged again. "It seemed that we were matched in temperament at least."

"And well accustomed to each other."

"Aye."

Bronwyn held his gaze and Rowan knew 'twould be a question of import that fell from her lips. "Did you love him?"

Rowan would have preferred to deny such an emotion, but he did not have the resolve within him to lie to her. Not here, not now. His gaze trailed to the empty sea, before meeting hers once more.

"I suppose I did," he admitted softly. "But then, there was naught at stake between us, naught one could win from the other. There was no declaration that might have been a lie, no need for such a pledge. We simply were together."

Rowan stared out over the sea for a long moment, mustering his ability to grin with insouciance before he turned. When he thought he could manage the deed, he did turn, though the smile felt unwelcome on his lips.

And Bronwyn's steady gaze saw too much.

Rowan propped one hand on his hip and made a jest before she could read too much into his concession. "I suppose such whimsy is worthy only of mockery.'' He spread his hands, inviting her to make a jest at his expense.

But Bronwyn stepped closer and framed his face in her hands. She smiled when he looked down at her in surprise, the glow of admiration in her eyes nigh stealing Rowan's breath away.

''You forget,'' she chided softly. ''I am the one who holds love in high esteem.''

Before Rowan could reply, she stretched to her toes and kissed him, her salute so gentle and coaxing that he could not step away.

He parted his lips and closed his eyes, accepting solace from her tenderness. She slanted her lips across his and leaned against his chest, her warmth a welcome weight against him. There was no need to hasten, her leisurely kiss seemed to whisper, no need to apologize, no need to be anything other than the man he was.

Acceptance was the most seductive gift she might have offered.

Rowan locked his hands around her waist and deepened their kiss, marvelling at all Bronwyn had learned when she flicked her tongue against his own.

She met him, touch for touch, returning his kiss with a vigor that weakened his knees. She twined her hands into his hair, urging him closer, her kiss beguiling and bewildering him as never before.

Bronwyn kissed Rowan as if she could not get enough of him, as if she would devour him whole, and Rowan responded in kind. He was harder than he had ever been in all his days, his blood pounded in his ears, he could feel the twin nubs of her nipples against his chest.

When she pulled her lips from his, they both were breathing erratically. ''I seem to recall we had a wager,'' she said, her words ragged.

Rowan could not conceive of what she meant, his thoughts clouded from her passionate kiss.

She smiled and flicked a fingertip across the tip of his nose, echoing his favored gesture. "A shower of kisses for every slave freed," she murmured, some mischief lighting her sapphire gaze. "I counted forty-two on the beach."

Rowan stared, incredulous, even while his blood heated.

"Here," Bronwyn insisted. Her eyes shone and she smiled with such ardor that Rowan's heart thumped painfully in his chest. "Here and now, I want you, Rowan de Montvieux." She ran one hand through his hair, her lips twisting at the sight he knew he must be. "Precisely as you are."

Her words redoubled his desire, but Rowan tried to think with good sense.

'Twas not easy. "The others will see."

"They are asleep and distant." Bronwyn's eyes sparkled and her lips quirked as she pulled back to study him. "Surely I do not have to *dare* you to see my will in this?"

She was beguiling as never a woman had been. She was at once strong and vulnerable, determined and feminine. Her eyes sparkled, her hand rose to trace a path across his jaw. Rowan turned his head without breaking their gaze and caught her fingertip in his lips, loving how her eyes widened.

And Bronwyn smiled, welcoming and unafraid, offering all he could ever imagine wanting.

Rowan chuckled and caught her close once more. "Consider me at your service." He bent and took his teeth to the tie of her chemise, then burrowed beneath the cloth. He captured her hardened nipple between his lips, inhaling deeply of her sweet scent and savoring her gasp of delight.

Rowan gasped in turn when her fingers found the tie of his

chausses, her hands busily freeing him to the breeze from the sea.

Before he could speak, Bronwyn peeled off her kirtle and chemise to stand bare before him, the sight chasing all thought from his mind. The sunlight turned her flesh to gold, her laughter sparkled like the sea shining behind her.

And when she pivoted, as gorgeous as a mythic woman made flesh, and beckoned to Rowan, she did not need to make the invitation twice.

She would win Rowan's heart, Bronwyn knew it well. Aye, their mating had been explosive, for she had given every measure that she had. 'Twas like touching a match to the tinder, for Rowan had responded with a passion that left them both exhausted in its wake.

It had been no small thing for him to admit that he cared for the destrier, and Bronwyn intended to reward the knight for that admission. Aye, and she would encourage him yet further along the course of love. He cared for her, she guessed, for he was protective of her, concerned for her fate, and defensive when she questioned as much.

The way to disarm Rowan was with her touch, for when they mated Bronwyn saw more of the secrets within his heart. She would seduce him a hundred times a day, and with each coupling come closer to making him her own.

She only hoped that she did not run out of time.

After their return to the others, the entire party walked that day along the narrow beach, finally finding a narrow niche where they could climb to the summit of the cliffs.

'Twas not a long climb, which was of splendid fortune, since the weaker of the ex-slaves had to be carried to the summit. Bronwyn could not imagine how they would pro-

ceed from there, for all were growing tired and the day
drawing long, but reaching the summit provided no solace.

There was naught but endless green to the north and
south, those mountains erupting to the west. The sea lapped
on the shore behind as Bronwyn strained her eyes, trying to
find some hint of habitation.

But there was none.

The ex-slaves clearly assessed their predicament as well
and many might have faltered there. But Rowan made a jest
and seized Bronwyn's hand, leading her in a merry dance.

"North to Dublin?" he murmured.

" 'Tis my best guess."

"Then, north we shall go." Determination flashed in his
eyes before he conjured a flower from behind one woman's
ear. He juggled a trio of stones and had Thomas join him in
a bawdy song.

Though the slaves did not understand the words, with
Rowan's encouragement, they were soon doing their best to
join the chorus. Bronwyn watched as he coaxed smiles and
lifted spirits with effortless ease. And when Rowan gestured
north, every ex-slave rose to match their steps to his.

'Twas a far cry from Rowan's recollections of a life lived
unfettered. He stared at the stars above long after the others
were asleep that night and thought hard about his choices.
Truly, he had always believed that this life had been perfect.

But he was hungry and he was cold, and there was naught
he could do about either. A song seemed a paltry entertain-
ment in such circumstance, and, indeed, Rowan was starting
to wonder what he might do for a fine meal and a warm
hearth.

How could such a life have been fostered by the life he
recalled? He watched the stars overhead and wondered, for

the first time, whether happiness had flourished in his mother's troupe not because of their circumstance but in spite of it.

Midmorning brought new hope. Not far away, perhaps half a mile inland, Bronwyn spied the silhouette of a keep. She cried out, the ex-slaves cheered at the sight, and all found new strength to reach their objective.

And not a moment too soon. All were tired and haggard, all were starving, Rowan alone still smiling and singing as they walked. But then, this was the life he adored. Bronwyn watched him from the corner of her eye and could find no hint of dissatisfaction in his manner.

While she was ready to cede anything for a meal and a warm hearth. Truly she had led a sheltered life!

A new doubt took root in her heart. What if they were too different to ever find common ground in love? Would she lose Rowan to this troubador's life?

Bronwyn hated that she did not know for certain.

Once they arrived at the small holding, Rowan's charm stood them in good stead, for the gatekeeper might have turned them away immediately. But with astonishing haste, Rowan had convinced the gatekeeper to dispatch a runner to fetch the lord himself to hear his plea.

He winked at Bronwyn and urged her to his side while they waited, his attention making her pulse leap. "You are a dangerous man," she charged beneath her breath, as much in reference to his skill with the gatekeeper as his effect upon her.

Rowan looked surprised, though he smiled. "Aye?"

"Aye. You have a gift for making one do the opposite of one's intention, and proceeding to do so willingly."

He chuckled, his gaze rising to the advancing noble party. "I thought this was your weapon of choice."

"Me?" Bronwyn protested, though her heart warmed. "There is none who could compel you to proceed as you did not desire!"

Rowan turned a sparkling gaze upon her and dropped his voice low, his fingertip brushing her cheek. "Nay, keep that smile in reserve, *ma demoiselle*. 'Twill blind and befuddle our potential host if you loose it too soon." And he kissed her quickly, before stepping forward to address the glowering lord.

Bronwyn dared to be encouraged by his compliment.

The lord was not a small man, nor a young one. A scar adorned his cheek, and his eyes were narrowed as he surveyed the bedraggled party. Bronwyn guessed that he saw them as an army of beggars, come to fleece him. He was broad and tall, his leather jerkin dark from use, his arms and legs sheer muscle.

This was a man who fought for what he desired, and oft won. Browyn feared they would find no shelter here.

"Aye?" that lord demanded. "And who might you be to disturb my midday meal so boldly?"

Rowan bowed low, apparently untroubled by his garb or the other man's manner. "Chevalier Rowan de Montvieux, sir."

"You are no knight!"

"I most certainly am, though the tale of my misfortune is a long and complicated one. I should not trouble you with the details, as you are at the board."

Curiosity flickered through the lord's eyes. He frowned as his gaze dropped and Bronwyn knew he noted Rowan's spurs. "You have no blade, no steed, no squire. No doubt you have stolen those spurs!"

"Stolen! Sir, I assure you I am no thief, simply a knight in less than ideal circumstance.'' Rowan made to turn away. ''Please, do not let me keep you from your meal.''

The lord gripped the wooden portcullis. ''But how did you come to be here? And without your steed?''

''We took passage on a ship destined for Dublin, which sank just off the coast.''

The lord folded his arms across his chest. ''I have heard a tale this morn of a ship floundering.''

''Well, 'tis sunk now, you have my personal assurance.'' Rowan stepped back with a smile. ''But by all means, return to your meal. I would not trouble you with a tale of adventure.''

The lord surveyed them silently, then frowned. ''You could tell who the rest are.''

''I would not delay you overlong. Does the meat grow cold?''

The lord's eyes flashed and Bronwyn appreciated how Rowan had guessed he might be anxious for bold tales. ''Tell me!''

Rowan snapped his fingers and Thomas bounded to his side. ''My squire, Thomas of Deneure.'' Thomas bowed low. ''Surely you know of the Deneure clan?'' And he descended into a dizzying recitation of genealogy that even Bronwyn could not manage to follow.

It ended with a link to the Norman throne and Thomas's proud smile. Bronwyn could not tell whether he told the truth or not, though she suspected the latter by Thomas's silence.

The lord's eyes narrowed. ''So, you would have me shelter you and this fleet of beggars, purely on a tale of a link to the king? Presumably with no compense to me or my house?''

''No compense! Why, I have a tale which will entertain

those at your board mightily.'' Rowan offered a confident smile.

The lord snorted, the glimmer in his eyes belying his stern words. "A tale is a fleeting gift and one which does naught to assure my holding.'' He turned and walked away, sparing a heavy glance for the gatekeeper. "Pray do not disturb my meal again for such frivolity.''

Bronwyn's shoulders sagged. She wondered how far they would have to walk when Rowan cast a merry glance her way.

"Ah, well, then,'' he said with a shrug. "I shall have to offer this prize of a tale to your neighbor.''

"My neighbor!'' The lord spun, his eyes flashing. "That fool would not appreciate a fine tale.''

"And 'twill be his all the same.''

The lord hesitated, his hands bunching into fists at his sides. "You could tell me some of it, then I could better assess the merit of the tale.''

Rowan scoffed. "I *know* the merit of the tale. 'Tis well worth a meal and accommodation for all of my party.''

The lord's gaze sweeping over the ranks of the ex-slaves. "Why should I feed all of them? They are fit for naught.''

"Because they are hungry, tired, and dirty,'' Rowan retorted. "Is it not your Christian duty to show compassion and hospitality? And they travel with me, so my tale sees to their welfare.'' He made an expansive gesture. "Not that 'tis of concern to you. Nay, your meat chills even as we linger. I would not presume to delay you further.'' He cleared his throat. "Thomas, run ahead to that neighboring estate and warn the lord that we are fast coming to his gates.''

"Aye, my lord.'' Thomas bowed and made to duck away, no doubt to do Rowan's bidding, even though Bronwyn could not imagine where that neighboring estate might be.

The lord hesitated for only a moment before he strode

back to the gates. Bronwyn could see him counting their ranks. "I could take their burden from your hands. How much do you want for them?"

"Me?" Rowan looked astonished. "Naught!" The lord grinned before Rowan leaned closer. "For they are freemen again and freemen they will remain, wherever they abide."

The lord gritted his teeth. "I would have slaves."

"Then you will not have these men beneath your hand. They are contented enough with me and my tales. Why, your neighbor will undoubtedly welcome us." Rowan turned to walk away, beckoning the party with one hand.

They made no more than a dozen steps before the lord cried out. "Come within the hall and savor the fare. I would hear your tale!"

But Rowan turned cautiously, his gaze running over the gates. "You shall give me your pledge, upon your own blade, that none will forget themselves and secure the gate behind us."

The two men stared at each other for a long moment, then the lord spun to stride away. "Agreed!" he roared. "Let it not be said that Leon of Aulnay does not keep his word!"

Bronwyn was tempted to shout with delight, but she kept her voice low. "You have found a home for them!"

"Not yet." Rowan shrugged. "Let us hope some of them will choose to remain."

"How did you know about his neighbor?"

Rowan grinned crookedly. " 'Twas naught but a guess. In my experience, a petty lord most always has an equally petty lord as a neighbor and they two are fiercely competitive. He may desire the tale for its own merit, or purely to be the first to hear it."

"Do you think he would be a cruel master?"

The knight looked after the lord, then shrugged. "I suspect he is one who bellows mightily but whose heart is good. Only time will reveal the truth, of course. In the end, if these people remain as freemen—and I shall ensure the documentation is correct—then they have the right to flee any onerous circumstance.''

''You intend to remain here?''

Rowan sobered. ''Aye. They will need someone to negotiate terms.''

''What of our year and a day?''

He studied her carefully, his expression inscrutable. ''What if I were to absolve you of that obligation?''

So, this then would be where they parted. Bronwyn's heart sank to her toes. Far from winning Rowan's heart, she had satisfied his desire for her and he would be rid of her. The end of their journey together came far too soon for Bronwyn.

'Twas no sweet revelation that he shed his pledge to her as readily as he shed all other obligations. Had her father not always said that a man could not be changed, however one might will it? Rowan confessed readily that he wanted naught to his name. She had been a fool to believe her touch could change his thinking!

Bronwyn averted her face, not wanting him to see how his dismissal hurt her. But Rowan touched her chin with a fingertip, coaxing her to meet his gaze.

''What would you do?''

She swallowed and tried to look indifferent. ''Return to Ballyroyal, of course.''

''So soon? But I shall have need of your gift for language, in order that they are asked their opinion. 'Tis too long these people have been denied any choice in their circumstance, and I would not deny them that now.''

Rowan hesitated most uncharacteristically, then lifted his gaze to lock with hers. ''I should be honored if you would

accept my accompaniment to your home, even with that
obligation between us dissolved.''

Bronwyn's heart skipped a beat at the intensity in his
eyes.

Then Rowan grinned mischievously. "After all, 'tis the
only way to ensure that you indeed arrive there, let alone
that you arrive hale and hearty. Truly, *ma demoiselle,* you
have a gift for finding unwelcome circumstance.''

But Bronwyn could not take offense at his charge, not
when he smiled so warmly at her.

Nor did she have it within her to decline. After all, it
could be naught but encouraging that Rowan was so intent
on ensuring her safe journey. Indeed, his protectiveness of
her was one consistent thread since they had met.

And her father also said that a man strives to protect only
what he loves.

Bronwyn could build upon that.

Leon of Aulnay's motte and bailey fort was still being con-
structed, only the palisade complete at this point. The ten-
ants' huts were clustered in the distance, and the few fields
that had been sown waved with crops coming to their fru-
ition. There were few vassals about, though, and Rowan had
guessed aright that Leon might had dire need of more help-
ing hands.

'Twas good import for the future of these souls.

Leon stood at the doorway of his hall with his chatelain
and greeted each ex-slave individually. They told him their
names, at least Rowan assumed that was what they said, and
Leon tried to repeat them, to much hilarity.

Inside the hall, the board groaned with dark bread and a
wheel of cheese, pickled fish and pitchers of ale, all of
which were met with delight. Rowan was pleased that mat-

ters resolved as well as they had, and was relieved that the lord was good to his word.

'Twas a good sign.

And 'twas a merry evening that ensued. Leon proved to have a pair of minstrels in residence, and they took up a celebratory tune once the ex-slaves were within the hall. Though all was simple, there was a joy bubbling from all of them that could not be denied.

This was the life Rowan recalled! Aye, there was ale and laughter, music and dancing, smiles upon every face. Rowan recounted the tale of Brianna of Ballyroyal's bride quest, the adventure that had brought him all the way to this hall, and Leon was well pleased.

The ale flowed and lanterns were lit as night fell. The dancing began after Rowan's tale was complete, no need of language to see the more hale ex-slaves on their feet. Truly, this arrangement suited both Leon and these homeless souls.

But it was not the ex-slaves the knight found himself watching. Rowan was captivated by Bronwyn's laughter, her features alight with a happiness he had never seen in her before.

" 'Tis good to be close to home," she offered as explanation when he asked, then smiled so brilliantly that he was struck dumb by her beauty.

Leon demanded her hand to dance and Bronwyn was on her feet. The minstrels picked a complicated tune, the ex-slaves clapped in time, Leon and Bronwyn's feet flew as they danced a merry dance, which was obviously traditional since both knew the steps. The lady's cheeks were flushed and she danced with an exuberance that heated Rowan's blood.

Aye, it reminded him of how much she had unexpectedly granted him on the beach. Rowan sipped his ale and found his thoughts turning to their splendid mating—no less how they would couple again this night.

There was a change in his lady, a liveliness that seized her step now that they were upon Ireland's shores once more. He was fiercely glad that had he had offered to accompany her home, for this Brownyn was doubly intriguing. As he drank his ale and watched her dance, Rowan realized that their inevitable parting would not be an easy one.

Though he would never so much as hint to Bronwyn of the truth. Nay, he was not the man for her, regardless of this recent and undoubtedly fleeting assumption of duties. He had abandoned his own good counsel; while "Ibernia" might have been a woman with naught to lose and who expected naught of him, the same could not be said of Bronwyn of Ballyroyal.

'Twould be infinitely better for the lady if their paths parted soon and forever.

Aye, Bronwyn had called the matter right. Rowan was no suitable spouse for an heiress like herself. He should find himself a dancing girl, one who would savor a life without responsibilities, as he did.

He drank deeply of his ale and refused to acknowledge the disappointment within him. Perhaps 'twould be easier to abandon Bronwyn to her fate if he had weaned himself from her seductive touch before they reached Ballyroyal. Rowan was by no means convinced of that, but he would try.

He was a man, after all, who was fond of long odds.

As night settled over the coast, the shadows falling long and cool on the beach, a length of the *Angelica*'s mast was finally washed against the shore. 'Twas farther to the north than the beach where Rowan and Bronwyn had come

ashore, even farther than the spot when Troubador's saddle
had been cast.

Clinging to that length of wood was a certain Venetian
man. He was pale from loss of blood, and his chattering
teeth gritted against the chill that permeated his flesh.

He should have slipped from that length of wood long
before. He should have drowned, as he had seen so many of
his men drown. He had watched them weaken and slip beneath the waves, never to rise again. He had watched his
ship fall prey to the crashing sea, even as his blood seeped
from his body.

'Twas anger that kept him alive.

'Twas anger that kept his grip tight on the length of wood,
anger that refused to let him fall into a slumber from which
he would never awaken, anger that had him alone drifting
toward Ireland's shore. Baldassare di Vilonte had been
deceived, he had been within a breath of winning all he
sought, and he had been cheated of that victory.

Worse, he had been cheated by Niccolo's own kin.
Baldassare would ensure they all paid—Niccolo, Bronwyn,
and all the rest of Niccolo's kin. After all these years, justice
would be served

Baldassare di Vilonte, after all, was not the manner of
man who accepted failure without a fight.

Baldassare nearly wept when his foot first brushed the
sand below. He did weep when he opened his eyes and
realized how close salvation lay, but that he was too weak to
avail himself of it. He was yet a toy of the sea, destined to
wait until the waves cast him fully upon the beach. Baldassare prayed, as he had never prayed before, that the tide
would abandon him upon the coast, instead of tugging him
back out to sea again.

He did not know whether it was a dream to feel sand
beneath his feet, whether he imagined that his knees grazed

solid ground. When he heard the woman's cry, Baldassare knew that could not be truth. He drifted alone, after all, a victim of the sea's caprice.

But the woman did not go away. Though her words were indistinguishable, he felt suddenly warm. Strong hands hauled him ashore, he heard someone run.

The woman murmured to him all the while. Gentle fingertips landed on his cheek. Heat caressed his face and Baldassare opened his eyes, nigh blinded by a golden glow.

A woman with hair the color of a flame bent over him, and Baldassare wept in truth at the realization that he had not survived his ordeal. Nay, this creature could be none other than an angel, an angel of mercy dispatched to save his soul.

But even as he was lifted toward the stars, Baldassare knew that eternal bliss would not be his own. Nay, his dark soul would not be easily retrieved—for indeed, hatred yet burned within him. He had been cheated, cheated by the kin of an old foe and a knight determined to defy him, and left to die.

Yet, even knowing he was to meet his maker, Baldassare di Vilonte still wanted vengeance, not salvation.

# Chapter Fifteen

O BRONWYN'S SURPRISE, ONE TALL BEARDED EX-SLAVE was a cleric. His name was Mikail and it was soon established by Leon's priest that Mikail read Latin, though he could not speak it with any clarity.

Once this was realized, Leon seized ink and parchment, and much discussion ensued. According to Mikail, the former slaves had been captured in a northern Polish principality as their homeland was rife with war. Baldassare di Vilonte had taken advantage of the chaos there and pounced upon the remote village. Many had been killed, the remainder herded aboard Baldassare's ship, ultimately to be sold as slaves.

Bronwyn noted the shadows in many eyes as Leon's priest translated the tale and read it aloud, and her heart ached for what these folk had endured. Their village had not only been ravaged but had been burned to the ground. No one wanted to return.

With the exception of Marika.

Mikail asked Leon to accept them on his lands, giving his assurance that all would labor hard to make this place their new home. He asked for protection and Leon swore to provide it. A ripple passed through the ranks of the ex-slaves, a glint of hope lit more than one face, and Bronwyn knew that they would find a good home here.

For Leon also had need of the labor.

Then Rowan stepped forward to negotiate on behalf of the Poles, to ensure they did not grant Leon more than his due out of gratitude.

'Twas four days before he pronounced himself satisfied, four days and nights that Bronwyn hoped to have his attention and did not. During the day Rowan sat at the board with lord and clerics, while at night he spoke with Thomas so long that she inevitably fell asleep. Though she knew this was of import, Bronwyn missed his touch and his company.

Marika alone had been adamant that she did not wish to remain.

Mikail wrote solemnly for the priest, who then translated the writing for Bronwyn. "He says that Marika has seen much pain," the priest confided gravely. "And that perhaps 'tis best that she begin anew, without familiar faces to remind her of all she has lost."

"What happened?"

Mikail shook his head slowly, then wrote, not waiting for the translation of Bronwyn's question. The priest glanced over the parchment, then met Bronwyn's gaze. "The tale, he insists, is not his to tell. He asks that you be patient with her and ensure that she is not without spiritual guidance."

The priest smiled and laid a hand on the larger man's shoulder. "He is a good cleric to worry over the fate of those who have been in his care. I believe that Mikail and I will have many interesting discussions over the winters ahead." The men smiled at each other with mutual admiration.

But Bronwyn's thoughts were full of Marika. Marika had already confided part of the tale in Bronwyn. It had to do with a child, a babe named Vassily, and perhaps a rape. 'Twould be easy to lay at least one crime at Baldassare's feet.

Bronwyn turned to find Marika watching her, anxiety in that woman's eyes. Clearly she knew that her course was being decided, and she wrung her hands in uncertainty.

Bronwyn resolved in that moment that she would find Marika a man who could push that woman's ghosts into the past where they belonged—just as Rowan had done for her. Marika would have a good husband, if Bronwyn had to scour all of Ireland to find him. She smiled and offered her hand, catching the woman in her arms when Marika began to weep in gratitude.

The other ex-slaves signed their contracts at Mikail's dictate, many of them doing so with a simple X, then a vessel of wine was uncorked in celebration.

They passed a chalice, saluting Leon, Rowan, and Mikail, and then drinking heartily. Bronwyn was proud to be associated with Rowan, to have been a part of the good deed he had done here.

Again she was struck that a man so disenchanted with responsibility should perform such obligations so well. But then, perhaps Rowan had only desired to see his obligations to the ex-slaves fulfilled.

Bronwyn wished she knew the truth of it.

'Twas just past midday, five days after their arrival, when Bronwyn and Rowan departed Leon's abode. Thomas tagged close behind the knight and Marika's face was streaked with tears from her farewells. They walked out the gates, the sun warm on their backs, and began the long walk toward Ballyroyal.

The road unfurled before them like a ribbon winding a course across the vivid green of the land. The wind was fresh from the sea sparkling to their right; the mountains rose loftily on their left. The range was indeed the Wicklow Mountains, as Leon had been quick to confirm, and they were less than two days' ride from Dublin.

Ballyroyal was a day's ride beyond or less, though, indeed, they did not ride.

'Twould not be a short journey and her feet would be aching by the end, but Bronwyn found a bounce of anticipation in her step. She was glad to be almost alone with Rowan again and looked forward to a measure of privacy for the two of them. Once again she was buoyed with optimism that she could win this man with her touch, his recent deed persuading her yet further that he tended care overmuch instead of not at all.

Their small party was well provisioned, courtesy of Leon, who had insisted upon seeing them compensated for bringing such labor his way. They each carried a pack, filled with bread and cheese, and though their garb was simple, it was clean and most welcome.

They walked in silence for a good hour before Rowan suddenly halted and frowned.

"What is that?" he demanded, gesturing to a dark figure in the fields ahead.

The distance was too great to be certain, but before Bronwyn could say anything, Rowan cast his pack to Thomas and began to run. Bronwyn cried out, the trio racing after the knight but unable to match his speed.

But as they ran, Bronwyn studied the dark silhouette, gasping when she recognized it. A steed stood grazing in that green field. It was an uncommonly large beast, no small mare or palfrey was this. 'Twas bereft of saddle and unattended, and it had one white sock.

And there was crooked white star upon its brow.

"Troubador!" Rowan bellowed jubilantly. A palfrey lifted her head at his cry, revealing her presence behind the destrier. "You feckless beast! You were swimming for England."

Troubador surveyed the knight with indifference, his

chewing never slowing. Then he blew out his lips and bent to graze with apparent nonchalance.

Rowan began to laugh. "Ah, you impossible creature! You did this only to grant me grief, I know it well." There was a warmth in his teasing tone, and Bronwyn knew he was relieved that his destrier had survived.

Bronwyn guessed that the stallion's more base instincts had ultimately won out over its fear. Troubador had followed the palfrey, for whatever reason, after she had turned for shore. The pair must have reached the shore this far north.

Bronwyn wondered whether Rowan would have another steed in his retinue shortly and started to laugh herself.

Rowan was beside the destrier in no time at all, his features alight. The other three remained on the road, Bronwyn holding Thomas back that Rowan might have a moment of reunion alone. He strode around the stallion, assuring himself that the beast was unhurt. His expression turning cocky, Rowan halted before the horse while Troubador continued grazing.

"Remind me," he informed the steed, "that your instincts are better than they might otherwise appear."

Troubador snorted and pulled deliberately at the grass, though his tail began to flick. His ears twitched, as if he kept track of the knight's location, but he had no intent to reveal his interest so clearly as that.

Bronwyn grinned to find that steed and knight were so similar. Rowan evidently also saw humor in this, for he winked at her before he spoke.

"Well, old friend, 'tis good to see you well." He patted the destrier's rump as Troubador strolled out from beneath his hand, evidently intent on a choice clump of grass a few steps away and oblivious to the knight's presence. "Fare well, Troubador. I trust you will find another, perhaps finer, master."

And he walked back toward the road, a whistle on his lips.

"But, my lord," Thomas cried. " 'Tis your steed!"

Rowan waved off the protest. "But, Thomas, the beast did not heed me. He must prefer to seek his own fate, a path I can certainly admire."

As the knight joined them and made a show of retrieving his pack, Troubador lifted his head and stared after him. The beast looked as surprised as a horse could look by this turn of events.

The palfrey similarly lifted her head, and Bronwyn realized that something had changed between these two creatures. Where once the palfrey had taken her lead from the stallion, now she stepped forward and nipped at his hindquarters, as if urging him to do something while Rowan walked away.

"But . . ." Thomas began to argue.

"But naught." Rowan ruffled the boy's hair and smiled. "I am persuaded to live unfettered, and a destrier is no small obligation to see fed. 'Tis clear enough that Troubador sees the merit of finding another master, for he did leave me." He granted them all a mischievous smile. "Come along, then. Dublin and Ballyroyal await."

Rowan began to stroll down the road, apparently unaware of the destrier staring after him. Troubador's ears twitched as Rowan began to recount a tale of his travels to Thomas. The palfrey whinnied, seeming to chide the stallion.

And he stepped forward.

Bronwyn watched from the corner of her eye, knowing Rowan well enough to guess that he only challenged the steed's indifference. The destrier took one last defiant mouthful of grass. Rowan laughed and prompted Thomas's chuckle, apparently unaware of the horse so close at hand, his long steps taking him quickly away.

Troubador snorted, then loped after the knight, his baleful

glance fixed upon that man's back. When Rowan did not halt or acknowledge him, Troubador snorted noisily.

Rowan continued with his tale, though Bronwyn noted his smile.

Troubador whinnied.

Rowan walked as if he were unaware of the steed.

A rush of heavy footsteps warned Bronwyn of the steed's advance, and she darted out of the way just in time. The destrier lumbered up behind Rowan, neighed loud enough to strike a man deaf, then seized Rowan's tabard in his teeth.

"Oh!" Rowan feigned surprise at finding the destrier behind him. " 'Tis *you*." He shook his tabard free and eyed the beast, hands on his hips. "I thought you had found greener pastures."

Troubador blew out his lips, then leaned closer and nudged the knight in the chest. His ears twitched and he eyed the knight as if to make a silent appeal.

"Oh, you great foolish beast," Rowan murmured with affection. He scratched the steed's ears, smiling as Troubador leaned against him with satisfaction. "I would not have left you, even though you did leave me."

Troubador nuzzled him, as if apologizing.

"Know that circumstances may see your belly empty if you follow me," Rowan warned. The steed nickered and seized another mouthful of grass. Rowan laughed. "I suppose there is enough on this isle to content you for the present."

Troubador rubbed against him and Rowan grimaced. "You smell like a brothel," he chided, though he did not move away. "And not a fine one either. But I suppose we have little enough choice." He regarded the steed sternly. " 'Twill be your fate to bear us to Ballyroyal."

He captured the reins that hung loose, making a face at the salt that had turned the leather much rougher than it had been. Then he turned to Bronwyn with a smile. "*Ma demoiselle,* can you ride without a saddle?"

"Of course!" Bronwyn grinned and stepped toward the destrier. " 'Tis the blood of Celts that runs in my veins!"

Rowan gestured to the palfrey. "Then I can offer you your own mount on this journey. Truly we shall reach Ballyroyal in fine style."

Bronwyn's heart sank to her toes. She would not ride with Rowan. No less, they would reach Ballyroyal sooner than she had anticipated. And if she and Rowan rode separately, then she would have little enough chance to persuade him to her view.

But then, 'twas not appropriate to ride with a man when there were no marital vows between them. Bronwyn appreciated that gossip would plague her name if they rode otherwise and supposed she should appreciate Rowan's thoughtfulness.

Even if she did have an eerie sense that there was more than that at root here. Was it the circumstance of Leon's hall that had kept Rowan away from her these past nights?

Or was it a portent that he intended to escort her to Ballyroyal, then leave her side for all time?

Despite Bronwyn's desire to know the truth, no opportunity arose for private discussion with Rowan in the three days that it took to journey to Ballyroyal. Each night he found them shelter and disappeared, purportedly to tend the horses, but he never returned before Bronwyn was asleep.

After one instance, she wondered. After two, she had strong suspicions. On the third morning, when he would not meet her gaze, she knew the truth. Bronwyn knew that it was no coincidence that matters kept them apart, and she chafed that Rowan had granted her no opportunity to win his heart as she had pledged.

She could only wait and see what he would do, when the final choice was upon him. 'Twas not Bronwyn's preference by any means—but then, she knew well enough that no one could be compelled to love another.

Still, her helplessness chafed.

At noon on the third day they spied Ballyroyal in the distance. Bronwyn could not decide whether they reached her home too soon or too late—she wanted desperately to know Rowan's decision, yet she feared he would quickly depart, leaving her to mourn this short journey for years to come.

'Twas one of those peculiarly Irish days, when the rain falls gently and ceaselessly, but a beam of sunlight toys with all around. The light burst from the clouds at unexpected intervals, highlighting a cottage in the distance, or illuminating the distant sparkle of the sea, or turning all around them to the vibrant hues of rare emeralds.

Her first sight of home in more than a sixmonth startled Bronwyn with the power of her response. She reined in the palfrey for a moment simply to look. There was the river she had splashed in as a young girl; there was the field where she had learned to ride.

Her mother's prize mare had indeed foaled, for Bronwyn could spy the smaller horse following behind the chestnut mare. Though she was distant, the creatures were as familiar as brothers and sisters might have been. Other horses grazed within the stone walls, many more than she recalled. Either her father had been buying gifts for her mother again or Ballyroyal had guests.

Rowan cast an inquiring glance her way and Bronwyn smiled for him. She felt a sudden urge to be home, to be safe, to be among those who loved her dearly.

Aye, she owed an apology to them.

"What will you do, now that we are at Ballyroyal?" she asked softly, half dreading, half anticipating his answer.

Rowan's hands tightened for a moment on the reins, the gesture drawing her gaze to his strong fingers. Bronwyn's mouth went dry as she recalled the magic he had roused from her flesh with those fingers.

He shrugged then, his manner cool and composed. "I had thought to find a travelling troupe of entertainers."

Bronwyn could barely force the words past the lump in her throat, let alone make them sound light and indifferent. "Aye? What of your heiress?"

Rowan's smile did not reach his eyes. Indeed, his gaze was curiously flat, though he quickly supplied the reason. "I will have no heiress."

"So you will lose your brother's wager?"

"I forfeit it and all its victory would have entailed." Rowan shook his head and looked away. "You called it aright, Bronwyn. To win would bring only that which I do not desire." He met her gaze again, his words falling tonelessly between them. "I thank you for showing me the folly of that path."

His gaze was steady, perhaps even dispassionate. Bronwyn stared at him, his manner unfamiliar. Where was the merry Rowan she had come to know? Where was the determined knight, the man whose anger flashed when she showed no regard for her own welfare? Rowan in every guise was passionate, his eyes flashed and twinkled, his smile was never far.

But this Rowan was an indifferent stranger, a man whose thoughts she could not guess.

"And what if I wished I had not warned you of that?" Bronwyn asked, for indeed, in this moment she did.

"Words once uttered can not be left unsaid." Rowan's

gaze was unswerving. "It seems you shall witness me losing the quest for Bronwyn of Ballyroyal's hand just as you desired." He arched a brow and smiled coolly. "Does it not please you?"

Please her? Anger swept through Bronwyn. Not only would Rowan abandon her, pretending there had been naught between them, but he would lay the blame at her own feet.

How dare he care *naught* for her, after all they had shared?

At least, Bronwyn knew the best way to bring back the Rowan she knew and loved. She would have one last glimpse of him with his eyes twinkling, to savor over the years.

For it seemed that was all she would have of him in the end.

"I shall race you!" she cried, and gave the mount her heels before he could see her heart break. "Indeed, I *dare* you to beat me to the gates!"

Marika squealed and clung to Bronwyn's waist as the palfrey leapt forward, but Bronwyn leaned low over the horse, loving the feel of muscles rippling beneath her. The steed needed no more urging to race like the wind.

Bronwyn heard Rowan's cry behind her but did not slow. She could ride like none other and was content to let him eat her dust. Oh, there was so much he did not know of her—so much he apparently did not *want* to know. His rejection stung, but Bronwyn would give Rowan no hint of that.

By the time they reached the gates, she would be composed again. Troubador's hooves thundered on the road behind, but she was away first and she would beat him to the gates.

And beat Rowan Bronwyn did, though any triumph she might have felt faded fast.

For none other than her father's partner Marco opened the gate to Ballyroyal's bailey. Marco, with his grim expression and disappointment in his eyes; Marco, who had always disapproved of Bronwyn's wild inclinations; Marco, whose hair silvered at his temples.

Marco, the fiancé from whom Bronwyn had fled

"Welcome home," he said, his voice dry as dust. " 'Tis no surprise that you return with all the impetuous haste you showed in departing."

Something was amiss.

One moment Bronwyn had been challenging Rowan to best her, her full lips set with defiance, the glint in her eyes making him regret the course he had chosen.

And the next, she had been wide-eyed and somber, her smile gone. She introduced Rowan stiffly to her father's partner, Marco, and said not a word more than that.

The lady was not often silent and Rowan did not care for the change. Indeed, he had been prepared to argue with her. He had been surprised by his own regret on their arrival to her home, for 'twould be only a matter of moments before he could safely deliver Bronwyn to her parents' care, then be on his way.

But he had not wanted to hasten, had not wanted to race to the gates, and now he did not want to leave.

Bronwyn paled beneath her tan in most uncharacteristic way. Rowan frowned as he followed her, Marco's polite chatter flowing over him unheard. Indeed, Rowan had been so stunned that Bronwyn asked after his plans, so surprised at the hopeful glint in her eyes, no less by the disappointment that followed when he pledged to leave.

Had she not wanted him to lose her hand, after all?

And why did Bronwyn's disappointment trouble him, as

no other woman's disappointment had ever done? Was it merely the way she addled his wits, the quick deceitful game that lust played on a man's thoughts.

Or was there something more at stake? Rowan was not certain he wanted to know.

Without doubt, 'twas good their paths parted now, before his thinking grew even more muddled.

They were only just within the gates, when a tall man stepped into what might have been generously called a bailey.

"Marco, who comes at this time of the day? Surely every guest we can accommodate is already here?" The man surveyed the arrivals quickly, then suddenly gasped aloud. "Bronwyn!"

"Hello, Father." Bronwyn stood and smiled.

Relief washed over the features of Nicholas of Ballyroyal and he let out a hoot of delight. He crossed the yard with quick steps, wonder on his face.

"Bronwyn!" he cried, then caught her in his arms. "Daughter mine!" He made a sound of speechless joy and swung her high, as if she were naught but a child. He clasped his daughter close and closed his eyes, as if he could not believe she had returned. Bronwyn locked her arms around her father's neck, her tears spilling even as she smiled.

So, this was what it was like to be welcomed home with love. Nicholas's delight nigh brought a tear to Rowan's eye, and he tried to recall if anyone had ever greeted his return anywhere with such pleasure.

Not at Montvieux. Margaux was more likely to roll her eyes and demand to know what he wanted of her *this* time.

But Nicholas framed Bronwyn's face in his hands and eyed her, as if he would see the evidence of anything foul his daughter had endured. He touched her cheek, her shoulder, he smiled that her feet were bare, he kissed her brow.

He seemingly could not believe she stood before him.

"God in heaven, I never thought to see you again," he whispered, his voice hoarse. "You are well? You are unhurt? You are none the worse for wear, despite your foolery?"

"I am well enough," Bronwyn admitted with a demure smile. She turned and gestured to Rowan, the disappointment that clouded her eyes making his heart sink. Was this not what she wanted? "This is Chevalier Rowan de Montvieux. He escorted me home."

'Twas true enough, Rowan supposed, though her tone gave no hint of all that had been between them. He stepped forward and accepted Nicholas's hand, feeling an urge to set matters straight, to claim the intimacy that he and Bronwyn had shared, regardless of the price that might bring.

But that was foolish. Their paths *must* part here.

Even if he preferred not to leave her.

Rowan felt Bronwyn's expectation heavy upon him, though he was not entirely certain what she wanted of him. Aye, the woman had always addled his wits!

Bronwyn's father was a man of perhaps forty-five summers, though he was hale and tanned like a younger man. His grip was sure and Rowan liked the man immediately. Nicholas's green eyes snapped with a vivacity unexpected, though his wavy mane of hair had turned to shining silver. He smiled, a man confident in his looks and his abilities, and gripped Rowan's hand warmly.

"I cannot thank you enough for your service in this," he declared. "The world is no place for a woman alone, and 'tis beyond good fortune that an honorable man should find Bronwyn and ensure her safe return home."

"Bronwyn is not without influence on her own fate," Rowan dared to suggest, earning Nicholas's hearty laugh.

"And she is her mother's daughter for all of that," he declared, chucking his daughter affectionately beneath her chin before he sobered. "When I think of what might have happened to you . . ." His voice faded and Bronwyn kissed his cheek hastily.

"I am fine," she murmured, and looked away.

Nicholas frowned briefly, then recalled his manners. "I thank you, sir, I thank you a thousand times, and welcome you as my guest. Before you leave this hall, I shall see you compensated richly for the wondrous gift you have brought me."

Nicholas wrapped an arm around his daughter's shoulders and hugged her tightly against him. "The greatest gift of all," he murmured, and kissed his daughter's temple. "We shall have a fine celebration this night!"

Bronwyn flushed scarlet, her gaze meeting Rowan's for a heady moment before she stepped away. "Where is Mother?"

Nicholas rolled his eyes. "With the foals, of course. Three this year, and you missed the arrival of them all."

Bronwyn's smile looked tight. "I would excuse myself."

"Go! She will be thrilled." Nicholas's gaze followed Bronwyn's course, a proud smile curving his lips. "I cannot believe it," he murmured, then flicked a bright glance to Rowan. "Indeed, I feel a decade younger on this day, thanks to you! I am certain 'tis no small tale that brings her back here, nor you by her side."

"We but made a bargain," Rowan said smoothly, wishing he could pursue the lady and learn what precisely troubled her. " 'Twas naught."

"Aye? And what was your wager? If she promised you coin, I shall see you paid this very moment!" Nicholas flung out his hands. "There are not enough riches in all of Christendom to compensate for this!"

"Nay." Rowan shook his head. "The lady kept her bargain herself. She is most resourceful. The stakes are of no issue at all."

Marco cleared his throat, reminding the other men that he was still at hand. "Unless she granted something that was not hers to grant."

Rowan found the man's tone and his insinuation annoying beyond all. Bronwyn could choose what she would tell of their adventures, but truly, whatever indignity she had borne, she had borne with grace. And whatever she had granted to Rowan, he would not have sullied by foul rumor.

Rowan turned to meet Marco's assessing brown gaze and held it stubbornly. "The lady granted me a tale, no more than that, you may be assured."

Marco arched a brow but held his tongue.

"A tale?" Nicholas asked.

"Aye, I sought a bride in this land." Rowan shrugged, seeing no need to provide details. "She told me of Irish women in exchange for my returning her home."

"Did she tell of herself?" Marco demanded tightly.

Rowan flicked a glance to that man. "Nay. She confessed that she was betrothed."

"You must not mind Marco," Nicholas interjected smoothly. "I fear that when Bronwyn fled, he took the matter personally."

"And who could not?" Marco said tightly.

"I do not understand."

Nicholas smiled. "Marco was Bronwyn's betrothed."

"Indeed." Rowan looked to that man with newly assessing eyes. Though Marco was not foul to look upon, he was markedly older than Bronwyn, of an age with her father. And his manner was less than appealing.

Indeed, he could well understand Bronwyn's choice.

"Did she not tell you?" Marco challenged. "Or did she lie?"

"Nay, Bronwyn spoke little of herself." Rowan reined in his temper with difficulty. Indeed, he managed a cool smile for this man who thought so little of the incomparable woman he had been pledged to wed. "I expect that any who truly knew Bronwyn would know that she has no gift for deceit."

"I fear my old friend was wounded by my daughter's protest," Nicholas said quietly. "Truly, Marco, one could misinterpret your manner."

Marco smiled and took a deep breath. "I apologize, *chevalier*. This has not been easy, believing it my fault that my friend lost his sole daughter."

"I can well imagine that."

"Aye." Marco's gaze trailed across the yard in Bronwyn's wake. " 'Tis most reassuring that she is safely home."

"Indeed." Rowan turned his smile on Bronwyn's father, noting again how closely that man observed him. "There is but one obligation that will undoubtedly be yours as a result of this, and I pray 'tis not an onerous one."

Marco sniffed, but Rowan continued undeterred, gesturing to the maid behind him. "Bronwyn felt compassion for the fate of this woman, who was enslaved. Marika has been Bronwyn's maid. I pray the burden of supporting her does not trouble you overmuch. She speaks only her own tongue, though she and Bronwyn have developed a strong bond."

Marika seemed to understand that her fate rested in Nicholas's, hands, for she dropped to her knees before him. She tried to kiss his fingers, but he would not permit it, so she kissed his shoe.

"Child!" Nicholas cried. "Marika!" She looked up at him fearfully, but he smiled and offered his hands. "Come to your feet,'' he urged with a gesture. ''We have no slaves here and you shall not be treated as one.''

He took her hands in his, kindly in his every gesture, and shook his head as he urged her to her feet. ''Look at this, you have been hungry so long that there is naught upon your bones. Do not tremble, Marika, all will be well.'' Nicholas smiled deliberately and the tiny woman seemed slightly more at ease.

''Cook!'' Nicholas called, and a blond man robust and tanned appeared, ducking around the side of the house. He carried a basket heavily laden with greens. His thickened midriff hinted to Rowan that the fare might be very good in this hall.

''This is Marika,'' Nicholas supplied, his voice low and even. Marika bowed slightly, apparently understanding. ''My daughter believed her to be in need of a home like ours. She will not understand your words, but try to reassure her, perhaps with some of your fine broth. She looks hungry to me.''

The cook stepped closer, his blue gaze sweeping over the tiny woman. ''Aye, and lonely, my lord,'' he amended.

''Can you find some labor for her in the kitchen?'' Nicholas asked, and the cook waved in reassurance.

''Of course, sir. There is always labor for another pair of hands.'' He smiled slowly, his manner that of a very gentle man, then beckoned to Marika. He made an eating motion and she bit her lip, clearly tempted. She looked to Nicholas, who nodded, then hesitantly stepped toward the cook.

A woman's delighted squeal echoed in the distance, the three men turning as one to look. Nicholas grinned outright when a woman with blond braids streaming past her hips burst into the yard, Bronwyn tucked fast against her side. The two woman shared similar coloring and beguiling smiles, though the one with the braids was markedly older.

"Niccolo, you sorry wretch!" she cried laughingly. "How could you not have told me sooner?"

"How *could* I have told you sooner, Adhara?" that man retorted. "I have only just learned the truth myself."

"You should have shouted it from the hills," Bronwyn's mother charged. Adhara pivoted and raised her arms skyward, shouting with glee. "My child, my Bronwyn, my own precious babe is home!"

Nicholas started to laugh as servants suddenly poured from the hall to see the truth of it themselves. Vassals came from the village, their eyes alight with curiosity, then smiled and shouted to others to join them. Young boys and girls came from the fields, the horses trotted closer to look, and soon the yard was filled with the sounds of laughter and love.

Bronwyn was home, and everyone was rejoicing.

'Twas nigh time for Rowan to go. He told himself that he lingered only because he so loved a merry celebration.

But even Rowan knew that to be a lie.

# Chapter Sixteen

ARIKA WATCHED THE MAN ESCORTING HER, UNABLE TO decide why he inspired her trust so readily. He had kindly eyes, and he moved with such restraint that naught he did was alarming. There was a tranquility about his manner that coaxed her to relax in his presence.

His low voice was soothing, though, indeed, she could not understand what he said. She had grown accustomed to that, and found herself listening to the rise and fall of his words.

'Twas like music, the way this man spoke. Perhaps that was what entranced her, for Marika dearly loved music and had heard precious little of it of late.

She followed him around the building that was clearly Ibernia's home, marvelling at the gentle green beauty of the hills on all sides.

"Well, now, you would be hungry after all the journeying you have been about and no wonder 'tis." The man's words flowed over her uncomprehended. He opened a gate and gestured Marika through it, as if she were a fine lady, not a peasant enslaved and stolen across the seas.

She found herself smiling at his gallantry, then caught her breath at the array of herbs and flowers growing in the enclosed space. He whistled and she glanced back, watching as he deliberately fastened the latch. He gave her a sharp look, tapping the latch, and Marika understood.

She was never to leave the gate unlatched. She echoed the locking gesture with her hands and nodded, winning a fleeting smile from the man.

''Have to keep the gate fastened, as you can see, for my lady's horses are nibblers of the worst sort. Lost nigh all of the elecampane last month, if you can believe the fact of it, and who would have been guessing that a horse would savor the taste of elecampane upon his tongue!''

He waved broadly to the hills beyond the garden walls and Marika noted the number of horses grazing in the meadow. She had no eye for horseflesh, but their coats were glossy with good health.

''Cursed stupid beasts they are, perhaps they do not taste at all, for, indeed, they trample every single thing flat in their haste to make a meal of what they should not be eating.''

He bent then and with gentle fingers lifted a snapped blossom. The tiny blue flower was trodden upon and he clucked his tongue disapprovingly.

''Borage,'' Marika said, naming the flower in her own tongue before she thought.

The cook looked up with surprise. ''You know this plant then, do you?''

'Twas obvious what he asked, and Marika was suddenly anxious to prove her usefulness to this household. She repeated the name of the plant, mimicked the making of a tisane and drinking it deeply. Then she straightened, giving as good an impression as she could of a knight emboldened by the brew. ''Valour,'' she insisted, and tapped her heart. ''Borage is for courage.''

Her companion chuckled and named the plant in his tongue. She repeated his word carefully, taking several tries to get it right. She knew when her pronunciation was correct, for he smiled.

He straightened then, his gaze drifting over the garden as he visibly saddened. "Reminds me of my Anna, it does, every time I am crossing the threshold to this place. Loved her plants, did my Anna, though she did not know what to do with the half of them." His voice dropped low and he fingered a blossom absently, sorrow in his blue eyes. "She loved the flowers so."

Marika did not know what had happened, though she feared she had done something to offend him. Quickly she scanned the garden and found another plant with which she was familiar. He had been pleased that she knew the borage; perhaps 'twould work again.

"Feverfew!" The plant heavily laden with tiny daisylike blooms could have been naught else. "For the headache." Marika tapped her temples emphatically, rolled her eyes at the feigned pain, then pretended to nibble the leaves of the feverfew plant. She blinked, as if her headache cleared, spread her hands, then looked to him.

"Truly?" He strolled closer and eyed the plant. "Indeed, I had no thought of its usefulness, for surely 'tis a foul-tasting plant and I would never put it into a stew." He made to seize a handful of leafs but Marika quickly stopped him, deliberately counting three into his palm. She gestured that he could have no more.

Understanding dawned on his features. "Ah! 'Tis of import how much is consumed. Aye, there are many a plant beneficial in small doses and less than beneficial in greater. That foxglove now, I know well its charms and its danger."

He pointed to a tall bloom Marika did not know and tapped his heartbeat. He indicated a tiny measure, then fluttered his hand against his breast as if his pulse raced. He marked a larger measure, then pretended to freeze in shock before toppling to the ground. His tongue was hanging out and his eyes wide open in a parody of death.

'Twas not a reminder Marika needed. She nodded once and turned away, haunted by the memory of her murdered baby, not a month old and stolen away from her. Bile still rose in her throat at the memory of the blood, so much blood from such a tiny child.

Her babe was dead and she was alone as she had never been alone before. To be sure, Marika had been alone even within her village, but that was naught compared to this. She had not been inclined to make a life among those who had shunned her for bearing a child without a spouse, even in this new land.

But she would never cease to mourn her child. At least they two might have faced the others together—if the babe had been granted a chance to survive.

Marika felt the weight of a hand upon her shoulder and might have hidden her tears, but her companion turned her to face him. Eyes filled with compassion, he truly had the most expressive features she had ever seen. Marika was amazed that a man could look so strong and reliable yet have his gaze tempered with understanding.

She had never met the like of this man. He was pleasant to look at, but that was not the root of it. She had a sense that he had endured much, for he did not accept his own good fortune with the foolish confidence of one who does not understand that matters could easily be otherwise. Yet no man with eyes so clear could be embittered by what had been his due.

Indeed, the lines in his tan indicated that he oft laughed.

"Aye, 'twas not too wise of me, was it then?" he said now. "If you were taken slave, then you must have seen those you loved die before your very eyes. I apologize to you, Marika, for that was less than thoughtful of me, and I know well enough the burden that the loss of a loved one can be."

Clearly he was sincere, and he apologized for surprising her. Marika nodded and might have turned away, but the man before her bent slightly to hold her gaze, an appeal in his own.

"Apology accepted then?"

He smiled tentatively and she tried to respond in kind. This seemed to relieve him, though he did not release her shoulders from his warm grip. He was slightly taller than she, though he was not a big man, and Marika found herself noticing the way the sunlight glinted in his fair hair. She had never seen hair such as these people possessed.

"Was it your husband that was killed, then, Marika? You are a pretty girl and I cannot imagine that you were not happily wedded wherever 'tis you were living."

Marika eyed him blankly, the cadence of his voice indicating a question, though she could not imagine what he asked. He grimaced and frowned, then shrugged. "Well, the truth of it will come out soon enough, I suppose, though only if we learn to speak properly to each other. Are you hungry, then?"

Marika stared at him, feeling like a fool for not understanding whatever he asked so earnestly.

He rubbed his belly, then wiggled his fingers as he made a funny growling sound. He looked to his belly, as if it had made the sound and startled him, and Marika laughed despite herself at his antics.

He grinned. "Hungry?" he repeated, and she knew what he meant.

She tapped her belly and nodded agreement, not because she was hungry but because it seemed to matter so much to him. "Hungry," she echoed carefully, and he smiled.

"Marika is hungry."

'Twas clear enough what that meant, given that she knew two words he uttered, so Marika repeated the phrase. They smiled at each other, both well pleased with what they had managed, then he was off.

"Well, there is much to be done this day, that much is certain, and if you are not minding a bit of a delay, I would have your help in bringing some herbs into the kitchen. Then I might labor while you eat your fill."

Marika trailed behind him, not certain what he was doing.

He tugged at an herb. "For a stew of chicken?" At her blank stare, he tucked his thumbs into his underarms and began to cluck like a barnyard fowl.

Marika laughed again and quickly indicated the sage she recognized. It grew lavishly along the edge of one bed, thyme directly behind it. She gestured to both, and he took his knife to generous handfuls of each as he taught her the names of the plants in his tongue.

She asked his name, just as she had done with Ibernia, and he grinned in that boyish way that was starting to affect the beat of her heart.

"Connor," he confessed, and Marika was glad she could say his name correctly the first time.

Indeed, Connor was so charming and attentive that it was easy to forget her painful memories for the moment. Marika found herself enjoying the sunlight and the plants, remembering her garden and wishing she could stay in this place forever.

But she did not know whether her mistress intended to remain or to continue on, though she knew that Ibernia was known here. Marika would remain with the woman who had won her freedom, for truly, she owed no greater loyalty to anyone else.

They were leaving the garden, their arms laden with herbs for the meal Connor must be preparing, when a child shouted from afar. Marika turned at the cry, the way Connor's eyes lit telling her much.

The young boy's resemblance to Connor told her the rest. He could have been no more than five summers of age, his hair the same golden hue as Connor's. She might have hated this child, if he had been closer in age to her own, or darker of hair as her own had been, simply for the crime of being alive.

But Marika was fiercely glad that she did not. She watched the play of emotions on Connor's face, though, and felt like a voyeur. She felt she lived vicariously by watching him.

And envying him.

The boy burst into the garden, a torrent of incomprehensible words falling from his lips and a tears upon his cheeks. He went straight to Connor and pointed to the line of blood upon his knee.

Connor crouched down before the boy after hugging him tightly, his words flowing low and soothing once again. " 'Tis hardly a scratch, though I can imagine it hurts like the very devil."

He ran a thumb across it and the boy winced. "Were you out in the brambles again? You know well enough that you are not to go there alone. The river is too close at hand and who knows what manner of mischief a boy can find himself within."

As Marika watched, Connor reached up and affectionately wiped a purple stain from the boy's chin. He smiled. "You were there, were you not?"

The boy shuffled his feet, clearly caught at some crime, then looked to Marika for the first time. Connor followed his gaze. "This is Marika." Marika bobbed her head at the sound of her name. "She has come to live here but does not understand all we say."

The boy studied her with open curiosity. "Why not?"

"She is from far away."

The boy's eyes rounded with wonder and Marika wondered what was being said of her. Her grip tightened on the herbs she carried and she did not doubt that Connor noted her uncertainty. The boy opened his mouth, no doubt to ask more questions, but Marika pointed to his wound. It was not overly deep but could do with some tending to halt the bleeding.

With Connor's encouragement, the boy followed Marika. She quickly found the plant she sought, plucked a few leaves, and crumpled them in her hands. Connor spoke to the boy, perhaps endorsing what she did.

They were in the kitchen shortly, the boy's eyes round with curiosity as Marika bruised the leaves, cleaned his cut, then bound the leaves over them. He thanked her prettily, then Connor dispatched him to some errand.

They stood, this man and woman, eyeing each other in the shadows of the kitchen. Before he could ask any questions, Marika pointed after the boy. She pointed to Connor, then rocked her arms as if she held a babe.

Connor smiled. "Aye, he is my son, that is the truth of it." He looked after the boy and his smile faded. "Though 'tis true enough that God gives with one hand and takes away with the other. 'Tis a sorry price to pay, to gain a son and lose a wife, but I cannot say that I would have preferred to be without him."

He smiled sadly and Marika wished desperately that she could have understood what he confided in her. " 'Tis the nature of all of us, I suppose, to want only all that is good and naught that is bad. I do miss Anna sorely, that much is for certain, but I cannot imagine not having my son."

He looked to Marika, as if asking for her endorsement of words she had not understood. Clearly he told her much, and she was suddenly impatient to explain herself to him.

She touched her own heart, she indicated the roundness

her belly had taken, then rocked a babe again. "Vassily," she said, naming her child for this man who listened so well.

He nodded, his gaze intent. Then Marika snatched the knife from the counter, her vision blinded with tears as she slashed at the mock babe in her arms. She choked on the tide of her tears and bowed her head as they flowed, ashamed to have shown so much of her pain to a virtual stranger.

But Connor stepped closer. He touched her shoulder, his expression sympathetic beyond all, and Marika found herself turning into his embrace. She found comfort there against his warmth, and she let herself weep for all she had lost.

When she was done, Connor wiped her tears and took her hand. He cupped her chin in his hand and spoke to her earnestly. "It seems we have much in common, though the fates have been more cruel to you. We have both lost what we held dear—come with me, Marika, and let me try to explain."

But Marika understood all too well when Connor bowed his head before the green mound marked by a wooden cross. And when his expressive eyes clouded with tears for Anna—a woman's name, without mistake—Marika offered solace this time.

'Twas no wonder she felt drawn to Connor, for this man understood how it stung to lose a loved one.

The sky was darkening when the family retired to privacy from the chaos of the hall, Rowan and Marco among their select number. Ale was brought in as well as bread, cheese, and a hot stew. Rowan ate his meal with gusto, as, he noted, did Bronwyn. The conversation rolled around him in that Irish tongue, but Rowan cared little for what was said.

Bronwyn was glad to be home, no doubt of that, and her family were more than delighted to see her again. She flitted around the table, sharing laughter with this one and another, spreading the delight of her smile. She had been sorely missed, Rowan could see the truth of it.

'Twas good to he here, and in such company. He glanced up once or twice, smiling to himself at the way Bronwyn fairly glowed. He had thought her a beauty before, but surrounded by the love she so treasured, she shone like a rare jewel.

The very sight made his heart ache with the knowledge that he would depart, never to see this lady again.

Suddenly Rowan guessed that the topic had changed, for Marco's comment brought silence over the board.

"What did he say?" Rowan asked Adhara.

She did not smile, and her words came low. "You will be wedded now, Bronwyn of Ballyroyal, he said. It must indeed be why you are coming home."

Bronwyn straightened and looked to her father, who sobered in turn. He did not reply in Irish and Rowan wondered if this was so he could understand, or whether Nicholas preferred not to speak that tongue.

"I understand, daughter of mine, that you did not want a spouse as old as me," Nicholas said carefully. Rowan noted how tightly he held Adhara's hand, how solemn that woman was. "I thought only of securing the future of all I had built and did not consider your feelings on the matter."

Bronwyn bowed her head.

"I wish that you had spoken to me before you fled."

The lady's chin shot up and her eyes flashed. "I did speak to you, but you would not listen!"

Nicholas cleared his throat and looked at his fingers entangled with his wife's own. " 'Tis true enough, I fear." He looked at his daughter again. "But now I have listened. I have cancelled your betrothal agreement, at not inconsiderable cost.''

Bronwyn's shoulders sagged with obvious relief and Rowan noted how Marco stiffened. The man was not surprised, though, making Rowan wonder what had been agreed.

''And I have made another arrangement, one equally suitable to me and one that you will hopefully find more fitting.''

''Another!'' Bronwyn gasped, twin spots of color burning in her cheeks. ''But I had thought to make a love match. I had thought to wed for love as you did!''

Adhara shook her head. ''There is too much at stake for such frivolity, Bronwyn, and you know the truth of it well.''

''But—''

''But naught,'' Nicholas interjected. ''Your opinion has been heard and my choice adjusted accordingly. You will wed Marco's son Matthew, a man but two years your senior.''

Bronwyn paled, as sure a sign of her dissatisfaction with the new arrangement as any. Before Rowan could protest that she should have some right to name her future after all she had endured, the lady lifted her chin and spoke. ''I cannot.''

''Whyever not?'' Nicholas said impatiently.

''I am no longer virginal,'' Bronwyn declared, standing straight and tall even as the assembly whispered in horror. ''I would not shame Marco or his son thus.''

Nicholas swore. Marco swore. All gazes pivoted to Rowan, but Bronwyn spoke clearly and distinctly. ''This knight showed me naught but courtesy, *after* I was raped by an unscrupulous sea captain. The blame for this lies at my own door alone, for being an impetuous fool and losing what I had to bring to a wedding as a result.''

Nicholas ran a hand over his brow and muttered something under his breath. Adhara took a deep breath and turned to Marco. "Marco, what do you say to this?"

That man, though he looked older than he had moments past, nodded grimly. "It does not affect the intent of our agreement. I shall speak to my son and ensure he understands the greater import at stake here."

"Matthew will see sense," Nicholas agreed. The two men held each other's gaze, then nodded once, their course agreed. Nicholas cast a glance back to his daughter, one that was not without affection for all its steadiness. "Indeed, Bronwyn, you may find that Matthew is a good match for you."

"Nay!" she cried. "This is not my desire!"

"You have a responsibility and you will see it done," Nicholas retorted.

Adhara stepped forward when father and daughter glowered at each other. "All are tired," she said with a gracious smile to the assembly. "And all are surprised by what has been witnessed this day."

Adhara laid a hand on her husband's arm. "Bronwyn, you know that your father wants only to ensure your future comfort, that you are wed to a man upon whom you can rely. I beg of you, do not set your thoughts so surely on refusal before you have considered the matter fully."

Bronwyn's lips set stubbornly, no good sign to Rowan's thinking.

"Consider this agreement until the morrow," Adhara proposed. " 'Tis all we ask of you."

"And on the morrow?"

"After all have slept well and tempers have soothed, we shall discuss this choice, as a family, and decide our course."

Bronwyn took a deep breath, looked between her parents,

then nodded once. ''Until the morrow,'' she agreed, then turned to march into the hall.

''You bend to her will in this,'' Nicholas muttered.

''And you will drive her away,'' his wife retorted in an undertone. ''I have persuaded horses to mate who would not tolerate each other's presence when I began. Trust me in this.'' She cast a brilliant smile at Marco and raised her voice slightly. ''All will be resolved to your satisfaction in the end.''

But Rowan was not so certain of that. Nay, Bronwyn was not the kind of woman who readily changed her thinking, and certainly not over a single night. She did not want this spouse, and given the disapproving manner of that man's father, Rowan could not truly blame her. Though clearly her parents meant well, it seemed a travesty that after all she had endured, the lady would be denied the only thing she wanted.

Impulse—or perhaps too many years in chivalrous company—demanded that Rowan do something about the matter.

All for naught.

'Twas all Bronwyn could think as she returned to familiar chambers, a familiar bath in a familiar tub, familiar maids, familiar garb, familiar rituals, and an all-too-familiar dilemma.

After all she had experienced, her father was still determined to wed her to a man she did not want to marry. She did not love Matthew any more than she loved his father, Marco.

And there was the crux of the matter. She had made her plea and it had been rejected. Beyond fleeing Ballyroyal again, a course she was reluctant to take, Bronwyn did not know what to do.

'Twas not a situation she savored.

The bathing chamber was at the back of the hall, the timbered ceiling low to hold the heat. The room was wedged between the kitchen and the hall proper, so that the warmth of both hearths would heat the air.

But the stone floor and lack of sunlight in this windowless chamber made the room dark. The maids had lit a trio of lanterns and a pair of braziers, the golden light and sputtering heat turning the chamber into a humid retreat.

The great wooden tub had already been rolled in, the liner inserted to ensure no slivers found their way into Bronwyn's hide. Maids were filling the tub to the brim with steaming water, chattering all the while. The steam clouded the air of the room, and the trio of lanterns flickered fitfully in the dampness.

Such a familiar scene should have soothed Bronwyn's agitation, particularly considering how dire her need for a good bath had become. Her mother's maid brought brushes for her nails and a finely milled soap, displaying them with pride, as well as lengths of linen for drying herself afterward.

No expense was spared, but instead of being pleased, Bronwyn simmered. She supposed she should not blame her father for wanting to ensure her future security, but still his choice rankled. How could he have made this commitment without her consent? How could he have failed to understand the root of her complaint against Marco as a spouse?

'Twas unfair, given that her parents had wed for love themselves! Too much at stake, indeed. Bronwyn fairly growled over the injustice of it all and thought rather more favorably of Rowan's disregard of obligations.

Her responsibility to her family's wealth was at root here, the truth of that more than clear.

And Bronwyn's happiness was as naught in the bargain. Oh, she was certain her parents believed she would find happiness in any match and that they longed only to see her well cared for until her dying day.

But 'twould be impossible to be happy in any match other than one with the man she loved.

And that man had made it most clear that he did not want her. Curse Rowan de Montvieux!

Bronwyn smiled thinly for the maid, who was not to blame for any of this. She shed her blue striped kirtle, wrought of a gift from Baldassare, and shivered at the unwelcome reminder of what she had done. Indeed, she never wanted to see the garb again.

"Oh, the wool is so lovely a hue!" that maid cooed. "I have oft heard tell of the weaving of Flanders—and to be sure, I have glimpsed on occasion the fine wares that my lord Nicholas does exchange. Never though have I had the chance to touch—why, even filled with salt and dirt, the cloth is wondrously fine!"

" 'Tis yours," Bronwyn said, sinking into the hot water with a sigh. The girl gasped with delight. Bronwyn accepted her gratitude politely but found herself glad when she was finally alone.

Though soon enough she would not be.

She frowned, realizing that she had been so disappointed that she had not even asked her father about the date for the wedding. Would it be soon? Bronwyn guessed as much, for no one would want to chance her fleeing in defiance again.

She scowled further at the realization that she could not even recall Marco's son particularly well. That was not a good sign! To be sure, Matthew had visited Ballyroyal, but he was quiet and had a tendency to linger behind his father.

Bronwyn grimaced, unable to help thinking of a man who insisted upon having all eyes upon him. She doubted she could even come to love a man whose presence was as substantive as a shadow.

Bronwyn splashed unhappily in the bath, her thoughts filled with memories of a certain roguish knight. It was all too easy to recall the last bath she had had. Never mind the pleasure Rowan had introduced to her that afternoon. She almost wished he were here, that they could share this moment and each other.

But that was not to be. Indeed, he had probably left Ballyroyal already.

Bronwyn's heart sank and she deliberately let herself think upon happier moments. Aye, she could fairly see Rowan's strong hands upon her flesh, feel his reverential touch, taste the heat of his kiss. Bronwyn took a deep breath and closed her eyes, recalling the amber flash of his eyes when she surprised him, the way the sunlight danced in the russet waves of his hair, the way his lips twisted when he teased.

But Rowan was surely gone, his task completed and the desire for adventure hot in his chest. No need for farewell between them—nay, such a show of tenderness would not be his way.

Bronwyn sternly told herself not to be a fool and yearn for what she could not have. Truly, if Rowan were not precisely as he was, he might not have captured her heart so completely.

'Twas cold comfort.

Well, there had to be some merit in this adventure. At least Rowan had taught her that there was naught to be feared abed. And he had never pledged to do more than that. Rowan had not lied to her. He had not deceived her in any way.

But Bronwyn would miss him sorely, for all her days and nights, just the same. She suspected she would always measure men against Rowan's standard, no less that Matthew would fall well short of the measure.

That was not a promising prospect for her wedded bliss.

The door to the bathing chamber opened behind her, but Bronwyn was not prepared to be sociable. She waved a wet hand dismissively, scattering water droplets across the floor. "Leave me be, if you please," she said in the Irish used in the household. "I would have a moment alone."

"I have no idea what you are saying," the object of her thoughts retorted cheerfully, and she jumped. "Though I can make a decent guess by the way you are waving your hand."

Bronwyn sat up hastily, certain her ears played tricks upon her, She cast a glance over her shoulder, only to find Rowan closing the door, that familiar mischief in his eyes. "What are you doing here? I thought you had left."

"You thought wrong." He winked and shed his tabard, kicking off his boots at the same time.

"What are you doing?" Truth be told, Bronwyn was delighted to find that Rowan had lingered at Ballyroyal. She might have protested his familiarity in coming to her side here, but no sound came out.

Nay, the sight of his bare chest silenced her.

How could she have forgotten how splendidly this man was wrought? Rowan winked, then dropped his chausses, granting her a sight guaranteed to ensure her silence. He leapt across the floor, showing the muscles of his legs to advantage, even while he made a face at the coldness of the stone.

"Ye gods, I should hope that bath is mightily hot! My feet shall be as ice by the time I am in it."

The sight of his bare flesh distracted Bronwyn and quickened her blood. Aye, she had missed him! Pleasure surged through her that her thoughts seemed to have summoned him here, that he was not gone after all. She wondered fleetingly if there was indeed a bond between them, despite what he said—or did not say.

*In the tub?*

Too late, Bronwyn realized his intent and recovered her tongue. She gasped in outrage. "You are not sharing my bath!" She retreated to the far side of the large wooden tub, but Rowan showed no signs of halting his progress.

"Whyever not? We shared the bathwater before."

Though that was true enough, matters had changed. "But not *here*!" Bronwyn flicked a glance to the door, half expecting her father to enter and chastise them. "You must leave!"

"Selfish woman," Rowan teased, clearly having no intention of going anywhere. "A fine deep hot bath like this and you will not share." He wiggled his eyebrows playfully as he climbed over the side, though Bronwyn could not help but note the lean strength of his legs. "I should have guessed your measure when you stole the cloak that morn."

"You cannot do this!"

" 'Tis too late, for I already do." Rowan winked, then caught his breath in appreciation as he sank beneath the steaming water. His eyes drifted closed as Bronwyn sputtered, unable to find words for his audacity. His expression was one of pure bliss. "Oh, this is marvelous indeed. A bucket does not compare." He opened his eyes and grinned at her. "Have you any soap?"

"I will not share soap with you. Now get out, before someone finds you here!"

Bronwyn was not surprised to find Rowan's expression turn mischievous. She did not miss his quick glance toward her breasts, nor indeed the way his gaze brightened, as if her nudity was visible through the water and steam.

Aye, a cautiously exploring toe brushed against her leg.

"You are overly audacious!" Bronwyn pulled back her legs and folded her arms across her chest. "You would make trouble for me in my father's own house!"

"Me?" Rowan pouted with mock disappointment, the merriment in his eyes unceasing. "Surely there is no need for modesty between us," he mused, then sidled around the tub, clearly intending to bump shoulders with her.

Oh, Bronwyn knew very well what he was about! Part of her was intrigued; the rest of her knew very well that she could not indulge in temptation. Not here in her father's home with her betrothed's father in the hall!

She scooted away from Rowan, knowing that if he touched her, she would be lost. "Do not touch me," she warned, less conviction in her tone that she might have hoped to hear.

"Whyever not?" Rowan's voice was low and unhurried, as though he would tempt her to tarry with him. "We have touched afore." He eased alongside her, but Bronwyn darted away, the pair of them circling the perimeter of the tub like a pair of dizzy crabs. The warm water swirled around her, teased into currents by their movements, the steam and the lanternlight making the room impossibly intimate.

Bronwyn was only too aware of how tempted she was.

Rowan arched a brow. "What has changed?"

"Oh, the cheek of you!" Bronwyn cried. "Everything has changed and you know it well! I am to wed Marco's son."

Rowan sobered and stilled as he watched her closely. "And you do not want to."

'Twas not a question, and Bronwyn supposed there was no

doubt of her opinion, after her very public protest. She shrugged as if her heart was not hammering at his proximity and apparent concern. " 'Tis clear that my desire makes little difference."

"Perhaps it should," Rowan suggested silkily, his eyes dark. "What do *you* desire, Bronwyn of Ballyroyal?"

Her heart leapt and she met his gaze, the steam rising between them and making her hair stick to her brow. The golden light of the chamber suited him well, making him look virile and mysterious, less playful than Bronwyn had known him to be. Yet there was a glint in his eyes, a hint of unpredictability that was all too familiar.

Bronwyn's mouth went dry beneath Rowan's perusal. She could not look away; she felt that the bath was suddenly too hot. And remarkably, she could not bring herself to utter the truth of what she did want.

Because she knew that Rowan would not grant her desire.

So Bronwyn held her tongue, though she could not look away. She did not know what Rowan found in her eyes, but finally he smiled that languorous smile that she knew better than to trust.

"I have a better solution," he whispered wickedly.

Bronwyn's breath caught in her throat, but she could not even form a question before he winked again.

"Trust me!" Rowan dove across the tub, a purposeful gleam in his eyes. His move launched a wave of water over the rim. He caught Bronwyn in his arms and she had time only to squeal in protest before the tub rocked on its considerable weight and slowly tipped. 'Twas not an easy deed to topple a full tub of this size, and she had no doubt that Rowan forced it over by his own choice.

Then everything happened very fast.

Bronwyn screamed as they fell backward, Rowan's cursedly confident chuckling in her ear. He held her tightly against him, rolling them so that he landed beneath her. Bronwyn saw him wince when his back hit the floor, saw the tide of water roll across the floor and under the door. Servants cried out in the hall and the door was thrown open, just as Rowan rolled her beneath him and captured her lips in a soul-stirring kiss.

Then Bronwyn cared for naught else but his touch. His kiss was everything she recalled and more, as if he poured his heart into the embrace. He kissed her with a thoroughness unexpected, and Bronwyn could hold back no longer.

God in heaven, but she loved this man. If this was to be her last taste of him, she would make it a kiss to cherish always.

Her father, however, had a rather different perspective.

"What nonsense is this?" he bellowed in outrage.

His roar compelled Rowan finally to break their kiss. Bronwyn caught her breath, eyed the knight's cocky smile, then followed his gaze to the portal.

The whole household had gathered around, their expressions uniformly shocked. Bronwyn realized belatedly that she was not only nude but entangled with a similarly nude man who was *not* her betrothed. Her cheeks burned with embarrassment, but Rowan seemed completely untroubled.

'Twas only then that she wondered what he did.

Rowan grinned confidently before her father's glower, as if there was naught untoward about the circumstance, even as he shielded Bronwyn from curious eyes. Bronwyn closed her eyes at her father's stunned expression and soundly cursed Rowan's self-assurance. Twittering rolled through the ranks of the household, and she knew this moment would be the talk of half of Ireland before the week was through.

Aye, 'twould take every measure of Rowan's charm to talk them free of this scandal!

# Chapter Seventeen

HERE WAS SOMETHING ABOUT BRONWYN OF BAL-lyroyal that made a man lose his course toward his goals, that much was certain.

Typically—at least in this woman's maddening presence—Rowan had thought only of saving her from the fate she did not desire and had not considered matters beyond that. She did not want to wed Matthew, so Rowan intervened.

'Twas simple enough.

The delight of holding Bronwyn close again surprised him with its intensity, as did the feel of her curves pressed against him and the taste of her kiss. Rowan realized he had never yearned for any other woman as he had for her, especially not after several bouts of lovemaking. But everytime he touched Bronwyn, it seemed he only wanted all the more.

This was more than desire at root. Aye, he loved the sound of Bronwyn's laughter, he loved how her eyes flashed when she was angered, how she pursed her lips when she puzzled a matter through. He loved her concern for others, regardless of their rank, and he loved how she made a gesture akin to flicking back her hair.

She had no hair to flick, since it had been shorn so short, but the gesture hinted that her tresses had once been long like her mother's. Indeed, he wondered how she would look with silken locks of red gold and was tempted to remain in her company long enough to see.

When had he ever wanted to remain *years* by a woman's side?

Rowan looked down at the lady, flushed and wary, and his heart skipped a beat. He loved more than the sum of these attributes—he loved the lady herself. And that love, a love he was so very afraid to trust, was what prompted Rowan to act against his own interests, time and again.

He loved Bronwyn.

There was a light in her eyes that made him wonder whether she might love him. The very possibility was staggering. A treasure Rowan had not even known he coveted was offered to him, with no price upon it except his declaration of love.

He stared into the lady's eyes and his confusion gave way to clarity. Rowan loved Bronwyn of Ballyroyal, which made his course remarkably obvious.

Meanwhile, the chattering of servants had risen to a din that was nigh enough to drive a man mad. Bronwyn's father shouted, his wife tried to interject a voice of reason, Marco frothed about the unsuitability of Bronwyn for his son.

Nicholas turned upon Rowan. "And what," he demanded frostily, "do you intend to do about this circumstance?"

"I shall wed your daughter, of course," Rowan said smoothly, and heard Bronwyn catch her breath before chaos reigned anew.

"What?" She gasped.

"What?" Nicholas demanded.

Adhara stepped past her spouse, her gaze glittering as her daughter's own often did, and asked the most pertinent question to Rowan's mind. "Why?"

Rowan grinned, then looked down into Bronwyn's wary

gaze. "Because I love her," he declared. "And I would wed her."

But if Rowan imagined that his sweet pledge would make all come aright, he was sorely mistaken. Bronwyn's eyes flashed and she planted both hands in the middle of his chest, giving Rowan a push that startled him with its strength.

He fell back and she bounded to her feet, seizing a length of linen and wrapping it around her nudity with a savage gesture. "You lie like a hide before the hearth!" she cried. "You do not love me!"

"Bronwyn!" her parents chided in unison, even as the servants pressed closer for a better view.

"Bronwyn," Rowan appealed as he got to his feet. "I do love you, I swear it to you."

The lady's marvelous blue eyes narrowed. "Were you not the one to warn me that a pledge of love cannot be trusted, especially when one wants something from the other?"

Rowan did not flinch from the accusation in her eyes, though he immediately guessed the root of it. "I told you that I had sworn off my quest."

"Until you had sight of Ballyroyal," Bronwyn retorted bitterly. " 'Tis a fine holding, is it not? And one upon which a man could live at leisure, if his wife turned a blind eye to his roving?"

She made to push past him, but Rowan seized her arm. "I know I said many things, *ma demoiselle,* but they are no longer true . . ."

"But words once uttered cannot be recalled, can they, *chevalier*?" she demanded, tossing Rowan's own words back to him. She lifted her chin, the valkyrie with the cold eyes he had admired all those weeks ago. "I am not your *demoiselle,*" she said with resolve. "You had best seek your heiress elsewhere."

She pulled out of his grip and strode out of the bathing chamber, the servants parting before her like a biblical sea. The lady had stated her terms, and Rowan needed only a chance to persuade her that she had convinced him of their merit.

But it seemed he was not to have it. Rowan gritted his teeth and lunged after Bronwyn, determined to have his hearing, but her parents closed rank against him.

Nicholas's expression was considering. "I would expect then that you will withdraw your suit?"

"Of course not," Rowan retorted, annoyed that Bronwyn's father should think his affections so fleeting as that. "She will wed me in the end."

He was so busy looking after the departed Bronwyn and plotting his course that he did not notice the smile Adhara cast sidelong at her spouse.

Matthew had not taken the news well.

But then, Matthew never took news well that was not to his own clear advantage. Marco sat in his establishment near Dublin's wharf, amid all the lengths of cloth, a day after departing from Ballyroyal and wondered how he might have explained the situation better.

He sighed and rubbed his temples, certain that his son would have stormed into the night no matter how he had presented the truth. Though Niccolo's daughter was impetuous, Marco could not have said that his son was of any more stable temperament. Increasingly, Matthew was vocal about his dissatisfaction the change in a once-shy child most startling to Marco.

Perhaps it was better Matthew and Bronwyn would not marry.

But then there were practical matters. Marco was skeptical that this knight who would wed Bronwyn could manage Ballyroyal, once Niccolo was no more. The noble class was oft beyond such mundane concerns, and this knight seemed less sensibly inclined than others.

Though Matthew might have done no better. Marco supposed he should not have kept the boy and his new moods hidden from Niccolo. Aye, Marco had been convinced that the boy would grow out of his inclinations.

He had been wrong. It seemed Matthew would never be sensibly inclined. Though few were as sensibly inclined as Marco. His lips twisted with the certainty that his son was undoubtedly gambling and drinking already, the two least sensible activities in which he might have engaged.

Sweet Jesu, but where had Marco gone awry? He buried his face in his hands, puzzling over the possibilities—or distinct lack of them—as the sounds of activity faded beyond his doors. The wharf stilled as night fell, even the whores' calls fading as the time passed. He did not know how long he sat there, but he straightened in shock when his heavy oak door was suddenly kicked open.

It slammed against the wall, revealing a slice of midnight sky that made Marco wonder whether he had slept. Then his fears returned and redoubled at the sight of his son, eyes alight with that fey optimism that oft seized him these days.

At times like this that Marco could not believe this man was his own child.

"Father! I shall have Ballyroyal in the end!" Matthew cried, punching his fist into the air. "You promised it to me, Father, and truly 'twill be mine!"

Marco shook his head. "Matthew, I have explained that matters have changed . . ."

"But we shall change them again. I will have the untold wealth of your concerns, I will be a king among traders."

"Matthew," Marco said wearily. "I have explained to you, and truly it may be for the best. You have never had much aptitude for trade, and 'tis clear I have indulged you overmuch . . ."

Matthew laughed and stepped farther into the chamber. "No aptitude? But I have a new friend, Father, a friend who insists I have precisely the qualities required. He insists that I should not stand aside and lose what is my rightful due."

Marco rubbed his temples. But any admonition froze in Marco's throat when his son tugged this new friend into the open portal.

It could not be!

He blinked, he looked again, and could not believe the evidence of his own eyes. Marco gripped the arms of his chair and stared, struck dumb to find a spectre from the past before him.

He knew Vincente di Vilonte was long dead, yet it seemed that very man stood before him once again. Perhaps 'twas Vincente's ghost, for he looked as if he had not aged a day.

Marco blinked and looked again, his good sense slow to assert itself. The answer, once it came to him, was painfully evident. 'Twas Vincente's son who stood before him, Vincente's son whose eyes filled with the same madness that had spelled his father's demise.

Baldassare folded his arms across his chest and grinned wolfishly, no good intent in his expression. Vincente might be dead, but his son was not.

Worse, Baldassare was *here.*

A man of wits could guess why all too well.

"Sweet Jesu, Matthew," Marco whispered. "What have you done?"

'Twas a fine summer morn, and on a day so clear, a man so fortunate as Padraig could have no complaints about his fate. Nay, Padraig had seen misfortune aplenty, and a fine little tavern upon the very wharf of Dublin and no lack for clients prepared to pay for an ale was a fine fine fate indeed.

He appreciated all that had come his way, that he did. Though a good measure of his success was due to solid labor, he did not forget to light a candle in the church each week, say his prayers, and let his Mary do whatsoever she felt was necessary to keep the fairy folk happy.

Life was good and Padraig savored every moment. His girth and his three chins were a testament to his success, as were Mary's padded hips. Aye, life was good, and since it could well be short, neither Mary nor Padraig was inclined to deny themselves whatever pleasure they might seize.

Padraig had unlocked the door facing the wharf and was just in the act of pouring himself a measure of his own ale— just to ensure that it truly fine enough for those inclined to pay—when a shadow fell across the doorway.

He took a hasty gulp, then pivoted with a welcoming smile. Mary whistled over the hearth in the room beyond, the smell of her meat pasties already wafting through the air.

The man who entered the tavern was no more grizzled than most, his ruddy beard shot with a healthy sprinkle of grey. His eyes were narrowed with impatience, and looked as if they were seldom any other way, though it might well have been the sunlight on the water that forced his expression. He scanned the room, as if he were half certain foes awaited him in every corner. To be sure, the man had seen more than one fight, for there were scars upon his face and his leather jerkin.

But Padraig was used to all types. Tough they might well

be, and he had seen more than one bloody fight, but every man alive liked a cool measure of ale in his throat and a warm morsel in his belly.

"Good morning to you, sir!" Padraig cheerfully rattled through his offerings and associated prices, his first guest silent.

"Ale," that man said succinctly when Padraig finally finished. He chose the one chair that backed against the wall and sat down, his eyes gleaming in the shadows when he looked to Padraig again. "And whatever 'tis I am smelling."

"Ah, my wife is a marvel of a cook, that she is. 'Tis a pasty like none other she conjures, 'twill melt in your mouth and make your heart sing from here to eternity."

Padraig filled a crockery mug with ale and presented it to the man. The man nodded once, sipped, then nodded again. He cast a glance through the door to the bustling wharf, then leaned back against the wall. He stretched out his legs and crossed them at the ankles, looking dangerous indeed.

Perhaps his silence was unnerving, perhaps it was simply Padraig's nature to talk, or perhaps just that keeper's merry mood was at root. Whichever way, Padraig found himself chattering.

"You would be a foreigner, then, by your garb." The man glanced up, but Padraig only grinned. "Ah, do not be looking so very surprised. 'Tis a busy wharf and I have eyes in my head enough to know who is of here and who is not. And truth be told, there are foreigners aplenty in Dublin these days—and many folk who think 'tis not as matters should be. Me, though, I have no quibble, for 'tis good business when foreigners come to town."

Padraig leaned on a table. "Aye, the locals, they go home to eat or to their friends for an ale, but those from abroad, even the cursed Normans, have need of a sip and bite. 'Tis what binds all of us together, shows a man that there is little difference between men, and truly, if you sailed all the way to Jerusalem, well, I imagine even *they* would have need of a sip and a—"

"Have you had many foreigners of late?"

Padraig was startled by the interruption, though he recovered himself quickly. "Oh, aye! To be sure, down Wexford way it has been worse, but we have had our measure here, that much is certain. More Normans than a man can shake a stick at, although I have to be wondering how 'tis they are different from the Vikings."

Padraig set to rinsing his crockery mugs. "Aye, there were tales aplenty when I was a child, of Viking raids in days long past and thieving of the churches and all, but every Norseman I have known here has been decent enough. Tall and blond they are, though, big men, if you take my meaning, and truly there are many among these Normans with much the same look about them . . ."

"Any other than Normans and Norse?"

Padraig blinked. "Well, the Welsh, of course, though they are a wickedly roguish lot. Always chasing the women, they are, and leaving their debts unsettled. Surly with coin, if I must say as much, and deceitful beyond other races. 'Tis something in their blood, I think, to covet what is not their own and to take what is not their right to take. Why, that Strongbow himself has a hearty measure of Welsh blood in his veins. 'tis said, which is proof enough for any thinking man of . . ."

The stranger cleared his throat pointedly. Padraig glanced up and realized to his dismay that this man's ruddy coloring might put him among Strongbow's countrymen. Before he could summon a question, the stranger asked another.

"Any other foreigners?"

Padraig felt his eyes narrow in turn. "And why would you

be wanting to know? You have a merry lot of questions this morn, for a man disinclined to share so much as his name.''

The man smiled, an expression that did not seem at ease upon his harsh features. ''I seek a friend.''

Padraig did not believe him, not for a moment, though there was something about this man that reminded him of another. ''A friend is it, then? Well, there was only one that put me in mind of you, that much is certain, and I suppose there is little harm in setting one foreigner after another.''

''Aye?'' The stranger leaned forward, his curiosity obvious.

''Aye, and a strange one he was, I have no quibble in telling you as much as that. A Venetian, 'twas my guess, though the boys they had a wager upon it, one that was never resolved. Dark of hair and dark of eye, but not of these parts. His eyes were nigh black, not that merry brown as the girls are oft having here. Nay, and there was something about him, something that put one in mind of a snake was what my Mary said of him, and she left the room when he was here. I cannot blame her—when the man looked upon you, you were wanting to shiver.

''Come to be thinking of it, he was asking after strangers as well.'' Padraig regarded his guest with newfound suspicion. ''Is it another invasion then?''

The man sipped and shrugged, his gaze unswerving. ''I would know naught of the doings of Venetians, much less any desire they might have for Dublin.''

Padraig snorted. ''Well, to be sure, he was not very mysterious about it all. That was why I did not wager upon him being from Venice, for he was the most outspoken foreigner I have heard in years. Aye, he went on and about, fairly hounding me with his questions of some knight or other.''

Padraig tapped his ample chin. ''The name, now, the name. A French name or a Norman one, though one I had not heard afore.'' He snapped his fingers suddenly. ''Chevalier Rowan de Montvieux, that was it, and how would I be knowing a knight with a name the likes of that, let alone where that man might be found?'' Padraig snorted at the foolishness of it all. ''Though I suppose in the end I did aid him, for I knew well enough where Ballyroyal could be found, though any fool in this town could have told him that.''

''Ballyroyal?''

''Aye, 'twas where he intended to go, though I cannot imagine why. Truth be told, though, Nicholas of Ballyroyal has that same uncommon coloring.'' Padraig leaned against the counter and drummed his fingers. ''I shall have to be asking after that, for perhaps they too were old friends and I was wrong to be so suspicious. Goodness knows that Nicholas is a fine and generous man, his wife was born and raised on that fair holding, though indeed her parents came oft to town. I would not want to be offending Nicholas of Ballyroyal, for 'tis said that his arm is long and though he seems amiable enough—''

''Where *is* Ballyroyal?''

Padraig started, telling himself he should become accustomed to this one's abrupt manner. ''Oh, a good day's ride north and west. 'Tis a fine old holding, though one that benefitted greatly from the bounty Nicholas brought to the marriage with the holding's daughter. Aye, 'twas said that Adhara of Ballyroyal was a beauty so beyond compare that men would come from across the seas merely to gaze upon her. Why, would that not be a marvelous tale if Nicholas had done precisely that?''

Padraig chuckled to himself. ''I had not thought of it before, and, indeed, there is something about Nicholas that prompts a man to refrain from asking bold questions, though perhaps when he is next in town, I shall ask him of his origins . . .''

Padraig turned to find the stranger gone. He frowned and crossed the tavern, then poked his nose out the door.

There was no sign of the man or indeed any evidence of his passing.

Padraig ducked back inside and checked the crockery mug, noting that it was empty. He snorted and picked up the vessel, the experience doing naught to disprove his opinion of Welshmen.

But there was single coin left beneath the mug. Padraig picked it up and turned it in the sun, bit the silver and was pleasantly surprised.

''Mary, you will not be believing this, but that man paid for both ale and pasty, without ever having the latter.''

Mary came to the door to the back room, her expression surprised, her hands busily wiping on a cloth. ''Aye?''

''Aye.'' Padraig spared another glance out the door. ''He cannot have been a Welshman, after all.''

Three days after Rowan's feat, Bronwyn was still furious.

She paced her chamber, uncertain whether to kiss or kill a certain russet-haired knight. Aye, she loved him despite all he had done, and truly her heart had stopped cold when he confessed to loving her. 'Twould have been a sweet moment, if not for one critical detail

Rowan sorely wanted to win his wager with his brothers. That was impossible to forget. As much as Bronwyn would have preferred to believe his sweet confession, it came at too convenient a moment to be credible.

Her mother had been and gone several times, having extricated the entire tale and tried her mightiest to convince Bronwyn to grant Rowan a chance. Bronwyn was surprised

to learn that Rowan had not already departed from Ballyroyal, to seek another more biddable heiress, but then he
could be cursedly stubborn.

And he wanted to win this wager.

The maids had told of Marco's departure and her father's
annoyance with the whimsy of women, both tales that
Bronwyn did not particularly care to hear. She paced her
chamber, impatient with its confines and even more impatient with Rowan for not simply leaving. There was no
chance of forgetting him while she knew he lingered in the
hall.

Perhaps there was no chance of forgetting him at all, but
Bronwyn chose to see him and his presence as the obstacle.
How like Rowan to capture her attention and not relinquish
it. She drummed her fingertips on the furniture and cursed
that knight soundly for tying her innards in knots so readily.

'Twas late before Bronwyn finally fell asleep that night,
and perhaps because of her recent restlessness, she slept
more heavily than was her wont. At some point, she was
vaguely aware of the chamber door opening and was certain
another maid or her mother was intent on persuading her to
abandon "this stubborn course." Bronwyn frowned and
rolled over sleepily, having no intention of arguing the issue
again.

When the feather mattress dipped beside her her eyes flew
open, but by then it was too late.

None other than the knight who so determinedly occupied
her dreams stretched out beside her, his confident manner
implying that there was naught untoward with visiting a lady
in her own chamber. Bronwyn gasped and might have sat
up, but Rowan leaned across to kiss her deeply.

'Twas unfair by any accounting, and, curse the knave, he
knew it. Bronwyn melted beneath his embrace, despite her

urge to do otherwise, and by the time the knight lifted his head, she could not recall what she might have said.

Her chamber was flooded with moonlight, a beam falling through the open window. The sounds of the evening carried to her ears, the muted rustling of insects, the occasional nicker of horses. The stars were out in abundance, and the warm breeze held the promise of rain.

But the man lying beside her, so annoyingly sure of himself, seized Bronwyn's attention.

"You!" she managed to utter before Rowan poked something into her mouth. Her eyes widened in astonishment, but he tapped a fingertip upon her lips, his eyes sparkling.

" 'Tis a fig, a rare treasure to find so far abroad," he confided, the low cadence of her voice making Bronwyn's pulse speed. 'Twas far too private here and she yearned too much for this man to trust herself alone with him.

But Rowan stretched his length out beside her, crossing his booted ankles on her fine linens, and grinned down at her. That fingertip tapped gently on her lips.

"And I know that you are too well bred a lady to waste such a luxury, no less to speak despite a mouth full of food." His fingertip traced the outline of her lips, the way the moonlight etched his handsome features almost enough to make Bronwyn imagine she dreamed.

But dreams were not irksome in forcing one to eat figs. And dreams did not touch one's lips with such gentle heat that one longed for more.

"And of course," he continued with a crooked confident smile " 'tis unthinkable that you would be so vulgar as to spit it out."

Bronwyn made to pull the dried fruit from her mouth with one hand, but Rowan entangled their fingers, easily holding her hands above her head.

Bronwyn made a wordless of protest and struggled

against him, but to no avail. She knew he would not hurt her—it was simply that he bested her so readily that annoyed.

Indeed, the man knew her too well.

*"Ma demoiselle!"* Rowan chided, enjoying himself far too much. "I am appalled that you would even consider such a course. My own foster mother swore that a lady of merit swallowed whatever she bit, regardless of what it might be."

Rowan leaned down and kissed Bronwyn's earlobe, teasing her with his touch. "And I had so hoped that the lady I would take to wife might comport herself as a lady of merit," he whispered.

Bronwyn wriggled to no avail, took one look at the mischief in his eyes, and began to chew with a vengeance. She was not his *demoiselle,* she would not wed him, and she would have her say!

"No doubt you are wondering why I have come to your chambers so boldly as this," Rowan said easily, as if they held a conversation in perfectly normal circumstance.

There was naught normal, though, about the press of his length against her, nor the quickening of Bronwyn's pulse at his presence. There was certainly naught normal about the tremble that spread through her when his free hand landed on her waist, nor the way she could feel the heat of his palm there despite the layers of linen between.

'Twas the toughest fig she had ever had the misfortune to eat.

She did not doubt that he had chosen it apurpose.

"But you see, if you would not come to me and hear my case, then I could only come to you."

"Because you do not intend to lose your dare," Bronwyn declared. She managed no more before Rowan rummaged between them, then dropped another fig into her mouth.

Bronwyn protested but Rowan grinned, his teeth flashing in the moonlight.

Then he dropped a sack upon her belly, Bronwyn's heart sinking with certainty at its contents. 'Twas not a small sack, by any accounting. She chewed with haste, even as she knew he would best her in this.

"I intend to be heard," Rowan declared, his voice low. "And I come prepared to keep you silent until 'tis done. You may chew quickly, or you may chew slowly, but you will hear me out."

Bronwyn soundly cursed his determination. She heaved a sigh meant to be heard, but Rowan's grin did not waver.

"Then we understand each other." He propped himself up on his elbow, his gaze running over her with obvious appreciation. Bronwyn wiggled against his sure grip once more, her back arching slightly, and watched Rowan catch his breath. 'Twas encouraging that she was not alone in being acutely aware of the intimacy of this situation.

"You should not distract me so," he murmured, his free hand falling upon her breast as she swallowed her fig. "I might forget my chivalrous intent."

"Lust is no mark of chivalrous intent!" Bronwyn declared, winning another fruit for her outspokenness. She granted her knight a mutinous glance and chewed with vigor.

"Indeed, you have an uncommon affection for figs," he mused. "I shall have to keep that weakness in mind that once we are wed."

"We will not be wed," she argued, disregarding the cursed fruit in her mouth. "And I loathe figs."

Rowan chuckled. "Then I would advise you to chew slowly, for I am not nearly done." He poked the bag he had brought. "And even one who adored figs would be heartily sick of them by the time all of these were eaten."

Bronwyn laughed despite herself. "You are stubborn."

" 'Tis a trait we have in common." Their gazes locked and held, the moment stretching long and warm between them. "And there is that beguiling smile." Rowan traced the curve of her lips with a fingertip, the glow in his eyes nigh stopping Bronwyn's heart.

She thought he might kiss her, but suddenly he was unaccountably serious, his hand sliding to her waist once again. " 'Tis not merely lust between us, Bronwyn, and you know it as well as I."

A smile flickered across his lips as Bronwyn dared to hope. "Indeed, you probably guessed the truth of it sooner, given your greater familiarity with love. 'Tis a marvelous gift your parents granted you in creating this home so abundant in its love."

Rowan paused for a moment, his brows drawing together, and Bronwyn did not have the heart to interrupt him. "Truly, I am more familiar with lust and its fleeting influence, and perhaps that is why I mistook my interest in you for a more base desire. 'Tis the nature of lust, though, to be readily sated."

Rowan lifted his gaze to meet hers and she thought unaccountably of that boy who believed he was not lovable. Her heart twisted in a most unwelcome way and her hope redoubled.

"But my desire for you seems to only grow more each day," Rowan confessed, his gaze searching hers. "And 'tis more than lust. 'Tis for more than your touch, 'tis for the simple pleasure of your company and the sound of your laughter."

"You have a gift for pretty argument," she said softly, wanting to believe but not daring to do so.

"Shh! I am not done." Rowan pushed a fig into her mouth with a wink, then nodded acknowledgment. " 'Tis true enough, though that has had little influence with you. My foster mother always said that the truth of a man's intent was revealed in his deeds, and there are matters you should know.''

Rowan frowned and Bronwyn waited, her heart pounding in anticipation. "Your father is disinclined to grant your hand to man who travels with troubadors, and truly, I cannot blame him for this. All these years, I considered that life ideal, having forgotten how often I was cold and hungry as a child, no less how young those I loved did die.''

Rowan cleared his throat and spoke hastily, his gaze fixed upon the sack of figs. "I have decided that to live a life unfettered is a course overrated. To that end, I have accepted a task offered by your father—that of his marshall.''

Bronwyn blinked in astonishment. "You took a responsibility? Willingly?''

Rowan clicked his tongue with mock disapproval and dropped another fig between Bronwyn's lips. " 'Tis not so surprising as that. A man must be prepared to work for what he desires.''

"What do you desire?'' Bronwyn demanded, despite the fig. Though her words were unclear, the knight seemed to understand.

"Such manners!'' he chided. "I shall make you a wager, *ma demoiselle*. Pledge to hear me out and I shall rid you of that vexing fig you loathe so very much.''

"Gladly'' was all Bronwyn had the chance to utter before Rowan rolled atop her. His lips captured hers, his tongue diving between her teeth to lay claim to the fig. He released her hands and Bronwyn wrapped her arms around his neck, sensing his need for reassurance on this unfamiliar course and determined to grant it. They were on the cusp of a confession, and she hoped against hope 'twas the one she longed to hear.

After all, Rowan had accepted an obligation.

Bronwyn giggled as he made a game of fetching the fig and losing it again, drawing out their kiss in a most pleasurable fashion. When he lifted his head and chewed despite his impish grin, she laughed aloud. "You are incorrigible."

"Ah! So much for your pledge! I shall have to take a penance for the breaking of your word."

And Rowan kissed her again, his touch so thorough and so gentle that Bronwyn forgave him much.

They were both flushed when he lifted his head and she reached up to push the hair back from his brow, letting her fingers tangle within it. "You willingly took this obligation," she mused, still marvelling. "Do you intend to fulfill it?"

"My word is not worth so little as that," he teased, then sobered anew, his gaze searching his. He cupped her shoulders in his hands, bracing himself over her, his gaze searching hers. "Bronwyn, you have shown me that there is naught to fear in pledging oneself to another, naught to fear in admitting tender feelings. I would have you certain that the only treasure I seek in this match is your love in return for mine."

Bronwyn stared at him, her heart thundering.

"I would wed Ibernia as readily as Bronwyn," Rowan pledged. "For 'tis the lady I love, not what is linked to her name."

Still she said naught, for she could not summon a word to her lips.

"Bronwyn," Rowan murmured, his eyes bright. "I love you as never I imagined a man might love a woman. Will you be my bride?"

"I will not keep you like a courtesan," Bronwyn warned, knowing full well that was not what he wanted any longer.

Rowan shook his head. "I would not be so kept. Indeed,

your father's offer has appeal, as I have wasted a perfectly good education.''

"I will not share my spouse," Bronwyn whispered, knowing she had to make matters clear and willing Rowan to see the strength of her feelings in this.

He sobered in turn. "And I will not share my bride."

His sincerity could not be doubted, and Bronwyn's heart began to sing with delight.

"Then I will wed you." She smiled, loving the way his eyes lit with pleasure, but not quite prepared to grant him such an easy victory as this. "Indeed, I should dare you to love me for all your days and nights!"

Rowan laughed aloud. "Nay, *ma demoiselle,* the odds of failure are not nearly long enough." Bronwyn's heart sang as he dipped his head to kiss her and she knew she could ask for naught more than this. There was a new ardor between them, a spark that Bronwyn knew would burn for all their days and nights.

Rowan lifted his head all too soon, his expression rueful.

"What is amiss?"

"Naught yet, but soon a great deal." At her puzzled expression, Rowan arched a brow. "Your father made it clear that a certain part of me would be forfeit"—he grimaced comically—"if I did more than talk to his beloved daughter before there was a ring upon her finger. He is protective of his womenfolk, your father."

Bronwyn smiled, knowing that a similarly protective man was in her bed and liking that very well. "Aye, that he is. I am surprised he made no mention of a priest."

Rowan's expression turned thoughtful, then he chuckled. "As always, Bronwyn, you see to the root of the matter. A ring is an issue readily solved." He pulled his mother's ring from his finger, the band of gold catching the moonlight as he slipped it onto the middle finger of her left hand.

Bronwyn was touched that he would entrust her with such a treasure. "You are certain I should have this token of your mother?"

"I can think of nowhere else it should be." Rowan leaned closer, his eyes dancing wickedly. "Do you truly think a ring alone will satisfy your father?"

Bronwyn smiled, liking that he concerned himself with her family's approval. "Marriage is made in the heart, not at the altar," she whispered. " 'Tis what my mother always says."

"Then our marriage is well and truly made, *ma demoiselle,*" Rowan murmured, kissing her soundly. When he lifted his head, she had only a moment to note the trouble-making glint in his amber eyes.

Then the figs were tumbling beneath the linens, rolling across her flesh, and hiding in the dips of the feather pallet. "Aha!" the knight crowed as he dove beneath the linens. "Fortunately for you, I do love figs. It shall be my quest to find them all."

Bronwyn closed her eyes in pleasure when he checked her navel with unexpected thoroughness, his tongue coaxing the heat to rise beneath her flesh.

'Twould be long before she slept this night, and Bronwyn did not care.

# Chapter Eighteen

ROWAN AWOKE TO THE COLD EDGE OF A KNIFE AGAINST his throat.

The moonlight that had caressed Bronwyn's flesh while they made love was gone, the sky greyed. 'Twas before the dawn, he guessed, and he was reassured that his lady still slept safely beside him.

For the moment.

He tried to feign sleep while he assessed the situation. His breathing must have changed, though, for the blade bit deeper.

"I will kill you, for taking what should be mine," his assailant muttered in his ear.

Rowan gasped as the knife bit into his flesh. Bronwyn stirred and he tried to warn her, but to no avail. Her eyes flew open, her expression changing to astonishment as she looked from the knife to Rowan's attacker.

"Matthew! What are you doing?"

She might have intervened, but Matthew stepped back, hauling Rowan with him. The knight stumbled to his feet, hating that there was naught he could do to aid himself.

Let alone his lady. What would Marco's son do to Bronwyn once Rowan was dead? Rowan did not want to consider the matter.

"I am taking what is my due!" Matthew cried. Rowan

hated that he could not accurately guess the man's height and strength. He could not even manage a glance over his shoulder with this blade at his throat.

He closed his eyes and guessed by the angle of the blade that Matthew was shorter than himself.

Bronwyn sat up in the bed and Rowan nearly groaned aloud. Her chemise was wrought of linen so sheer that it hid none of her many charms, though she was blissfully unaware of that.

Matthew might not be.

"What is this you say?" she demanded, propping her hands upon her hips. "There is naught here that is yours. Surely your father explained the truth to you?"

"He told me that you had spurned me, that you would wed this one instead."

Bronwyn shook her head and made to rise, Matthew's resulting agitation making Rowan nigh choke on the knife. Her eyes widened and she held her ground, much to Rowan's relief.

"I had no idea the betrothal was of such import to you, Matthew," she said carefully. "Indeed, we have seen little of each other in recent years."

Matthew laughed. "Betrothal? I care naught for you—'tis all of our fathers' holdings that are due to me and me alone."

Rowan thought of the dagger in his belt, now buried in his discarded garb. He tried to gauge the distance to those clothes without truly casting a glance that way.

He would not put it past Bronwyn to guess the direction of his thoughts and strive to set matters to rights. The woman had a rare determination to affect her own fortunes—but Rowan would not grant her any means to win this disenchanted man's ire.

The knife bit deep again. " 'Tis this man who means to

steal all from me. I shall kill him, then you will wed me, then all that wealth will be mine.''

"Nay, Matthew, 'tis not a course of good sense,'' Bronwyn protested, and put one foot on the floor.

"Nay!'' Matthew screamed suddenly, and the knife moved slightly away.

'Twould be Rowan's only chance before the last blow was struck.

Bronwyn screamed in the same moment that Rowan dug his elbow into Matthew's gut. The other man fell back; Rowan pivoted but halted at the sight before his eyes.

Blood ran from Matthew's left shoulder yet he held his knife before himself, the blade wavering. He was smaller than Rowan, though built solidly. His eyes were wide with fear and he had backed away to face another opponent.

Aye, Matthew faced an unexpected foe, one who had entered the chamber silently, one who had wounded Matthew already, and one Rowan knew was more formidable than any Matthew could have faced before. The older man with blood on his blade was not to be underestimated; truly he seemed to smile in anticipation of his next kill.

'Twas Rowan's own father.

"Gavin?'' he asked, stunned that the mercenary should be here.

"Aye, 'tis me, that is clear enough.'' Gavin growled, his gaze unswerving from Matthew.

Rowan shoved a hand through his hair, relieved as Bronwyn's arms closed around him from behind. She was trembling and he closed his hands over her own. "But why? Why are you here?''

Gavin's gaze flicked his way. "I have a missive from your foster mother.''

Matthew took advantage of Gavin's averted attention and

lunged. Rowan cried a warning, but the younger man's knife slashed at Gavin's neck. The mercenary roared and turned on Matthew with a vengeance.

Their blades met with a clang, they grappled at such close range, then threw off each other's weight. They circled warily as Rowan retrieved his chausses, boots, and dagger.

"I have killed a thousand, boy," Gavin purred, and beckoned to Matthew with one hand. "One more is as naught to me."

"You have no reason to kill me," Matthew whispered.

"Every reason," Gavin corrected. "You alone have tried to kill my son. 'Twould be a novelty to kill for the cause of righteousness."

Matthew might have surrendered and saved his own hide, but there was a wild light in his eyes. He attacked Gavin suddenly, his blade flashing with vigor. Gavin dove for the younger man. Matthew fought with surprising strength and managed to drive his blade into Gavin. Rowan leapt into the fray but, before he could strike, Gavin bellowed with rage.

He drove his blade deep into Matthew's belly and jerked it up into the younger man's chest. Matthew made a little cry, then sagged, his blood pooling on the floor.

Gavin withdrew his blade, wiped it on Matthew's chemise, then flicked a cool glance toward his fallen opponent. "I had expected better sport of one who began so well."

He turned then to assess his son, his eyes narrowing as he studied Rowan. Rowan let him look, in no way inclined to make more of the meeting than might otherwise have been. He was all too aware of Bronwyn's presence behind him and guessed she was mightily curious.

"I thank you for your aid," he acknowledged when his father said naught.

''You would have had matters resolved in short order.'' Gavin grinned. ''My son, after all.''

They stared at each other, neither apparently having the words for this meeting, and the older man's smile gradually faded.

''You look well,'' Gavin said finally, his voice gruff.

Rowan folded his arms across his chest. ''You are bleeding.''

Gavin wiped at the blood and shrugged. ''Better than dead.'' He nudged Matthew, as if ensuring the man was truly dead, and nodded approval. He shoved his knife back in his belt and surveyed their surroundings so openly that Rowan cringed.

''What do you want of me?'' he asked, not troubling to hide his impatience.

''Must I want something of you?''

''Aye.'' Rowan almost laughed. ''Otherwise you would not be here.''

Gavin snorted. '' 'Tis a fine welcome for a father who has travelled far in search of his son.''

Rowan had no chance to argue further, for the morning silence was suddenly shattered.

''Niccolo!'' a woman screamed from below. ''Niccolo, nay!''

''Mother,'' Bronwyn whispered.

The three of them fled the chamber as one. There was no use counselling Bronwyn to remain behind, for Rowan knew she would not heed him, not when someone she loved was in fear.

Aye, 'twas one of the traits he most loved about his betrothed. He would not, however, let her take the lead. Rowan seized the lady's hand and held her fast to his side, pretending he was immune to the plea in her eyes when she glanced to him.

"I am not about to lose you now," he said grimly, and was relieved that she remained in his shadow.

For now.

They rushed into the hall and Bronwyn gasped in horror. Her mother stood, wide-eyed with terror, her hands twisted behind her back. Her father stood helpless in the middle of the hall, staring at a man who should have been dead.

Baldassare di Vilonte traced patterns against Adhara's fair flesh with a bloodstained knife.

Bronwyn had not killed a man, after all.

She had little chance to be relieved. Three more strangers immediately stepped out of the shadows, their blades rising to the men's throats. They divested Gavin and Rowan of their knives, one pulling Bronwyn's hand behind her back as her mother's were held. She refused to give him the satisfaction of crying out.

Baldassare glanced across the hall, his gaze alighting on the recent arrivals. "Do join us," he said smoothly, as if they had any choice. "But remain where I can see you clearly, for I have learned well enough that you are not to be trusted."

Bronwyn stood tall before the captain's cold gaze.

"I must assume that my protégé proved himself to be cut of the same cloth as his father."

Niccolo froze. "What have you done to Marco?"

Baldassare smiled. "He outlived his usefulness after winning me access to your gates. 'Tis his blood upon this blade—you will find his corpse in the gatehouse."

Bronwyn found her horrified gaze following the movement of that knife. Her mother swallowed.

"And what of these men?" Her father gestured to the other men aiding Baldassare.

Baldassare smiled, nodding to his companions in turn. "One can always find men who are tempted with the prospect of gold. You should have been more careful with your reputation, Niccolo—many in town knew of your wealth, no less coveted it for themselves."

Bronwyn's father paled. The three men who aided Baldassare—one dark, one fair, one in between—grinned in anticipation of the spoils.

"Coax the fire to life, Niccolo," Baldassare invited amiably.

Niccolo shook his head. "I will not watch you hurt her."

"Then you must do my bidding. I would have a blazing fire upon the hearth." Baldassare's voice hardened. "And I would have it now. Surely 'tis not too much hospitality to grant a guest?"

Niccolo's hands clenched and unclenched, his gaze not straying from the knife. "You will not hurt her."

"Not if you cease to tempt me." Baldassare dug the blade deeper and Adhara blanched as she gasped. Niccolo stepped closer, but Baldassare did not ease his grip. Bronwyn could hear her mother's frightened breathing. "Stoke up the fire, Niccolo, if you want your wife to live."

Her father looked suddenly elderly, but he lingered only another moment before kneeling at the hearth. Silence reigned until the flames were coaxed to life.

" 'Tis done," Niccolo said flatly and stood. "Now release her."

Baldassare laughed. "I will do no such thing!"

Bronwyn watched her father's dismay, hating that she could do naught to aid him or her mother.

"Then exchange my life for hers."

But Baldassare regarded him coldly. "Do you not understand, Niccolo? You cheated my father and left him dead in a foreign land, taking his share of the profits from that journey for yourself and leaving his reputation shattered.''

''I did no such thing!'' Niccolo retorted angrily. ''He tried to kill us all, that he might have a greater share! Your father was seized with madness for the gold—you were there! You saw the truth of it! He would have stolen from all of us—'twas your own father who dared too much, who wanted too much!''

''Nay, he wanted only what was rightfully his, but you betrayed him, as men who have shared meals should never do.'' Baldassare's voice was grim. ''But that journey made your name, Niccolo the Falcon, it made your fortune and your reputation. All you built should have been my father's, and thence should have been mine—'tis as if you stole it from me.''

Niccolo did not correct him this time, though Bronwyn knew the charge was unfairly made. A trickle of blood broke from Adhara's flesh and she bit back a whimper. Bronwyn watched her father blanch and hold his ground with difficulty.

A dull flush of anger rose over Baldassare's face. ''It took me long to find my way back to Venice, only to find that you had destroyed my family name with malicious lies. I vowed then to have my due of you, but you disappeared, as if you knew yourself to be hunted.''

''I wanted only to find peace,'' Niccolo asserted quietly.

''By living on stolen spoils for which there could be no accounting?''

''Your father could not have imagined that all the profit would fall to him!'' Niccolo protested.

''It should have! He deserved it. I deserved it!'' Baldassare's voice rose. ''But I found you in the end, I proved to be the better hunter than you were prey. And now, Niccolo, you will destroy all that should have been mine.''

"Release my wife and all I have will be yours."

" 'Tis not enough. Not now."

Bronwyn's father frowned. "What nonsense is this?"

"I have decided 'twould be sweeter for you to be the one to destroy all you love." Baldassare nodded toward the hearth. "Take a torch and light it, Niccolo. The first thing you will destroy is your own hall."

Niccolo frowned. "Of what sense is that?"

"Shall I kill your wife while you linger, then?" Baldassare's gaze turned cold and Adhara cried out as the knife jabbed into her. Her blood mingled with the remnant of Marco's blood on the blade.

"Nay!" Niccolo cried.

"Nay!" Bronwyn cried.

"Do it, Niccolo," Adhara whispered fervently. "I beg of you."

Bronwyn watched her father's shoulders stoop. He took a glance around the hall, then gazed at his wife for a long moment. Bronwyn feared neither of them would survive this day, and guessed that they both came to the same conclusion.

Then Niccolo bent to touch the torch to the flame. He straightened and started to turn.

"Now!" Rowan cried in the same instant that Niccolo cast the burning torch at Baldassare. Gavin drove an elbow into the ribs of the fair-haired man beside him and Rowan attacked the dark-haired seaman behind him.

Bronwyn jabbed her elbows back with vigor and managed to escape her captor's grip. She pivoted and kicked him in the privates, sending him to the floor writhing in pain.

Adhara similarly took advantage of Baldassare's surprise. She stamped on Baldassare's foot, ducked, and ran. The torch hit the wall behind them and the timbers began to burn, the flames licking greedily at the dry wood.

The men paired off to fight. Bronwyn noticed all too quickly that the battle was mismatched—Rowan had no blade, nor did her father or Gavin. She saw her father snatch another torch and light it, closing on Baldassare with resolve in his eyes.

Bronwyn ran for the hearth without hesitation and seized another torch. She lit it and raced to Rowan, who waved it immediately under his opponent's gaze. The dark-haired man was blinded by the light and danced backward.

Adhara similarly took a torch to Gavin. The hall was lit with flickering orange light, and though they should have roused the others and fled, Bronwyn and her mother remained to watch.

Gavin first swung his torch with gusto and caught his blond adversary across the midriff. The man cried out as flames licked greedily at his clothes. He fell scrabbling to the floor, and Rowan's father stepped forward to seize the knife from that man's belt.

The blond man rolled suddenly though and stabbed upward, catching Gavin beneath the ribs. Bronwyn saw Gavin catch his breath, his complexion paling as he stumbled. The fair man leapt to his feet and dove on the older man, despite his burning clothes, and the pair went down.

"Rowan!" she cried.

Rowan took one look and shoved his torch toward his opponent's face, taking the opportunity to seize the man's knife. Rowan stabbed quickly at the man's throat and the dark-haired man went down, to move no more.

His clothing burned and he rolled into the wall, the flames quickly feasting upon the timbers.

But Rowan had turned on his father's opponent. He leapt into the fray, drawing the man's attack. The man fought with unexpected vigor, though both he and Rowan were clearly tiring.

Gavin, meanwhile, did not move, and Bronwyn feared for his life. She and Adhara tried to carry him from the hall, thinking that the morning air would revive him. They managed to drag him only a few feet before Rowan bellowed and felled his opponent.

But the man who had held Bronwyn stumbled to his feet, hatred in his eyes. Bronwyn stopped to stare, her heart in her mouth as Rowan turned on that man. He attacked him in a sudden burst, torch in one hand and blade in the other, and the man was quickly vanquished.

Rowan bent over and dispassionately ensured the man would not rise again, then spun to meet Bronwyn's gaze. He looked past her to her father, swore and raced to that man's aid.

Niccolo and Baldassare battled on the high table itself, dancing back and forth as they parried and struck. Bronwyn was shocked to see her father being driven back, blood running from his face, but Rowan's cry made Baldassare glance up in alarm.

'Twas all it took for him to err. Baldassare stepped forward, clearly intending to strike down Niccolo, and slipped. Niccolo took advantage of the moment and battled anew, slicing Baldassare across the throat with a sweeping gesture.

Baldassare fell to his knees before Rowan reached the dais. Niccolo drove his blade into the other man's heart, the effort costing him dearly.

Indeed, Niccolo fell back, his features drawn and his flesh pale, his bright gaze locked upon the fallen Baldassare.

"Tell me," he urged Rowan huskily, "that this villain will never threaten my family again."

Rowan bent down and touched Baldassare's throat. "He is dead," he acknowledged, and Niccolo's shoulders sagged in relief.

Adhara fled across the hall and caught him in her arms,

her tears flowing at the gash upon his face. His fingers traced the line the knife had made, his kiss falling on her wound.

"I shall live, Adhara," Niccolo declared, his gaze rising to the timbers that burned all around them. "But only if we escape the hall soon."

Bronwyn had time for one glance only at the hall where she had been raised before Rowan seized her hand. He hastened her before him, seeing her safe before returning for his father.

Bronwyn found her mother by her side as she worriedly watched for Rowan's return. "You will do well with this man beside you," Adhara said softly, then smiled quickly. "I shall dance long at your nuptials." And she gave Bronwyn a tight hug as the men came out once again.

They gathered in the fields beyond Ballyroyal's gates, the red of the rising sun echoing the embers that glowed where the hall had once stood. All of the servants and vassals within the hall had awakened in time, and Rowan had carried his father to safety. Adhara had fussed over Gavin's wound, the wrinkle in her brow telling all that her hopes were not high.

Finally, Adhara sat back on her heels and tugged Gavin's cloak over the wound, which still bled. "There is no need to torment the man," she said softly, and all knew the import of that.

Rowan sat vigil beside his father, his expression grim. Bronwyn joined him, hoping he would have an opportunity to mend matters with his father and uncertain he truly wanted to.

Indeed, Rowan seemed to have naught to say, though his grip upon her hand was sure.

Bronwyn and Rowan both jumped when Gavin suddenly spoke, his voice hoarse. "I would tell you a tale, while I yet can."

He did not open his eyes, though he clearly knew who sat beside him. "Once there was a man, born of a saddlemaker in a small town in Wales," he said gruffly. Bronwyn and Rowan exchanged a glance, then Rowan frowned as he watched his father.

"The name of the town is not of import, but the saddlemaker was named Gerald. He was a man of uncertain parentage, a hardworking man who was uncommonly proud of the birth of his first and what would prove to be his only son. He believed he had built something for his son, a saddlery of repute, one that serviced knights and lords, a place of craftsmanship which generated a reasonable measure of coin."

Gavin took an unsteady breath. "But that was not enough for his son. Nay, that son was ambitious beyond all else; no mere saddlery would suffice for him. He left his family as soon as he was able, he fled to fight and to win his fortune, for a fortune was surely the only thing he deserved.

"He was victorious at first and returned home a wealthy man. His father, thinking this lust for adventure was satisfied, arranged a match for his son with the pretty daughter of a local man. The deed was signed, the dowry exchanged and spent, before the son discovered the news."

Gavin began to cough, a fearsome amount of blood in his spittle. Rowan braced his father's back and held a crock of water for him, winning a grunt from Gavin when he had had enough.

"The son"—he continued as if there had been no interruption—"was enraged. No country wench would do for him—he intended to wed a lady of the court, no less would suffice. Father and son argued, as fathers and sons are wont to do. The family could not return the dowry, and yet more important, the father Gerald refused to break his word. He insisted the son stand by the pledge.

"The son took this news in poor temper, for he was not one who preferred to be denied his will. Perhaps his parents had indulged him overmuch, as he was their only child, perhaps it was his nature. It matters little—what matters is that he vented his rage upon his new wife. He was drunk when he bedded her." Gavin swallowed. "God in his mercy spared this fool the memory of what he had done. His bride likely never forgot it.

"He left with the dawn, vowing never to return. 'Twas years before he realized that the weight upon his heart was shame."

He fell silent then, his eyes opening as he seemed to watch the clouds scuttle across the morning sky.

"And the wife?" Bronwyn prompted.

Gavin flicked a glance her way. "She died, bearing his son."

" 'Twas then he felt remorse?"

"Not he." Gavin shook his head. "Nay, he turned his back upon the place of his birth, holding naught from there but the memories he denied and a small golden ring that had been dispatched to him. It was the ring he had put on that bride's finger. He remembered the ring, for it had been his mother's own." Gavin frowned. "He could not remember the bride."

Bronwyn realized belatedly that Gavin made his confession before he died. Not to a priest, to be sure, but clearly he intended to set matters straight while he yet could.

Rowan sat beside her, his gaze fixed on the distant hills, his features so still that they might have been carved in stone.

But she knew he was listening.

Gavin cleared his throat. "So he sought another bride, one more fitting of his ambitions, and he found her at the court of the French king. A cold beauty and an heiress, he knew he could win her, and he set to the chase with diligence. She succumbed to him and wedded him, much to the shock of all the nobility, with a passion that shocked her new spouse. Indeed, he had made a rare bargain, though he realized that later than he should have.

"He might have given her the ring, but he thought she would have mocked him for saving such a tiny sliver of gold. She had far finer jewels already."

Gavin smiled and shook his head. " 'Twas years before he realized that she only wedded him to take vengeance for her own father's lofty ambitions for her."

He looked to Bronwyn, clearly expecting her to comment. "That is terrible."

Gavin seemed to find that comment amusing. "Nay, they were of the same ilk. Indeed, they had much in common, these two with their burdens of bitterness and ambition. Perhaps they deserved each other. At any rate, they had a son, a fine boy, despite the anger between them, and I suppose their match was not all bad. In the end, though, 'twas the husband who spoiled all."

Rowan's lips tightened, his hand closing over Bronwyn's again, and she guessed this was the part of the tale that concerned him.

"That mercenary spied a wench in a dancing troupe and she was a beauty. Flashing eyes the color of sunlight and hair as fiery as the dawn. She laughed like a goddess and danced like a firefly—he was bewitched the moment he saw her. He followed her like a dog in heat and was astounded when she yielded to him. He was further astounded at the sweetness that blossomed between them.

"But, of course, such stolen treasures are not destined to

last. The troupe of entertainers moved on, and she went with them, slipping away in the night. She had his heart, though, and she had that sliver of gold, that ring he had once put upon another finger. He sought her, without success, but this woman, this one who had never been his bride, he never forgot.

"And when, five years later, the call came that the troubadors were at the gates, he ran there with all the enthusiasm of a child. She was not there." Gavin's voice broke over that confession, though he stared diligently at the sky. "But there was a child, a red-haired boy with his mother's eyes and the man's own ring on a chain around his neck."

He paused and swallowed. "This was his son."

Bronwyn glanced quickly to Rowan.

" 'Twas a gift he had never expected, and it humbled him that this woman had borne him a son, unbeknownst to him. Indeed, 'twould have been easier to deny the boy, to turn him away, but the man could not do it. The dancer had melted his heart and the revelation that she was dead broke it. So he took the boy into his home and his rich wife promptly cast him out. She kept the boy, for she was not an overly cruel woman, and, indeed, she had the grace to raise him with her own child.

"Though she never could explain to him the origin of that ring."

Gavin's roughened fingers closed over Bronwyn's left hand. He lifted her hand to his view, a smile slipping over his lips. He brushed his lips across Bronwyn's knuckle just below the golden ring that Rowan had slipped onto her finger.

"So, you see, in the end, the man won all he roundly deserved." Gavin's smile faded to naught and his voice faltered. "He left his home with little and ended his life with naught; he had pushed aside every soul who had ever cared about him, and he had lost even that sliver of gold.''

Gavin turned a bright gaze upon Bronwyn, and she found her vision clouded with tears. '' 'Tis your tale now, just as 'tis your ring. I would not have you think its legacy a wicked one.''

'' 'Tis far from that,'' she said quietly, and saw a smile of reminiscence touch his lips briefly.

Then Gavin looked to Rowan, the two men's gazes holding long. ''I have never asked you for anything,'' the older man said. ''But now I would have your pledge.''

Rowan caught his breath. ''In exchange for the tale?''

''Is the wager not fine enough for you?''

Rowan smiled slightly, his own gaze suspiciously bright. '' 'Tis more than fair. Name what you would have of me.''

''Go home to Montvieux. Go to Montvieux and tell Margaux that I would grant her the only thing she ever desired of me.''

Rowan frowned. ''But what would you have me take to her?''

Now Gavin smiled in truth. ''Naught. Naught but your bride and the man you have become.''

Bronwyn and Rowan exchanged a glance of confusion, but before either could ask, Gavin began to cough. Adhara came to his side, but 'twas all too soon that he slipped from awareness.

And not long after that, Gavin Fitzgerald ceased to draw breath at all.

'Twas Rowan who dug his father's grave in the hills near Ballyroyal; Rowan who dressed his father for burial; Rowan who lingered by the freshly mounded grave to weep in solitude. When Bronwyn went to his side, he took her hand, his thumb sliding back and forth across the slim band of gold.

"Let us pledge to each other at Montvieux," Rowan said quietly, a question in his words.

"If you wish it thus," Bronwyn agreed, knowing he would keep his vow to Gavin. She leaned against him, wanting to tempt his smile again. "But you should know that your wager is surely lost."

Rowan looked at her in surprise.

"I am an heiress to precious little now, and certainly not the most wealthy heiress in all of Ireland."

Bronwyn was rewarded with Rowan's slow smile. "Then there are no questions left between us," he murmured, brushing his lips across hers. "For we will wed nonetheless."

# Epilogue

IT WAS SNOWING WHEN THEY RODE THROUGH MONTVIEUX'S gates. Rowan thought that no place in Christendom could compare with the estate where he had been raised. He had never before appreciated its beauty, but in showing it to Bronwyn, he rediscovered its marvels again.

And he was very glad he had waited to take their vows in Montvieux's chapel.

Their party was not small, Adhara and Niccolo having chosen to accompany them. Bronwyn's parents thought to make a change, to begin anew, and Rowan suspected they would not be far from their daughter. It suited him well enough to have a family and a family's love surround him, for, indeed, he grew used to their open affection.

He liked that he was included within their circle, just as he was.

Many of the servants from Ballyroyal came with them, including Connor and Marika, who seemed much enamored with each other. Thomas talked nigh twice as much as he had before, and the boy was learning languages at a ferocious rate. Adhara's horses had been brought as well, many of them sold to fine families along the route to cover the cost of passage.

Niccolo had made a strong case for visiting the city of his birth, and they came to Montvieux by way of Venice and the

Italian cities. Rowan had sworn he would never willingly board a ship again after that journey, and he heartily doubted that Troubador will permit himself to be led into a ship's hold again. Indeed, Rowan would be satisfied to remain home for years, after such an adventure.

If he still could call Montvieux home.

'Twas Christmas Eve and the bells were ringing, the snow falling in massive flakes, the sky perfectly black overhead. The horses halted in the bailey and Rowan's arrival was greeted with cheer by the ostler. Rowan captured Bronwyn's hand in hers and led their party to the chapel, knowing that his adopted family would be at mass.

And so they were. The chapel was garbed in greenery for the occasion, the smell of the fat beeswax candles as warm and welcoming as ever a smell could be. Burke was here, his wife, Alys, ripe with child; Luc and Brianna and their cooing babe on the other side of the chapel. Margaux knelt at the altar, accepting the priest's blessing last as was her habit.

Rowan halted in the portal, waiting for his foster mother to turn. She had aged, he noted, and she needed Burke's aid to rise to her feet once more, despite her cane. She turned regally once on her feet, though, her chin high, and made to lead the recessional as the priest began to sing once more.

Then she halted to stare.

"Rowan." His name left her in a breath so filled with hope and delight that Rowan felt his throat tighten.

He stepped into the chapel, Bronwyn's hand fast in his own. "Margaux." He bowed, then closed the distance quickly between them, out of courtesy for her. "I would have you meet my lady, Bronwyn of Ballyroyal, and her parents."

Margaux greeted them politely, her gaze returning to Rowan's face. "You did indeed arrive for the Yule," she declared, her usual authoritative manner restored. "Though only in the barest margin of time."

"I was delayed in courting a bride." Rowan winked and was reassured when his foster mother snorted.

"How like you to . . ."

"To bring my betrothed home to be wed at Montvieux." Margaux blinked. "You are not yet wed?"

Rowan smiled slowly, his thumb sliding across the ring Bronwyn wore. "It seemed only courteous to let my mother attend a ceremony of such import."

Tears welled unexpectedly in Margaux's eyes and Rowan could not bear the sight of them. He cast a glance over the chapel. "And indeed," he found himself saying, "I could not imagine taking such a pledge anywhere else."

"Tell her of Gavin," Bronwyn prompted.

"What of Gavin? Where is he? Have you seen him?"

"He died, defending my betrothed's family," Rowan said quietly. He watched Margaux bite her lip and marvelled that she would come so close to tears. "He said something that made no sense to me." Margaux met his gaze with open curiosity. "He bade me return here, to grant you the only desire you ever had of him. Do you know what he meant?"

Then Margaux did cry in truth. Rowan was so astonished by this that he did not know what to do. Bronwyn nudged him and he caught his mother's shoulders in his hands, letting her lean against his chest while she wept.

He was certain he had never seen Margaux cry, nor indeed show any vulnerability before others.

"Miserable man," she muttered against his tabard. "He would die just to ensure that I could not thank him for this."

Rowan looked at his brothers, both of whom shrugged. "I do not understand."

Margaux wiped her eyes and flicked a telling glance at Rowan. "Your father's son, there is no doubt of that." She fumbled at her belt before Rowan could reply and lifted a tiny chamois sack.

He had seen it many times before, though she seldom carried it with her. "Why do you have the seal of Montvieux with you at mass?"

"I thought to surrender the estate to the church on this night, but in the end, I could not do it." Margaux tipped her head back to hold Rowan's gaze. "And 'twas a good thing, for my son has need of a holding."

Rowan's gaze flicked to his older brother. "I thought Burke had a holding, by way of Alys."

"He does."

Rowan stared at her, incredulous at his intuitive guess. "You would never entrust me with anything of import," he whispered.

"Perhaps that was my mistake. Galling as 'tis to admit, Gavin Fitzgerald taught me a simple truth this day." Margaux smiled thinly. "A son is not wrought of blood alone. You are my son, Rowan de Montvieux, for I raised you to be my son." She took the sack and pressed it into his hand. "And you will be my heir."

Rowan looked up, only to find his brothers grinning.

"He was always her favorite," Burke teased, affection in his grin.

"And that despite his mischief," Luc agreed. "His betrothed is probably pregnant."

"What?" Margaux demanded, then pounded her cane on the floor. "Is she?"

"Of course," Rowan agreed with a smile for Bronwyn, whose eyes began to shine. "Bronwyn is no longer the most wealthy heiress in all of Ireland, if indeed she ever was, but I will have her as my bride all the same."

Burke cried out in delight. "Ye gods, we have won a

wager with him, after all these years.'' And Luc began to laugh.

Margaux started muttering about bastards, but neither Bronwyn nor Rowan were listening to any of them.

Rowan lifted his hand to Bronwyn's cheek, amazed that she would be his bride. ''I love you, Bronwyn,'' he murmured. ''Would you make Montvieux your home?''

Bronwyn smiled the smile that would always make his heart leap and leaned against him. ''Would you take such an obligation as this?''

Rowan shrugged. ''There would be a great enough risk of failure to suit me well.'' He winked at her. ''Perhaps the longest odds of all my days.''

''My home is wherever you are,'' Bronwyn whispered, and lifted her face for his kiss. Rowan bent to claim Bronwyn's lips with a triumphant kiss, knowing that she alone could have opened his heart to the treasure that was love.

Aye, though he might have lost his brothers' dare, his heiress had brought him the richest legacy of all.

And that was a far, far better prize in the end.

Dear Reader,

Once upon a time, three Fitzgavin brothers set out on a Bride Quest, never guessing that they would lose their hearts along the way. Certainly I never guessed how many readers would thoroughly enjoy their stories. Thank you for writing! In response to your questions, yes, the Bride Quest will continue in spring 2000 with *The Countess*. But the quest will move in a different direction—north to medieval Scotland.

You may recall that the countess Eglantine de Crevy tried to seduce her brother's friend, Burke Fitzgavin, but failed because Burke's heart was already claimed by the damsel Alys. Nonetheless, the romantic knight gave Eglantine a great deal to ponder in his eloquent defense of love. Eglantine has been thinking all these years, and now that she is widowed for the second time, she has taken to sitting on the corner of my desk. She drums her fingers very loudly. She sighs when I ignore her. She taps me on the shoulder and reminds me of her responsibilities.

Eglantine, you see, has two daughters of her own—one from each marriage—and a stepdaughter by her first marriage. She is very concerned for their futures, and rightly so—three daughters without dowries is quite a challenge for a penniless widow. Determined and beautiful (yet considered beyond her prime at the age of twenty-eight!), Eglantine vows that her daughters will know the romantic true love that has eluded her all of her life. So she takes matters into her own hands and moves her household to a remote Scottish estate she inherited from her late husband. There, inspired by the brothers Fitzgavin, she intends to persuade men of honor to embark on their own Bride Quests. The prizes for the most worthy men in Scotland will be Eglantine's lovely daughters.

It seems a perfect plan, but Eglantine has yet to meet Duncan MacLaren, the chieftain who will challenge her, defy her, and infuriate her. Little will she guess that this handsome warrior is on his own Bride Quest, intent on winning the hand of the most intriguing, stubborn, and beautiful woman he has ever met—a foreign noblewoman and widow named Eglantine.

As you can imagine, it will be quite some time before these two negotiate a cease-fire, let alone manage to live happily ever after! I hope you will join us on the next leg of the Bride Quest. Enjoy the following excerpt from *The Countess*! I look forward to hearing from you.

All my best,

*Claire*

P.O. Box 699, Station A
Toronto, Ontario
Canada M5W 1G2

http://www.delacroix.net

# The Countess

*Manor Arnelaine—*
*October 1176*

E GLANTINE HAD BEEN CERTAIN THE FUNERAL WOULD BE the worst of it, but she was wrong. When she awoke to the gray slant of rain, she had feared that she would not be able to provide the example of strength and dignity that the villeins of this small manor expected, that she would fail to mask her own feelings before her children.

Eglantine had managed the deed, though only just, but she lay the credit before her brother's wife, Brigid. That sweet woman was so heavy with child, so sympathetic to Eglantine's loss, so obviously missing Guillaume that it had been easy to be strong in her presence.

'Twas what Eglantine did, after all. And 'twas a mercy that she had not had to witness the awareness of her mistake in her brother's gaze. 'Twas bad enough to know that she had wed foolishly, without the reminder that her ardor had cost her brother. 'Twas with every good intention that Guillaume had entrusted the penniless Theobald with the manor of Arnelaine, though Theobald had not reciprocated in kind.

Guillaume was a brother beyond compare—he had never complained of his vassal's poor management, or his drinking, or his gambling, but Eglantine knew that her brother knew the truth. For the first time in her life, she was glad that Guillaume had been called to the royal court, for she could not have faced him this day.

'Twas later—when all the well-wishers were gone, when she fleetingly believed that the worst was over—that Louis, the manor's chatelain, stepped out of the shadows. Without a word, he summoned her to the chamber where the manor's books were kept, something in his manner making her heart stop, then race anew.

How badly had Theobald managed Arnelaine? Eglantine was not certain she wanted to know, though 'twas unlike her to be a coward. 'Twas painfully evident to Eglantine that she sat in the place of her spouse in that room—in his chair, at his table, with his papers arrayed before her—while Louis reviewed matters he should have discussed only with a man.

And 'twas there that Eglantine realized she would never hear Theobald de Mayneris roar for more wine again. She blinked back unanticipated tears, unwilling to admit that she would miss the man who had so carelessly torn her life asunder. Marriage was a journey for fools. 'Twas clear, no matter what illusion one had when embarking upon the voyage. She had tried it twice, neither journey having turned out any better than the other, and knew all she needed to know.

Mercifully, Eglantine would not have to endure marriage again.

She cleared her throat and eyed Louis deliberately. "I beg your pardon, Louis. I did not heed your inventory of the estate."

The older man glanced up, his gaze sharp. "There is no inventory."

Eglantine frowned, knowing that Louis had always kept impeccable records. "How can that be?"

Louis looked discomfited. "Because the estate was not held by your spouse upon his demise."

Eglantine frowned. "Louis, Theobald was invested with the estate at my brother's behest. Has Guillaume retrieved the manor due to some disagreement?"

Louis shook his head. "Nay, Lord Guillaume has done naught."

Eglantine straightened. "This is a poor jest, Louis. We both know that a vassal has no right to relieve himself of a holding held in trust for his overlord."

" 'Tis no jest, my lady. There is no inventory because there are no books, and there are no books because there is no seal."

"What nonsense is this?"

"The books of the manor are no longer in my possession." Louis glanced up and held Eglantine's astonished gaze as his voice dropped. "My lord Theobald may not have had the right, but he had the seal of this manor in his hand. He wagered it and he lost."

Eglantine blinked in shock. "But that cannot be!"

"Nonetheless, 'tis."

"But there must be an error, Louis. Theobald would not have been so foolish." Even as the words crossed her lips, Eglantine knew very well he could have been. 'Twas why her heart hammered so.

But Louis said naught more.

"Theobald would not have left our daughter Esmeraude with naught!" Eglantine argued as though she would convince herself, rising to her feet in consternation. "There is a dowry to be bought and bellies to be filled. There is my dowry held in trust, which is mine alone! Theobald would not be so remiss in his responsibilities as this!"

The chatelain rubbed his chin as he surveyed her, the gleam of sympathy in his eye telling Eglantine more than she wanted to know. 'Twas clear Theobald would have done as much.

Eglantine pushed away from the table, rising to stare blindly out the narrow window, rubbing her temples with her fingertips.

The seal was gone. Her brother Guillaume would have to pay the debts left by his vassal and brother by marriage or lose this part of his holding. Eglantine knew that Guillaume would never suffer the loss of even a corner of the family holding he had inherited. Crevy-sur-Seine was his pride and joy, a close second only to his blushing bride.

Eglantine dreaded having to tell Guillaume the truth and ached in anticipation of what her own folly would cost him. Why, oh, why, had she been so smitten with Theobald? Andy why had she begged her brother to grant Theobald some small holding so that they might make a match?

Oh, she had cost her family dearly, there was no mistake of that. And for what? A man who drank and gambled and cost her all.

And left her penniless to raise three daughters. Eglantine heaved a sigh and turned back to the patient chatelain. "All of it, Louis?"

He shook his head, no more happy with the truth than she. "Every denier, child, every last cursed denier. Do not imagine that I did not try to stop him."

Eglantine forced a smile. "I am certain that you did. Your loyalty to Crevy is beyond expectation."

The chatelain bowed slightly. "I thank you, my lady."

Eglantine straightened. "I shall ensure that Guillaume understands your efforts in this. 'Twas not your error and I shall do my best to ensure that you do not pay for it."

"Again, I thank you. You have always been most gracious." Louis met her gaze steadily. "I would dare to suggest, my lady, that 'twas not your error either."

Eglantine shrugged and took her seat again. "But I shall bear the price of it, you may be certain."

"If I may be so bold as to ask, what will you do?"

There was no point in artifice, for this man knew Eglantine's circumstances even better than she did. And she trusted the older man, for he had served their family for years. "I do not know. Somehow, my duaghters will need dowries, and I cannot turn away Alienor even though she is not my own blood."

Three unwed women. 'Twas a somber prospect. They shared a moment's silence, then Louis offered a piece of parchment. "This missive came from Charmonte this morn. 'Tis addressed to you."

"Charmonte!" Eglantine recoiled, meeting the chatelain's gaze with alarm. It seemed that matters could grow yet worse.

"I am afraid so, my lady. Sadly, the betrothal agreement for your daughter Jacqueline is not missing from the former Lord d'Arnelaine's papers."

"That would have been rather against my current run of fortune." Eglantine accepted the missive, distrusting that word came from this man so quickly.

Reynaud de Charmonte was the man her first spouse had chosen as a betrothed for Eglantine's first child. Jacqueline had been but a babe, Reynaud older than Eglantine even when the agreement was signed, an arrangement too painfully familiar for Eglantine to find acceptable.

Her much older spouse had not been interested in her views.

'Twas not reassuring that Jacqueline, now a beauty at fourteen, had called Reynaud "the old toad" when he'd last visited. Eglantine had called her first husband by the very same appellation. She turned the missive in her hands, hating that she would be compelled to honor this old agreement and condemn her beloved daughter to the same unhappiness in marriage she had known.

She could not ask Guillaume to buy out the arrangement, not now that Theobald had served him so poorly. She had no coin of her own. She had no champion of her own with Theobald dead, not that he had been much of one while he still drew breath. Her first husband's heir, a son by the same previous marriage that had spawned her stepdaughter Alienor, had already shown that he had no compassion for women. 'Twas why Alienor had come to these gates, her own brother having cast her out for lack of a suitor. Eglantine did not particularly care for the girl, but she could not have turned her aside.

And she still had a babe in need of a dowry, Theobald's own blood, little Esmeraude. Four women with nary a coin among them.

Eglantine heaved a sigh. Sympathy gleamed once again in Louis's eye, and he conjured another document from his ledger. 'Twas tucked into the endpaper, this one, and written upon fine vellum. Eglantine's heart skipped a beat when she spied her name scrawled across it in her spouse's familiar hand.

"Naught but a letter, a letter for you." Louis handed it to her, then stood and bowed. "I hope it will explain matters more satisfactorily than I ever could."

A letter, its seal unbroken. Eglantine turned it in her hands, not certain she wanted to open it. 'Twas no less than Theobald's last words to her, and there would be only silence after this.

She did not trust him not to make matters even worse.

Eglantine squared her shoulders and realized that the ever-tactful Louis had left her alone, having closed the door behind himself. Eglantine crossed to the narrow window, taking a deep breath of cool breeze as she tore open her spouse's letter, surprised at the spark of anger that lit within her. He had betrayed not only her, but her daughter, her stepdaughter, and the child they two had brought to light.

And he had not even told her the truth.

Theobald's letter was dated four months past.

*My dearest Eglantine,*

*'Tis oft said that a man may not savor the view after a night of drinking and that is true enough of me on this morn. I have been foolish, not for the first time and probably not for the last, but I fear that this foolishness cannot be set to rights.*

*Months past I took a wager, thinking it an easy one to win. 'Twas to ensure Esmeraude's future that I took this gamble, for I worry overmuch about that child's choices. I would have her wed a king, a prince, a lord of lords, and knew 'twas my responsibility to ensure she had the dowry to win the best man to her side.*

*'Tis the irony of such matters that my deeds may well have precisely the opposite effect. 'Tis the way of the wine to make me feel that Dame Fortune rides beside me, and more than once these past months, I have tried to set all to rights. Instead, I have only made matters worse—last night, I lost the manor of Arnelaine itself.*

*I know 'tis not mine to lose, I know I had no right, but with the seal in my purse and the dice falling my way, I dared overmuch. 'Twas my intent to see this corrected, though I know now that I hoped overmuch. There is naught left to my hand, naught with which I might wager, naught with which I might buy, no honor left in my name which might compel others at least to courtesy.*

*This morn, I am faced with a dark realization. It is not unlikely that I shall fail in this task.*

*And so I write this confession to you, my own wife, the one destined to make something from naught. If I succeed in correcting what I have done, then I shall burn this* missive and you will never know the truth of my sorry secret. If you are reading it, then 'tis only because I have failed.

And you, you who loved me for what I pretended to be, will surely be dismayed. Though truly, Eglantine, if there is any who can make the most of little, 'tis you. Here is all I have to grant you, the title to a distant holding, one which I have never seen. 'Twas granted to my father years ago, and truth be told, if any believed it had any value, I would have wagered it and likely you would not even hold it in your hand. The property lies in distant Scotland though it carries a tale perhaps worth the journey.

'Tis the way of the Celts to make a handfast in this place, and that is a pagan wedding ceremony. A couple in love pledge to live as one for a year and a day, and if all goes well, they swear at the end to keep all their days and nights together. 'Twas said by my father that this holding is believed a fortunate place to make such a vow, that locally all clamor to make their promises there.

Perhaps you and I should have taken our pledges each to the other in such a place. Perhaps then I would not be writing this missive, perhaps I would not have failed so badly, perhaps you would yet regard me with other than disappointment in your lovely eyes. Perhaps then I might have been the man you always believed me to be.

But we did not and I am not. And instead of a fine fat dowry for Esmeraude, I leave you only the deed to a property held to be worthless, at least on these shores.

Forgive me, Eglantine, if you can find it within your heart to do so. 'Twas not my intent to fail.

Eglantine ran her fingertip over Theobald's signature, the enclosed title falling to the floor unheeded. She traced the swirls of ink as tears obscured her vision, remembering all the hopes she had once had. Then she buried her face in her hands and wept, alone but for her responsibilities and one worthless title, feeling more like a young girl than a woman widowed once again.

When the thunder rumbled in the distance and the sky darkened, Eglantine straightened. She wiped her tears and found her composure once again.

She opened Reynaud's letter, every word feeding her dawning conviction.

*My lady Eglantine,*

*Be advised that I shall arrive ar Arnelaine in a fortnight's time. It is my understanding that your spouse has recently passed from this earth—please be advised that arrangements can be made with the Abbess of Courbelle for your acceptance there as a novitiate. You may linger at Arnelaine, as my guest, until the nuptials between Jacqueline and myself are celebrated two months hence. I shall, with your agreement, be delighted in your stead to arrange for Esmeraude's marriage when she comes of age. Please ensure that all is made ready for my arrival and that the keys to Arnelaine are entrusted to Jacqueline.*

Reynaud had not signed his missive beyond a lazy *R* but had marked it heavily with red wax imprinted so deeply with Arnelaine's seal that she could not have doubted the image. A second seal bore the arms of Charmonte, his home estate.

Eglantine's lips drew to a tight line. So this was who had taken Theobald's wager! It seemed that Reynaud de Charmont did not heed her objections to his marriage to her daughter. Time and again, she had protested that Jacqueline was yet too young—now Reynaud had ensured that she had no right of protest.

And a convent for her! Eglantine would join no convent!

How dare Reynaud suggest such an arrangement? How dare he dismiss her from her daughter's life?

'Twas as though Eglantine were only so much baggage, and baggage that must be removed. Jacqueline would have much to say about the arrival of "the old toad," that much could be relied upon. At fourteen, she believed she knew all there was to be known. As for Esmeraude, well, Eglantine heartily doubted that Reynaud's choice of spouse would suit when the time to wed came.

Family loyalty prompted Eglantine to turn to her brother, but she knew that Guillaume would only uphold Jacqueline's betrothal agreement. She had asked him about it repeatedly since her first husband's demise, and repeatedly he had quoted the law to her, albeit with apologies. 'Twas the way of a man of honor to uphold the law, and Eglantine knew that her brother would not be swayed to her side.

There was a time when she might have thought Burke de Montvieux would champion her cause, but those days were gone. He was in love with his wife and enamored of his young son, and Eglantine knew she no longer had a right to intrude on that happy scene. Burke had persuaded her once of the merit of love—though his argument had won her naught, she was still tempted to find such love for her daughters.

What if even one of them might win the hand of a man like Burke?

What right had she to stand aside and condemn each of them to unhappiness, knowing full well what she did of marriage?

'Twas too late for Eglantine, twenty-eight summers and the bearing of two children behind her, but she would not stand aside and let her daughters be compelled to match her own sorry course. They would not marry old men, they would not be trapped in households hostile to them, they would not be so much chattel in men's lives.

They would have the love of which Burke so eloquently spoke, the kind of love that Burke himself and even her brother Guillaume had found with Burke's aid. Eglantine would ensure it.

After all, Theobald had unwittingly granted her the means to make a difference. Eglantine picked up the Scottish deed, a smile playing across her lips as her decision was made.

They would go to Scotland, a place so far that she could barely imagine it. Louis would go with them, Eglantine was certain, along with his family, for there was no future for him beneath Reynaud's hand. Aye, she would take any of the household willing to travel with them, and Reynaud's wishes be damned!

And then she would begin her own Bride Quest, not unlike that of the brothers Fitzgavin. Eglantine straightened at the sheer good sense of the thought. Aye, she would summon men to her court, she would persuade them to undertake tests of valor, she would coax them to win the hearts of their ladies fair!

Three particular ladies fair did come to mind. Eglantine would ensure these men competed, the best of them winning the hearts of her daughters three. 'Twould be just like an old tale, just like the Fitzgavin tale of the Bride Quest that already was recounted in the halls hereabouts.

Perhaps Theobald's legacy would bring more than he had hoped. She lifted her chin and strode from the chamber, her footstep light with her surety of the future. Perhaps Eglantine truly *could* wring something from naught.

She certainly intended to try.

DELACROIX Delacroix, Claire.
X
        The heiress.

$6.50